ONE RICH REVENGE

SOPHIA TRAVERS

For my friend M. Thank you for your support and for lending me something very important.

Copyright © 2024 Sophia Travers

All rights reserved. No part of this publication may be distributed or transmitted without the prior consent of the publisher, except in the case of brief quotations embodied in articles or reviews.

All characters and events depicted in this book are entirely fictitious. Any similarity to actual events or persons, living or dead, is purely coincidental.

The following story contains mature themes, strong language, and explicit scenes, and is intended for mature readers.

www.sophiatravers.com
Developmental editing: Jennifer Prokop
Copy editing: HEA Author Services
Cover design: lorijacksondesign.com

1

Callie

I have three rules in life, and in business:

1. Never print a lie.

Sure, I might embellish a tad for dramatic effect, but I never lie. Lies come back to bite you.

2. Always be able to look at yourself in the mirror the next morning.

That means no stories that could hurt someone. I don't expose cheating scandals if the people involved are nice people. I don't write about people's kids. I have a moral code, and I like to think it puts me head and shoulders above everyone else in this business.

3. A little fun never hurt anyone.

I really try to live this one every day. I go to bed with a smile on my face and hope in my heart for the morning. Even on my worst days, I ask myself what I have to look forward to. Stupid? Maybe. But it's worked for me so far.

Until today.

I squint at my phone screen, hoping the number will change. It doesn't. $25,000. *How can we still owe that much on the line of credit?* We did not need that printing contract. I told Dad to focus on digital distribution and social media, but he thinks a newspaperman isn't a newspaperman without a physical paper. The big red deadline is just two weeks away. I could have sworn we were making payments on time and the balance should have been close to zero. Another thing I should have been monitoring instead of letting my father "handle it."

I put the phone down and pour another cup of coffee. It's lukewarm. Dad was up early today. He must have brewed it before the sun rose. It's just peeking over the horizon now, filtering in the east-facing living room windows, weak and watery at this time of year. He's probably in his office right now, holed up with three or four papers, sucking down the daily news and gossip like a drug.

"Dad," I call.

"In here." His voice comes from behind his office door. I weave through the haphazardly organized and cozy living room, past the worn couch and around stacks of books. There's a huge sofa, a record player, and a big TV—all the comforts of home—at least according to my father. But not a feminine touch in sight. My mother's never been in the picture, so it's always been just me and Dad against the world.

When I push open the office door, his typical chaos greets me. An actual typewriter, our fat orange cat Samson, stacks of papers, a few decorative paperweights. My father is settled in his leather armchair, thumbing through the *Post*.

"Anything good in there today?" I lean against the doorframe.

He lifts his head. He might be slowing down, but his jovial-seeming face hides a sharp mind and intelligent eyes. They never miss a thing.

"They printed your photo of Jonah." He flips the paper so I can see one of my photos from last week. In it, Jonah Crown, Manhattan's favorite billionaire, is striding across the street, coffee in hand, looking deadly and handsome.

"I should hope so, with how much they paid for it."

My father is silent. He hates talking about money, but it's the root of all our problems these days. Irritation flares.

"Dad. What's going on with the loan we took out?"

His eyes flick up and back down, his bushy brows drawing together. "It'll get paid, Callie, don't you worry." *Don't you worry.* Like I'm a child who shouldn't bother her pretty head with serious things. Except this paper is my business and my lifeline, and ultimately, my legacy. And I want to save it. If only he will let me.

"It's coming due. We got an email from the bank today. We have two weeks to make the payments. I thought we'd been paying consistently. How can we still owe $25 grand?"

"It's okay," he repeats absently, and thumbs to another page.

"We can't just ignore this. We don't have enough money coming in from the paper. The photos I'm taking are the only things keeping this business afloat. We need a strategy." All the plans I've shared push to the forefront of my mind. A better website, digital subscriptions, higher quality photos, different branding, a focus on celebrity gossip. Something, *anything* to get us out of this funk. Ideas my father has refused to implement over the years.

"We'll figure it out."

"I'm not letting this go. I refuse to stand by and watch this paper fail."

His jaw tightens but he doesn't respond. My stomach sinks. This is how my father deals with everything. We never talk about my mom leaving. We never talk about his failing health or the doctor's appointments that we can't afford. We certainly don't talk about how the paper is on its last legs.

We've had numerous versions of this conversation. I push him, but he shuts down. I don't want to lose our paper because we were too cowardly to talk about its problems.

I wait for him to say something, before I walk out of his office with an aching heart.

I spend the rest of the day nervous and sweaty at the thought of twenty-five grand. Our business checking account shows that we have enough to cover our expenses for next month. That's it. The $7,093 I have in my personal account stares at me with accusing eyes. Maybe if I make the payment now, I can get an extension? It's worth a shot. I fill out the information for the e-check with shaking hands. This seven grand is my independence. I've fought so hard for it, and paying off this stupid loan I didn't want in the first place...ah, it hurts. Another year living with my father. I squeeze my eyes shut and click the button to pay it before I can chicken out.

Nausea churns out as I click out of the page and focus on getting this week's issue ready and brainstorming items for the website. We're going to need to sell a lot of photos and papers if we want to make eighteen grand in the next six months, much less the next two weeks.

I better get out and take photos then. I grab my jacket and my camera bag, settle my ball cap on my head, and run out the door.

∼

Forty-five minutes later, I'm leaning against a parked car outside the restaurant Jonah Crown goes to every Tuesday night. It's a quaint Italian place not far from his apartment. It's impossible to get a table from what I hear, though I've never tried.

Numbers run on loop in my head. I started the paparazzi side hustle five years ago when my dad couldn't pay rent. Five years has taught me that exclusive photos will rake in at least $1000 each, but they have to be good—like a celebrity doing something salacious, or photos of someone who never lets themselves be photographed. *Except I never get those photos.*

I never get them because I hate doing what it takes to get them. I love being a reporter. I like reporting gossip alongside our usual articles. It's fun and light in a world filled with too much darkness. Street fashion photos, articles about celebrities in the neighborhood, fun tidbits about their dogs — all of that deserves to be reported right alongside the news about the latest construction delay on the subway station near our apartment.

But I hate following people. I hate invading their privacy, running from their security teams, seeing the shocked look on their faces when they've been caught doing something. I hate following people with kids more than anything. It's one of the reasons I started photographing Jonah. He's single, and he rarely sees his family. He doesn't do anything secretive or exciting.

In fact, following Jonah is boring as hell most of the time. The man is utterly predictable. Early morning wake-up, black car to the office, the occasional dinner. He rarely goes to events. He never goes on dates. If he weren't so hot, I wouldn't even bother. Hot and famous. He's self-made, ruthless and loaded.

I never see other paparazzi taking photos of him. Maybe because they don't know his routines like I do. We live pretty close to each other, even though the twenty blocks between our apartments make a world of difference. Paparazzi are typically tipped off because they cultivate relationships with restaurant hostesses, security staff, and employees of the celebrity in question, but I've never heard of anyone betraying Jonah's trust. I smile into my scarf as I scan the restaurant facade. Not surprising. He has a *kill quickly and hide the body* sort of vibe.

I tap my fingers on my camera, trying to look casual. He went into the restaurant with a woman forty-five minutes ago, and I have to know who she is. If I can get a photo of him with a date, it will be a major scoop. *In my dreams.*

I've never seen him with a date. Not like some of the other celebrities and rich people I photograph. There's one guy who lives in the skyscraper on 55th and Broadway who has a new woman on his arm every time I see him. Not Jonah, though. And not his business partner, Miles Becker, either. He rarely saw women before he started dating Lane Overton, and now she's his entire world. At least judging from the way he can't take his eyes off her.

Even with his boring life, Jonah's photos still sell better than anything else. It must be the arrogant way he looks at the world, or his permanent sneer. Men want to be him, and women, well, judging from the comments on our articles, they want to do lots of unprintable things to him.

A guy walking by gives me a weird look, and I duck my head to fiddle with my phone. I'm in all black, like I usually am on the job, with my hair tucked in a ball cap and a giant camera on my hip. It's obvious I'm here to take photos. Most New Yorkers don't care. It's a badge of honor to shove rudely through a celebrity's entrance to a hotel and throw your hands up like *they* are in *your* way. But a sketchy looking girl leaning against a parked car? That will draw attention.

Luz and Adriana are texting me, asking if I'm free for drinks, speculating about whether Luz's new boss has an actual stick up his ass or a metaphorical one. I grin and tap out a response that implies Luz should fuck around and find out.

I'm lost in my phone when I hear, "You."

My head jerks up. It's him. Jonah. *Ah, shit.*

2

Callie

Did I ever wonder if Jonah Crown would happily murder me and stash the body? Well, now I know the answer. He strides forward, eyes black with rage, face set. He crowds me against the car, and I freeze. I've spent at least a year following his every move, but I've never been this close to him before.

His attention is a physical thing. Heavy, unwavering. When our eyes meet, I shiver. I can't decide if it's unpleasant or not.

"I've been looking for you."

I've heard him speak before, but never directly to me. Hairs go up on the back of my neck. *Must be the cold air.*

"Do I know you?" I will not be intimidated by him, and I'm definitely not blowing my cover. My stomach clenches. My body is poised for fight or flight. This is the worst part. I've been accosted before, and it's everything I can do not to apologize to the subjects. Usually. Right now, I just want to run away.

"You're the one taking the photos."

He's huge up close, bigger than I thought, actually. His shoulders are broad, and he's taller than I realized. Tall enough to make me feel dwarfed by his presence. I tip my chin up to meet his flinty gaze again. His eyes are dark in the dim light of sunset. His hair is black and silky. His forehead is high, regal almost, and his nose is a straight slash. Solid cheekbones, dark brows, a jaw that could cut glass. Lucifer himself. A fallen angel on this mortal coil.

Think, Cal. Why would you be out here? "You got me. I'm a real estate photographer." *I'm definitely not, and sunset photos of real estate make no sense, but whatever.* I press my lips together to keep from saying or doing anything else that might make me look nervous.

His scoffs. "Stop following me."

"I'm not following you. In fact, I'm really busy. I need get a photo of this building." I give him a calm smile, when in reality, my heart is thundering.

He looks furious at my words. He's probably not used to being defied.

"Jonah. Come on. It's cold and you're being insane. Is he bothering you?" The woman he's with pipes up from behind him, and I lean over to make eye contact. *His sister, Christine.* I knew it. I snapped a photo of them going in to the restaurant earlier, but I couldn't catch more than her profile. *Boring.* Why can't the man just go on one date and let me take a photo of it?

"Don't look at her." His hand comes down on the car next to me, and I startle. "Don't even breathe in her direction." He's *angry*. Understandable, but irritation rises all the same at the way he's crowding me. I've been threatened before, sometimes while taking photos, other times just because I was asking questions for an article. The general public might read the news, but they sure as hell don't trust reporters.

I suspected he was an asshole, but this confirms it. *Presumptuous jerk.* He's way too handsome for his own good. Those black eyes invite you to sin. That silky hair makes your fingers itch to touch it. Not my fingers, of course. I don't go for assholes. Not anymore.

My eyes narrow on him. I might hate being a part-time paparazzi, but I also hate how celebrities think they're better than you. Jonah Crown thinks he can threaten me into stopping. He has no idea what my life is like. No clue that I need these pictures and this money. I take a deep breath. *Don't be mad. Don't give him ammunition.*

"I have no idea what you're talking about," I say with admirable calm. "You're blocking my shot."

"This isn't over." He backs away, eyes flashing, jaw clenched so hard it looks like he might break a tooth.

"Have a great night," I call out as he strides away.

As soon as he's out of sight, I slump against the car, shaky from the adrenaline. *Damn. I can't believe he saw me.* I was distracted by the texts, and I didn't think he'd eat so fast. I've never been spotted before, though Jonah might be the first person who has ever cared to try.

Great. I settle my camera bag on my shoulder and start the walk back to my apartment. I'll have to get a new hat now, or a disguise or something. Jonah isn't going to let this go, and I'm not going to quit. *It seems we're at an impasse.* I smile to myself. One crazed billionaire isn't going to stop me.

~

It's a healthy forty-minute walk back to the apartment I share with my dad. We might only live twenty blocks north of Jonah, but it's a world away. From what I've seen, his townhouse is the epitome of luxury, while our apartment is the definition of faded comfort. When I enter into the living room, my dad is on the couch with a baseball game on, his trusty Mets cap settled firmly on his head.

"How's the game?"

"They're not playing well," he grumbles. "Benitez can't get his head out of the clouds. Oh, come on." He throws his hands up at the TV, and I grin. My father yelling at baseball is a staple in this house.

"Did you eat?" I set my camera bag on the dining table. Our living space and kitchen are connected, like they are in many New York City apartments.

"Yeah. I had some pizza. And before you start in on me, I took off half the cheese."

"Dad, come on. You know you're supposed to be eating vegetables." After his heart attack over the summer, the doctor put him on a strict diet, one I've been trying to enforce while living here.

"Tomorrow, Cal." He waves his hand in the air. "There's some pizza left for you if you want it."

I sigh, but grab a slice from the box on the counter. It's from our favorite place on 98th and Broadway. I've been eating pizza from Little Italy Pizza since I can remember. It's thin crust, with lots of cheese, in big pies. Just the way I like it. I chew and flip through my photos. I was downtown yesterday, trying to get shots of an A-list actress who was filming in the West Village. She's known for her public tantrums, but I didn't get more than a few boring shots of her in full makeup and hair for the shoot. The photos of Jonah are great, though. Him ducking out of his car, looking elegant and annoyed. Him hugging his sister. Her outfit is perfect—bright red boots, blue denim, a cropped jacket. He's intensely private, so photos of him with family will sell. Matt over at Green Media might even be interested. They'll want an exclusive, though, so I'll need to be back out there tomorrow getting more photos. I have some shots from yesterday of Jonah at lunch with a stunning brunette, but I want more information on who she is before I publish them.

I finish my pizza and settle in at my laptop to upload the photos and email Matt. I hate dealing with Green Media, but no one pays more for photos. They might be picky, but they are always eager for photos of Jonah.

Matt responds to my email with a *yes* in all caps, which makes me smile. Matt's a good guy. He went to Columbia with me, and he was a total fish out of water. Just a guy from Indiana trying to make it in the big city. I took him under my wing, and now he helps me out when he can. He hates Green Media, though. They're known for firing people if you make even one wrong move. Matt needs the money, with his student loans, so he's stuck in a shitty situation.

Can't say I blame him. My student loans are set to the minimum payment right now. Even with all the grant money I received, and the fact that I lived at home, journalism school was not cheap.

And I'm so not going to think about that right now. I'm just going to edit the photos from dinner tonight and make sure they're as good as possible for Matt. And for the money. Maybe I'll make a dent in those student loans after all.

3

Callie

He's late today. It's 5:03 a.m. and Jonah Crown would normally have ducked into his chauffeured car three minutes ago. I tug my beanie down onto my forehead and pull the hood of my jacket up. It's only October in the Upper West Side, but it's freezing at this hour. And my butt is going numb. I resettle on the steps of the brownstone across from his townhouse and try to shake some warmth back into my legs. I'm partially hidden by the low wall that extends from the steps of the building, but I have a clear shot to his front door and the reserved parking space in front of his building. I have no idea who he had to bribe to get a reserved parking space, but it's the only one I'm aware of for an individual on the entire island of Manhattan. And he doesn't even drive. No, he has one of a fleet of stealthy black cars pick him up every morning and bring him home every night. At least four different cars. I know, because I've made note of the license plates. Not intentionally, because I'm not a stalker, but idly, because I pay attention to details and have nothing better to do in the dark morning hours.

5:05 a.m. *Come on, Jonah.* All this waiting for one photo, maybe two. If I'm lucky, he'll be wearing a suit with no jacket. He looks like a fashion model in those bespoke suits, even with that perpetual frown. One spring morning, I was lucky enough to catch him in running shorts with no shirt. I finally needed to turn the comments off on that article, because they were getting explicit. One woman even put her cell phone number down.

5:07. *Maybe he isn't coming.* I groan into the crisp air. Getting up at four a.m. for this is bad enough, but to come home empty-handed? Not an option. Green Media is paying handsomely for the photo from yesterday, but I have nothing to print in our next run. I haven't published anything about Jonah in weeks, and we're overdue. He's our star.

The door to his townhouse swings open and I sit up straighter, camera at the ready. *Oh, he looks good today.* He always does, which is why these photos rake in more money than anything else, but today he looks especially gorgeous. Gorgeous and cold. Almost like he knew I would be here. I lift the camera and view him on the screen. Dark, silky hair, those cut cheekbones and full lips, a navy bespoke suit, fathomless eyes. *Satan himself.* I shiver and snap photos as quickly as I can. I don't want another confrontation. Not because he intimidates me, because he doesn't, but because it will definitely blow my cover this time.

He has two tumblers in his hands. *Odd.* I've never seen him do that before. Maybe he's meeting someone? His driver pulls forward, but Jonah steps into the street and looks right at me. My hands jerk, and the shutter clicks. The shot won't be usable. *How can he even see me?* I'm hidden by an absurdly large planter and half of a wall. But he's stalking toward me and I scramble to stuff my camera into my backpack and whip out my phone, like I'm just another resident of 87th Street and Central Park West.

He stops at the bottom of the steps, his expression icy with distaste. His brows are drawn low, his lips sneering. I have the absurd urge to scramble to my feet, but it will make me look guilty.

"Hi." My voice sounds weak. Ugh.

"I thought I'd give you the rundown for my day to spare you the trouble." His voice is smooth and rich and makes something uncomfortable churn in my stomach.

"The rundown?" I blink up at him as he mounts the steps, each deliberate footfall creating a symphony of movement under his suit.

He holds out the tumbler of coffee. I stare at his hand. *Is this a trick?* I finally take it, careful not to touch him, and a faint expression of satisfaction crosses his face.

"My first meeting is at seven a.m., then I'll have lunch at my desk, then dinner tonight with my business partners at The Charlatan downtown. You should take notes." His voice is even and cool, but I feel like I've been transported into another dimension.

"I have no idea what you're talking about." I swallow hard, staring up at those depthless eyes. They're a brown so dark that they're almost black. "I live here, and I'm just waiting for my friend to pick me up." *There's no way he's going to believe this.* I feel like prey. My pulse is speeding and my gaze darts while he watches me.

He smiles humorlessly. "I know you're not my neighbor, Ms. Thompson. This building is owned by the ambassador from Pakistan to the United States. And he's away on business right now. He's also unmarried. So either you're a house cleaner, or a stalker. And you don't look dressed for housecleaning."

"How do you know my name?"

"Private investigator." He gestures. "Your hat is from Columbia University. It's amazing what you can do with facial recognition technology and an unlimited budget."

My mouth drops open. He leans down so we're nearly face to face. I shiver slightly, but quickly steel my spine. His breath puffs out against my face, minty and not unpleasant. Up close, I can see lighter brown flecks in his otherwise dark eyes. The lines of his face are classic, elegant, and cruel. Especially with the flatness of his expression.

"I've been searching for you, Ms. Thompson. And trust me, being found by me can be very bad for your health."

I freeze, my pulse fluttering. "Are you threatening me?"

He rises, smiling again, more real this time. *Maybe the threats are doing it for him.*

"If you publish anything else about me, I'll ruin you." He raises a brow. "Understood?" He's so smug, so satisfied that he has this in hand. All in a day's work. *Jerk.*

I lift my chin. "You're a public figure. I'm not doing anything wrong." I'm not. I write about his company and its founders, but the articles are well-researched and always truthful. And I'm not taking photos through his window. He's on the street, just like everybody else, though I suspect he spends very little time among the masses.

His face tightens. I get a brief glimpse of the rage boiling beneath his facade. "I could sue you to prevent you from publishing anything else." His voice is icy, bored.

"Sue me," I say flippantly. *Please don't sue me. I don't have money for a lawyer. I have student loan payments and doctor's bills for my dad and rent and the printing contract. Oh god.* I swallow hard, but lift my chin. "The law is on my side."

He snorts softly like he sees through my false bravado. "Tell me, Ms. Thompson. How did you get Green Media to print those photos of me? Has it been you selling them photos?" He cocks his head, and I freeze.

He looks like he would murder me in cold blood and leave me on the ambassador's doorstep. My tongue darts out to lick my lips. *Why does he care? Fuck it.*

"Yes. Well, for the past year." Once I figured out his routines.

He inhales sharply. "Wrong answer."

He turns around and stalks toward his waiting car. When he's gone, I lift the tumbler to my mouth with a shaking hand. I take one tentative sip before spitting the coffee all over the steps. *Ugh.* He salted it. I narrow my eyes at his car, where it waits at the light. *Childish asshole.*

I'll just have to be more careful next time. Because I'm not going to stop reporting on Jonah and his company.

∼

I MEET Luz for breakfast near our apartments. She's an ER nurse, and my weird hours suit her even weirder hours. She lives a few blocks north of my dad's apartment, and our favorite bagel place has no line at this hour, just a few construction workers laughing loudly and ordering soft drinks at six a.m. In the hierarchy of New York bagel stores, this one is near the top. I am, of course, biased, as a lifelong Upper West Side resident. I've been eating bagels from Bagel Frenzy since I could chew.

Luz is petite with bleached blonde hair, and her movements are always a little frenzied. She claims the intensity of the ER calms her, but I think the adrenaline overload has fundamentally broken something. She waves manically at me from the corner, and I grin.

"Are you heading to the hospital or leaving?"

She chokes down a bite of bagel and coughs. "Heading to. Another shift with Dr. Davenport. Blech." Dr. Davenport is her new boss and her nemesis. To hear her tell it, he's hairy and oafish and always in her way when she's trying to save patients' lives. "What about you?"

I scoot my chair closer to the table so I can whisper. "I just had a weird run-in with Jonah Crown."

Luz's brown eyes are round. "Ooh, the Crown Prince himself," she says, using the nickname I came up with for Jonah.

"More like the Prince of Darkness." I snort.

"Good one. You should start using that. What happened with him?"

"He caught me taking photos of him. Last night and again this morning." I scrunch my face. "It was pretty unpleasant. Last night, he went crazy when he saw me. And then today, he found me sitting on the steps across from his townhouse. I hid my camera but he totally knew who I was. And he threatened to sue me."

"No way. How does he know who you are?"

"Billionaire. Duh. He used facial recognition technology and a private investigator." I take off my worn Columbia ball cap. "Apparently the hat gave me away."

"You're just too pretty to be stealthy," Luz says supportively.

"I just don't think anyone has ever bothered to look." I make a face and sip my coffee. It's lukewarm, not very strong, and hazelnut-flavored. The taste of home.

Luz scoffs. "He's deranged. It's not like you've ever done anything to hurt him. The worst thing you've ever printed is that one day when he looked like shit."

"Come on. I made up a nickname for him. Yeah, I mostly write articles about how hot he looks, or speculate about his whereabouts, or the women he's with, but it's not exactly flattering. He's probably embarrassed."

She rolls her eyes. "He's a public figure. What does he expect?"

"Exactly what I said. Come to think of it, it seemed to be the photos I sold to Green Media that really tipped him over the edge."

Luz rolls her eyes. "It's not like you're taking pictures through his windows."

I shake my head. "You know that goes against my rules."

"You're like the most ethical paparazzi in New York. He should be *thankful* to be stalked by you."

I wince. "That makes it sound even worse."

"Whatever." She waves a hand. "All I'm saying is you're one of the good ones. You've never sold his home address, or revealed information that could hurt him. What's a few photos of him looking wind-blown and sexy? He should be *flattered*."

"Well, he's definitely not flattered." I grimace and take a bite of my cinnamon raisin bagel. It's soft but chewy, just the way I prefer it.

"You're not going to stop, right?"

"No way. You know I can't afford to stop. I'm still getting back on my feet after the mess with Eric."

"I know." She makes a small face of distaste at my ex's name and chews her last bite of bagel. "Jerk," she mutters. We've been over Eric's general awfulness on many a wine-soaked evening. The humiliation of our very public break up has dulled after a year, but Eric still came out on top. I'm better off without him, but I still hate the way he invaded every aspect of my life, until I lost myself along the way.

"He's a jerk who still lives in my apartment." I loved that apartment, but it wasn't worth the pain of fighting with Eric to get it back. I should have known. He screwed his previous ex over too. He used to tell me she was crazy and deserved how shitty he was to her during their breakup. Fat chance. She was probably great and he was taking advantage of her, just like he did to me. Men don't change.

"Well, now you live on the Upper West Side instead of all the way in Brooklyn, and you get to live near me." She gives a winning smile, and I can't help but smile back.

"You have poppy seeds in your teeth, Luz. And living near you is of course, the very best part of breaking up. Living with my dad, not so much. I'm twenty-nine and I live with my father. It's pathetic." My shoulders slump. "I thought I'd be out of there by now."

"Getting back on your feet is harder than it seems. Besides, situations like the one you were in before don't come along every day." Luz is referring to the apartment I had downtown. A gorgeous, old one bedroom for a great price. I don't want to go down this road with her, because she and Adriana think I should have kicked Eric out, but he wasn't going to leave unless I physically forced him out. Part of me thinks taking my apartment was part of his plan all along.

"I know." I sigh. "I'll be able to move out next year."

"I'm proud of you, Cal." Luz smiles at me. "You're doing what you have to do."

"I know. It's just…stifling living with my dad."

"That bad? He's not trying to tell you what to do, is he?" Luz has been friends with me since college. She knows all about my dad's parenting irregularities.

I shake my head. "No, nothing like that. You know he's never been a worrier." As much as I wish someone in my family had been. I had way too much independence, even at eighteen. I shake my head. "But I feel accountable to him. Like a little kid. And also, like I'm his parent? Especially when I have to tell him to take his heart medication." I make a face. "It's weird watching your parent get old."

Luz nods thoughtfully. She's constantly worried about her parents, especially her mom. "Is he still working like crazy?"

"Yep. Twelve-hour days holed up in his office or out tracking down information for one of those long think pieces he loves so much. I swear, that heart attack changed nothing for him. He still eats crap and drinks way too much coffee."

She shakes her head. "He should retire. You could take over the paper."

I want nothing more. But even though I'm my father's longest-running employee, he won't treat me like a business partner. In his mind, I'm still his little girl, and he wants to protect me from the trials of running a failing business. Even if I grew up loving the feel of crisp paper between my fingers. Even if I helped him format articles at age eight and helped him write them at age twelve. Even if my idea to start our paparazzi side hustle saved us five years ago. My father is too blind to see I have ideas that could catapult us into the future.

I sigh. "One day. You know he's stubborn."

She smiles sympathetically. "You'll win him over. I'm sure of it."

~

I SPEND at least an hour starting and restarting articles that night. The paper runs Friday and we need something beyond our usual fare. We need to be better than ever if we're going to make 18 grand. My pulse skips at the thought of all that money, and I shove down the anxiety and refocus on the screen.

We're a weekly paper, but I try to put fresh gossip up daily. It drives the most traffic to our site. More traffic means more ad dollars. And I like to stay top of mind for the editors heading up New York's biggest gossip columns—Page Six and Green Media. I've established myself at this point.

I click through the photos I've taken in the last week. We've already run most of them. Before yesterday's photos of Jonah, I have some great photos of the rat infestation in Riverside Park. We haven't run those, but I don't have it in me to write the article required right now. The photos of Jonah and the unknown woman appear on the screen. *Who is she?* I told myself I wouldn't print the photos until I figured out who she was, but part of me felt slimy printing them.

Their meeting seemed clandestine. Jonah kept looking around as if he were worried about being spotted, and she wore her sunglasses even though it was raining.

I chew my lip uncertainly. She's probably an actress, or maybe a politician. Jonah's not known for being a playboy, but when he does go out with women, they're always stunning. She fits the bill. And yet, something in me doesn't want to print the photos, even if it's a harmless date. *If I expose his secrets, will I be able to look myself in the eye tomorrow? And why do I feel such stupid loyalty to a man who threatened me?* I set the camera down and rub my temples. A stress headache is starting behind my eyes. I click to the next photo. It's one of Jonah's sister, Christine, before she went into the restaurant with him. She looks trendy and rich, stepping out of a vintage yellow Mustang. *Good enough.* I do some googling and jot down what I can find about her before putting a fluff piece together about her outfit and her mysterious wife, who I know is named Mia. I've become an expert at figuring out brands. The women who read us love a celebrity style piece.

I pull together the little background I have and then go digging for more. I just need to put a little more in about Jonah and his family. I click around until the articles about the embezzlement come up. I forgot about these. Jonah was involved in some sort of embezzlement scandal years ago. There aren't many articles about it. The websites I click on lead to nothing. He must have shut it all down, by bribery, or maybe by force, if his reactions this morning are anything to go by.

I've been down this road before, and I can recite the facts I know about him from memory. He was twenty-four when he started Kings Lane, right after the embezzlement charges became public knowledge. He was never arrested and the charges were dropped just as quickly as they arose. Not a month later, there were nude photos of him leaked to the press. Hot nudes. Photos I definitely haven't lingered on when researching him. They're hard to find now, but not if you know where to look, and I always do.

I add some background about Jonah to the fluff, hit publish, and move to the comments sections of our latest articles.

Our comments section is pretty lively, and I check it a few times a day. We get the occasional troll who wants to rile people up about city politics, or neighborhood denizen who thinks the local deli really needs to stock better coffee and takes things too far. I've had to ban a few people, but it's usually pretty tame. But today, we have fifty-three new comments on an article from a few days ago about Miles Becker, Jonah's business partner, and his new girlfriend. This is the type of gossip I enjoy printing. It's a cute piece—just a photo of them outside his office building. He has her up against a sleek black sedan and he's kissing her like he's drowning and she's air. I thought it was sweet, and the accompanying article just includes a few tidbits about Miles, Jonah and their company.

I scroll to the bottom and see a thread started by someone with the name "Prince of Darkness." *Jonah? It can't be.* That would be a crazy coincidence—the name I used just today to describe him, though it's one step from what I typically call him—the Crown Prince, Satan, Lucifer.

Prince of Darkness

Can this gossip rag even get its facts straight?

Then he proceeds to correct all the minor errors concerning Kings Lane Capital, Jonah and Miles' company. Apparently, there's a third owner, which I didn't realize. My face heats as he continues. Each line is punctuated with a disparaging comment. He ends the tirade by saying, "I'm not sure why I even click on this crap anymore. You're better off reading the *Post*."

My fists are clenched so tight that the bones stand out against my skin. *It's Jonah. It has to be.* He told me to stay away, and now he's making it clear what happens if I continue.

A loyal reader of ours gets into the mix, noting that we were the first to break the news about the broken benches in Riverside Park and the city's plan to fix them. *Thanks, Marsha. This is my turf, Jonah. Back off. Go back to making billions and leave me alone.*

Hope soars for a brief moment, and then a new comment pops

up. Oh no, someone is agreeing with him. "Quality has gone down in recent years." *Since I took over.*

The Prince of Darkness immediately responds, "Was it ever there to begin with?"

Asshole.

A new comment pops up on the article about Christine. The Prince of Darkness has commented again.

Prince of Darkness

Was my message not clear earlier?

With shaking hands, I turn off commenting on the article, and then pull up a new page. I can draft this article in just a few minutes. I drag and drop photos of Jonah and the lovely woman at lunch. I pick the ones where he looks particularly furtive, and then stab out a title. "The King of Hell: Looking for His Queen?" It's not much of a takedown, because I know nothing about the woman, and I refuse to make up facts, but I add some idle speculation that Jonah is lonely and jealous that his business partner is happily settled and he isn't. The speculation is real. Mrs. Winters down the hall asked me just the other day if he was single. Close enough.

I add the most salacious background I can find. I can't bear to publish leaked nude photos, but the embezzling goes into the first sentence. It's worse than anything I've ever said about Jonah before, but none of it is untrue.

I check for typos and hit publish with sick satisfaction. Take that. The Prince of Darkness comments one minute later. He tags me, under my pen name.

"You'll regret this." The comment is meant for my eyes alone, because it's deleted not two minutes later.

I slump back against my chair, heart racing and a little ashamed of myself. Printing that article was a mistake. I should not have engaged with him. Something tells me he isn't going to let this go.

4

Jonah

"You really need to let this go."

I raise my head to see Miles in the doorway of my office. He strolls in, relaxed and loose, typical for him now that he's living with Lane. Must be the regular sex. It's made him more self-satisfied than usual, and I grunt an acknowledgment. I don't want to deal with his good cheer this morning.

He drops onto my office couch, uninvited, and I raise a brow.

"I'm serious, man. George told me about the comments you left on the article last night."

"George has too much time on their hands."

"They'd have even more if you'd just hire an assistant already."

"That's quite the enticement. Besides, I haven't found anyone remotely competent."

"Your standards are too high."

"Yours are too low," I snort.

He rolls his eyes. "What happened with the last candidate? Did he ask for vacation days or something?"

I tap my finger on the desk. "His social media was filled with political rants. And vacation days are allowed, so long as they align with my schedule."

Miles grimaces, but drops the subject. We both know George is stretched thin, managing expansion plans, seeing to our travel, interviewing candidates. When they requested an "army of minions," we both quickly agreed. Turns out those minions are harder to find than I anticipated.

"She printed an article about Christine." The words drop between us like a grenade.

"I saw it," he says carefully. "She mentioned the embezzling rumors too, but she didn't mention that the charges were dropped. That was low."

"This is how it starts." My hand clenches around my pen. "Idle speculation, then looking into Mia, then discussing the family, maybe photos of the baby. Mia's due in February. Fuck."

Miles's mouth twists in sympathy.

"Don't give me that look." I shove back from my desk. "I'm going to handle it."

"Handle it how?"

"I'll figure it out," I say shortly. "But she's not going to stop unless I make her stop. I confronted her twice this week. I made it very clear what happens if she continues. And she continued." I shrug. It's that simple. Callie Thompson is the enemy, and I will stop at nothing to protect my family.

Miles sighs. He's not going to argue with me. We have very different ways of looking at the world, but he understands me. "Will there be any fallout from what she published about your meeting?"

Callie fucking Thompson should never have seen that clandestine meeting with the COO of Green Media, and she sure as hell shouldn't be printing photos of it.

"I don't know. I'm waiting for a call."

"Have you thought about just…moving on?"

"Out of the question." I give a sharp shake of my head, and his mouth turns down. Even when he was mired in grief and guilt, Miles has always wanted the best for his friends. He's a better friend than I deserve.

"It was a long time ago."

"Don't start," I say shortly. "Our feud may have started years ago, but it's not over. Dylan tried to contact Christine just last year. What would you do if he contacted Lane?"

Miles's face hardens. "I'd take him down. He's a piece of shit." Miles would kill for Lane. He's said it many times.

"So you understand. I will never forgive him. Christine was in therapy for years after those articles. My mom had her arm broken trying to escape from reporters outside the house." My stomach churns at the memories. The fear in my mother's voice when she told me they were being followed, the anger and sadness in Christine's when her girlfriend broke up with her because of Dylan.

Miles sinks deeper into the couch. "That was unforgivable. I'm not saying to forgive him. I'm just wondering if maybe success is the best revenge. Happiness. You should try it sometime." A pause. "Don't give me that look. You're going to say something douchey to push me away, but you know I'm right."

I swallow down my retort. He's right. The itch to lash out is always there, even at my best friend. "Happiness. What do I know about happiness? I wouldn't recognize it if it grabbed me by the neck."

Miles huffs a laugh of agreement. "Come to the Montauk house next weekend. Enjoy yourself. It would make Lane happy."

Miles and Lane invited me days ago, but the two of them together are unbearable. So in love. Their eyes practically shoot hearts when they look at each other.

"So I can watch you make calf eyes at your girlfriend? No, thank you."

"Don't be a dick. She's your friend too. She invited some of her friends. The artist who shares Mallory's studio is coming. She's pretty and really smart. Talented." He shrugs, but his eyes are watchful.

"Me. With an artist." I snort. "Unlikely." And even more unlikely that I'd mess around with one of Lane's friends, when it would only end in heartbreak. My assignations are short and to the point. A means to an end.

"Won't know until you try."

"When have you ever known me to try?"

Miles leans forward. "Not since Annalise. That's the point. You've been alone since her. You work at all hours, you see your family, you work out like a man possessed. I'm worried about you. Lane is worried about you. And I know Christine is worried about you." He shoves a hand through his hair, and I feel a twinge of guilt at the mention of my little sister worrying about me.

"I'm fine."

"Really?" He looks skeptical.

"Really. I just have a lot to do. And I'm not interested in a relationship interfering with my carefully planned existence." Not another Annalise, that's for fucking certain. She was like a bomb waiting to detonate. I learned my lesson—to be the best, you're better off not letting anyone close. I might not be at the top, but I'm damn close, and I intend to stay there once I arrive.

Miles opens his mouth to argue and I raise a hand. "I hear you. I'm glad you have Lane. I'm glad you're happy. But a relationship is not for me. It's a distraction I can't afford."

My best friend looks mutinous, but presses his lips together in a flat line.

"Suit yourself," he says shortly. "But think about the party. And tell me if anything happens as a result of the article."

I sigh heavily and see him out. Miles will never understand. He was always waiting for Lane. He's driven, yes, but not in the way I am. And now his life is complete, and he's gone...soft. My mouth twitches unhappily. Now, he'd shackle me with the same weakness. I can't think of anything worse. We're not on top, not yet, and I won't rest until we are. We have competitors, rivals. Miles is happy with our success, ready to move on to the next phase of his life. I will never move on. *This* is where I want to be. In this glass tower, controlling everything around me, on top of the world.

Unless Callie Thompson ruins it for me.

The speculation in that asinine article last night was enough to make me laugh. The implication that I'm lonely and jealous of Miles, and looking for a woman. Denise Silverman wants less than nothing to do with me, unless it can help her get back at her boss. Callie doesn't know that though. I turn back to my email. The article better not have fucked things up for me. *If it did...* My fist clenches around the mouse briefly. *Not a possibility.* I didn't get where I am today by doubting. I always come out on top.

An hour later, I get the call I was dreading.

"I'm done, Jonah." Denise's voice is hushed but steady. "He knows it's me and he's going to come after me."

"You said you wanted to expose him."

"I do. But this job—" Her voice cracks a little and she inhales. "I need this job. I can't afford to be involved with you anymore."

I tap my fingers on the desk. "Denise. You promised." I have nothing on her. I can only rely on begging or bribing her.

"I can't." She hangs up and I call back immediately. Straight to voicemail. I leave her a brief message saying I'll make it worth her while. Whatever she wants, I'll pay it.

I hang up and set my phone carefully back on the table. I want to throw it across the room, but I settle for shoving back from my desk and pacing to the windows. They're floor-to-ceiling and give the impression that you're going to fall into Manhattan. I press my palm to the glass. *Fucking hell. Again.* My fingers curl against the cool surface. So fucking close. Just like two years ago, when Dylan countered my bid to acquire shares of Green Media by installing his idiot of a brother on the board. And a year before that when he sued me to prevent disclosure of his shady business dealings with Belarussian billionaires.

Fucking Callie Thompson. She couldn't even have the decency to have a boring name. *And those eyes.* So blue they unsettle me up close. That sinfully lush mouth. That silky dark hair. I shake my head. She couldn't have the decency to be ugly, either.

Callista Thompson, born to Maggie and Arnold Thompson in New York City. Twenty-nine years of age. Writes under the pseudonym You Know Who. Mother lives in California. Father is the owner of The New York Star. Resident of the Upper West Side. Responsible for ruining my life.

How dare she? Rage heats my blood. Resentment is a heady rush. I've worked too long and too hard for this revenge to have some fucking reporter rip it all away from me at the last second. Not to mention all her lurking around, going after Miles. Going after Christine. My hand twitches against the cool glass. *Christine.* That was the last straw. Dylan is business. Christine is family. And now she's in Callie's sights. Green Media's too. Dylan and his evil minions have stuck to printing things about me for years. I'm used to the articles. They're mostly lies. Until now.

Until Callie.

She sold that photo of Christine to them. It had to be her. She admitted to selling photos to them over the years.

Damn her. My body is taut with the need to find her, make her stop, protect my family. *No.* I take deep breaths to beat back the rage rushing through me.

Is Callie in cahoots with Dylan? Or is she a pawn? There's one way to find out. I turn the facts over in my head. Callie knows Dylan, or someone at his company. I'm back to square one with ruining Dylan. And time is running out if Christine and Mia are being targeted. This has to be solved before the baby. Callie is smart. She knows my routines. She'll never stop, unless I make her stop.

Make her stop. And use her.

I stalk back to my desk, my movements tight and controlled. I shove the rage down and focus on the list I keep in my desk drawer.

Every name is crossed off except for one. Dylan Green. The man I hate the most. I pull out a fountain pen and add one more name to the list. Callista Thompson. The harsh pen strokes make dark slashes across the page and satisfaction coils in my stomach.

Revenge. For my family's honor. For my sister's suffering. For mine.

And I know just how to obtain it. Kill two birds with one stone. Get back at Dylan and use Callie to do it. Keep her close. Make her pay for the articles and the photos. Dangle her in front of Dylan when I'm done. Her paper will be caught in the fallout.

I pick up my phone and press 1 to reach George.

"How can I help?" Their voice is smooth, unbothered. I could ask George to hide a body and they would simply ask if they could get reimbursed for the shovel. The person we hire for me needs to have that quality in spades. It is, unfortunately, incredibly difficult to find, which is why Miles acquiesces every time George asks for an obscene pay raise.

Callie Thompson should never have tangled with me. I can't wait to destroy her.

"I need you to find out everything you can on Callista and Arnold Thompson."

∼

THE BEST PLACE TO discuss revenge is a quiet Italian restaurant near my Upper West Side townhouse. If only I could get my sister to focus.

She crunches a seeded breadstick while I glare at her.

"I'm not giving this up, Christine."

She swallows and sighs. She's the spitting image of our mother. Wild, dark hair, dark eyes, a strong jaw. Christine says it makes her look too manly, but to me she's just my baby sister.

"It's in the past, J. Why are you so focused on this?"

By *this*, she means my revenge against Dylan Green. He deserves to be ruined for what he did. I slowly take a bite of my bolognese. Slowly, because I want to rage, but we're at my favorite place near my apartment, and I'm not about to upset Silvio with my antics. My icy calm would have a business rival scurrying, but my sister simply sips her wine.

My hand tightens on the fork, and I set it down carefully. "I will never forgive myself for letting him into our lives. He hurt you. And now he's taking an interest in you again. What if he goes after Mia or the baby?" Christine flinches at my words. It's her worst nightmare. "I didn't make him pay at the time, but now? I can't let the baby be born into a world in which he escapes with no consequences." My voice is rough, and Christine's expression twists in sympathy.

"It's not your fault."

"It *is* my fault. I brought him close to the family. I told him about your girlfriend. I *trusted* him." I spit the words, the force of my anger and shame making it hard to breathe. "He made you miserable for a year. We had to move because of all the reporters at the house. Mom loved that house." Christine did too. She wanted her future kids to grow up in that house.

Christine's face takes on the haunted expression she wore after Dylan began publishing articles about the family. "I don't want to talk about this," she says. My chest pinches at the fear in her eyes. "He doesn't merit any more of your time."

"After what he did to you? To me? You hate him. You've wanted to get back at him for years."

She leans forward. "I can't afford to hold on to grudges now. Not with the baby coming." She points her fork at me. "And don't try to blame this on me. What he and Annalise did to you..." She shakes her head and goes back to eating. "That was worse. It's okay to be mad for yourself, J. It doesn't make you weak to admit how much they hurt you."

My throat is tight, until I sip my wine to clear it. "It took me years to claw my way back to the top. Dylan and Annalise fucked me over. And they deserve to pay." Each word makes rage boil through me, just like the events of six years ago did. "I nearly had him. His COO was *this close* to giving him up for tax fraud until that reporter from the New York Star published the article."

Dylan has weaseled his way out of every trap I've set for him, thanks to his mommy being a federal prosecutor and his dad the CEO of a Fortune 500 company. Tax fraud is a big fucking deal and goes straight to the IRS. The taste of victory was on my tongue, and now all I can taste is disappointment.

"What reporter?" Christine cocks her head. "Wait, the one who published those photos of you jogging last spring?" She grins. "Man, the comments on those were so good."

"The very same." Callie Thompson has been a thorn in my side for far too long.

Christine is still smiling when she sips her wine. "You know, I should make a calendar this year for Christmas. Ma would love it. I could sell them online. The half-naked photos could be June, just in time for your birthday."

"Shut it," I growl. "Don't even think about making a calendar."

She laughs and takes a bite of her tortellini. She gets it every time we come here, and it never fails to remind me of when we were kids. Mom working two jobs, Dad coming home late. *How many times did I put Christine to bed?* I made her tortellini with butter on the nights she missed our parents. She's always been the soft one compared to me, and I intend for her life to be good and happy. She deserves it. Which is where Callie Thompson comes in.

"I have a plan," I say after a few moments of eating in silence. "That reporter is going to help me get back at Dylan." *And she's going to suffer for invading my privacy.* I have plans for Callie Thompson. I'm not getting into that with Christine, though.

"How?" Christine raises a brow.

"I'm going to hire her and use her to get close to him." *Make her serve my every need.* The thought of revenge against Callie is a pleasant buzz through my body. "She can dig up information. She has a connection to him. Maybe I can even get him to hire her and funnel information back to me. She could plant false information about Kings Lane, and I could sue Dylan for libel later." Christine looks skeptical, but I know Dylan Green. "He's always wanted what I have. I just need to dangle her in front of him, and he'll bite." My lips curve at the thought of him falling for Callie's big blue eyes. He's a covetous bastard. One glance at her with me, and he'll be panting to hire her.

"I don't think this is the right path." Christine sighs. "I want you to be happy, not obsessed with revenge."

Happy. I don't bother telling my sister that this is as close to happiness as I'm going to get. Work. Revenge. More work. The way I prefer it.

I ignore her and she gives me a pointed look. "Ma has been asking about you. You missed dinner last Sunday. Even Dad started complaining." She raises a black brow. Complaining is unusual for my easygoing father. My mother? Not so much.

"I've been busy." It's the truth, though I'm no busier than usual. *You're a bad son,* my conscience whispers. I rub at my temples, where a headache is starting behind my left eye.

She rolls her eyes. "It's the same excuse every time. You have to be there for family, J."

"Don't start," I say shortly. "I am there for you. But you know how our parents are." They're always asking when I'm going to settle down, trying to set me up on dates with their friends' daughters. My mom still thinks I might move back to New Jersey. I'd rather eat glass.

Christine winces slightly. "I know. We miss you, though. Mia misses you."

I snort. "Mia does not miss me." My sister's wife and I get along as well as we can, which is to say, a careful state of détente.

"I had to try." Christine grins unrepentantly, but her smile fades. "I worry about you, J. Everything is falling into place for me, but I don't want you to be left behind."

My chest pinches. "You deserve it. Don't worry about me. You have enough on your plate. The baby, your new job. Oh, and it's not too late to divorce Mia. I know a really good divorce lawyer, I swear." I change the subject and she rolls her eyes, but she's smiling. She's used to me ribbing her about her wife, and she knows I love her too much to care who she married.

We finish and pay. I leave a generous tip for Silvio, who always makes space for me, even when it's busy. Christine gives me shit about the fact that I'm thinking about heading back to the office, and I nag her about why she insists on driving her awful, old Mustang.

"I love that car," she protests, as she shrugs back into her jacket.

"You need something safer for the baby. I told you that. Let me get you something more reliable." I'm already pulling out my phone to email George.

"Relax, J. Mia has one of those big SUVs with all the safety features. I don't think a car seat would even fit in the Mustang."

"Let me just get you something newer. It could even be another Mustang." *Like hell it will be.* I button my overcoat against the cool night on the other side of the glass.

She shakes her head and pushes open the door into the crisp air. "Stop worrying, J."

"I don't worry."

She grins and gives me a kiss on the cheek. "Try to be happy, okay? Less revenge, more walks in the park."

I snort and hug her goodbye. Not fucking likely.

5

Callie

A few mornings after my confrontation with Jonah, my dad and I exit the subway at Columbus Circle, and shoulder past tourists on our way to 57th Street.

My dad hasn't given me much information, but he was approached by an investor this week. We're on our way to the meeting now.

"Just tell me where we're going," I say.

My dad shakes his head. "I want you to go into this with fresh eyes. You'll be biased if you google the building, and then the owners. I don't want that."

I roll my eyes and speed up so I can keep pace with him. He's right. I would totally do that.

"Just tell me who the investor is."

He shakes his head again, and I sigh.

"You know how I feel about being independent. I thought you never wanted to sell the paper." *Why not let me take over instead?*

"We're not selling out, Cal, we're looking at our options. An investor could be exciting. Try to look on the bright side." He's trying to be cheerful, but his eyes are shadowed. He sees it too—this is one step on the path to defeat. One step until we're just a subsidiary of some giant company, or worse, totally wiped out of existence.

"I can run the paper. I can grow the business." Even as I say the words, I know they're a mistake. We've been over this before, and every time, his reaction grinds me down a little more. But I have to try.

"Cal, no."

"Why not? And don't tell me we can't do more digital, because that's exactly what an investor is going to push us to do."

My dad's mouth flattens into a stubborn line. "You don't want to be like me, Cal."

"What is that supposed to mean?"

"I want more for you. There are so many careers you could have."

"I'm not a kid, dad. I love doing this." We stop at a crosswalk and I give him a direct look.

"Don't follow in the footsteps of an old man and this failing paper." His shoulders sag slightly and my ire is quenched by sympathy. I know my dad is lonely, but I try not to think about it. He's stuck in his routines, no matter how much I try to shake him out of them. It's probably the only good thing about being forced to move back home, even if I'm reminded every day of my teenage years.

"That's not how I see you or this. I love this paper. I love this business. Think about all the loyal subscribers we have. We get hundreds of comments on every article. We have letters to the editor talking about real issues for the neighborhood. This paper matters. Let me do this." My voice is fierce with emotion, and my stomach dips while I wait for his response. In the back of my mind is the ever-present doubt—he doesn't want me to take over the paper because he doesn't trust me.

"Let's just see how the meeting goes," he says with a sigh.

With any luck, this investor will take one look at us and kick us out. I don't want to be part of a conglomerate.

We stop in front of a steel and glass tower. 555 57th. I recognize this address. *I've been here before.* I hand my ID to the security guard while I think. Then it hits me. 555 57th. Jonah.

My dad and I speak at the same time. "Kings Lane Capital."

The awful realization makes my head spin. I'm going to be sick. My breath comes out in a choked gasp as we walk to the elevator bank. "You didn't. How could you? Jonah? Really?" He hates me, hates us. Nothing good will come of his involvement.

"What's wrong with him?" We step into the waiting elevator and my father turns to me. He removed his ball cap for this, and I'm wearing a dress, but we still look woefully out of place. This is a world of sharks and we're minnows. Or krill. Whatever is smaller than krill.

"Everything is wrong with him," I argue. "He's totally ruthless and has no moral code. This is not someone we want to be in business with." I turn to face my father and cross my arms over my chest.

"He'll offer us a fair price. He respects us and what we do. He wouldn't have invited us here otherwise."

"No." I shake my head. This is about revenge. But I can't say that. My dad will freak out about Jonah's threats. "He does not respect us. Jonah Crown respects no one but himself."

"Miss Thompson. How lovely to finally meet you." Jonah's voice rolls over me, drawing a shudder from inside me.

My stomach plummets like an elevator breaking free of its cables. I shut my eyes briefly. When I open them and turn around, Jonah is there, holding the elevator door, looking devastating in a gray suit and blood-red tie. His expression is as bland as his tone is frosty.

"Nice to meet you as well." I attempt a smile. It falls when he gives me a short nod and introduces himself to my father much more warmly. *Interesting that he also doesn't want to acknowledge that he met me last week. What are you hiding, Jonah Crown?*

He leads us into a conference room that I'm sure is designed to intimidate. It's right off the elevator bank, so we can't see any of the interior office. There's coffee, fruit, mini bagels, and tiny croissants. My father, who has never turned down free food in his life, fills a plate. I take some coffee and sit at the conference table, right in the middle and facing away from the floor-to-ceiling windows. The view makes me feel ill and a little too exposed. And with the way my stomach is knotted, I don't think I can eat. I wish I were hungry, so I could have something to do with my hands instead of wiping my sweaty palms down my second-best dress. Jonah leans against the credenza, casual, at ease, like a men's fashion model turned cutthroat billionaire. I bet he never wonders what to do with his hands.

When my father is seated next to me, Jonah smiles, though it doesn't reach his eyes. "Shall we get started?" He doesn't sit but crosses his arms over his stomach. "I'd like to buy your paper."

I knew it. This is the worst possible outcome. Going corporate is my nightmare. I can't think of anything worse than a giant company polishing away our honesty, carefully managing our opinions, until we're nothing but a mouthpiece for Jonah and his business partners.

"Why?" The question pops out of my mouth, and my dad shoots me a look.

"What Callie means is, how did you become interested in our paper? We don't report financial news or anything of the sort."

I nearly choke but swallow the sound. How can he even ask? Is he not paying attention? *I guess not.* My stomach clenches. I know Dad is mired in the one or two long-form articles he writes per week, but he doesn't even know we're publishing articles about Jonah. Does he think I'm just taking photos and selling them to the Green Media and the Post?

"Your paper caught my eye. I'm an Upper West Side resident myself, and Kings Lane is looking to expand into news media over the next five years. We believe firmly in the power of small, local outfits over national chains. We're hoping to leverage synergies between papers to get better advertising deals and transform the subscription model into something more sustainable."

My dad looks suitably impressed and I want to shake him. Jonah's words are meaningless corporate speak, and his eyes glitter while he talks. He's greed, malice, and ambition wrapped in one beautiful package. With a silver tongue to match.

"Well," my dad says slowly. "Callie and I had never planned to sell. We don't want to become a faceless paper. We're local, and we think it's important that we maintain a connection to the community."

Jonah nods, thoughtfully. His brow is appropriately furrowed, but it all seems fake.

"How much?" I interject.

Jonah's brows go up. "Ready to discuss price so soon, Ms. Thompson?"

My face heats. "That's why we're all here, right?"

Jonah considers me, his eyes calculating. "Twenty-five thousand dollars."

He knows. My head nearly jerks back, but I stop myself. He knows about the debt. This was planned. I was the impetus for this meeting, and the debt is the leverage. The Devil wants his pound of flesh. But there must be more. My pulse speeds, and I shift in my chair. *Think.* He wants revenge. *This isn't just a sale. He's going to destroy you.*

"That's ah, very generous," my father replies. He's not remotely prepared for this.

"No. It's not. The paper is worth more." I press my lips together before I can insult Jonah to his face.

Twenty-five thousand dollars. He knows we'll do anything for the money. *Bastard.* My reaction must show on my face because Jonah's lips tilt. *He enjoys this.* He enjoys toying with us. I feel sick.

"Ms. Thompson. Would you like to negotiate?" He says the word "negotiate" in a tone that almost makes it sound *sensual.* He probably gets off on intimidating people. I won't win by forcing him, as much as I want to rage. I can tell he'll take pleasure in doing something just because he knows it will cause me pain. I've spent a long time observing Jonah Crown. He's known for his ruthlessness and his drive to win.

While my father hems and haws, I take a calming breath and force my shoulders to relax.

"Twenty-five thousand is less than the revenue we bring in each year," I say mildly.

Jonah's eyes flare with interest. *Is it worse for him to find me interesting or worse for him to want to ruin me?* Hard to say.

"Mr. Thompson. Would you like to see the rather impressive art collection we have at the office?" He asks the question of my father, but his stay glued to me.

"I'll stay," my dad says.

My lips twist. My father wouldn't trust me to negotiate on his behalf.

"I'd like to speak to Ms. Thompson alone, if that's okay."

"Callie?"

I look over at my father, worried but determined. "It's okay, Dad." I sigh. "It's fine. I'll talk to Mr. Crown. I'm sure it won't be long."

Jonah shows my father out and George collects him with a polite smile. When Jonah turns back around, his eyes are hard and his jaw is set. He'd be pretty if the harsh planes of his face weren't so masculine. His lips are full, even when set with displeasure, his eyes thickly lashed. His hair is impossibly dark and silky. He could be imposing if I let myself be cowed by him, especially with the way he towers over me. His suit is impeccable, tailored for his broad shoulders and lean waist.

"Done staring, Ms. Thompson?" He arches a black brow.

"Are you done looming?"

His lips curve in a cold smile before he unbuttons his suit and smoothly seats himself just a few chairs away. I catch hints of spicy cologne. *Delicious.* I will the thought away. Nothing about this infernal man is delicious.

My heart thuds uncomfortably under my dress as he stares me down, turning a pen in his long fingers. My gaze flicks to his hands. Large, lightly dusted with hair, an expensive-looking watch.

"What price would you propose, Ms. Thompson?" As he speaks, his full lips reveal straight white teeth. *The better to eat you with, my dear.*

My gaze meets his fathomless eyes. They draw me in, as if he's trying to reach my soul. I shiver. *What price is high enough to compensate for our dignity?*

"Five hundred thousand dollars," I say boldly. It's ten years of work and a nest egg for my father. Maybe I can finally convince him to retire.

"Bold," Jonah murmurs. "I'll accept that offer, but I have one condition."

"What is it?" I ask warily. This will be something awful, I'm sure.

"You have to work for me for one year."

I frown. He probably wants me to work in the mailroom or something. "I'll have conditions," I say, at the same time as Jonah speaks.

"As my secretary."

6

Jonah

Callie's eyes widen with delicious surprise at my statement. Triumph heats my blood and I force my hand to still on my leg. Negotiating with Callie is an unexpected rush. She's smart. I can see her mind whirring behind those dark blue eyes.

"As your secretary?" She repeats. Her cheeks are pink. I'm sure she's picturing all manner of depraved things. My stomach tightens. *Not happening.* I don't fuck people who plan to betray me. Because that's exactly what she's planning. She would be a fool not to, and I can tell Callista Thompson is no fool.

"Get your mind out of the gutter, Ms. Thompson." Her eyes flick to mine, as if surprised at how easily I can read her. "Yes, I know what you're thinking." I smile humorlessly. "But no. I have a secretary position for which I have been…unable to find a suitable candidate."

"I'm shocked," she mutters. I nearly smile. It seems I've cracked her pleasant facade.

"Yes, well, good help is so difficult to find these days."

Her eyes narrow. "Why would you do this?"

Revenge. You stole mine and now I'll take it any way I can get it.

"Why not?" I shrug, like her answer doesn't matter, when in reality, my skin is buzzing and my neck is prickling. I can't remember the last time I had this much fun. If tormenting her in this meeting is good, I can only imagine how it will feel to have her at my beck and call.

She tilts her head. She's right to be wary. *Come on, sweetheart. Say yes.* I try for a casual expression. I'm well on my way to killing two birds with one stone—using her to get to Dylan and making her suffer along the way.

"If I do this, I want more money. A million dollars. And I have conditions."

I dip my chin. A million dollars is nothing. "Name them. And then I'll tell you mine."

"I want to see the contract first."

Smart. "If you'll excuse me. I have it in my office." I actually have a copy of it in the monogrammed leather folio sitting on the conference room table. I've been prepared for this meeting since yesterday. But letting a negotiating opponent stew can be useful.

I buzz George and pace my office while the phone rings.

"Have security pull the conference room feed up."

"Spying on Ms. Thompson?" Their voice is amused.

"Just do it."

They laugh and hang up. A moment later, the feed is up on my computer. I've done this before. Once, I made a particularly annoying investor wait for fifteen minutes while I answered emails and enjoyed a latte. It's amazing what you can learn when someone thinks they're alone. People will shift in their seats, pace, take notes, call their partners. Ms. Thompson doesn't do any of that, though. The video is good enough quality that I can see her teeth digging in to her full lip. She's still for a full minute, then she looks around furtively and pulls the folio toward her. I loose a choked laugh.

Of course she starts snooping. Typical fucking reporter. Can't mind her own business. The dark thought makes my hand clench. There's nothing significant in that folder. She must realize that as well, because she pages through the contract, then places the papers back in the folio and aligns it precisely where I had it. *She's good.* Observant. Unwelcome respect floods me. *She's a reporter. It's her job.* And I can use her skills to my advantage.

I grab the contract and head back to the conference room, shoving down any unwelcome feelings about Ms. Thompson.

When I push open the door, she's sitting calmly, like she wasn't just going through my personal items.

I slap the contract unceremoniously on the table and drop into my seat. She's getting to me. Already. Like any reporter would. They're the lowest of the low. *I can't wait to crush her.* The thought fuels me as she pulls the contract toward her and gives me a strange look.

"Go ahead. Take your time."

I intend to enjoy this.

7

Callie

The contract is long, so I skip past the boilerplate and look for juicy details.

"I'm on call twenty-four hours a day?"

"Seven days a week."

Asshole. The stare he gives me is unyielding. I'm going to have to pick my battles with this one. I keep scanning. Compensation is listed as a lump sum at the end of the term. The amount to be filled in.

"You're not paying me?"

"No. You're getting the lump sum. That's enough."

I keep my face impassive but my stomach sinks. This might actually be an issue. I have a little left in my personal account, but I won't be able to take many photos while I'm here. Ad income pays our rent, but those photos pay for everything else. I chew my lip. Jonah's face is hard, his eyes chips of black ice. I'm playing at being a negotiator, but I'm so far out of my depth that I can't even see the surface.

"Can I fill in the lump sum?" I want it in writing before I start asking for things.

"Go ahead."

My hands shake slightly as I write. One million dollars. Pocket change to him. Everything to me.

"Conditions, Ms. Thompson?" I can practically hear him rubbing his hands together. *He loves this.*

I lift my chin. "I want my paper back."

His eyes flare. "And why would I do that? I'm paying a million dollars for it, after all."

"No. You're paying a million dollars to humiliate me."

He almost smiles. *Bastard.* "One year. One year of working for me, and you can have your paper back."

One year with this asshole? No way. Not even for the Star. "One month."

He laughs, and my insides flutter. I dig my fingernails into my palm. If I'm going to work for him, I need to stop noticing how handsome he is. "Bold." He cocks his head, a ghost of a smile still on his face. "Six months. And you can't quit. If you quit, I get the paper. If you get fired for cause, I get the paper."

"Define cause," I say flatly.

"You'll see it in the contract. But generally speaking, it means no disparaging the company, no breaches of confidentiality, no egregious behavior."

Egregious behavior will not be an issue. And I can avoid disparaging him. But breaches of confidentiality will be tricky. I need to be able to run the Star while I work for him, or we'll lose all our readers.

"I need to be able to publish articles while I'm here."

"Really, Ms. Thompson? You think you'll have time for that? Whatever will the people do without their pizza rat videos?"

My face flames at his words. "Our paper is more than that. It's a lifeline for a lot of people. There are residents who rely on us."

"Somehow, I doubt that."

The faint, mocking smirk on his face makes me want to stand up from the table and leave. *I hate you, Jonah Crown.* My feelings must show on my face because his smirk broadens into a knowing smile.

"If I can't publish while I'm here, the paper will have no value when I get it back." Something he should understand. I hope he understands, because I have very little bargaining power here. I want to run and hide. I hate being the subject of his mocking scrutiny. I'm the face behind a pen name, not a woman who goes toe-to-toe with billionaires.

"*If* you get it back. And as you say, Ms. Thompson, I'm paying a million dollars to humiliate you. Your gossip rag's value can go to zero for all I care."

His cruelty takes my breath away. Everything we've worked for over the years. My father's dream. Mine. All the loyal readers who depend on us. "Why?" I ask. My voice trembles a little. *Get it together.* "Why do you hate us?"

He leans in, his dark eyes holding mine. "You took something from me. Something I waited years to achieve. You went after my family." His nostrils flare, his eyes flash. He's angry. Angrier than he's willing to let on. He sits back, and his impassive mask falls back into place. "You stole my revenge. And now I'll get it any way I can."

His family? I never went after his family. "What do you mean went after your family? I've never done that." I'm pretty ethical for a paparazzo, not that he seems to care.

"Oh? What do you call it when you sell photos of my sister to Green Media? What about when you start writing articles about her? Following her? What about when the photos you sell turn into this?" He reaches into the leather folio and pulls out the article I saw while he was in his office. He smacks it on the table accusingly.

"What does the title say, Ms. Thompson? Read it for me." His voice is low and vicious.

I clear my throat. "Christine Crown. Cheating Scandal and Weight Gain—is She on the Brink?" I look back up at him. His eyes are flat and cold. The article goes on to imply that Christine's wife is cheating on her and that she's getting fat as a result.

Sympathy rises for Christine. I know what it's like being publicly humiliated. This is why I don't publish articles like this one. I focus on the good, the light and fluffy. I'd talk about where Christine gets those cute shoes, speculate about whether her baby will look more like her or her wife, even though obviously both their genes aren't present. That kind of thing.

"Nothing to say?" He scoffs. Guilt twinges. Matt asked me for details about Christine, and I gave them. I should have known Green Media would twist the plain facts into something mean. This is how they operate. Takedowns, not fluff. Jonah has been in their sights for years. I knew it, and I knew a photo of his sister would bring in big money. I chose to ignore the likely consequences.

My mind whirls. "I'm sorry your sister was hurt," I say carefully. "That wasn't my intention."

"Intention and result are two very different things."

"Maybe I can help you get your revenge." I do feel bad that Christine is getting caught up in this. And clearly, he really cares about her. She might be the only person he cares about, from what I can see.

His eyes flare with interest. "You're going to help me get it. On my terms."

"*If* you let me publish." I cross my arms. This is my line in the sand.

"You think you have that kind of leverage over me? How much do you think you're worth?"

"Enough that you want me to work with you." I shrug, even though my stomach is tight with nerves.

He smiles without humor. "Do I, Ms. Thompson?"

Our eyes lock. I need him to crack. I need the paper. I need to be able to publish. The dark pools of his eyes flicker with little flecks of golden brown. His mouth parts slightly, like he's about to speak. But instead he just stares, until the weight of his gaze grows heavy. My skin prickles. Finally, I slump and pick up my pen and paper from the table.

"All right. I wish I could say this was a pleasure, but I think we both know it was incredibly painful." My eyes flick up to his and for a second, he looks *hungry*. Ravenous and unsettled.

"You're leaving?" His voice is lower than before. *Does he want me to stay?*

"There's no reason to stay. I'm selling the most important part of my life, and in exchange, I know it will be run to the ground and I'll be tormented by you for six months. No amount of money is worth that." I push back from the table and move toward the door. My steps are deliberate. *Say something, Jonah.*

His chair creaks, and then I hear, "Wait." He clears his throat. "You can publish. As long as you don't disclose anything confidential. And you can't say anything negative about us."

I turn, finally. His cheekbones are colored slightly, tinged pink. *I got to him.* I, Callie Thompson, a mere beat reporter, ruffled Satan's feathers.

"What about you? Can I write bad things about you?"

His eyes go flat. "I'd advise against it, Ms. Thompson." His voice is silky, and I shiver. I hate that I shiver. I hate how he affects me.

"Anything else?" I ask.

"No fraternization." His eyes glitter.

"Define fraternization."

He takes a step forward. His dark eyes hold mine, and his full lips tilt up at the side. "Sexual relations, Ms. Thompson. With fellow employees." His voice is low, tugging at my insides. *How can he make such a clinical word sound delicious?*

I covertly wipe sweaty palms on my skirt and force myself not to shift on my feet. *Why is he getting to me?* "I'm glad to know that serving your every need won't include *every* need," I say.

His eyebrows go up and he looks like he might laugh again. "Don't worry, Ms. Thompson. I wouldn't ask that of you." And then he gives me an insulting once-over, from the top of my hair, down my body, to my feet in my only pair of heels. His gaze makes my skin heat with awareness. *Bastard.*

"Is that all?"

He taps his index finger on his leg. "You'll have the signed contract by the end of the day. There will be no further negotiating. One million dollars. I buy the paper and sell it back to you. But we aren't partners. You're mine for six months. No acting out, no quitting."

I will my arms to stay at my sides instead of coming up to protect my stomach. I'm shaking slightly at his words. *You're mine.* But I can't let him see how he affects me. "Mr. Crown. This is a challenge for me. And I didn't get where I am today by backing down. Game on."

8

Callie

"He wants you to work for him?" My father is incredulous as we walk home. It's a warm October day, and the walk across Central Park is one we've done many times. The lull between tourist seasons means the park is quieter than usual. The tourists mostly come in the summer, when New York smells like warm trash, and in the winter, when the park is too cold to enjoy. The fall is just for us.

"He agreed to let me run the paper while I'm there at least. It's a temporary role. And if I do this, he'll let us keep the paper." I'm intentionally vague on the details. My father is a proud man, and I'm not sure how he'll react to the arrangement Jonah and I have. One million dollars for the pleasure of six months of torment. His pleasure. Not mine. I shiver a little, even though the day is warm. "You really want to sell to this guy? I mean, we said yes, but we haven't signed anything."

He's silent for a second, as we wend our way down the path by the baseball fields. "Without him, I'm not sure we can pay the loan off."

"At least we're in agreement, for once."

"It was a mistake." He settles his baseball cap more firmly on his head, a nervous tic he's always had. "I can admit that now. We should have looked for a cheaper method to distribute."

I can't believe this. "No, Dad. We should be modernizing. We don't need to distribute physical papers. With the print run we're doing, the cost per copy is almost as much as the price our customers are paying. Not to mention all the time you're spending formatting it for print. If we move to online-only distribution, we can run more ads. It will turn a profit. I just need to—"

"No." He shakes his head. "We need a physical paper. We'll make it work."

I clench my jaw and take a deep breath through my nose. I'll never be able to convince him. I want to scream that *making it work* means selling our souls to the Devil, but I don't. It's just my soul that's being sold, and I'll do anything to help my father.

"I don't want to be involved with him either, Cal."

My eyes flick to him. He looks small and old, and regret twists my insides. I loop an arm around his shoulders. It's been my dad and me against the world for most of my life. My mom is a vague memory at this point. She left when I was six, and we haven't heard from her since. I can't lose him too. And now that he's getting older, it's up to me to be the tough one. "We'll figure it out."

I have to. I can't let Jonah win.

∼

LUZ AND ADRIANA are appropriately shocked by the identity of our buyer when I meet them for drinks later. We're tucked into the corner of a wine bar we like. It's equidistant from our apartments, and bottles are half off on Thursday nights.

Adriana is furiously searching his name, her dark eyes intent on the screen. She's a management consultant and she excels at ferreting out nuggets of information. I always tell her that she should have been a reporter.

"Says here that he's never seen in public. What's wrong with him?" Adriana asks.

Luz laughs and takes a sip of her wine. She's in her weekend clothes, since her four-day shift finished yesterday. "Probably why our girl here has to stalk him at his apartment."

"That's exactly right," I say primly. "He's known for being a recluse."

"What else is he known for?" Adriana wags her brows. "He's hot as hell. Does he have a girlfriend?"

I shake my head. "Not as far as I can tell. He's almost never seen with women. His business partner, Miles, goes out a lot, especially with his new girlfriend. But Jonah doesn't attend many events. He seems to work and go home, or eat the occasional dinner with family or his business partners."

The girls laugh. "Okay, so he's a workaholic recluse. Sounds like working with him will be fun." Adriana wrinkles her nose.

"I know." I grimace. "Here's the thing. I think he sought the paper out."

"What do you mean? As payback for the other morning?" Luz's eyes are wide.

"Maybe," I say slowly. "But I think it's more like revenge for reporting on him. Selling photos of his sister was the final straw, I think. He knew the exact amount of our debt. And he approached us, not the other way around. But the worst part is that he wants me to work for him."

"He what?" Adriana's mouth drops open.

I take a hearty gulp of red before continuing. "This is how I know he wants revenge. He told me if I work for him for six months, without quitting or getting fired, I can have the paper back at the end."

"Well, that seems reasonable," Luz cuts in. "Right? Adriana don't you think?"

Adriana narrows her eyes while she thinks. "What does the contract look like?"

"Fairly standard, I think. I'm at his beck and call for six months.

And if I last, I get a million dollars." I shrug. "I think he'll keep his word. He doesn't care about the paper. He hates me. You should have seen his eyes. Like looking into a pool of darkness. He likes the idea of having me at his beck and call."

"Wait," Luz interjects. "Does this mean you know—" she waves a hand in the air. "*Stuff?*"

"Sex," Adriana says flatly. "Does he want sex?"

I think back to the flatness of his eyes, the insulting expression on his face when he looked at me. "He said he would never ask that of me. He made it pretty clear that he thinks I'm not his type."

"Dick," Adriana says, tipping her wine back angrily.

Luz snorts. "Look on the bright side. If he thinks you're gross, at least he won't be making *advances.*"

I laugh. "That is a bright side. Thanks."

"Okay, so all you have to do is lie low for six months and you'll get the paper back." Adriana nods decisively.

"How does your dad feel about all this?" Luz asks. She knows what disappointing your parents feels like. Her mother's eternal shame is that Luz is a nurse, not a doctor.

"Well, he doesn't really know." I fiddle with my napkin before meeting the knowing eyes of my friends. "He was the one who took the meeting. He agrees we can't pay the loan off."

"Here we go." Adriana rolls her eyes. "You never should have taken it to begin with."

"Believe me. I know." I sigh. "But during the meeting, Jonah asked to speak to me alone. So my dad doesn't know about the whole secretary thing. He knows I'll be working for him." Luz is giving me a knowing look. "Come on, guys. He would freak out if he knew what Jonah was planning. I mean, I don't really know either, I just know it will be bad. Dad can't handle the stress."

"She's doing it again," Adriana says.

"Yup." Luz sips her wine. "Classic Callie."

"You can't do everything on your own." Luz's eyes are sympathetic. My friends are convinced I have some sort of hero complex.

"You guys are crazy. All I have to do is survive, and then I get my paper back."

"And then what?" Adriana flings her hand out. "You do all of this and then your dad takes back over and runs it into the ground?"

I wince. "Way to call me out."

Luz leans forward. "We just hate seeing you do so much when he's so resistant to change."

"Determined to fail, more like," Adriana grumbles into her glass.

"I just need to prove to him that I can take over. He's already doing less and less. The paper is his baby. I need to show him that I can do it in a way that he supports."

Adriana rolls her eyes, but Luz looks thoughtful. "Okay. So, what would it take?" she asks.

I lean forward. "A really big article. An exposé. My dad loves those. We've never had the time or the staff to do anything investigative, but now I'll be getting the inside scoop every day."

Adriana's mouth drops open. "You're going to write about Kings Lane. You're going to spend every day gathering information. And then, what? Air his dirty laundry?"

I smile. "Depends on what I find. But Jonah Crown is too much of an asshole to not have some bodies buried."

"But then you'll definitely get fired." Luz frowns.

"Not if she waits until the end," Adriana says. I can see her mind whirling behind her eyes. She tilts her head. "It's a good idea."

"But what if you get sued?" Luz cuts in. "I don't like it, Cal. Jonah doesn't seem like the kind of person to take this lying down. He threatened you, for fuck's sake." She leans forward. "He's basically buying you as a servant." Her eyes are huge and worried.

"Well, when you put it like that, it sounds bad." I wrinkle my nose at her.

"That's because it *is* bad." She nearly knocks over her wineglass as she gestures. "He could ruin you."

"He already has," Adriana murmurs. Her eyes cut to mine, and my lips twist in acknowledgement.

"It's true, Luz. He could ruin the paper over the next six months.

And even if I do get it back intact, who knows what the readership will look like. I need insurance. In case he decides to bully me. And to prove to my father that I can be taken seriously."

"I don't like it," Luz mutters.

"Me neither." I give her a half smile. "But I can make this work. It's six months. How bad could he be?"

9

Callie

The tower housing Kings Lane Capital looked evil when I first took the elevator to the meeting with Jonah, but today it seems to pulse with ill will—a black monolith against the bright blue October sky. I pull my skirt down and lean against a support pylon to slip on my pumps. My skirt is definitely too short, but my heels are comfortable enough and my plain green blouse shouldn't draw any attention. I don't have the budget for fancy new office clothes, so Jonah is going to have to deal.

I suck in deep lungfuls of air as I ride the elevator up to the top floor. Kings Lane owns the entire building, but the executives sit on the 52nd floor, where we had our meeting. Since I'll be working with Jonah, presumably I, too, will sit in those hallowed halls. My ears pop as the chrome elevator rockets upward, and I crack my jaw.

When the elevator opens, George greets me. I met them at the end of our meeting last week, and they seem nice enough. The once-over I get today and single brow raise speaks volumes.

"Ms. Thompson. Welcome to your first day at Kings Lane." They flick a glance at my pumps.

"Is something wrong with my outfit?"

"You'll see," they say ominously and whirl, in a cloud of spicy cologne and draped silk.

"I'm not really a business casual girl. I'm here against my will, after all," I mutter.

"I'll let you take that up with Jonah," they shoot back.

The hall is nearly all floor-to-ceiling windows, and soft sage-colored carpet. It's hushed and elegant, with artful arrangements of armchairs, coffee table books, and paintings.

George points out their desk, in front of Miles's office in the northeast corner, and then leads me down the hall to Jonah's office in the opposite corner, and my desk standing guard outside the door. While George's desk is a command station, my desk is tiny, and the light above appears to be *out?*

"Problem with the lighting?" I ask.

A flash of humor crosses George's face. "I suppose so. You'll need to contact facilities."

So that's how it is. George isn't a part of this nonsense, but they aren't going to help me either.

"Is Jonah here?"

"It's Mr. Crown actually," a deep voice says. *Jonah's voice.* George leaves me with a faint smile, and I finally turn. Jonah is leaning against the door to his office, arms crossed, a mocking smile on his face. He looks absolutely edible in a gray-blue suit that skims over his broad shoulders. His dark hair is pushed off his forehead, and the hollow of his throat is bared above his collared shirt. No tie. Casual. The Devil off duty. Ruthless ambition with a veneer of civility. He really is beautiful. I give myself a mental shake. *Don't think about how hot he is.* I need to focus on getting through the day.

"So nice of you to join us." His smile fades as he scans me. His jaw tightens as he takes in my skirt and my sensible heels.

"Problem with my clothing?"

"Skirt's a tad short, but it'll do." He shrugs and my face flames. My fingers twitch to tug at my skirt, but I clench them into fists. I refuse to play his games. Not when insubordination could get me fired, along with a whole host of other things.

"Apologies," I say stiffly. "Business casual isn't my normal attire. It won't happen again." It most definitely will happen again, because I have about three appropriate outfits and no money to buy more.

"See that it doesn't." His voice is hard, like his word is law. And I guess in this building at least, it is. *Prick.* I force my shoulders to relax.

"So, Mr. Crown, is it?"

"Oh, it most definitely is," he replies silkily. "Come in, and let's chat about your new role."

My stomach dips as I follow him into his office. The floor-to-ceiling windows make it look like we're in a sea of office buildings. The water to the west sparkles in the distance. His furniture is not what I would have expected. There's a sleek wooden desk, a velvet couch, a bar cart.

"Look your fill, by all means. I don't have anything else to do." His voice comes from my left.

I whirl. Jonah is sprawled in his desk chair, flipping a pen. I sit stiffly across from him and tug surreptitiously at my skirt.

"I assume I'll be answering the phone, filing things, getting your lunch. General degradation. The usual." The last bit pops out, and I almost wince. I've never been known for holding my tongue, but I told myself this morning that I would try.

He makes a surprised sound. "Degradation. Is that what you think?"

I press my lips together. I'm sure he'll tell me that I deserve this, or pretend he's not here to make me miserable. He leans forward, his eyes glittering.

"You will do whatever I tell you to do. And I never use this word, but *literally* everything. It's up to you whether the request constitutes degradation. But if it does—" He shrugs. "Not my problem. Refusing requests constitutes cause. Check the contract."

My pulse is thudding uncomfortably while he stares me down. "I read the contract. I understand. I'm yours for six months." And damn if I don't still feel guilty for selling those stupid photos, but the guilt is replaced by anger at Jonah.

His eyes flare at my words, and he dips his chin. "That's right. If I'm here, you are too, even on a weekend. If I call you or text you, I expect a response within five minutes."

"What if I'm out with friends? Or away for the weekend?"

"That's not my problem."

I snort. "So all you do is work then? You're never out with friends or away for the weekend?"

His head jerks back, just the barest amount. *Ha.* I struck a nerve.

"My personal time is none of your concern. I'm paying you to serve my every need." An irrational flash of heat goes through me at his words. My traitorous brain pictures serving his every need right here in this office. My tongue darts out to lick my lips.

"Thompson."

My eyes refocus on his face. His perfect face. Those full lips, that strong jaw shadowed with stubble. "Where did you go?"

"Ah, sorry." I will my cheeks not to redden. *Just picturing giving you a blowjob under the desk. And I didn't hate it.* I press my lips together to keep from laughing. If I'm lusting after this awful man, it is beyond time to get laid.

"I expect your full attention when we're at work together. Do I make myself clear?" His words cut through any lust I might have felt. His tone says he doesn't think I can handle this. I hold his dark gaze. *I'm going to survive you, Jonah. I'm going to triumph and leave the rubble of your company in my wake.* His eyes narrow.

"Thompson?"

I hate that he's using my last name, like I'm some sort of servant. *Ill-mannered asshole.* I want to scream it in his face, but instead I calmly reach for a pen and paper. If I'm going to get through this, I need to be the Callie who charms the pants off interview subjects, not the Callie who wants to claw her boss's eyes out. Fun Callie. The girl I am to most people, though Jonah makes me want to break things.

I smile winningly and click my pen. "Crystal. Now why don't you tell me your lunch preferences?"

"I have a salad or a wrap from the deli on the corner. On Mondays, they have a special and I almost always eat that."

I know he goes to that deli a lot, because I've seen him there, but every day?

"You never try anything else?" I raise my head to see Jonah watching me intently. "What about one of the carts on Park Avenue?"

He shrugs. "I like the deli just fine."

Boring. Eats the same thing every day. I make a note on my paper next to his order.

"What else do I need to know?"

Jonah taps a single finger on his polished wood desk. "I get to the office every day at 5:45 a.m. Depending on traffic. Though it's rare at that hour. I guess you already knew that, though." He cocks his head and I shove down a shiver. He's eyeing me like I might be lunch, instead of a wrap from the deli.

"Let's play a game, Thompson." He leans forward.

I freeze. "I don't think we need to do that." *This won't end well for me.*

He laughs softly. "Why don't you tell me what I do every day?"

I wince. "Really?"

"Why? Embarrassed? Someone finally caught you and now you can't own up to it?"

"No," I reply evenly. "Why would I be embarrassed?"

He snorts, like my question isn't even worth answering. "Go ahead." He crosses his arms over his chest and raises a brow.

"Fine." I sigh. "You take a car to the office every morning at 5 a.m. One of several. Four, maybe?"

"Five."

"Five. All are the same make and model, but the license plates are sequential."

His eyes glitter. "Very good, Thompson."

"You arrive at the office around 5:45 a.m., though you used to get here earlier."

"Very good." His voice is low. "Why do you think that is?"

I tilt my head. He's punctual and a man of habit. He would take the same route, so it's not traffic. There are no road closures to deal with. He changed his routine.

"You make a stop," I say. His nostrils flare. *Ha. I'm right.*

"Continue," he grits out. He won't acknowledge that I'm right, and I tuck the information and his reactions away for later.

"You work out every day. I assume before work but at the office." At his questioning glance, I say, "The gym bag."

"Right." He nods. "I'll expect you to join me for those workouts, by the way."

"You're going to make me work out?" I frown. I guess it makes sense as some sort of torture, but it seems odd, even for him.

His lips tilt up at the side. "No. You're going to hold my towel while *I* work out."

My pen slips briefly against the paper. *Hold his towel.*

"Is that a problem?" His eyes are lit with unholy fire when I meet his gaze. He wants me to say yes. This is the tip of the iceberg. If I crack now, he wins. Holding his towel is nothing. I tilt my head, observing the way he's comfortable under my gaze. He flips his pen in his fingers, idly, but there's tension coiled beneath the surface. *What would it be like to see him crack?*

"Thompson?"

"Not a problem," I say calmly. "So after your workout, presumably you putter around this office all day, with a brief break to get your lunch."

"Putter. That's right."

"And you pick lunch up yourself, or someone fetches it for you?" I feign calm while I make notes on the page.

"If I'm busy, I'll expect you to get it for me."

Why does it sound like he'll be busy a lot of the time? I smile placidly. "Duly noted. Most nights, you leave the office late. On the days I've observed you, it's been past 8 p.m. I don't usually work that late, but I've seen you occasionally."

"Does gossip stop after sunset?" he asks snidely.

I clench my pen. "No, but my photos do."

"Touché." He dips his chin for me to continue.

"A different car picks you up. And I don't know where you go after. Maybe to your apartment? I know you don't date. And you don't seem to see your friends very frequently. Do you have friends?"

"That's enough," he says shortly. He pushes back from the desk, and I scramble to my feet. His eyes flash under lowered brows. "I don't need a clueless paparazzo speculating about my social life."

My lips press flat. *Or lack thereof*, I almost say. But instead, I force my shoulders to relax. "Anything else I should know?"

10

Jonah

Callie Thompson makes me want to scream. *Anything else I should know?* She's playing a game, and she might be just as good as I am. Maybe. I'm a ruthless negotiator, but I can't figure her out. She was spitting fire when she walked in, but she's gotten it under control.

"That will be all," I say slowly.

She gives a crisp nod and turns toward the door. My gaze drops helplessly to her ass, again. My hand flexes against the wool of my suit pants. That skirt is way too fucking short. Her long legs are bare and the curve of her butt makes my blood feel hot. *Shut it down.* I'm not going to lust after this woman, and certainly not now that she's an employee.

"Thompson."

She's nearly at her desk, but she turns. "Yes, Mr. Crown?" My name on her full pink lips makes me tense. They're sinfully full, under a small, lightly freckled nose and high cheekbones. Her long, dark hair curls over her shoulders, and her eyes are the color of my favorite navy suit. She looks like a fucking Disney princess and it makes me want to scream. Or better yet, make *her* scream.

"I have a task for you. Please see George. I expect it completed by the end of the week." She inhales. She's gathering her patience. *Not as calm as she seems.*

"And your lunch?"

"I'll be far too busy to get it today. Coordinate with George. And you have thirty minutes to eat, so I expect you to get mine and finish yours in that time." A rule I just made up, but it feels right. I couldn't care less how long my employees take for lunch, as long as their work is completed.

I can see the protest in her eyes. They're flashing with anger. *Come on, sweetheart. Let's see you crack.*

"Understood," is all she says, before she walks away, her hips swaying and her long legs carrying her confidently down the hall.

I force my gaze back to the papers on my desk. Term sheets, projections for next quarter, an email George thinks I need in hard copy. I have no business lusting after Callie Thompson. Not when she wants to ferret out my secrets and use them against me. I'm intimately familiar with the hot agony of betrayal. It's a dull knife hacking at your insides, not a clean cut. A back alley stab in the back, not a surgeon's scalpel. I've been left raw and bleeding before.

To be the best, I need my wits about me. I can't afford to let anyone close. Which means staying the fuck away from Callie. I narrow my eyes in concentration, even as words swim before my eyes.

I won't let her get to me.

11

Callie

Four hours in to my "task," and I'm fairly certain I'm going to cry. I'm buried in a storage room down the hall from Jonah's office, sorting papers, like a corporate Sisyphus. I have twelve boxes to categorize and alphabetize, but each is packed to the gills. There are thousands of papers in here, and no rhyme or reason to the contents.

"Who even uses paper anymore?" I grumble. I'm starting to lose it. My arms are tired from sorting, and my back hurts from bending down to add papers to my various piles. *Fuck you, Jonah.* I think the words but I'm not brave enough to utter them. He probably has cameras in here.

I squint at the beige drop ceiling, like something out of a 90s movie. A little black camera stares back. Yup, definitely cameras. I put my back to the camera and drag the next box toward me across the gray carpet. There are no windows in here, no clock. I listened to music for the first few hours, but my phone is nearly dead now, so I sort in silence.

The next box is packed so tightly that I can barely pull out the first folder. *Ugh. Is this how every day is going to pass?* Locked in a closet while Jonah lords over me? He would love that. Despite his beauty, he's as cold as I suspected he was. I flip idly through the folder. It's full of financial statements. Not something I know how to analyze, or I'd stop to read them. I put them in the pile with the others. More financial statements, meeting notes, then emails. *Emails.* My eyes catch on one dated almost six years ago. It's from Jonah to Dylan Green. *Of Green Media.* I've never met him, but Matt has talked about him a bunch. *Jonah knows him?*

This email isn't recent. The words *call me* are in bold, nothing else. Presumably, that's typical Jonah brusqueness. I drop the email into a new pile. The next one stops me in my tracks.

It's a response from Dylan and all it reads is, "you got what you deserved." *Holy shit.* My eyes dart guiltily to the camera before I sink to the floor with the whole stack. I scan the pages quickly, looking for anything that could give any clue as to what happened. There are a few cryptic exchanges between Jonah and Dylan, each using their personal email addresses. *Why are these even here?* I am definitely not supposed to see this. The thought spurs me to read faster.

You'll pay for this. Jonah to Dylan.

I'd like to see you try. Dylan to Jonah.

Jonah knows Dylan Green. Jonah *hates* Dylan Green. And I sold him photos of Jonah's sister. *Ah shit.* The familiar guilt about my photos flares, and on its heels, dread. This is worse than I thought. *What have I gotten myself in the middle of?*

I rifle through the rest of the emails but find nothing useful. The door slams open. My head jerks. Jonah. No jacket, hair mussed. His eyes narrow.

"Do I pay you to sit on the floor, Thompson?" My pulse speeds at his hard tone. He's angry. *At me?* Hard to say. He always seems to be angry.

"You don't pay me at all actually," I mutter, but I shove to my feet. An email flutters to the floor, and we both watch it hit the carpet.

"What is that?" His voice is low, silky, wrapping around me.

"Just trying to file the papers," I say lightly.

He takes one menacing step forward, and my back hits the shelf. I teeter on my stupid heels, my knee buckling. Before I can grab the shelf, Jonah is there, crushing the emails under his loafers and steadying me with two warm hands on my waist. Mine land on his chest, over the smooth cotton of his white shirt and the hot skin of his chest. He's firm muscle and spicy cologne and a carefully shaved jaw. He's also way too close. His breath puffs out against my face, and when I shift my hand over his heart, he inhales sharply. *His pulse is racing too.* I tilt my head back to watch him. The hunger is there again, in his dark eyes, before he shutters his expression.

"Saving me?" I ask with a smile. Maybe he's not as bad as I thought he was. Maybe there's a kernel of goodness under that cruel exterior. And suddenly, I would dearly love to find it. I would love to worm my way beneath his skin and figure out what makes him tick. See if there's more of that hunger beneath all his layers.

His hand tightens on my waist. His eyes harden.

"Not likely. Making sure my property doesn't get damaged."

I frown. "But you stepped—oh." My breath catches as realization sinks in. My stomach bottoms out. "Me," I whisper. "You mean me." I shove at his chest and he steps swiftly back. "You think I'm your property?" I choke out the words. *He's worse than I thought.* I may not survive this. The realization hits me with stunning clarity.

He smiles coldly. "For five months, thirty days, and—" He checks his watch. "Six hours. And my lunch is late." He raises a brow. "Hurry up, Thompson."

My chest is tight. I suck in a breath, and he smirks. His eyes are black fire.

"Something wrong?" He expects me to back down. *Never.*

I dig my nails into my palm and force a smile. "Let me just grab my purse."

It takes twenty minutes to get Jonah's sandwich. It's a Monday special and half of Midtown Manhattan seems to be getting the same thing. I'm surrounded by a sea of blue suits and construction workers in dusty vests. When they finally call his order, I slump in relief. I have ten minutes to get upstairs, deliver his lunch, and eat the food I brought. I race back to the office, as fast as my heels will allow. *I should have changed before leaving.* I won't make that mistake again.

By the time I duck out of the elevator on the fifty-second floor, I'm limping. Jonah's door is closed, so I slump into my chair in relief. I send him an email to let him know his precious sandwich has arrived and start shoving carrots into my mouth. I've just crunched into the fourth when his door opens.

"Thompson."

I squeeze my eyes shut. I'm so hungry, and I just want five minutes without Jonah's imperiousness. But I force myself to swallow the carrot and stand. Jonah appears in the door, Miles behind him. Miles's beauty is approachable, warm, not like Jonah's cold fire.

Jonah eyes my lunch. "Lunch break is over." He steps forward.

I step back, protecting my food. I wordlessly pass him the bag with his sandwich. Miles's lips twist in what looks like sympathy. Jonah takes another step. I put my hand over my carrots and leftover pasta.

"I need you to finish sorting those papers, Thompson."

My stomach lets out a growl. My face flames. "I'll just finish my food and I'll be right back to it."

Jonah leans in, and I suck in a breath. *What is he doing?* His eyes glint with sick pleasure, and then he reaches around me and swipes my lunch into the garbage.

I slump back against the desk. I dig my fingers into my palms. *Don't react.* I refuse to give him the pleasure.

"Hurry up, Thompson. You only have until the end of the week, so you better work quickly."

I hold his black gaze, my pulse thudding uncomfortably under my shirt. He gives me a smirk and heads back into his office.

Miles eyes me uncertainly. "You're the reporter, right? From the New York Star?"

"That's me. Come to punish me as well?" I ask bitterly.

"I should," he says crisply. "You've certainly printed enough articles about me, but—" He grins. "You brought my future wife back into my life, so I can't be mad at you."

My eyes widen. I knew he and Lane were together, but I didn't realize it was the articles I published about him that pushed them into it. *Future wife.* Wow. "Thank you. You seem very happy together."

"We are." His eyes are soft and far away. Something that feels a lot like jealousy twinges. I've never had anyone who got that look on their face for me. "Anyways. Say the word, I'll get you out of whatever this is." He waves his hand at Jonah's office.

"No." I shake my head. "I don't want to get out. I want to go over the top." My eyes narrow as I take in Jonah's door.

Miles barks a laugh. "I approve. But good luck. He's the most hard-headed person I know."

I give him a small smile. "Good thing I am too."

An hour later, George appears at the door of the storage room with an annoyed look on their face and a protein bar in their hand.

"For you." They hold it out to me.

"Why?" I eye it suspiciously. "Is it poisoned?"

A smile curves their glossed lips. "Jonah wishes. But no, Miles sent me. Lane has made him into a soft-hearted fool. He said Jonah trashed your lunch." They grimace. "That's shitty."

I accept the protein bar. "You don't think I deserve it? For reporting on the company?"

"No. It made my job more interesting." They grin, full and open. "Though I think I deserve a little more attention in the press."

A surprised laugh tears from my throat. "I'll see what I can do. Have you done anything scandalous lately?"

They tap a manicured nail on their chin. "I'm happily partnered up, so my days of tearing up the West Village are over. I could make a scene on 57th Street?"

"No, no. Jonah would probably string you up by your ankles."

"Unlikely." They roll their eyes. "He needs me too much."

"Maybe a fashion spread? Our readers love those. And your outfits are great." I eye their smooth, dewy skin. "Or a skincare regime. Assistant to the billionaires and how I stay beautiful. That could work."

"Ooh. Yes. I'll do a sheet mask tonight and make sure I'm looking fresh tomorrow."

I smile. "I'll bring the camera."

George watches me unwrap the protein bar. "I thought I was finally going to get some help around here. And he has you sorting papers that we could easily digitize and shred." They purse their lips.

"They keep you busy?"

"Like you wouldn't believe. Miles is easygoing, in his own way, but Jonah is exacting. Nothing is good enough for him. He's particular and demanding. The staff are terrified of him. And so are his interview candidates. You're not, though. I can tell."

"Sorry." I give them a sheepish smile. "I think I'm here to be punished, not here to work. Not really. I serve at the pleasure of the Prince of Darkness."

George lets out a surprised laugh. "I like the nickname."

"At least someone does."

George says goodbye and a tiny spark of hope flares. If this is how the next six months go, I may survive.

12

Jonah

"You're being a dick. I mean, more than usual." Miles swirls his whiskey so the amber liquid catches the dim light in the bar at Kings Cove. The back room is reserved for our exclusive use, and the secret hideaway makes a convenient meeting place, since it's on the ground floor of our office building. The wall sconces shed dim light, and the red velvet upholstery shines like rubies.

Jason snorts. "Has anyone quit yet?"

I scowl at my friends. "She can't quit. Besides, she deserves it, and you know it."

"Wait. She who?" Jason leans forward. His eyes are bright with curiosity. "Are you seeing someone?"

I roll my eyes. "Hell, no. What is with you two? Last week, Miles practically tried to push me down the aisle."

Jason spreads his arms out. "Look how it's working out for me."

"Yes, you're very relaxed now. You're almost as bad as him." I jerk my head at Miles, who is sipping his whiskey and texting Lane.

"He's a goner," Jason agrees. "So who is *she*?"

"The reporter from the New York Star. Callie Thompson. Callista, actually." Her name rolls off my lips, full and sinful, like her body. My hand tightens on the whiskey glass.

"The one writing the articles? You've been trying to figure out her identity for months."

"More like a year. Though after the nonsense with Miles and Lane last month, I increased my efforts." More like I bullied our security team into using less than ethical methods, but why split hairs?

"The very same reporter," Miles agrees. "He found her."

I grin savagely. "Through sheer force of will. And a slip-up on her part." She never should have shown me her face. She never should have worn that hat.

"Don't even ask about the facial recognition technology." Miles shakes his head.

I sip my whiskey. The burn used to make me cough, but I suppressed that reaction years ago. Just one more thing I shed on the way from being a townie from New Jersey to being the man I am today. "It was worth it."

Jason's brows go up. "What are you planning?"

"Planning? He's already implemented it. He has the poor woman upstairs sorting files," Miles interjects.

"Where did you even find files?"

"George dug them up for me."

"George has important duties to attend to. You can't keep monopolizing their time with your petty schemes. You were supposed to hire someone." Miles is annoyed, and perhaps rightly so. George is technically the Chief of Staff, but they work for Miles more than me. "You should have Callie actually help you."

"I don't want her snooping." I sip my drink. "Besides, she's distracting. I don't want her near me all the time."

Jason cocks his head. His ice blue eyes are calculating. "You're attracted to her."

"Don't lawyer me," I say shortly.

"Just calling it like I see it," he says mildly, but he's smirking.

"No, wait. You might be right." Miles leans forward to watch me.

"Knock it off," I growl.

"Callie is pretty," Miles agrees. *Pretty doesn't begin to cover it.* I clamp my lips together. "She's tallish for a woman, curvy. Freckles, full lips, dark hair. It's long, too, and wavy." *The perfect length for winding around my hand.* I quickly sip my whiskey before I can get caught up thinking about how hot she is. "Thick lashes. Brown eyes."

"They're blue," I say shortly, and then groan.

Jason barks a laugh. "You do think she's pretty. This is great."

Miles and Jason raise their glasses and knock back the rest of their drinks.

"Why do you even care?" I ask.

"It's just that you haven't been with anyone in years. You've been contemplating revenge against Callie for what? Months? Almost a year? And now that you have her, you want to fuck her."

"I do not want to fuck her." *I so do.* I haven't admitted it to myself, because it's the road to perdition, but fuck, I want to bend her over my desk. I want to spread her out like a feast and shove that short skirt up to her waist. I want to bury my face between her legs until she's sobbing my name. And when was the last time I felt like that? Years maybe?

Jason flicks a glance down at my hand, where it's tight on the crystal tumbler, and raises his brows.

"Sure. You don't want to sleep with her. But if you did, what's so bad about that?" The question is carefully phrased, but he and Miles are watching me. I glower at them, but Jason just stares.

"Because we don't sleep with employees. Well, Theo might have once or twice, but he's in Australia right now, so he doesn't count." Our elusive playboy of a co-founder hasn't been at the office for over a year.

"Oh, come on, she's not an employee," Miles says.

"You're shockingly cavalier for someone whose reputation was just in the dumpster," I say crisply. Callie's reporting on Miles ruined a deal he'd been after for years. She implied he broke a woman's heart, and it caused him no end of trouble. Trouble that resulted in his best friend's sister coming back into his life. The asshole always comes out on top.

Miles leans over to smack me on the shoulder. "Don't be a dick. And you know I'm right. She's not an employee."

"Worse," I growl. "She's a reporter."

"Ah." There's a world of meaning in that word as Miles sits back against the booth.

"Not everyone is Annalise. Or Dylan," Jason says casually.

"What's that supposed to mean?"

"Just that you could be forgiven for not wanting anything to do with reporters after the way they used you."

"And that you should keep an open mind. Instead of looking for betrayal around every corner." This from Miles.

"It works for me," I say tightly. "And it works for you too. Look how successful we are."

"But at what cost?" Miles leans forward. "I know you were at the office at 9 p.m. last night. On a fucking Sunday. Don't you have family dinner on Sundays?"

I do and I didn't feel like going because Christine was going to badger me about coming to her baby shower again, and my mom was going to ask me if I was eating enough, and I couldn't do it. All the family time and Christine's happiness and the darkness swirling inside me, so at odds with the cheery brightness of her life.

"I was cleaning up the mess Callie made."

Jason cocks his head questioningly, so I add, "Dylan's COO was going to sell him out, until Callie reported on us being seen together. I'm back to square one."

"I see," Jason says. He and Miles share a look, and I roll my eyes. They're scheming. I can tell.

"Knock it the fuck off. I'm right to be worried about her. She could very easily sell company secrets to national news and fuck us over. Just like fucking Dylan did. She's supposed to spy on Dylan. She's not here to spy on me." *Just like Annalise.* But I don't mention my ex, because Miles and Jason will start in on me and how I need to let the past go, even more than they already are. "At least if I keep her close, I can monitor her."

"Monitor her. Is that what they call it these days?" Jason chuckles, and Miles bumps him with his shoulder.

I shake my head. "Callie Thompson is staying firmly where she belongs. Out of my sight and with her nose out of my business."

"Famous last words," Jason adds. He looks far too smug. But what happened to Jason will not happen to me. I like being alone. I like my organized life. Love is messy. Christine's life is endlessly complicated by her brash wife, Mia, and their future son. Miles and Jason always have plans now—group texts, trips with their little families, dinners out. It's a wonder Miles gets anything done.

I ride the elevator back up to the office in silence. The building lights flicker on as I stride down the hall. No one is here at this hour. I settle in my desk chair and bring up the proposal I was reviewing. Two hundred million dollars for an investment in our next project. The words swim before my eyes, even though I only had one whiskey. I increase the font size and refocus. This needs to get done tonight. I spent the day in meetings, trying to find information about the board members of Green Media, and torturing Callie.

Callie. Is she still here? I could find out easily. *No.* I'm not going to think about her. I need to work. I read the same sentence six times before I give up and call building security.

"Mr. Crown. How can I help you?"

"I'd like the feed for the camera in 52A."

"You'll have it shortly." My computer flickers on and the hellish storage room appears. My eyes catch immediately on her, still surrounded by boxes. She yawns and pulls something out of her purse. A phone charger, maybe? She bends and I get a perfect view of her ass. She's delicate, but curvy. It's an appealing combination. Even on the slightly grainy video, she looks good.

Stop. I squeeze my eyes shut. *Don't be a creep.* I click out of the camera's feed. Not a minute later, I hear the storage room door shut. I turn guiltily back to my work. I'm reading without understanding the words when she comes down the hall, humming something.

"Oh. You're still here." She's in my office doorway, and I raise my head slowly, like I haven't been monitoring her every move and fantasizing about her in my free time. My gaze flicks helplessly over her before I meet her eyes.

"Was there something you needed?"

Irritation flashes over her face. *Good.* "Nope. I'll just be over here."

She settles into her desk chair. I can make out just the side of her body and her screen. *Don't even look at her.* She's tapping diligently away while I refocus on the term sheet. Millions of dollars deserve my full attention. I will not be distracted by her. Until she starts humming again.

"Can you not?"

"What?" Her head snaps up.

"Stop. Humming. People who hum in public should be shot."

Her eyes narrow. "Do you hate all happiness, or just mine specifically?"

"Yours is particularly distasteful to me." And she seems to be so damn happy all the time. Singing under her breath, maintaining that pleasant facade. And I'm sure it's a facade. Which means I can crack it.

"At least you're honest." She snorts and turns around.

"Why are you even here? Don't you have files to finish?"

"I'm working."

"Right. On the paper." Derision is heavy in my tone.

She swivels in her chair, and frustration is written on her face, before she smoothes it away. "I'll do my work. And you do yours. Unless I'm making it difficult for you to focus? You could always give me the million now, and I'll be out of your hair."

I nearly smile. "Nice try. Now turn around and do that work you so desperately need to do."

Thirty minutes later, I have to admit she's relentless. Disorganized but intelligent. She scrawls quick notes on a pad of paper as she types, then turns to editing a photo. *Of me?*

I get up for a closer look, and she startles. Those huge blue eyes are surprised, her lips parted. The scent of her shampoo is in my nose. "What are you writing about?"

"Not you," she says shortly.

I see a photo of an older woman, but not much else. "I thought you mostly covered celebrity gossip."

"You know, I'm not surprised you've never read the paper. Did you just look for things about yourself and then go straight to the comments section?"

Embarrassment heats my face, and *what the fuck?* I'm never embarrassed. "I'm more of a Financial Times kind of guy."

"At least it's not the Journal." She shrugs, unimpressed, before digging around in her bag. "Here. The latest copy." She passes a slightly dog-eared paper to me, and I take it gingerly.

"It won't bite."

"Wouldn't want to get ink on my hands," I say smoothly. In reality, I want nothing to do with this. Seeing your face looking at you from every publication in New York City will do that to you. Callie might not even realize how widespread the articles were, because I eradicated every mention of me from the press after the incident with Anna and Dylan. Every copy burned.

She snorts and turns back to her computer. Ignoring me. And like a little kid, I want more of her attention.

"So, what are you writing about today, if not me?"

She huffs and scrolls up. "It's an interview with a documentary filmmaker. She's a lifelong resident of the Upper West Side, and she just finished a documentary about the neighborhood and how it's changed over the years."

I'm silent as I scan the interview questions. *What do you remember about being a child in the neighborhood? What have your own experiences of change been? How did that influence your work?*

Good questions. Insightful, intelligent. Begrudging respect fills me. I assumed Callie wrote exclusive gossip and fluff pieces, but I was wrong. Callie yawns as I read.

"Tired?"

She rubs at her face. "Yeah. I was nervous about today. I didn't sleep much last night. And I need to finish this before I send it to the proofreader."

"Good. You should be nervous."

She rolls her eyes. "Yeah. Yeah. Punishment. You're going to make my life miserable. Right? Is that the plan?"

That's not even half of it. "I should be tormenting you right now," I mutter.

"Believe me. You started strong." She smiles slightly, like the file sorting didn't bother her at all.

"Not strong enough, if you're still smiling." *Fuck, this woman.*

"Why? Does it bother you?" Her smile grows as she rises from her chair, putting her right below my chin. Foolish desire twists in my groin.

"It drives me insane." My voice comes out hoarse. *With irritation.*

"I'm so glad," she says. "What exactly about me drives you insane? I'll take notes." She reaches for her pen, and my hand lands over hers.

"Don't," I growl. "No notes about me. How are you so cheerful all the time?" *I hate it.*

"That's my secret to know, and yours to find out."

Her blue eyes shoot fire and I step closer, until I'm in her space, soaking her in like a plant in the sun. Her lips part. Her breath hitches.

"I don't want to find out." I brush my thumb over the skin of her hand, and she shivers. *Good.* I will my body's reaction away. "I want you to suffer." My words are quiet, spoken like a lover, but the words of a villain.

"Then we're aligned." She smiles, like she's already won.

Her words light something inside of me. A match to a fuse I thought was long dead.

"Game on, Thompson," I whisper.

I turn back to my office, unsettled by my new knowledge of Callie. *Ms. Thompson.* Unbelievably beautiful, a body made for sin, and a sharp mind. Everything I want in a woman. If only she weren't out to destroy me. I watch her work. She twists up her hair, baring the long column of her neck. I want to bite it. She slicks on lip balm, and I want to lick it off. I'm not even pretending to work. I'm just watching her and *wanting*.

This needs to stop.

I grab my papers and my briefcase, then my overcoat. I need to get this under control. I can't afford distractions. I need to stay focused. Revenge on Green Media. Conquer the world. I'm close. And to start, I need to stop fucking thinking about Callie Thompson.

13

Callie

I wake to a hand on my shoulder. I snort inelegantly, and flail. *Where am I?* My head throbs and my mouth feels fuzzy. I jerk my chin up and see Jonah Crown smirking at me. *Jonah. The office. The sorting. Finishing the paper. And then more sorting.* I shut my eyes and groan softly.

"Tell me this is a nightmare," I mutter.

"Believe me, Thompson. You're not one of the top five people I want to see on a Friday morning. This is, unfortunately, all too real. And I'm late for my workout." Jonah's crisp voice cuts through the haze in my brain.

"Start without me. I'll catch up." I let my head drop back onto the desk.

A warm palm closes around my upper arm. "Let's go." Jonah pulls me out of the chair and swiftly steps away. His eyes glint as he takes me in.

"Are you planning to work in that?"

I look down at my outfit. I asked Adriana to bring me supplies last night when I was stuck at the office again, and she came through with an overnight bag and dinner. I'm wearing yoga pants and a cropped sweatshirt. There's a small strip of skin that shows above my waistband, and I tug at the hem.

"I'm not sure there's much you can do. That garment seems to be missing several inches." Jonah cocks his head. "Though it may even be an improvement over yesterday's outfit. It's hard to say." By yesterday's outfit he means the same dress I wore on Monday. *Asshole.*

He turns on his heel without so much as a "follow me." I stick my tongue out at his back as I shuffle after him. I follow him into the elevator and lean against the wall, with my eyes shut.

"One would think that you'd be an expert at waking up early, what with all the early morning skulking you do."

"I don't skulk," I mutter.

"So, what do you call it when you stalk innocent men and wait for them outside their apartments?"

"My job."

Jonah snorts. "Ah yes, informing the residents of the Upper West Side about the latest celebrity to move to the neighborhood. A real public service."

My eyes snap open. Jonah is watching me as the elevator ticks down. He looks feral in the dim light. His gaze is predatory, his eyes flickering with malice. His arms are crossed in his black sweatshirt.

We do more than publish celebrity gossip, and he knows it. We'd be able to do even more if I wasn't spending twenty hours a week trying to make ends meet taking photos. I could focus more on the lifelong residents of our area instead of its most famous ones. My eyes narrow.

"What public service do you provide, Mr. Crown?"

His nostrils flare briefly. "Plenty. We have numerous charities we support."

I snort and lean back against the wall. "I'm too tired for this today. I didn't sleep. Your papers are sorted, your highness."

Jonah leans in, gaze sharpening on mine. His nearness makes my pulse thud. His cologne smells delicious and his lips are parted slightly. He stares me down like I'm the only thing in his universe.

He's the first person to ever do that, and I hate it. I hate how much of his attention I garner, and how he wields it like a weapon. "You don't get to be tired, Thompson. And I prefer Your Majesty."

With that, he sweeps out of the elevator and beckons for me to follow. Like I'm some kind of dog. *I hate you, Jonah Crown.*

I swallow my words as a gleaming row of exercise machines unfurls before us, backlit by the lights of Manhattan through the floor-to-ceiling windows. It's not yet dawn, though the sky is lighter than it would be at 5 a.m. Jonah drops his workout bag on the ground and strips off his sweatshirt. His shirt rides up to display a hard stomach, and my belly tightens. I quickly look away as he prepares for his workout. *I want you to suffer.* I nearly laugh. I'm already there.

"Towel's in the bag. Water too. Work out if you want. Sit on your hands. I don't care." He walks away and through an unmarked door at the back of the room.

"Towel's in the bag," I mimic, before slumping onto the chair of one of the leg press machines and shutting my eyes.

I'm just drifting off when I hear, "Thompson" in Jonah's deep voice. *Too soon.*

"I'm pretending to be dead. Please go away."

"Much as I wish that were true, I need a towel. Let's go."

I crack my lids and promptly suck in wind. He's shirtless. He tips his water bottle up, and his throat works. My brain short circuits. A bead of sweat appears at his hairline and I follow it with my eyes, tracing over the column of his throat, the cut of his collarbones against his smooth skin. Then lower. Moisture seeps over the edge of his pec, just inches from the flat disk of his nipple. His skin glistens over slabs of muscle. My mouth is dry and I swallow hard. *Look away.* But I can't. I need to know where that droplet of sweat is going to go. It traces lazily over each ridge of his abdominals, tempting me to reach out and follow it with my fingers, until it finally lands in the crisp black hairs that lead into his shorts. I shudder when it disappears and lift my gaze to his. He's done drinking the water, and my face flames. *Caught ogling the boss.* I wait for a cutting remark, but he watches me under heavy lids. His breaths are coming fast, like mine are. Except I didn't work out. I stand on shaky legs.

"I'll just get that towel," I say inanely. I keep several feet between us as I rummage in his bag, pulling out the white towel. I pass it to him without looking and he takes it. *Could this be any more embarrassing?* Lusting after a man who wants to ruin me. I'm texting Adriana and Luz for backup the second I escape from this gym.

"What's wrong with you?" he asks.

I turn to see Jonah eyeing me. "Nothing. Just tired. You know."

He towels over the back of his neck and into his hair. "What time did you go to bed?"

"Bed? Oh no. I slept here. In case you couldn't tell."

He grins. "It was a figure of speech. It's obvious you slept here." That grin makes my skin feel hot. He's handsome beyond belief when he smiles. Even if it's at the thought of my misery.

"Ah, three maybe? I'm not sure. I went back to finish filing after I sent the paper to the printer because I realized I had filed the financial statements with the invoices, which obviously makes no sense. So I went back through all the boxes and filed them with investor reports. And then I had to label everything. By the way, there are some HR files included in there. Those should be shredded if it's past the retention date." My eye twitches from exhaustion, and I press a hand over it. "After that it gets a little blurry. I lost track of time. And I cut myself on the tape dispenser trying to seal up the boxes, so I had to deal with that. You should really have first aid kits readily available."

Jonah is watching me, a faint frown on his face. I'm rambling but I can't shut up. He probably hates rambling. I told myself I would be circumspect and smart. *Shut up, Cal.*

"Wait right here."

He turns around and walks to a carefully concealed closet. He moves economically through space, confidently. When he turns back, there's a first aid kit in his hands.

I put my hand out for it, but he keeps coming. I step back, and he follows, until the backs of my knees hit a weight bench.

"Sit." His face is impassive.

I sink to the bench. He sinks to the floor, kneeling before me like he's a supplicant before a queen. I press a hand to my mouth to keep from laughing at the absurdity.

"Where did you cut yourself?" His eyes snag mine, inscrutable. He looks like a fallen angel, but he smells like a man—sweat and faint hints of bodywash.

I hold my arm out, and he frowns. The jagged cut is an angry purple from the bruising.

"It looks worse than it feels." My voice comes out breathy. *Get it together, Cal.*

The brush of his thumb over my pulse makes me shiver. He tears open an antiseptic wipe.

"This will hurt."

He presses the wipe to my skin, and the sting makes me hiss a breath.

He smiles faintly. "Told you."

"Shut up," I mutter. "You're enjoying this."

He bandages the cut with steady hands, and I inhale deep lungfuls of his scent. I want to shut my eyes and press my face into his chest. I want to grab him by the neck and shake him for getting me into this mess.

"Why?" I whisper.

His head jerks up. For one delirious, awful moment, I want to press my lips to his. The rush of desire makes my stomach lurch.

"Because I take care of what's mine." His voice is low, a little rough.

"And I'm yours." I hate it, but his words still send a tendril of warmth through me. I've never belonged to anyone. The thought of belonging is seductive. It's a single grain of sugar. Delicious, bad for me, and not enough to satisfy. I search his face. *I can't figure you out, Jonah Crown.*

He pulls my arm into him, forcing me off the bench as he rises to his feet. "For six more months, you are. And I don't want any accidental injuries. We wouldn't want to impair your usefulness. The only one who gets to torment you—" He leans in, until his breath ghosts over my face. I can see the tiny lines around his eyes. "Is me."

I suck in a breath at his words, but he doesn't give me time to react.

"Now pick up that towel and grab the water. It's leg day."

I spend the next hour standing next to him while he lifts weights. I shift from foot to foot, sneaking surreptitious glances at his biceps as they flex, at his shoulders as they tense and release, at his abs as he does some sort of insane pull-up with a weight hanging from his waist.

"Why do you work out so much?" I ask, when he finally drops the floor.

"Do you not?" He eyes me as he pants. His haughtiness is still there, through the harsh gusts of his breath, but it's tempered by his exhaustion.

"Oh, come on. Does it look like I work out?" He jaw tightens as he comes up with a response. "Don't answer that, actually," I say quickly. I don't want to hear whatever rude thing he was about to say.

"I work out because I was scrawny once. Weaker than my peers. My inferiors. And now I'm not." He shrugs, but his eye are shadowed. "Simple as that. You should try it sometime."

"I can't imagine you that way." It's hard to picture him as anything other than dominating, filling every room with his presence, always having the last word.

"Believe it," he grunts, before he heaves himself up on the bar for a second set. "I'll never go back to that. I'd rather wake up at four a.m. every day than go back to feeling inferior. Regular." His arms flex obscenely. I quickly look away, and when he finally finishes the workout, I feel like I've been lifting weights right alongside him. I'm damp under my shirt and too warm.

I lock myself in one of the changing rooms and call Luz. She's on shift at seven a.m., so she'll be awake and walking to work.

"Hey girl. It's early. What's up?" I can hear cars in the distance, so she's definitely walking.

"Luz, help," I whisper urgently.

"Why are you whispering?"

"I'm hiding from my boss. Jonah."

"I know who your boss is." There's a laugh in her voice.

"I need backup. He hates me and this is worse than I thought."

"What did he do now?" Her voice hardens.

"I slept at the office three times this week, and he threw my lunch in the trash and made me hold his towel at the gym." My face heats as I talk, because it's so shameful—the way I've mortgaged my self-respect to save my paper.

"He's just trying to get to you. You have to rise above. Everyone loves you. You have to make him love you too. That's the only way to win."

I squeeze my eyes shut. "I'm attracted to him, Luz. Like really attracted. It's so fucked up."

"Oh no. Okay. *That* is bad. And not what I expected you to say. You *cannot* sleep with him, Cal."

"I know. I know. He's just so *ugh*." Beautiful, and brooding. Seething with rage and anger. Layered, I think. Strong hands and rippling muscles and feral intelligence.

"Don't even think about it," she warns. "I know you. You like the bad boys. You think you can change them. You're too softhearted. You cannot change him. He hates you."

"I know. I know." I press a hand to my forehead. Luz is right. Eric was a bad boy. Though definitely a boy, not a man. His social media was full of photos with his arm slung around models, in dimly lit Lower East Side restaurants where they let you smoke cigarettes if you know the owner. I'm so weak. And I'm no good at separating sex and attraction from feelings, but I need to do exactly that.

"This is why I called. What would Adriana do?"

Luz thinks for a second. "She'd fuck someone else and forget about him."

"Exactly. Which is where you come in."

"It is?"

"Yes. You're always saying the hospital staff is looking to mess around. You work long hours and have to let off steam. I could use a distraction."

"Like a date? I thought you were done dating after Eric." She sounds skeptical.

"I'm definitely not dating. I don't need another work-obsessed man who sucks me into his life and makes me forget about my hobbies." Like I did with Eric. Shame burns hot. I hate thinking about the way I forgot about my dreams. I even saw Luz and Adriana less. *Never again.* "I don't need a date, just a good time. Find me a nice nurse with capable hands. Or maybe a surgeon. You always say those are the crazy ones."

She laughs. "Surgeons are all egomaniacs."

"Sounds great." I can't keep the eagerness out of my voice. I have to forget about Jonah and the way he makes my blood rush. "I'm sure it's just that I haven't been with a guy in a while. If I sleep with someone else, I'll forget all about my asshole boss."

"Let's hope so," Luz mutters.

14

Jonah

"Are you even listening to me?" Miles's brows go up.

"Of course," I respond.

"What was the last thing I said?"

I glower at him. This is a ridiculous exchange. I'm known for analyzing information and making decisions quickly, and yet, today, I feel off.

The workout did nothing to make me want Callie less. I'm turned on and on edge. She's sitting right outside my office, and it's getting to my head. Miles is talking to me about an acquisition, and I can barely focus. That never happens.

"I don't know," I admit and scrub a hand over my face. "I think my workout made me too tired. I need to eat."

Miles eyes me like I've had a personality transplant. "I've never seen you like this. Maybe you're sick."

"I don't get sick."

"There was that one time during the conference in London."

"Five years ago." I shake my head. "No. It's something else."

A loud laugh sounds from outside the door and I tense. *Callie.*

She's winning over this office with her annoyingly plucky ways and her Disney princess smile. One thousand watts of shiny white teeth under plump pink lips.

Miles starts laughing.

"Not you too."

"Are you going to forbid our employees from having fun next?" He's way too pleased.

"No, but she's a bit *much* don't you think?"

His brow wrinkles in confusion. "What do you mean? She's perfectly fine."

"She is not fine," I hiss. She's far from fine. Fine is lukewarm. Callie is fire, sunshine, impossible curves, snappy retorts. Annoying as hell and addicting as chocolate. I hate it.

Miles is watching me with a faint smirk on his face. "What's wrong, Jonah? Don't like your routine being disrupted?"

"Did you know she went out and got fucking cupcakes for the staff? Apparently it was Tabitha's birthday and she wanted her to feel welcome since she started last month." I slash a hand through the air. "Welcome. Callie has worked here for one week, and she's welcoming people. It's ridiculous. And cupcakes? Honestly. Everyone is very distracted. I can practically feel the lack of work getting done."

"I thought you called her Ms. Thompson. When did she become Callie?" Miles asks.

"That's what you're taking away from this?"

He grins. "Seems relevant."

"Being in a relationship has made you soft." I snort. His smile grows. "Get out of my office."

He stands, raising his hands in the air. "George seems to think *Ms. Thompson* could do more."

"She's not here to do more."

"What's she here for then?"

"Whatever I damn well please." *Well, that sounded dirty.*

Miles guffaws.

"Not like that and you know it."

"Lighten up, you old bastard. Maybe you like cupcakes after all."

He saunters out, making small talk with Callie, who laughs again, a bright tinkling sound. My chest squeezes. She's never laughed around me. *What the hell?* I don't want to make her laugh. I want her to cry. I want to use her as a tool for my revenge against Dylan. I want her to regret ever printing my name in her paper.

I rise from the desk and arrive at her station in just a few long strides.

"Jonah," she says, surprised. "I mean, Mr. Crown. How can I help you?"

Miles is looking at me like I'm a crazy person, and I realize that most of the office is staring at us. They all have cupcakes on their desks or in their hands.

"Would you like a cupcake?" Callie plucks one from the box on her desk and offers it to me. It's yellow cake with blue frosting. *When was the last time I had dessert?* Christine's birthday maybe. Dessert is superfluous, but suddenly it sounds amazing.

"No, thanks." My voice comes out gravelly and awkward. I hate that Miles is looking at me with something like pity, that this woman has won over the entire office in less than a week.

"Okay." She puts the cupcake down and looks back at me expectantly. It's her and them against me. I'm the villain of this story. A fact I've always been comfortable with, until this very moment.

"You have frosting on your face," I say.

"Oh." Her tongue darts out to lick the pink sugar away and my breaths seize in my chest. I'm morally deficient, this I know. But in this moment, I so badly want to be a piece of pink frosting.

"I'll find you later," I mutter, before locking myself in my office.

∽

LATER TURNS out to be five p.m., when I've finally been able to refocus on my work and make meager progress. That stupid pink frosting and Callie's bright laugh drove me to distraction for most of the afternoon. I'm irritable and hungry when I finally crack the door. *To monitor the goings-on and make sure everyone is working.*

The sunset is blazing through the west-facing windows. It's my favorite time of day at the office, before the lights in the surrounding buildings go on and make you feel like you're utterly alone.

Callie is humming busily at her desk, googling things, making little notes. I watch her for a while. I can just see her through the door, unless she shifts too far to the right.

She seems to be looking through our files, though she's doing it casually. My eyes narrow. I knew this was a risk when I hired her, which is part of the reason I put her desk near mine. Between this bullshit and the cupcakes, her first week is not going well. It's time for me to teach Ms. Thompson a lesson.

I slink out of my chair on silent feet, moving closer, closer, until her screen is clear. She's browsing through a document. I can't really tell what it is, even as I squint. I'll ask IT to monitor her activity later.

"What's that you're looking at?"

She jumps in her chair, before she turns, face red and eyes wide. "You scared the shit out of me."

"What are you looking at?" I repeat, my voice tight.

"Just looking for an employee handbook. I didn't really get any onboarding."

Lies. She's trying to look innocent, but it's the same look Annalise had the night I found out she'd sold those photos of me to the press and betrayed me to Dylan. She played just as innocent as Callie is now. Her face superimposes over Callie's, even though they look nothing alike. Rage makes my vision blur.

"Do you think I'm that stupid?" I ask quietly, so no one in the office can hear.

"What do you mean?" She tilts her head.

I watch her react. Her tongue flicks over her lips. *Nervous.*

"I know what you're doing. You're poking around. Looking at things that are confidential."

Her eyes flare wide. *Gotcha.*

"I better not see anything like that printed in your paper, Thompson. Do I make myself clear?"

"Get a grip," she shoots back. "I haven't forgotten the terms of the contract."

Tabitha is coming around the corner. I don't want anyone to see me like this. I'm known for my icy facade, not cascading rage. "Get in my office," I respond.

"With pleasure." Callie precedes me and I shut the door with a little more force than necessary.

Her arms are crossed over her chest, and her face is pink with anger. *Good.* That makes both of us. I refuse to look at the way her full breasts are pushed up over the square neckline of her tank top. A fucking tank top. It should be illegal. I make a note to create a dress code policy for her. Mumus only.

She tips her chin up. "I was looking for a handbook. I got no information when I joined."

"You're lying." My voice is rough with anger.

Her mouth parts. "I don't lie. Ever. It's my job to be honest."

A sharp laugh tears from my throat. "Don't give me that bullshit. All reporters lie. Especially gossipmongers like yourself."

"I'm done." She turns to go, and in three swift steps I have her caged against the wall. My hands press hers into the plaster, and her pulse runs like a rabbit in her throat.

What are you doing? I have no earthly idea. "You are not *done*, Thompson."

"You said I could publish while I'm here," she replies hotly. Her eyes are spitting fire, but she makes no move to shove me back.

"Nothing confidential. Nothing damaging."

"You are deranged. I know, okay? I know. I won't do anything to hurt your company." She blinks quickly when she speaks, and my blood freezes. *Liar.*

I step in closer, so close that she's forced to tilt her head up to meet my eyes, close enough that my suit jacket brushes against her blouse. Her soft lips are parted, and I want to bite them.

"You would, little liar." I whisper the words directly into her ear, and she sways on her high heels.

"Don't call me that." Her voice is high and reedy.

She smells so fucking good. Like shampoo and soft skin, moisturizer and woman. My pulse is hammering under my jacket and fuck, I hope she can't see how she affects me.

"You *are* a little liar." My lips are so close to the lobe of her ear. Just one movement would have me kissing her neck, lower still. And hell, I want that.

"I'm not lying," she huffs. "I was looking for an employee handbook. But I *did* look through your files earlier. It's my job. And you should have thought about that before you hired me."

My blood runs cold. "I knew it." I no longer want her. Instead, I want to ruin her. My body disagrees, because her nearness still makes my collar feel tight and my hands itch to span her waist.

"Then you shouldn't have given me access to your files."

I step away, anger flaring. "You shouldn't be snooping."

"Make me stop, then." She lifts a brow. "Give me the million now and get rid of me. I'll be out of your hair faster than you can say Kings Lane."

"Not happening." I shove my hands into my pockets. "You're going to regret this."

She laughs. She actually fucking laughs. "You sound like a bad movie villain. Do your worst, Jonah Crown." She shakes her head and walks out, leaving me wanting more. My brain is buzzing, my body feels tight. I want to drag her back in here and press her up against the wall. I press my palms over my eyes. *No fucking people who plan to betray you.* Especially since sex with me would mean multiple orgasms for her, which she certainly doesn't deserve.

Callie Thompson needs to pay. And not with pleasure.

I press my lips together in a grim line and call our lawyers.

"Jonah. Good to talk to you." Aiden answers without pleasantry, which I appreciate.

"You too, Aiden." He's is whip smart and dedicated, a former colleague of Jason's, and someone I actually trust.

"Any update on that paper I asked you to investigate? The one we bought."

"Yeah." He shuffles some papers. "I'm actually preparing some documents for you now. You're dissolving it, right?"

My pulse speeds. Here it is. The reason it's so satisfying to be me. One word and I can ruin her business. *Do you want to do this?* Of course I fucking do. She's planning to ruin us. She's snooping. She admitted she was going to publish articles about us while she's here. She stole my revenge right from under me.

"What does dissolving it entail?"

"We can take a few courses of action. As you know, the paper is owned by the LLC you purchased. The LLC has a few assets. The trademark for the paper's name, the website, a printing contract, some debt. There's also a press pass issued by the City of New York. We can cancel the contract, shut down the website, pull the printing pass. A little leverage on the mayor's office will help you get it done faster. The trademark will take longer, and there's an appeals process. She'll need to be involved."

I stare out the window at the Hudson while I consider Aiden's words. If I do this, there's no going back. Callie will get nothing at the end of this. I press a hand to the glass. *She deserves it.* She came after me. She came after my family. But I still need to use her against Dylan. And who knows how long that will take? Better to have her paper intact.

The discomfort lodged in my chest dissipates. It's the logical choice. I'm still acting from my head, not my confused body.

"Prepare the papers. But wait to file them."

"Very good," Aiden responds.

We hang up and I stand at the window for a long while, admiring the sea of buildings, the streets below. I read an opinion piece once that said living and working up in the sky made it impossible to care about the people on the ground, who appear as so many ants. *Not true.* My fingers curl on the glass. I don't see ants. I see problems. A messy world and messier people. At least up here, everything is simple. I control this world, and nothing happens without my approval.

One determined reporter is not going to change that.

When I finally have the courage to look at Callie's chair, it's empty. I frown. She's supposed to be here when I'm here. Even if it's getting late.

I hit Tabitha's number and she picks up on the first ring.

"Yes, Mr. Crown?"

"Where's Ms. Thompson?"

"Oh, she had plans tonight." Tabitha's voice brightens at the mention of Callie, and my jaw clenches. *Another Callie fan.* Of course. It was the fucking cupcakes.

"Did she say where?" Not that I would go and interrupt her, because that would be insane.

"No. Sorry. Oh, and Mr. Crown? I'm going to head out for the day. My husband is taking me out for my birthday." She sounds nervous and it's probably my fault.

"Sure. Go ahead. Happy birthday," I say absently and hang up.

Plans. When she's supposed to be here. I should call her back to the office. An image of her laughing with a gaggle of faceless women fills my mind. And then an image of her in a dimly lit restaurant, charming a man with those huge blue eyes and that tinkling laugh. *Tomorrow.* I don't need her tonight.

So all you do is work then? You're never out with friends or away for the weekend?

Her words ring in my ears. And suddenly, for the first time in my life, I feel lonely.

15

Jonah

Callie is snooping again. I can hear her speaking with George in hushed tones. I'm going to call her into my office as soon as this conference call is over. Sean, my head of security, is explaining the measures his team is taking to determine the scope of a data breach this morning and the identity of the hacker. Sean has worked for me since the events of six years ago, and he's excellent at what he does. When Dylan got serious a few years back, Sean deployed around-the-clock monitoring for any mention of me, my family, or Kings Lane. Recently, that's meant waking to an inbox full of articles written by Callie.

I'm only half listening to Sean. I know the attack was from Dylan. I can feel it in my gut. It's been like this for years. All will be quiet, and then he'll pop up with a takedown article, or poach one of our employees, small stuff like that. Until two years ago, when he approached Theo about selling his shares. The attacks have escalated since then, become more personal. Now he's hacking our servers.

It's even more imperative that I take him down. Before he can cause real damage.

The call ends. *Time to see what Callie Thompson can do.*

"Thompson. Stop snooping and get in here," I bark.

She appears in the door, fidgeting with her hair. *She should be nervous.* I'm in a foul mood and seeing her does not make it better. I'm supposed to be using her, making her miserable. I should be halfway to ruining her and Dylan. There should be bags under her eyes. Instead, she looks fresh and unbothered in an electric blue wrap dress that makes her eyes seem brighter than usual and her curves more alluring. Her hair is down and just messy enough to make it look like she had good sex last night. *Did she have sex last night? She had plans. Maybe she had a date.* My stomach pinches uncomfortably. I shouldn't care about her, and yet, something about the line of her neck and the sweep of her thick eyelashes makes my palms sweat. *Fuck.* I'm turned on and awkward. I'm never awkward. Cool frustration is my default, and I sink back into that. I scowl at her and she stares calmly back.

"Did you find who hacked the server?" she asks, and my scowl turns blacker. *Little liar.*

"No. And I wouldn't tell you if I had. Nice try."

She smiles, unrepentant. "I had to. But anyways, it sounds personal, don't you think? Emails. Personnel files. It's what I'd go for if I had a vendetta. A thief would go for more valuable information, no?"

Does she know? Did she have something to do with this? I tilt my head as I watch her. "That's the conclusion our security team came to as well. How did you know?"

"Just a lucky guess." She shrugs, but she's still fidgeting with a lock of her hair. Either she's smarter than I realized, or in cahoots with Dylan.

"Thompson. You're going to help me today."

"No more files for me to sort?"

"No. I want you to find out everything you can on this man." I slide her a piece of paper with a name on it. *Let's see how you react to that.*

"Dylan Green?"

Her brows draw together in confusion. *Fake or real?* "You know him?" I ask. *Come on, sweetheart. Where are your tells?* She's too collected in my presence, and I hate it. My collar feels too tight and her scent fills my nose. I would do anything to unsettle her.

"I don't know him personally, no. But I do know of him." Careful words. The truth, I think, though maybe not the whole truth.

"I want a dossier on my desk by the end of the day. Everything you can find. And I don't care what methods you use to get the information. That shouldn't be a problem, right?" It's a ridiculous request.

She blushes but lifts her chin. *Stubborn woman.* "You know, I'm pretty ethical. I don't take photographs through peoples' windows. I only track public figures."

Anger twists my insides. "Like my sister?"

Her mouth flattens. *She's angry too. How quaint.* "She was with you."

I smile without humor. "I'm sure you can find it within you to drop the moralistic act for a few hours." I raise my brows. "Chop, chop, Thompson."

I let her get to the door before I say idly, "Oh, and I want that wrap again today. But it took you too long last time. The lettuce was soggy."

She tenses before turning neatly on her heel. I want to shout in triumph. "It's a special," she says crisply. "They have it Mondays and Thursdays. Tuesdays and Thursdays are the days they have a full construction crew at the new building on 6th Avenue. You and the construction workers have the same taste in sandwiches. If you want a fresher sandwich, choose something else. Or somewhere else." Her voice is even, even though her eyes flash. She's probably imagining throwing something at my head.

"How did you figure that out?"

"I'm observant."

She's damn observant if she gleaned all of this from ten days on the job. "What else do you recommend?"

"You want a recommendation from me?" She smiles. "You hate

me. I don't think we have the same taste in sandwiches. Where else do you like?"

My mind is blank. I don't know any other places near the office. I'm a creature of habit. She tilts her head, and I swallow uncomfortably. Never has the gulf between us seemed so large. I usually don't walk in Midtown, except to get into or out of my private car.

"I'll get you something you'll like," she finally says, putting me out of my misery.

"Thanks." She's being nice. Weirdly nice. That must be why I offer, "Why don't you get yourself something as well?"

She freezes. For a second, she looks like she would like nothing more. "No, thank you," she says carefully, and walks out.

∼

By five p.m., it's apparent Callie Thompson and I are playing a game. I ask her for help and she replies with ever-increasing speed. *She's halving the time between responses.* Just to piss me off, I imagine. Little does she know that efficiency makes me hard.

She flips her hair over her shoulder and huffs a little breath every time I send an email. I send one telling her to come into my office, just so I can watch her get annoyed. She stands in a rush and flounces in. I press my lips together to keep from smiling at her annoyed expression and pink cheeks.

"You know, I would be able to spend a lot more time on the dossier if you sent fewer emails." She glares at me.

"I didn't send that many emails, did I?"

"11:34 a.m. You asked for a coffee from the in-office barista. At 11:44 a.m., you told me it was the wrong order and asked for a new one. At 1:07 p.m., you wanted me to call and make a reservation for dinner for you. I begged the hostess at The Charlatan for a table until she relented. At 1:11 p.m., you asked me to call and cancel it."

She sucks in a breath to continue and I interrupt with, "Impressive recall." It is impressive. *If* I let myself be impressed.

She snaps her lips shut and glowers at me.

"What have you found on Green Media?"

"I filed a FOIA request."

"A what?"

She huffs, like I really should know what it is, but says, "A Freedom of Information Act request. The Green Media and Hartley Telecom merger last year was approved by the FTC. That means lots of public documents. Have you filed one before?"

"No," I say shortly. "We didn't. And we probably should have." Talk about a massive fucking oversight. *How did I miss this?*

"You should have," she agrees.

"How long for the results?"

She frowns. "It could take months. It's coming from a federal agency."

Not good enough. I need information and I need it now. "I want you to follow him. Tonight. See what you can find." *While I follow you.* I want to figure out Callie Thompson's connection to these people.

She opens her mouth to argue and I raise a brow. "Problem, Thompson?"

"I have a life, you know. Friends. A father. My business. I know you're mad at me about the photos, but I really need to be out there taking pictures for myself." She's nearly pleading, and guilt flares. I'm mad about the photos, yes, but nothing she's doing for me now will absolve her. She thinks she's working off a debt, when in reality, she's a pawn.

As it should be. She deserves this. I force myself not to back down. Instead I just stare, coldly, and say, "Better get moving, then."

She stomps off, and I follow, just minutes later. I don't need to tail her. I know where Dylan lives. She'll go there first.

∼

WHEN I GET DOWNSTAIRS, just minutes behind Callie, I settle in to the waiting car, grunt a hello at my driver, Lou, and prepare myself for a long night. Lou parks near Dylan's apartment, and Callie arrives twenty minutes later. Dylan lives in a townhouse in Tribeca. It's gut-renovated and modern, with a basement pool. I know because I've seen it. *Before.* I once wanted an apartment just like it. Now mine is infinitely superior.

Callie settles in across the street, on the steps of another townhouse, plopping on to them like she belongs. She takes out her phone, flicking through it occasionally, and sneaking surreptitious glances at the townhouse. *She's good.* And now that I can watch her in private, I can see just how good. The way she rests her chin on her hand says bored college student, but her camera is on her lap, hidden under a massive black scarf. *Remember, she's done the same to you.*

She pulls her coat closer. It's cold tonight. She must be freezing. *Let her freeze. It's what she deserves.* There was another article this morning about Christine, using photos Callie Thompson undoubtedly sold to Green Media. *After I told her to stop.* So let her fucking freeze.

Every car that comes down the tiny street makes her head jerk. She must be cataloging the make and model like I am. Dylan wants new and fancy only. So when a white Mercedes slows, we both straighten up.

His head appears first, sandy blonde hair gelled back. My hand is on the handle of my door before I even realize it, and I force myself to relax. Dylan's slender frame emerges after, clad in a long wool coat and black gloves. He's slightly paunchy. *Going soft,* I note with vicious satisfaction. Callie is already halfway across the street, camera snapping.

He sees her and he *preens*, he actually fucking preens. He smiles. I hate it. I crack my window in time to hear her say, "Mr. Green. A quote? I'm from the New York Star."

"You're too pretty to be a reporter." He leers at her, and my hand drops to the door handle again. *Mine. He's encroaching on what's mine.*

"What do you know about Jonah Crown?"

His face falls. "Jonah Crown? Fuck that guy." He turns on his heel and strides back into the townhouse. I slump back on the seat.

No recognition. Nothing. He doesn't know Callie and she doesn't know him. *Maybe she's not as bad as I think she is.* I watch her tuck her camera away and bury her chin in her scarf, and I steel myself.

I can't be making excuses for her. This is how she'll worm her way in. Cupcakes, those bright smiles, and the next thing I know I'll be spilling company secrets.

So instead of offering her a ride back to the office, I send her a text noting she better get her ass back to work after the assignment or I'll fire her on the spot.

She reads it, gives her phone the finger, and makes a frustrated sound. I laugh into the car's silent interior.

Game on, Thompson.

16

Callie

When I get back to the office on Thursday night, Jonah is still there. His shirtsleeves are rolled up and his tie is off. His hair is even mussed from him running his hands through it, or so I assume. It could have been from him brutally murdering an employee and hiding the body. *It looks like sex hair*, my traitorous brain reminds me.

He greets me with, "Anything?"

"No," I say shortly, shucking my coat. "Dylan wasn't happy to see me, and I don't know what you expected me to get. He lives in a beautiful townhouse, and he's just as creepy as I thought he was from his photos." My skin feels slimy from his leering, and I shudder.

"Creepy how?" Jonah's brows draw down. "Did he make a move?"

"Like you care." I snort. "Unless you need fodder for a lawsuit? Here. Grab my arm." I walk closer to Jonah, who freezes. "I'll never tell them it was you who hurt me."

"I'm not a monster," he says quietly. I just watch him, too irritated to respond. He treats me like his servant, he doesn't pay me, and he doesn't let me work to take photos I can use. *I hate you, Jonah Crown.*

"Creepy. How?" he repeats. His voice is hard.

"Just the look on his face. It unsettled me." Jonah doesn't respond, and I shake my head. "You know what, never mind. I don't want to get into this and have you dismiss me. Men always do."

His jaw works. "I wouldn't," he says with quiet intensity. "I wouldn't dismiss it."

I don't know what to say to that. It sounds a hell of a lot like a peace offering, and I know that's not the case. So instead I say, "What did you need me for? Do you want me to continue the dossier? I'm going to email LexisNexis to see what searches I can run on there. We can get public records. Unless your lawyers have a subscription we can use?"

"I'm not sure. I'll ask." For a second, he seems distracted, scanning me, his dark eyes lingering on my body. *Making sure I'm okay?* No way. "Do you want dinner? I'm going to order."

I don't have money for that. Just like I don't have money to order lunch. I have $11 in my bank account and a credit card bill to pay. Rent. Food. My dad's doctor's appointments. I also didn't bring enough food for dinner. *Shit.* "No, thanks," I say calmly, and go back to my desk.

An hour later, building staff drops by with a takeout bag. Jonah tips them handsomely from what I can see out of the corner of my eye. *Because of course he does.* Soon, the smell of pasta drifts from his office. My stomach gurgles hungrily, and I shift in my seat to cover the sound.

"Thompson. There's a ton of food in here. Do you want anything?"

"I'm good," I say, and go back to putting together an email for the lawyers on what documents I need. Just a few more minutes, and then I can work on the paper. The printer needs the final layout by two a.m., four a.m. if Ray is working, because he's a whiz with the press. *I really hope Ray is working.* I finish the email and start going through the photos I have for the week. We don't have a headline article. My dad's piece on the asbestos in the local school hit a snag when the school board denied our interview requests. I haven't been able to work for a week, and we just have...nothing. Maybe it is time for the rat infestation article. *Ugh.* My stomach growls again, and I leap out of my chair. There are snacks in the break room. I'll go, grab a bag of peanuts, scarf it in the bathroom, and keep working.

"Thompson." Jonah's voice comes from behind me, and I startle. "Eat something." He looms over me, arms crossed. His eyes are wary, and his body practically radiates irritation. "I don't want you collapsing on the job. Let's go."

"Fine." I follow him into the office and sit in the chair across from his desk. It's a mess of papers, with takeout containers scattered about. There's penne a la vodka, meatballs, broccoli rabe. My stomach growls again, and I blush.

"What do you like?" he asks.

"What? Oh. You're serious." He's staring at me. "Um, I'm not picky."

He raises a brow. "I asked you a question."

"Fine. I like penne and meatballs, but I hate how bitter broccoli rabe is. It's like broccoli's sad cousin."

His mouth tips up as he prepares me a plate. On real flatware. He must keep it in the office.

"Do you eat in here a lot?" I tip my head toward the plate.

"A fair amount." He passes me the plate and some silverware. It gleams like real silver and I want to laugh.

"More than you'd like to admit, then."

"Stop snooping and eat." His voice is milder than earlier, though. I don't think he's even annoyed at me, just reacting out of habit. Or maybe that's wishful thinking on my part.

"What if I'm trying to get to know you?"

He makes a disagreeable sound but doesn't respond. The food is good. Really good, actually, and I tell him that.

"It's from the place on the corner of Lexington. Italian Table."

"You order takeout from there?" I shake my head, smiling. "It's good to be you."

"Is this going to end up in an article somewhere?"

"Diets of the rich and famous? You'll never believe this one weird trick." I smile at him and there's a glimmer of a smile back. Hope springs in my heart, because I'm an idiot who can't stop trying to see the good in people. For a few minutes at least, Jonah Crown looks like he doesn't hate me.

I eat as quickly as possible, because Jonah doesn't seem inclined to let me go before I finish.

"Why did you turn down dinner tonight? And lunch?" he asks, as I'm chewing my final bite.

I lick my lips and look up to see his gaze rapt on my mouth. *Well, that's unsettling. And hot. Ugh, you idiot.* "I, uh, don't have meals out in the budget right now. And since I've been paying for your lunches, I doubly don't."

For a second, he looks stricken. "You didn't expense them?"

"Why do you care?" I don't mean it in a flippant way. I'm genuinely puzzled. "Torture means torture, right? I'm supposed to suffer. I assumed paying for your lunch was part of that." I didn't even ask because I assumed the answer would be no. I rise and stack my plate neatly on top of his. "Anyways, thanks for dinner. Do you want me to bring these plates to the building's kitchen?"

"Leave them." His voice is rough.

We don't speak for the rest of the night. Somehow, I fall asleep at my desk, and when I wake up around three a.m., there's a stack of cash next to me with a note.

Take the money, or you're fired.

~

Luz comes through for me the next morning and sets me up with a hot doctor named James. He lives in Midtown, so he can be close to the hospital, and he wants to meet at a wine bar that night. When Luz texts me that he's only free tonight, I sink into my chair and shut my eyes. I could sleep for a hundred years. Maybe more. It's Friday. I was looking forward to an after-work nap and some quality time on the couch with our cat, Samson.

But instead of sleeping, I shower and primp until my eyes are heavy under sooty makeup and my breasts are pushed together. And the whole time, I try not to think about Jonah Crown and his erratic behavior. He's hot and cold. Sexy and confusing. Feeding me, but also glaring at me like he wants to destroy me.

Unfortunately, after all the work on my hair and makeup, I come to the realization that James and I don't have much in common. We're tucked at a table in a dimly lit wine bar near the office, with velvet seats and little clusters of chairs. I'm persevering, but it's tough. The thing is, James is perfectly nice. Not an egomaniac, though a part of me wishes he had more of an edge. He asks about my day, pays for my glass of wine, pulls my chair out for me. I think back to Luz telling me that I like bad boys, and I push the thought away. I just need to try harder. James has long lashes, bright green eyes, and a chiseled jaw. I shift a little closer to him to see if something, anything, will spark between us.

"So where has Luz been hiding you away?" he asks, after we get a second glass of wine. He's interested. I can tell. He's leaning in toward me with bright eyes. He doesn't have much tolerance for alcohol, and his cheeks are a little pink. It's adorable. Or it should be.

I laugh awkwardly and take a hearty gulp of wine before responding. "I just haven't been dating much the last few months." *Try a whole year.*

"Why not?"

"I had a bad breakup." I shrug, like it was nothing, but my shoulders are tight. It was more than that. Leaving Eric was like stepping outside on the first day of spring. I didn't realize how much I'd lost myself until I was free of him.

"I've been there." James grimaces. I use the opportunity to ask him about himself. It's pretty obvious that he's a girlfriend guy. He tells me how he really wants to settle down. He likes to ski and camp when he can get time off, and he loves dogs. He's perfect. For someone. I so want it to be me. He's the opposite of Eric. Where Eric was brash and showy, James is quiet. He's not famous, but he's successful. The second glass of wine makes me bold, and I lean in more. *Maybe he'll kiss me.* His eyes snag on my lips, his hand lands on my thigh. I feel nothing.

And then my phone rings. My whole body jerks, and I nearly fall out of my chair. *Jonah.* I set a different ring tone for him. My phone plays the Death March from Star Wars.

"My boss," I say with a grimace. James laughs.

"Nice ringtone."

I pick up and hear, "Where the hell are you?"

Before I can lie, he adds, "I can hear the music, Thompson."

"I'm out," I say boldly. "Did you need something?"

He makes a low, frustrated sound. "Get your ass back to the office. I want to see you within ten minutes. Or you're fired."

My stomach bottoms out.

"Gotta go. Call me." I grab my coat and run outside. The air is crisp and I'm only a few blocks from the office. Walking it is. I stuff my chin into my coat and walk as quickly as my dainty heels will allow.

I'm out of breath and nine minutes have passed by the time I get up to the fifty-second floor. The hallway lights flicker on this side, a path of light leading straight to the lion's den. Jonah is leaning against the doorframe. My steps slow.

He waits, arms crossed, sneer firmly on his face, as I near. *Damn, he looks too good.* I want to pull out my camera and take a photo of his haughty face and the way his throat works. His hair is mussed and his tie is gone.

I stop in front of him and raise my chin. *Asshole,* my gaze says.

I'm on to you, his says.

I narrow my eyes. *I hate you.*

His mouth curves up. *Right back at you.*

"Why did you call me back to the office?"

"I need your help with something." His tone isn't mocking. It's genuine. *Weird.*

"You actually need my *help*? With what?"

"Don't sound so surprised."

I'm pleased is what I am. Maybe Jonah is finally taking me seriously. I can do more than he's asking me to do, and I hate being bored. *And I want access.* Maybe I'll learn something useful.

I press a hand to my chest and gasp dramatically. "What do you need from me? Perhaps you need me to trek across town to get you dinner? Are you fresh out of the souls of small children for your morning coffee? Did you want to insult me more?"

He almost smiles, but quickly presses his lips together.

"Knock it off and come into my office."

"Yes, your highness," I mutter.

"I told you, I prefer Your Majesty," he shoots back. I have to smile. A little tendril of warmth fills my chest, and I tamp it down. Jonah Crown is not someone I should feel anything but hatred for.

"Do most of your employees call you Your Majesty, or just me?"

"You're special," he mutters. My stupid stomach flips at the phrasing. *Silly, Cal. He doesn't mean you're special like that.*

I drop my purse onto the couch in his office and dig around for my phone.

"What's under the coat?" His voice sounds angry. My head jerks up.

"Why?"

"Were you working, Thompson? What's under the coat?" His eyes are hard and his jaw clenched. A total about face from just minutes ago, when he seemed almost normal.

Fuck it. I drop my phone and shuck my wool coat. Raw hunger flashes over his face before he tamps it down. *No. I must be mistaken.* His eyes trace the tops of my breasts where the corset-like top of the dress has pushed them together, then over the silky fall of material that ends at my upper thigh, down over my stocking-clad legs, to my heels.

His jaw clenches. "Were you on a date?"

"Am I not allowed to date?"

"Not when you're supposed to be working. I'm here. You're here. That's the deal." His voice is deadly quiet. *Where is the man from last night? The one who fed me and left me a stack of cash?*

"But you're always here," I counter. The wine is making me bold.

His eyes flash. "Funny, Thompson. I don't recall asking for your commentary on my private life."

He's such an asshole. My eyes narrow. He reminds me of a street dog, lashing out at anyone and everyone.

"What private life?" I counter. His brows go up. *Shit.* That was a dumb thing to say, and now I've backed him into a corner.

"What do you know about running a multi-billion dollar company? Do you think I have time to socialize like you do?" He cocks his head.

"I know it seems lonely," I shoot back. "I know you're here at all hours. I know you barely sleep. I know you don't see your family." I step toward him. "You forget. I know far more about you than you do about me."

His eyes glitter dangerously. "Is that true? I have very good private investigators."

"Okay. Let's hear it. You give me a fact and I'll give you one in return." I cross my arms and stare him down, even as my brain screams that this is a bad idea. One that might get me fired.

"I'll play." He leans against his desk, looking evil and beautiful all at once. "Your father went to college in Massachusetts. Amherst, specifically. He majored in journalism and had a full scholarship. Just like you did to Columbia."

I tamp down the surprise before it can show on my face. He really did have me investigated.

"On Saturday mornings, you go to the bagel place on the corner of Amsterdam and 90th street. And you always wear a ball cap so no one recognizes you. Usually a New York Royals hat," I respond.

His eyes narrow. "I've never seen you there."

"I'm stealthy and you're not observant. Next."

"You lived downtown until a year ago, when you moved in with your father."

Close. Too close to the truth. Which is that my awful ex lives in my apartment and I was left with nothing.

"You've lived at 87th street for four years."

"Your father is sixty-eight years old."

"You barely see your family. You don't invite them over, though I know they exist. What's wrong? Embarrassed by them?"

His gaze hardens. I've gone too far, hit too close to home. I tense.

"Your mother left you when you were six years old."

I reel back, my heart jumping in my chest.

"How? How do you know that?" *Why would you bring that up?*

"I know where she is now too." His face is cold, cruelly beautiful.

I squeeze my eyes shut. "I don't care." I know she's in California. I know she wants nothing to do with me or my father. I don't need to know her exact location.

"Are you sure, Thompson?" His voice is silky. Exactly the voice I imagine Satan himself has. Dark smoke and secrets.

"How dare you?" My eyes pop open. "I can't believe you would bring that up."

Emotion flashes across his face. He pushes off the desk. I step back.

"Stay away from me."

He stops, looking uncertain.

"I need to leave." My voice is high, panicked. "Fire me if you want. I need to leave."

"Okay, Thompson. Okay." He raises his hands placatingly.

I scoop up my belongings and practically run out the door. I sit on the cold subway seat and inhale shallow breaths. I don't think about my mom. It's a lost cause. She didn't want me and I don't want her.

You're mine. It's so fucked up how much I liked hearing that come from Jonah's mouth. And entirely fucked up that I can't stop thinking about his soulful eyes and his handsome face. I hate him so much it makes my hands shake, but I still find him attractive.

I pull out my phone and text Luz.

CALLIE

> It didn't work. Anyone else you can set me up with?

One more date. And then I can forget about Jonah Crown and just try to survive.

17

Callie

Jonah won't look me in the eye on Monday morning. I spent the weekend stewing and trying to get photos of an actress who just left her husband for her younger co-star. All I got was my arm twisted by her security detail and a shot of her eating a salad for lunch. I even checked my mom's social media pages for a few minutes before I had the good sense to shut my computer. *Thanks, Jonah.*

I meet him in the office lobby, and he silently passes me a coffee. I nearly drop it in surprise when our hands touch.

"Is it salted?"

"No." He grimaces. "That was...childish of me."

An apology. Of sorts. The coffee and the admittance that he feels a little bad. Probably all I'll get from him. I sip gratefully as we ride the elevator in silence.

His jaw is clenched and the hood of his sweatshirt is up. All black again today. Black hoodie, thin black pants. The Prince of Darkness works out. I laugh softly to myself.

"What's so funny, Thompson?"

"You don't want to know." I shake my head. "You'll hate it."

"Tell me." His expression is implacable.

"I was just thinking that your workout outfit is totally what Satan would wear if he went to the gym."

His eyes widen in surprise before he barks a laugh. "Satan at the gym, huh?"

I smile tentatively. "Totally. My readers would eat it up."

"So take a picture." He raises a brow, still smiling faintly. *Danger, Will Robinson.*

"What? No." I scowl. "You're just looking for an excuse to fire me."

The elevator dings and he gestures for me to step out. Ahead of him. Weird.

"I behaved poorly last week." He looks a little ill. *He's uncomfortable.* This is probably the first time he's ever apologized for anything.

"So to make it up to me, you'll let me print a photo of you?"

He nods shortly. "One photo. Shirt on."

"You saw that?" I redden.

"Saw it? Thompson, my sister had it printed on a card, along with the choice comments."

I wince. "That was inappropriate. I turned the comments off after a few hours. Sorry about that."

He nods and leans against the wall. His hood is up, his brows are lowered. I pull out my phone. Not the best camera, but it will do.

"Do you want me to smile?" He asks, like he'd rather cut off his own arm than smile in a photo.

"No, I want it to be true to life. Put one leg up on the wall and tip your head back. He complies and my stomach turns itself over. The strong column of his throat is bared, stubbled and bronzed. His lips are parted slightly, like he just got done fucking the viewer and he's out of breath. Those eyes are still arrogant though, and his body betrays no hint of softness. His arms are crossed impatiently. Prickly, broody, breathtakingly handsome. I shiver and snap the shot.

He immediately comes off the wall. "We done?"

"Yep." My legs feel a little weak, and I sigh when he disappears through the unmarked door. *What does he do in there?* I creep closer to the door, but I can't hear anything, even when I press my ear against it. No music. No movement. Must be soundproofed. Weird.

I tap out the beginnings of an article about his workout routine, which is ironic, considering I have no actual idea what he's doing. Readers are going to eat the photo up though, and that's what matters.

He bangs out of the door not thirty minutes later, sweaty and breathless. Without skipping a beat, he says, "Back and arms today. Let's go Thompson."

"Got your towel right here." I wave it in the air. *I'm ready for you, Jonah. Hit me with your worst.*

His brows go up, but he stalks to the weight benches. He selects dumbbells that look heavy enough to break a foot if they're dropped.

"So should I just stand here then?" I'm pretty sure that's exactly what he wants. He prefers for me to be as uncomfortable as possible.

He flicks me a glance as I shift from foot to foot. "You could work out if you wanted to. I won't yell at you if you touch the weights." He sounds utterly disinterested in what I do, but I'm surprised he's even offering.

I don't work out. I walk a lot, especially while working, but I've never lifted a weight.

"My sister finds lifting weights pretty empowering." He shrugs and settles back on the bench. "Says it clears her head. But suit yourself."

I could use that. Especially after Eric. Being empowered sounds amazing. I look down at my outfit. A black dress and stockings. Not exactly workout attire.

"Maybe tomorrow. I'll bring a change of clothes."

He nods and starts bench pressing the dumbbells.

"Does it clear your head?"

He grunts and presses the weights in the air again.

"I'll take that as a yes. Do you split by body parts?"

"Stop talking, Thompson," he grits out.

"I'll just stand here, then. Like a piece of wallpaper. Or a plant maybe. Two degrees from Columbia, but you want me to hold your towel. What luck."

He drops the weights on the floor and sits up. His gaze runs up my legs, before his expression shutters, even as his sides heave and sweat runs down his hairline. "Yes. A plant. Exactly. In fact, I would love if you were even less lifelike than a plant. Maybe a chair?"

My mouth drops open. Foolish hurt lances through me. I should know this feeling by now. "You're joking." He's such an ass. Apologizing one minute and then putting me down the next. The stray dog analogy fits. "Afraid that bringing me a coffee might mean I like you?"

His expression hardens. "Let me be clear about something." He stands, rising over me, smelling like sweat and man. "We are not friends." He gestures between us. "This is not a buddy cop movie. I am not going to suddenly change and become a nice guy."

He's too close. I so badly want to take a step back, but I tip my chin up instead. "I know you're not a nice person. Believe me, I've seen it in action." His eyes flash. *You asked for it.*

"I'm glad we're clear. Anything else?"

"Nope. I'll just stand here and hold this towel for you, since it's so heavy." I keep my voice sweet, and he glowers. "In fact, can I play some music while you work out? It would help me be more chair-like."

He growls and sits back down on the bench. I pull out my phone and put on some singer-songwriter music I know will annoy him. I can practically hear him rolling his eyes as he lifts. I keep my back to him, refusing to watch those muscles flex and roll under his shirt. The music was a mistake though, because now I want to sing.

I sing in the shower, when I'm alone in the park, at karaoke night. Basically wherever I can get away with it. I love it, and I'm a decent singer, but Jonah doesn't know that and I don't want him to. I don't want to reveal that secret, joyful part of me, so I hum faintly under my breath and sway a little.

A thump of a weight on the floor makes me jump. Jonah is glowering at me, a dark, sweat-slicked god. He pulls his shirt up to wipe his face, and I gulp.

"Here." I thrust the towel in his face. "Spare me the sight, please."

Endorphins do not make Jonah Crown any more pleasant, because in response, he strips his shirt off. Again. I keep my eyes carefully on his face. His cheekbone to be exact.

He takes the towel and spends an indecent amount of time rubbing himself down. I hold myself stock-still at his side, even as heat rushes through me. *You like the bad boys.* Heaven help me. I must, because even with Jonah telling me he'd prefer if I were a chair, I still want to jump him.

He leaves to shower, and I settle in at my desk downstairs. *I can get through this.* I take deep breaths. The man might think I'm lower than dirt, but I can still survive. I've survived worse, after all. My mom leaving, all the shifts I worked as a waitress in grad school, especially the overnight ones at the diner near Columbia, and my very public breakup with Eric. I click into a blank document and keep working on my article for later. I stab out the letters as I type. I'm fiddling with the photo of Jonah on my phone, editing his skin, even though he barely needs it, when he appears next to me. Just like yesterday, when he tried to scare me. I was looking for an employee handbook, though not ten minutes earlier, I'd been going through all the emails saved on the system.

He's such an ass. Letting me in and then keeping me at a distance. *Why does it matter?* Because I want him. I liked how he teased me in the office last week, all his focus on me, murmuring insults against my skin. *And what does that say about me?* I *liked* who I was with him. Even if I hate that he was using desire to unsettle me.

With Eric and his friends, I faded into the background. With Jonah, that would be impossible. *He meets me as an equal.* Even when he's demanding things from me, he acts like I'm someone to be feared, respected. Something Eric never did.

Except when Jonah pushes me away. Every time I get too close, Jonah reminds me of my place.

I'm distracted and flushed the rest of the day. Every time Jonah asks me to do something, I try to keep our contact to a minimum. I can't stop lusting after him, and it's ruining my brain.

I text Luz and Adriana while I wait for Jonah to get off the phone.

CALLIE

I can't stop wanting my boss, you guys. This is going to break me.

LUZ

Help is on the way! I'm setting you up with a new resident. Sam. I'll text you his number.

CALLIE

What's he like?

Please say mean, dark-haired and hot as hell.

LUZ

Brown hair, blue eyes, tall. Sweet, as far as I can tell. Driven.

Blue eyes. Ugh. I shake myself. I need to get over this infatuation with Jonah. It's bad for my health. I actually licked my lips while watching him talk earlier. It's obscene.

I text the number Luz sends me. A nice, normal message, asking if he wants to get dinner on Wednesday. Not the message of a madwoman who wondered what color her boss's underwear was this morning. *Black. Most definitely black.* I squeeze my eyes shut at the memory of Jonah hooking his thumbs under the waist of his shorts as he walked to the lockers.

"Thompson," he barks.

I take a deep breath and walk calmly into his office. *Don't look at him. Don't look at him.* I look. Mistake. His blue suit makes his hair look even blacker, shiny like a raven's wing. He forgot to shave this morning, because the hollow of his cheeks and his sharp jaw are covered with dark stubble. It makes him look rakish and hotter than usual. *Oh no.*

"Would it kill you to call me Callie?" I say, instead of something dumb. I give myself a mental pat on the back.

"Yes. Now come here and look at this."

"Near you?"

"Yes. I don't bite. Come on." He points at something on his computer.

I inch closer, and he growls under his breath. I huff and stand next to him. Heat radiates from him. The smell of his cologne fills my nose. I mentally calculate the cost of one spritz. Anything to distract me from leaning in to smell him.

"Are you paying attention? Look at this. We didn't get the FOIA results back yet, but Adam did pull the files you requested. The public records. This was among them."

"Sorry," I mutter and lean closer to the computer. "This looks like a court case. That's odd. I didn't see this when I looked at the lawsuits against the company."

"You wouldn't have. Because it names Dylan personally, and not the company. It's a claim of wrongful termination. I want you to see what else you can find on the person who filed the suit."

"No. No, no. I'm not getting involved in this." I back up as Jonah glares. I don't know what Jonah wants me to do with this information, but it makes me feel dirty.

"What's wrong?" he snaps.

"Wrongful termination is discrimination most of the time. I'm not going down that road. Whoever filed that lawsuit deserves to be left in peace."

His eyes flare in surprise. "So that's where you draw the line?"

"Yes," I choke out. "Of course. You really think I'm that bad?" All of my desire for him evaporates at the reminder that he really does hate me. "I think I need to take a break. I'm going to get a coffee." And take a walk. Maybe all the way back home.

"I'm sorry." His deep voice comes from behind me. I freeze, fists clenched, and then force myself to turn back to him. His eyes are shadowed.

"What did you say?"

"You heard me. I know you wouldn't use that. I believe you. And the suit isn't claiming discrimination. It's claiming Dylan assaulted his CFO and then fired him a week later because the CFO went to the police."

I inhale slowly. His face is sincere. "I'm sorry," he repeats. "Are you going to make me say it again?" He looks so annoyed that I smile against my will.

"I accept your apology. Now tell me about the lawsuit. Maybe it's something I can use."

∽

On Wednesday, I meet Sam right after work. He's fresh from his hospital shift, so we meet near my apartment, which is conveniently a short bus ride across the park from the hospital. He is sweet, like Luz promised. Handsome, with a square jaw and all-American man good looks. He cares deeply about his patients.

"Aren't you tired from being on shift?" I ask. His face is lined with exhaustion. "I know Luz sleeps for a whole day."

He smiles tiredly. "Nurses have it harder than doctors do. And Luz is a trauma nurse, so she's on her feet with adrenaline pumping. I'm an oncologist, so the exhaustion is frequently more emotional than physical."

He's sensitive. And he doesn't have that superiority Luz claims lots of doctors adopt. *I like it.* Or I should. I feel nothing.

He tells me about moving from Boston. He jokes about how he named his dog Frodo.

"You're funny," I respond. *I want to like him. Please, let me like him.*

Sam walks me home later, even though I tell him to go home and get some sleep.

When we get to the brownstone, there's a car idling on the curb, and a man in an overcoat leaning against it.

It can't be...Oh no. It is.

"J—Mr. Crown?"

In the space of a breath, Jonah's head jerks up and he takes in Sam.

"Friend of yours?" Sam mutters.

"My boss," I respond.

If Sam is weirded out, he doesn't say anything. "Hey, man. I'm Sam Cord."

Jonah ignores him and turns to me. "You weren't answering your phone."

My mouth parts in shock. "So you came to my apartment? Are you insane? Actually, don't answer that."

His jaw works. "You left it on your desk. I brought it back. In case I needed you." He makes no move to pass me the device, instead, he looks over at Sam, who is standing awkwardly to the side. I can see the exact moment realization dawns. Jonah's face shutters, the fire in his eyes hardens to icy distaste. I can practically see the walls being built back up.

"Clearly, I'm interrupting something. I thought you were—never mind." Jonah's voice is stiff. "I'll just get your phone from the car."

He was worried. Jonah came here because he was *worried*. Oh my god. It's nine p.m. and he just came from the office. I picture him there, his office the only one illuminated in the dark building. An ache builds behind my ribs. He's so lonely. And proud. Way too proud to admit he was concerned about me.

"You know what? I left some files at the office. Do you mind driving me back?" My words come out in a rush.

"Not at all," he says coolly. I expect him to get back in the car and let me say goodbye to Sam in peace, but he just waits.

I roll my eyes and turn to Sam. "Sorry about this. I had fun tonight."

"Me too." He smiles and gives me a hug. He doesn't even try for a kiss. *Because of Jonah?* I'm more relieved than anything. "I'll call you."

"Come on, Thompson." Jonah holds the door open for me, and I precede him into the quiet interior. The privacy divider is raised. The car smells like Jonah and expensive leather. I shut my eyes and soak in the scent. It's delicious and comforting. Better than Sam's hug. *Ah, shit.* My eyes fly open to see Jonah watching me with those black eyes. He's close, his heat and his size dominating the small interior. He's still wearing his overcoat. It frames his jaw in a way that makes me feel light-headed.

"Who was he?" Jonah's voice has a hard edge to it.

"A date. A doctor friend of my friend Luz's."

"A doctor," Jonah scoffs. "Well, how was it?"

"You really want to know?"

"Humor me," he says darkly.

"It was fine." I shrug. I'm being too honest, but I had two glasses of wine and I'm tired.

"Just fine? What was wrong with him?"

"Wrong?" I laugh. "Nothing was wrong. He was just so nice."

Jonah's mouth tips up at the side. "Is that supposed to be an insult? I mean, I agree. But that's me. I figured you would like a nice guy."

"Because you know me so well," I shoot back. I used to like nice guys, or I thought I did. But then there was Eric, who definitely wasn't nice, just weak. *And now Jonah.* The opposite of nice. The man I definitely shouldn't want, but the one who makes my pulse speed every time I look at him.

"Fair." Jonah taps a finger on the seat. "Tell me what you do like."

"You want to get to know me?" I smile at him. "I'm winning you over."

"It's a long ride back to the office," he replies evenly. "Don't read into it."

"Honestly?" I say. "I'm not looking for anyone. Luz, my friend, has been setting me up with guys who want to have fun. But I'm not interested in dating right now."

"Why not?"

"I had a bad breakup." I fiddle with a loose button on my coat. "I don't know why I even answered that. I need to figure out what I want before I date anyone."

Jonah makes a humming sound. "That's fair. If you had to, though, what would he be like?"

"You're being weird." I wrinkle my nose at him. "Why are you asking me this?"

"So I can use it against you later," he says blandly. "Now tell me."

I shiver at the way his gaze presses into me. He's totally focused on me and it makes me squirm. I shut my eyes and try to picture the perfect man, but it's Jonah in my head. *Physically.* Not personality-wise, because that would make me a masochist.

"Thompson."

My head is empty of everything but thoughts of him. His scent, his jaw, the way he watches me. Jonah feeding me, coming to bring me my phone, his dry humor. *Oh no. Say something.*

"Um. Blond. I don't care if he's tall or not. Blue-eyed. Funny. Works a regular job. Like a teacher or a doctor. Someone who will watch sports with my dad." Half truth, half lies. I'll let Jonah try to figure out what's truth.

"Regular, eh?" he says. I open my eyes to see his expression shuttered again. "Makes sense, I guess."

He looks out the window, hand clenched on his thigh, and I can't help but think I've disappointed him.

18

Jonah

When I descend from the gym that Friday morning, Callie is already at her computer.

"Working on your paper, Thompson?" My voice comes out icy with rage. I'm blowing hot and cold with her, and I can't help it. I hate her paper. And in the minutes that I manage to forget that she's a reporter who went after my sister, I actually like Callie Thompson. I like her and I hate that I like her. It's making me grouchy and snappish. My staff is avoiding me. Even Jason texted me telling me I was being a dick. I snapped at Lane at dinner last night, and Miles nearly punched me. Lane just laughed and said I must be losing my head over a woman. *I'm very much not.* I just need to work out more. Forget about Callie Thompson. Keep her at arm's length. Starting today.

"It's not nine a.m. yet," she says warily. Her big blue eyes and her pink lips are stamped in my brain. I don't even have to look at her to know the exact tilt of her head and fall of her hair. But I do look, because I'm an idiot. She's wearing that short skirt from her first week here, a black tank top, and a blazer. She looks sexy and forbidden. I glare at her and she glares back. I love it. *You sick bastard.*

"That's right, but I have something for you to get started on when the clock strikes nine." Something that will crush whatever is between us. Forever. Not that Callie will care. She doesn't want me. She wants a regular guy. A teacher or a construction worker. Someone like the guy she was with last night, who saves lives. Someone my family would approve of, someone who could drink beers with a guy like my dad and make small talk about sports. I know fuck all about sports, and I've never wanted to be regular.

When I pass her the stack of files, her brow wrinkles in confusion.

"More files?"

"I need these delivered."

"To where?" She's still confused. She thinks she's here to work for me, when in reality, she's here for me to use. She thinks we're getting closer, when in reality, just this morning I looked at charity events to attend so I could dangle her in front of Dylan as bait. I shove down the guilt that flares. It's high time she started proving her use. I've been weak where she's concerned. She's supposed to be helping me get back at Dylan, and I've made exactly zero progress.

"Various locations." I hand her a list, and she scans the addresses.

"New Jersey? You're joking. That will take hours on the train. Can I take a car at least?"

I laugh coldly. "Who do you think you are, Thompson? No, you can't take a car."

She sucks in a breath, looking like I punched her.

Nausea rises, like I kicked a puppy. "Thompson? Are you ill?"

"Give me the files," she says woodenly. Her hand shakes when she holds it out. *Don't feel guilty. This is what you wanted.* The desired result. Back to our assigned roles. Her, hating me. Me, lording it over her.

I scan her as I pass them over. For one sickening second, our eyes meet and I think I see tears in hers. *Oh fuck.* My stomach bottoms out.

"What's wrong?"

She ignores me and turns away. "I'll see you later. I have my cell if you need me." She starts walking, practically running away from me. *Don't let her leave.*

"Thompson. Wait."

She speeds up, her shoulders tense, her head down. I slump against her desk as she disappears into the elevator bank. I should have chased her.

~

THAT AFTERNOON, my cell phone rings and the name on the display makes me shut my eyes briefly.

Christine. I do not want to deal with my sister right now, but I've been avoiding her for days.

I accept the call and the sound of moody singer-songwriter music fills my ear.

"Now he picks up the phone." Her brash voice carries over the line.

"Are you driving?"

"On our way to the doctor. For Mia's five-month checkup. Which you'd know if you ever bothered to call me back. Or come to family dinner."

That's Christine. Blunt as ever. And I refuse to feel guilty, even if the pit in my stomach says otherwise.

"Hi, Jonah." Mia sounds unexpectedly calm today. "You should call your sister more." There it is. The fierce protection of my sister. The one reason I put up with Mia's nonsense.

"I've been busy."

"You're always busy," Christine protests. "You need to slow down and enjoy life sometimes. You're going to be old before your time. Mark my words."

"Did you just say *mark my words*? What are you, a fortune teller?"

She guffaws, and I know that I've earned a brief reprieve. Christine is just the vanguard, the canary in the coal mine. Soon, I'll have my mother calling.

"How's the baby?"

"Oh, you know, kicking the shit out of his mother. Glad it's not me."

Mia laughs. I was the sperm donor for them, so Christine couldn't use her eggs. She says she got the better end of the bargain, along with several other choice descriptions of female anatomy and the word *destroyed*. I prefer not to think about it.

"He's gonna look like you, J. I know it."

"You mean he'll come out of the womb scowling?" Mia snorts a laugh, and Christine joins her.

Christine has the same wild black hair that I do. My mom's Italian genes are strong. Their baby probably *will* look like me. And I'll have no fucking clue how to deal with it. I'm not a baby kind of guy. I've never held one, and I don't intend to start now. But I know Christine will hate me forever if I don't at least try to be an uncle.

"Hey, I spoke to the accountant about setting up that 529 plan."

"He's not even born yet," my sister protests.

"It's never too early to start planning for the future," I respond.

"You need to relax, J. You're all 529 plans and taxes and bonds and stuff. Stop and smell the roses."

Well, one of us has to be the responsible one. But I don't say that. Our roles were established years ago, and I'll only hurt my sister. One of a few people in the world I care about protecting.

"About that baby shower," Christine starts, and I groan.

"Stop your whining," Mia cuts in. "It's the twenty-first century. Men come to baby showers now. And it's not going to be a regular baby shower, it's going to be a fun one."

"Yeah, with an open bar," Christine adds.

"Which not all of us can enjoy," Mia grumbles.

"Maybe you can bring a date," Christine says slyly.

"A date. To my sister's baby shower. I don't know, Christine. Is that what women want these days?"

They both laugh. "Couldn't hurt. Is there someone you can take?"

"Nope."

"Come on, J. No one? Really? Let me set you up with Mia's sister."

"I'm good."

"If I didn't know better, I'd take offense to that," Mia mutters. Christine calms her while I'm silent. My sister's wife describes herself as "unhinged white trash," and I try to stay on her good side. For Christine.

"Anyways, think about it. And Ma is going to call you about dinner this Sunday. Be ready."

"I'll make sure my phone is off. Thanks."

We hang up and I scrub a hand over my face. I love my family. I do. But they're messy. Complicated. And not part of my world. Not really. Dinner with my mother means questions about my personal life that I don't want to answer, my father's well-meaning comments about my business, Christine's latest work drama, which she's usually right in the center of. If I'm lucky, my grandma will be there, smacking shins with her cane and pretending she can't hear when we chastise her for insulting people.

No thanks.

◦

"Ms. Thompson is underutilized here. I thought I would let you know."

I raise my head to see George at my door, their lips pressed into a thin, disapproving line.

Miles appears behind them, and I raise my brows.

"Is this an intervention?"

"You're wasting company resources," Miles says flatly. "She's smart. And George needs help. I need you to stop monopolizing their time."

"You were supposed to hire someone," George interjects. "But you scared all the decent candidates away. She's not scared of you. That makes her qualified for the job."

"The real job," Miles adds. "Not this crap." The meaningful look he gives me tells me he's on to me.

"I'm taking her to the charity event tonight. Is that good enough?" I take pleasure in the shock on Miles's face.

"You're what? I'm sorry, did you say event?"

"Do you want me to hit you to make sure you're not dreaming?" George asks him gleefully, and Miles grins.

"You'd love that. But no. I just—why the change of heart? You've never voluntarily attended a charity event. Last month, you told me you'd rather walk across hot coals than sit at a dinner and bid on things."

"Dylan will be there."

"Ah. So what's your plan? Show up and schmooze?" He looks skeptical.

"And she's going to help. She's a reporter after all. And besides, Dylan always wants what he can't have. If she's mine, he'll try to steal her from me."

Miles frowns. "And then what? You're not waiting for him to try and get her alone, are you? That's sick, man."

"No," I say with more force than is necessary. "I just want her to talk to him. I'm not a monster." *The same thing I said to Callie.* Unease churns my stomach.

"Have you let Ms. Thompson know? I'm sorry, I mean Callie." He says her name with a seductive lilt that makes George laugh.

"Knock it the fuck off. I have her running all over Manhattan right now, but I'll tell her when she gets back."

"Won't she need to get ready or something?" George asks. "You can't show up with her looking sweaty and disheveled."

I stand, ushering George and Miles out. "I appreciate the concern, but what part of *she will be punished* do you not understand? The point is not for her to be paraded around like a prize jewel."

Miles shakes his head. "I think you're making a mistake."

"I know you do, but you're not going to interfere, are you? Remember the articles she wrote about you? Merciless Miles? She stalked me, for fuck's sake. She wrote articles about Christine. She called me an embezzler. She deserves this."

Somehow, the events don't hit the way they used to. Miles seems to agree because he shrugs.

"She brought me Lane. Indirectly. But still."

"You're sick. Get out."

He leaves with a grin, and I drop onto my office couch. I trust Miles, even though we are very different people.

I shouldn't do this. I'd planned to force her to come to the event with me, sweaty and annoyed. Humiliate her. The final nail in the coffin of her animosity. I need her to hate me. Because if she likes me... I can't handle that. I can't have her close. She's too tempting.

I was prepared to go the rest of my life with just my work for company. But then Callie came along, with her dancing in the gym, and her cupcakes, and her winning smile. She's a vine creeping into the cracks in my facade, so I need to harden my heart, set us back to square one.

When was my last relationship? The women Callie has reported on in the paper haven't been dates, just business associates. Maybe Amy? A lawyer who helped on a merger about two years ago. We spent a few nights together, until she wanted more, and I immediately cut things off. And before her, Annalise. *Not going there right now.*

I can practically hear Christine now. *Why do you want to be alone?* My response is always the same—it's safer this way. No attachments means no betrayal. No one meeting my family means no one can hurt them. Christine is the risk taker, at least when it comes to her personal life. I might be willing to bet millions of dollars on something in business, but my family's feelings? Absolutely not.

I shove off the couch, my mind made up. There's no reason not to continue with my plan of tormenting Callie Thompson. Nothing other than damnable human frailty.

A momentary weakness. A passing fancy for a woman I know is bad for me. I need to shove any attraction down so deep that I'm practically a monk. I need to regain the icy calm I'm known for. I gulp the water George leaves on my desk every morning, savoring the cool slide down my throat. If I'm icy on the outside, maybe I can convince my insides to feel the same.

I RAISE my head from a due diligence report to Callie dropping a stack of three files on my desk.

"These were rejected."

"And why is that?" I raise a brow. Her hair is windblown, her cheeks are pink, and she's glistening with sweat. *This is what she'd look like in my bed.* I jolt. *Not fucking happening.*

"Recipients said they hated you," she says sweetly. I clamp my lips together, even as a smile threatens. Callie is funny, even when she's being a brat.

"Sounds like you didn't try hard enough, Thompson."

"Do *not* make me go back out there. It's some sort of Halloween bar crawl today." She shudders. "The things I've seen. I rolled my ankle avoiding a pile of vomit, and I was hit on by more frat bros than I can count. Don't they know I'm too old for them?"

"I'm sure they don't care," I say coldly. My hand twitches on my thigh. *She was hit on?* The thought fills me with icy rage. She's mine. No one else's.

"Can I sit?" She's oblivious to the clawing possessiveness in my chest as she sinks onto the couch and twists her ankle this way and that, wincing slightly. "I think it's fine," she mutters.

I'm halfway out of my chair and reaching for the closet with the first aid kit before I catch myself. The point of this is for Callie to suffer. This is exactly what *should* be happening. I push my doubts down and make sure my face is impassive before I speak.

"Thompson. We have an event tonight. We're leaving in twenty minutes."

Her head pops up. "An event?" She looks wary.

"A small one." It's not small. It's massive. But my plan depends on keeping her in the dark, so I can savor her shock when she realizes she looks like Cinderella at the ball, if she never got the makeover.

"And you'll let me attend?" She cocks her head. "What if I learn something useful?" Her eyes are calculating. *Shit.* I didn't think of that. I'm off my game. Distracted by her full mouth and thoughts of locking the door and shoving her up against the wall.

I shrug. "Fine by me."

"Okay, then." She gives a brilliant smile and pops off the couch. "Let me know when it's time to leave."

19

Callie

Finally. Something I can use. I don't even care that I have to spend more of precious personal time on company business, that I'll be attending looking like I just ran a marathon in my sheath dress. An event surrounded by billionaires? No one gets access like this. Especially if it's small, it means I'll actually get to talk to people.

It's weird that Jonah wants me to attend. I mull over his motivations as I pack my bag. I make sure I have my spare charger and my notepad, just in case. He probably wants to torment me more. Maybe I'll have to fetch him drinks. Maybe he'll make me wear a leash or something. I snort a laugh and cover my mouth.

"Finally losing it, Thompson?" My head jerks to where Jonah leans against the door frame. The breath leaves my lungs in a rush. He's wearing a tux that fits him like a glove. His hair has been tamed with gel, and it highlights the sharp planes of his face, his cut-glass cheekbones, his too-full lips, the shadowed edge of his jaw.

"Did you have that suit in your office?" Not the question I want to ask. *Is that material as soft as it looks? Why do you smell so good?*

"Of course. Let's go."

I follow him down the hall, rolling my eyes at his back. One of his fleet of black cars is idling outside the building. The driver opens my door and I give him a bright smile. Jonah huffs as we sink into the cool interior.

"Are you really like that with everyone?"

"Like what?"

His jaw tics and he looks out the window. "So...nice."

I laugh softly. *Only from Jonah would that sound like an insult.* "I'm always pleasant to people in the service industry. They have some of the worst jobs. Believe me. I know. I waitressed for years."

"When did you waitress?"

"Years ago. While I was in journalism school. I waitressed at a diner and lived at home. I had a scholarship, but I still needed to cover living expenses. Trust me, with the kind of customers you get overnight at some places, a smile goes a long way."

He looks back at me, his black gaze inscrutable. "You're like that with everyone at the office too."

I shrug. "I try to wake up on the right side of the bed. There have been times in my life when things weren't so good. When I get up, I try to think of one thing I have to look forward to every day."

The look of distaste on his face makes me laugh again. "I'm not a Mary Sue, if that's what you're thinking. I just decided one day that I could go through life angry at the world, or appreciative. The latter is far more pleasant."

"And today? What did you have to look forward to today?"

Very little, I nearly say, but it's not true. *That's surprising.* I guess going toe-to-toe with Jonah every day is exhilarating. I'm sure as hell not telling him that, though. "The weather is nice. I decided to walk to work and treat myself to a coffee on the way. There's a place near me that makes New Orleans-style coffee with chicory. I love it."

"And when things weren't so good?"

I pull my lip between my teeth, and Jonah's gaze arrows to my mouth. I'm not entirely sure I want to share this with him. It feels like ammunition. *Who do you think you are, Thompson?* "I've just had some times that were tough. That's all."

He hums noncommittally, and I think he'll go back to staring out the window, but instead he watches me. His attention is a physical thing, overwhelming when combined with the way he takes up all the air in the small space. Our hands rest next to each other on the seat, and I have an insane urge to run a finger over the back of his hand, his wrist. Would his skin be warm and rough? Would the hairs feel good under my fingers? Are his arms as heavy with muscle as they appear to be in the gym?

"What you thinking about?" His words in the silent car make me startle.

Um. Fantasizing about your arms. Shit. "Just thinking about the paper," I say airily. That will shut him up.

His jaw tightens. "Yes. The gossip. I'm sure you'll learn some interesting things tonight." He looks homicidal at the thought.

"Gossip isn't all bad, you know. It's fun. Light. Enjoyable. It provides an escape for people." I cut myself off before I can go further into my tirade about why things that primarily women enjoy aren't bad. Like reality TV, celebrity news, and romance novels.

He raises a brow for me to go on. "Don't let me stop your crusade, Thompson. What about gossip is good? I'm dying to know." He drawls the words like he can't possibly be convinced.

I turn to face him more fully. "Think of it like a juicy Netflix show, something you binge. When you have a long day, you just want to turn off your brain. It's healthy. Especially if you're an anxious person or working a high-pressure job, you just want to escape for an hour or two. Take my friend Luz, for example. She's an ER nurse, and she loves romance novels. She can fully immerse herself in the story after a day of saving lives."

"And you provide that?" Jonah looks skeptical, but maybe *understanding*? He's not arguing with me at least. Maybe I'm getting to him.

"I do. I try to. What's the harm in reading something frivolous?"

"Unless there's real harm to the subjects," he says bleakly. His jaw flexes, and he looks away. My cheeks heat, and guilt flares.

I open my mouth to apologize, but before I can speak, we're pulling to a stop in front of an ornate building with columns and glowing lights. When we get to the front, Jonah says, "We're a little late. Everyone is here already."

He motions for me to precede him and we ascend a sweeping staircase, his shoes tapping on the marble. The sound of a crowd grows as we approach the double doors.

"I thought you said—" Before I can finish the sentence, we're at the top of the landing, and the doors are being flung open. A sea of people is displayed before us, and our late arrival means every one of them is staring at us. At me. They glitter like peacocks, clad in jewel-toned gowns and tuxes. I'm wearing my least favorite flats and a blue sheath dress with sweat stains.

Jonah's face is set in vicious satisfaction. *He planned this.* My stomach bottoms out. This is my punishment. Being humiliated in front of all of his friends. I nearly laugh at the irony. It's the perfect torture.

My mouth is dry and my pulse is racing. I back slowly into Jonah, who grabs my arm and growls, "Come on, Thompson." A small laugh goes up from the crowd, and my vision blurs.

It's happening again. The whispers. The stares. I suck in air, but it's not enough.

"Thompson."

I shake my head. He'll make me go down there, and it will be awful. Like being torn apart by hyenas. Like it was every time with Eric. *But the last time*—I squeeze my eyes shut like it will make this go away. *The last time was the worst.*

"I can't do this," I gasp out, before I whirl and run for the hall. I stumble blindly down the stairs. *Not that way.* I can't bear for anyone to see. I turn right and push open an unmarked door into a quiet room. I lock it with shaking hands and lean against the wall, sides heaving.

Not thirty seconds later, someone tries the handle, and I hear, "Thompson. Open this fucking door."

20

Jonah

"Go away." Her voice is shaky and something ugly twists in my stomach.

"I will fire you if you don't open this door right now."

The handle rattles and then Callie's shocked face appears. I push into the room, a sitting room at the Davenport Club, and turn on her. The fire in me drains when I take her in. Disheveled hair, red face, glassy eyes.

"Please leave," she says. Her chest is heaving.

"Are you having a panic attack?"

"I don't—" She presses a hand to her chest, sucks in a gasping breath. "I don't know."

Something in me cracks at that. I can punish her later, but right now, she's so small and diminished and I just want that Callie fire back in her eyes.

I step toward her and she backs against the wall. "Go away. Please, Jonah." My first name slips out in her panic as she sucks in another breath. "I can't. You win, okay? You win. Fire me. I can't—"

You did this. You asshole.

In a swift movement, I haul her against me, my arms banding around her back, pressing her face to my chest. She pushes against me but I murmur, "Shh. Let me help you. My sister used to have panic attacks. I know what to do."

She finally relaxes and lets me sweep firm strokes over her back. "Breathe." Her inhale is shuddery and pain lances through me. *You failed her. She's yours and you failed her.* I shake the thought away. She's not mine. She's an employee. But my brain won't rest. *You claimed her. Like Miles and Jason and Theo. You were supposed to protect her.*

"What happened?" I ask softly. Her breathing is evening out, but it hitches at my question.

"My ex," she finally says. "He was a minor New York celebrity. An influencer. Stupid. Anyways, we'd go to parties and he'd always talk down to me. He let his friends be awful to me. I never knew how to dress, how to talk. And he preferred it that way. He liked having power over me."

Just like you. Fuck. "He was an asshole," I say. My voice comes out gravelly.

"Yeah. He was. Our breakup was public. He appeared at an event with another woman on his arm. And when I confronted him, he said *who do you think you are?* And then they all laughed." *The same words I said to her earlier.* She's shaking, and regret twists in my gut, ugly and black. *Christine would be ashamed of you.*

"I think I could have handled tonight. I'm not weak. But with my outfit, and the shoes, and then someone laughed." She tenses. "I couldn't do it."

I rub her back until she stops shaking. Only then do I unlock the part of my brain that won't stop clamoring about how good she feels in my arms. I shut my eyes for a moment, savoring the smell of her hair in my nose, her hot breaths puffing out against my shirt. I can feel them through the material, can almost feel the shape of her lips. I keep my hands to safe areas, but I want so badly to let my palm drift to the dip of her waist. I want to feel where it flares out into her hips, just once. *Just once.* It's wrong and I'm a sick fuck for lusting after her while I'm the one who caused her pain. My employee. My enemy.

She pushes against me again and I drop my arms. I have no reason to hold her if she's okay. Her eyes are wary, flat, when she meets my gaze. "I think I need to sit down."

She sinks onto the couch and looks up at me bleakly. "You're going to fire me now, aren't you?"

Shame lances through me. She believes the worst of me. *Of course she does, you fool.* "Why would I fire you?"

"This was the plan, right? Humiliate me in front of everyone? Make me bow to you? Your pet reporter." Her voice is hollow and she looks down to where her hands are knotted together, so tightly that the bones stand out against her skin. And suddenly my behavior, my regrets, come rushing at me like an avalanche. *Who do you think you are? He liked having power over me.* My pride. Her determination. My failures. Her vulnerability.

I crouch down in front of her. She won't make eye contact, and something shifts inside me. I press my forehead briefly to her clasped hands. "I'm sorry. I didn't know. And even so—" My breath stutters. "I shouldn't have done that. Forgive me." She tenses at my words. Surprise, maybe? I've surprised myself. I've never begged for a woman's forgiveness before. I've never cared enough to ask. *Not going to examine that right now.*

Our breaths are loud in the quiet room while I wait for her response.

"Okay," she whispers. My body sags. I rise, ill at ease with how relieved I am.

"Do you need me to go back inside? I mean, was tonight about me, or was there another goal?" she asks.

Dylan is in there. His board members. I can approach them about selling their shares. I can see if they know about the tax fraud. And if I don't, if I can't take down Green Media, if Christine and Mia's baby grows up in a world in which Dylan doesn't pay...the thought makes rage rush through me.

But Callie. She's so resigned, so small. And in that moment, I don't question it when I say, "No. There's somewhere else we should go."

21

Callie

"A diner?" I ask as the driver pulls up to the chrome and neon facade. "I pass this one all the time. I've never gone in."

"You're missing out. It's the last one left on the Upper West Side. Diners all over the five boroughs are disappearing."

"I know. My father laments this exact same thing." *I'm surprised you care*, I don't say. I'm wary of Jonah and his reactions, now more than ever. That party was my worst nightmare come to life, and while he couldn't have known about Eric, it's clear he still hates me, apology or no. I'm not sure what to make of him. He's arrogant and cold, but unflinchingly honest. Cruel, but caring, in his own way. He's too hard to predict, and I need to protect myself.

The middle-aged man behind the counter looks up when Jonah opens the door. "Hey, J, it's late for you. Dinner?"

"Wait. You *know* him?"

Jonah doesn't respond to me, but spots of red ride high on his cheekbones.

"Thanks, Paul. A table for two, please."

Paul leads us to a booth on the left, and Jonah slides in like he's been here a hundred times. And maybe he has. Our knees brush under the table, and I scoot to the side. I'm all raw and worn out from the party and his apology. *Forgive me.* No one has ever begged for my forgiveness before, like he would die if he didn't receive it.

"I'm surprised to see you this late. Everything okay?" Paul hands me a menu.

"Just wanted to show her the best food on the Upper West Side," Jonah says, and then he *winks*. I gape.

Paul's chest puffs with pride. "That's right. Pitas are homemade and the burgers are fresh."

"Thank you," I say, stunned, as Paul walks away.

My gaze flicks up to Jonah, who is watching me warily. He should be wary. I haven't decided if I want to sit across from him for this. I feel like a skittish animal, unsettled, nervous, and ready to bolt.

Jonah's midnight black tux is delightfully incongruous against the green vinyl of the seat. He's not looking at his menu. Probably because he knows it by heart. My eyes narrow in thought.

"Wait. Is this where you come every morning?"

His head jerks. "How did you guess?"

"I told you. I'm observant."

"It's uncanny," he grumbles. "But yes." He doesn't elaborate.

"What's your order?"

"Just a coffee most days. I don't eat before I work out."

I tilt my head. He's not looking at me. And he stops here for coffee every morning, when he has an in-office barista on the forty-eighth floor. Something is up. *I'm coming here to investigate.* I need to know the truth about Jonah Crown.

"What do you recommend?"

"How hungry are you?"

"Starving actually. I had a protein bar for lunch."

Something like regret flickers across his face, before he shutters his expression.

"Trust me, then. I'll get us something to share. Breakfast for dinner." He gets up to order.

I watch him walk, confident, loose, like billionaires eat at diners all the time. Paul grins and smacks him on the shoulder when he orders, and I jolt from the shock. If someone smacked him on the shoulder at the office, he'd probably fire them.

Jonah returns to the booth, cold beers in hand. I make a grabbing motion and his lips tilt slightly.

"Not so fast, Thompson."

He sits, holding the beers close. "I want you to tell me about your ex before I let you have one of these beers."

My truths. But none of his own. I was right about the layers. He's greed and ambition. Ruthlessness and anger. Protectiveness and intelligence. And now I'm seeing a different side of him, and I foolishly want more. *You like the bad boys. You can't change him.* He's a man who is willing to humiliate me in front of a crowd of people. But he's also a man who is willing to apologize. And I've learned that's rarer than anything.

"Let's play a game," I say. His eyes flare. He likes games, I think. "One of my truths, for one of yours."

"Fine," he says shortly. "You first. When did you and the ex break up?"

"About a year ago. The party was the last straw. I moved out the next day and in with my dad."

Jonah's jaw tics, and he passes me the beer. It's cool and bitter going down. Delicious. I put it in the center of the table when I'm done. Jonah is watching me with dark eyes, looking angry.

"Why not make him move out?"

Jonah would have. "I just wanted to move on. He would have made it hard for me. I needed to lick my wounds." My face heats with embarrassment. He must think I'm an idiot. Between my panic attack tonight and this shameful admission.

"Did you ever make him pay for what he did?" he asks tightly. Surprise rushes through me. No judgment from Jonah, just action. *I like it.* Too much. Even though it's not something I'd ever do.

"Make him pay?" I shake my head. "That is such a *you* thing to say. No. Why would I?"

"Sounds like he deserved it. And revenge can be...enjoyable." He smiles sharply.

"I'd be lying if I said it never crossed my mind. My whole life was upended by that breakup." I wince. "I loved him. Foolish, I know." Jonah is silent, waiting for me to finish. *He never interrupts.* Even with all his brash confidence, he waits and listens. Not like Eric, who always had to be the center of attention. "But no." I shake my head. "I'd rather live in the present than the past. Focusing on revenge won't make me happy."

Jonah snorts. "I can tell you it will." He gestures to the beer and I sip again. "Want me to ruin him?" he asks casually, and I choke on my drink.

"Excuse me? Did you just say ruin him?"

He shrugs elegantly. "I can."

"What would that involve?"

He raises a brow. "Bloodthirsty, Thompson?"

"Maybe I'm becoming more like you."

His fathomless eyes are intent on mine when he says, "Whatever you want." My heart thuds in response. "I'll buy up his debt and call it due, purchase his apartment building and kick him out, ruin his career."

"Why?" I whisper. My blood is rushing in my ears. *Why would you do this? You hate me.*

His brows lower. "I don't like people who prey on others. Men who wrong women are the lowest of the low."

Disappointment curls through me. *Stupid, Cal. Don't let yourself think you mean anything to him.* But after earlier, I can't help but soften. It makes me an idiot after he humiliated me. I'm sure of it. But instead of a cruel boss, I now see a man whose silky black hair pressed against my hands, whose lips caressed my knee as he asked for forgiveness.

"You sound like you're speaking from experience. And I don't mean your behavior earlier."

He winces. "I deserved that. But yes, I am." He reaches for his beer.

I jerk it back out of his reach. "I'm going to need more than that if you want to earn your beer."

"Thompson," he growls. I shiver at his tone. "Give me the beer."

"Give me more than a one word answer."

"You're determined to drag it out of me, aren't you?"

"I am." I tip up my chin. I want honesty from Jonah Crown, and this is the only time I might have any power over him.

"Don't push me." He glares at me through narrowed eyes.

"I'm not scared of you. You like me." I poke him with my toe again, and quick as lightning, he reaches down to grab my foot. My heel comes off in the process, and warm fingers wrap around my ankle as he pulls my foot into his lap.

"Take that comment back." His eyes spark and my breath catches. He's so unbearably handsome, and this is a side of him I haven't seen. Another one.

"Is it so bad? I won't tell anyone. I promise." I wiggle my foot and his grip tightens. The more annoyed he gets, the more I want to laugh.

"Thompson." His voice is gravel. "I do not like you."

"Sure." I wink. "You *don't like me*. Got it."

"You don't like *me*."

"I never said that."

"Well, you shouldn't," he shoots back. I have to laugh.

"Are you annoyed because I don't hate you? That's absurd." I shake my head at his glower.

"You have no sense of self-preservation. I exist to torment you. And you want to be my friend."

I shrug. "And yet here you are with me in a diner, giving me a foot massage."

He looks affronted. "I am *not* giving you a foot massage."

"Feels like you are, what with the way you're digging your thumbs in."

He immediately loosens his grip and just to needle him, I say, "Oh yeah, a little to the right."

"Thompson. You and I could not be more different. We are not friends."

"*Not friends* definitely grab each others' feet." I give another little wiggle and he hisses a breath.

"Stop that," he growls. His thumb presses into my arch, and a sigh looses from my lips. He tenses.

"Don't stop," I breathe, but he doesn't listen. He just shifts awkwardly and lets my foot drop back to the ground, before sliding out of the booth and heading for the bathroom.

When our food comes, the waitress delivers it with a huge smile for Jonah. I choke out a laugh when I see how much he ordered. Pancakes, waffles, sausage, fried tomatoes, bacon, eggs, toast.

We both reach for the same pancake, and Jonah yanks his hand back. "Yep, we could not be more different," I needle and he rolls his eyes, but wraps a sausage in a pancake.

He proceeds to eat it delicately with a knife and fork, while I watch. His brow goes up, daring me to say something. He swallows and makes another one.

I chew my food and he watches me eat. We both go for the last sausage and he pushes it toward me, shaking his head. *He can be nice. When he wants to be. Is it just regret from earlier? I don't understand him.*

"So, since we're *not* friends, does that mean you still plan to torment me?" I ask lightly, but I really want to know the answer. We've broken through a barrier tonight, I think. I hope.

He frowns around a mouthful of sausage and pancake. "I actually need your help."

"Oh, you do, do you?" Pleasure lights me up.

"Don't gloat." He pops a piece of bacon into his mouth while I crunch my toast.

"It's what you would do."

He smiles. "Fair."

"So you need me? And in exchange, you won't torment me anymore?"

22

Jonah

How do I respond? Callie is looking at me with those big blue eyes, asking if I'll stop tormenting her.

"Well?"

"I won't deliberately torment you," I say slowly. Am I really willing to make peace with Callie? To give up my plan of dangling her in front of Dylan? Is she better as an ally or an enemy?

She nods. "Okay, what do you need?"

I suck in a deep breath and meet her eyes. "I need you to help me destroy Green Media."

Callie's delicate brows go up. She spears a strawberry and pops it into her mouth while I watch her with barely leashed hunger. I'm half hard under my slacks from the touch of her foot, for fuck's sake.

I reach for the beer and she pokes my hand with her fork. I let out a low, frustrated noise. "I'm about to tell you everything, so relax. Fuck, Thompson. You're like a dog with a bone."

"Thank you," she says primly. "I appreciate that."

I take a long gulp of beer. She watches me the whole time, those pretty blue eyes intent on me, those delicate brows drawn low.

"Why do you need to destroy Green Media?"

My hand tightens on the beer. "Dylan Green betrayed me. He was my friend." Something ugly twists in my gut at the words. "He befriended me when I was the unpopular kid in school. I was on scholarship to his fancy private high school, and everything about me was wrong. My background. My clothes. My accent. Dylan was popular. Rich and athletic. He took me under his wing. We stayed friends through high school, and even though we drifted apart during college, we reconnected in business school. We started the company that would become Green Media on the day we graduated. I thought he was the real deal, you know?"

Callie grimaces and sips her own beer. "So, what happened?"

I nod. "It's cliché, but it was a woman. Annalise. An old friend of his, and someone he wanted to date, though he never told me." *Fucking Annalise.* Saying her name feels like swallowing poison.

Callie makes a pained face. "A woman. Ouch."

I turn my beer in my hands. "Dylan...changed. In college. Became crueler, more possessive. I didn't see it at the time. When this all happened, our business was doing pretty well. I was the CEO and co-founder. And I was admittedly better at business than Dylan was. He went to business school because his dad wanted him to. He didn't have the ambition required to really make it."

"But you did," she says. Her eyes are rapt on my face.

"Yeah. Of course I did," I scoff. "I came from literally nothing. Business school was my lifeline. I slept in the office every night when we started the company. And we were doing well. My star was rising in the business world, even if his wasn't. Until he told the press I was embezzling. You've seen the articles." My stomach tries to turn itself over at the memory. The article I'd opened with shaking hands. The allegations. The calls with feds, the overpriced lawyer I'd hired just so my mother would stop crying.

"No way." Callie leans forward. "No fucking way. That was a lie? I mean, I know the charges were dismissed. But that was him?"

"Yes," I say shortly.

"I'm sorry for printing it," she says bluntly. I freeze. The words are a white flag. I keep my face carefully blank, even though I'm surprised at her candor. *She's willing to apologize.* After everything I've done, she's still willing to apologize. She's a better person than I thought.

"I didn't know it all came from him. Did you get in trouble?" she asks.

"No. By the skin of my teeth. I kept meticulous records and our head of finance was a stand-up guy. He was able to prove that I'd never touched a dime. I still lived with my parents, for fuck's sake. It's not like I was skimming and living large."

"But you lost the company." Her eyes are calculating. She's always two steps ahead, this woman. And I fucking love it.

"I did. That company became Green Media."

"And this is why you hate reporters. Because of the way he weaponized the press against you."

That and everything that happened after. But I can't get into that with Callie. I dip my chin. "That's right. He weaponized the press against me, and in those articles, he said horrible things about my family, about my parents. And he outed my sister." Hot rage slices through me. Christine had been twenty-one at the time, and vulnerable as hell. She'd been testing the waters with her first real girlfriend, who had been a secret up until that moment. She'd been trying to figure out how best to break the news to our family. She'd told me at nineteen, and I'd kept her precious secret, for the woman I loved most.

"My parents didn't even know and he told the whole fucking world. Her girlfriend broke up with her. Her girlfriend's dad found out when Christine was at her house. He kicked her out and made her walk home in the snow, at least until I picked her up." I push my beer away before I break the bottle. "I sat next to her while she cried and made me promise I wouldn't kill him. She was devastated." My throat is thick at the memory. The hot shame I felt comes roaring back. I trusted Dylan, and he betrayed me. And Christine paid the price. "I regret that promise. I should have run her ex's dad over with my car and made it look like an accident. And I should have gone after Dylan next."

Callie presses a shaking hand to her mouth. "Dylan would have deserved it." Her eyes are murderous and in that moment, I want to crush her to me and kiss her. She looks like she'd kill on Christine's behalf too. "I want to help you take him down. Tell me what I can do." Her voice is fierce. *Ally instead of enemy.*

"There's nothing you can do tonight, Thompson. Ease up." I give her a rusty smile, a real one, and her eyes flare wide.

"Fine," she says. "But I *can* help, you know. I'm good at research. Really good. You've seen it in action already. I can find more information about Dylan. Whatever you need."

My chest aches at her words. Several hours ago, I was tormenting her for my enjoyment. I'm not totally certain I've given up my plan to use her. And now, she wants to help me.

"Thank you," I say roughly. "Let's talk about it tomorrow."

"Tomorrow," she groans. "It's already ten p.m. Are you sure you need to work out tomorrow? Maybe you should take a break." She sounds hopeful, and I press my lips together to keep from smiling and encouraging her.

"I don't take breaks."

She studies me. "What do you do for fun?"

I freeze on my way to spear a sausage with my fork. "You sound like my sister."

"Well?" She raises her eyebrows as I chew, stalling. She's way too fucking perceptive. Those blue eyes seem to look straight through me.

"I work out."

"We've established that."

"I see my family." Though not in weeks. "I watch New York Royals hockey. Theo's fault, really. I'm not a sports guy."

"Theo?" She cocks her head. "Oh, the other founder. The one you commented about on the site."

I wince. I'm not proud of those comments.

"That's him. He's been gone for a while, but he owns a minor stake in the team."

"So you're not a sports guy. Do you like to travel? Eat out? Go to concerts?"

I don't know. My chest is tight and my collar is cutting off my air. I shed my hobbies years ago. I sacrificed my personality on the altar of my ambition.

Callie's eyes soften and I hate it. She sees this weakness at the heart of me. *Why does her opinion matter so much?* She doesn't matter. She's someone I'm supposed to destroy. She's a fucking reporter.

"I don't need hobbies." My voice comes out harsher than I intend.

"Everyone needs—"

"I'm not everyone. Stop trying to fit me into a box, Thompson. I'm not part of your world. I don't want to be."

Hurt flashes over her expression and disappears. I hate it.

This is what you wanted.

"Why don't we get the check?" she says. She pushes back from the table before I can respond and walks over to where Paul is manning the counter that doubles as a bar.

He smiles at something she says and nods. Her face lights up. Something ugly makes my stomach turn. *Fuck this.* I chug the rest of her beer, then mine, but the alcohol doesn't make me feel better. It doesn't stop the ache sitting just behind my ribs.

I drop a crisp hundred on the counter on the way out and nod at Paul. "See you tomorrow." I stride out of the restaurant and Callie follows.

"Goodnight, J—Mr. Crown," she says softly.

I turn. Lou is already opening the door of the car. "Get in the car, Thompson." I jerk my head toward the interior. She bites her lip. I want to bite it too.

"I think I should walk."

The thought of her alone, walking home in the dark, makes my pulse thud. "Get in the car," I repeat. "You're not walking."

She sighs and precedes me into the space. It's too small inside. *How have I never noticed that before?* I make a mental note to get a bigger car. Maybe a limo. She could sit at one end, and I could take the other. That way I wouldn't be able to see her hands twisting in her lap, her wary eyes when she looks at me.

I'm too aware of my loud breaths in the quiet interior, her scent, her perfect cheekbones, her long lashes. I shut my eyes and press my head back against the seat. That makes it worse. The car is filled with her and I want to pull her onto my lap, suck on her neck, tell her I'm sorry, that I don't know how to be anything other than who I am, that I want her. That all I want is her. *Fuck.*

We ride in silence the ten blocks to her apartment. I help her out of the car before Lou can come around. I wave him away and shove my hands into my pockets while she loops her scarf around her neck.

"So this is where you live?"

It's a neat brownstone. Slightly worn around the edges, a little bit of stone crumbling on the steps, the bars over the first-floor windows rusted in one place. But there are lights on in most of the windows. A cat watches us from the second floor.

"There. That's our cat, Samson." She points. "But I guess you probably knew that."

"I didn't know about the cat." An asinine thing to say, but the rush of blood in my ears is making me stupid.

The side of her mouth tips up slightly and I want to roar in triumph. But her smile is gone as quickly as it came.

"Thompson, I—"

"Jonah," she says at the same time. "I mean, Mr. Crown."

"You can call me Jonah." *I didn't mean to say that.*

"Okay, Jonah," she says slowly, testing it out. She's pleased. The sound of my name on her lips makes me shudder.

Kiss her. I jolt, and she gives me a strange look. My brain is clamoring for me to claim her. She would taste delicious. I know it. My eyes drop to her lips. Her tongue darts out to wet her lips. *Would she let me?* More importantly, would she like it? Would she sway against me? Would she let me hold her up? Desire beats through my blood.

But kissing? *Fuck, I must be going insane.* I don't kiss women. I take a step back. *She's my employee. And a reporter. A fucking reporter.* I need to get a hold of myself.

"Jonah, I—"

"Good night, Thompson. Don't be late tomorrow."

23

Callie

It's surprisingly easy to sneak out of the house every morning when my father sleeps like the dead and snores loud enough to wake them.

"I can't believe I'm still doing this," I mutter, doing a silent dance around the kitchen to get my coffee and my lunch. *Why am I even sneaking? Because what I'm doing this morning feels forbidden.* It's been days since I went to the diner with Jonah, and I've been dying to know what he does there. This isn't work, just stalking. I don't want my dad asking questions. He'll see right through me. Luz would laugh in my face.

I used to sneak out at nineteen, when I had a fake ID and not a single worry. I'd sneak back in at around the same time as it is now. Five a.m. *And I'm going to be late if I don't hurry.* I bury my chin in my wool coat as I walk the short blocks to the diner. Five a.m. is the witching hour. The time in between the partiers and the early morning workers. Dark and silent, even in the city that never sleeps. Three a.m. sees crying couples still heading home from the bars. Four a.m. is bar fights and club goers finally falling into bed.

Five a.m. on a Thursday is still creepy, though, especially for a woman alone. I walk with purpose, my hand wrapped around the pepper spray on my keychain. There's the occasional drunk guy who hassles me on my early mornings, but it's mostly quiet. Broadway between 95th and 107th is my turf. I make it to the diner at 5:16 a.m. The windows are bright against the dark morning, and slightly fogged. Paul is at the counter and I grimace, thinking of how tired he must be. My eyes are gritty and my head is fuzzy. Last night, I came home and finalized a few articles for the print run of the paper before uploading the files to the printer. The article about Jonah's workout routine will run alongside photos of the mayor's new dog.

As I approach the diner, I spy Jonah with his back to me, in a booth. I creep closer, until I can see his face, taking in the overcoat he hasn't removed, the way his inky hair is pushed off his high forehead. My stomach does a stupid little flip at the smile he's giving his breakfast companion. He gave me a real one the other night. And he'd looked like he wanted to kiss me. *In between insults, you fool.*

Who the hell is he having coffee with? His black sedan is double-parked across the street, ready to whisk him to the office. *A woman? A date?* Something ugly claws at my throat. If it's a woman... I shake my head and press myself to the side of a lamppost.

It *is* a woman, but she has to be seventy, maybe older. Her hands shake slightly as she lifts the mug to her lips and a drop of coffee spills on the table. Jonah's expression twists with sadness for a bare moment, and then he hastily wipes the droplet up before she can finish drinking. He's smiling, really smiling at her, soft and gentle. She's smiling back, and she must make a joke, because he tips his back and laughs. *Holy shit.* I can't tear my eyes from him. He's so handsome, carefree in a way I've never seen him. Mr. Crown is gone, and in his place is just Jonah.

I want to make him laugh. My brain is a traitor. Luz would yell at me. Because if I'm the girl who likes bad boys, who tries to change men who can't be changed, then Jonah is the baddest of them all and I'm a fool. *I don't want to change him. I just want him to smile.* He leaves money on the table and kisses the woman on the cheek before he starts for the entrance. *Shit.* I need to go. I dart out from behind the lamppost, straight into the leering face of a man whose breath reeks of whiskey. He's wearing a suit with no tie and the blank look of someone who's spent the whole night drinking. I gag and step back swiftly.

He mutters something unintelligible, his hand reaching for me. I stumble back and he follows. My gaze darts. *Subway. No. Too far. Diner.* I feint to the left and move to the right, but his hand shoots out and grabs my arm. His grip is punishing. My pulse hammers in my throat. I push past the panic and take a lungful of air. No one pays attention to screams in New York, but maybe someone will this time.

I open my mouth and then I hear, "Get your hand off her or I'll kill you," in Jonah's seething voice. The nickname Prince of Darkness has never been more apt as he steps from the shadows, looking like a demon in his black coat. The man whirls, and Jonah raises a brow.

"You won't," the man spits.

"Try me." Jonah bares his teeth. "I have no morals and enough money to bribe the police."

The man draws himself up like he might say something else, but something in Jonah's face seems to stop him. He stalks off, ranting to himself, and I'm left shivering on the sidewalk while Jonah stares me down. His dark eyes are flat and angry.

"Thank you."

"Don't thank me. You're not going to like what comes next."

He turns on his heel and heads for his waiting car. When I don't follow, he turns in the middle of the street, forcing a cab to stop and lay on its horn. "Thompson. You're getting in this damn car."

"Yes, my lord," I mutter, but I scurry across the street into the waiting car.

Jonah's eyes are black with rage by the time I buckle my seatbelt. He drums his fingers on his thigh. Like every time I've been confined with him, he takes up all the air in the small space.

"Do you insist upon taking risks like that every morning, or is it a special treat just for me?"

"Are you *mad?*" My mouth pops open in surprise.

"Yes, I'm mad. It's not safe at five a.m. Don't you read the news?" He realizes what he's saying and shakes his head. "Don't answer that."

"Are you done lecturing me? I'm not a child. I'm working."

"Working?" he scoffs. "More like spying on me."

Think, Cal. "I'm doing an article on the diner. I was getting some photos before the streets get too busy." Paul already agreed to be interviewed for an article about the disappearing diners of New York, so it's not a lie.

"You're a bad liar."

"And you're very arrogant. It's not always about you." *It's totally about you.*

"So you don't want to know who I was having coffee with?" His eyes glitter. I practically shudder with the need to know, but I shake my head.

"You don't want to know what we talked about?" He cocks his head.

I press my hand to my thigh to keep my leg from jiggling. "Nope."

He huffs a laugh. "You're too curious for your own good."

I roll my eyes but stay silent.

"Let's make a deal."

I flick my gaze back to him, where he's watching me intently. The sky beyond his window is starting to get lighter. Dawn isn't for another ninety minutes, but it's no longer pitch black out.

"Okay," I say, against my will. "What's the deal?"

"You do whatever I tell you to for the next hour, without complaint, and I'll tell you who I was meeting with."

Whatever I tell you. I bite my lip. That could mean anything. His eyes flare as he watches my teeth worry my lip. His exhale is loud in the car.

"What do you mean by whatever you tell me?" Images fill my head. Him raising the privacy divider, pushing me down on the seat with those black eyes on mine. One large hand on my stomach, pinning me. Kissing him. In my imagination, he tastes like smoke and liquor. Sin. Forbidden pleasure.

"What are you thinking?" His voice is low.

I shut my eyes, trying to banish the images of his perfect jaw above the collar of his coat, the silky fall of his hair, the stubbled column of his throat.

"Thompson. Tell me what you're thinking or I will make your life hell." The sound of his voice wraps around me, drawing my nipples to points.

"I'm already there," I say.

I can practically hear him freeze. When I dare to open my eyes, his are heavy-lidded, watching me, analyzing. *Don't go there, Thompson,* his eyes say. *It's too late,* mine respond. I should be mortified, but I've never wanted anyone like this before. So when he says, "Do we have a deal?" I say, "Yes."

24

Jonah

Nerves jump in my stomach as I push open the studio door. The lights flicker on automatically, displaying the ring, the practice bags, the mats, the water station. No one comes to the studio, except Jason, Miles, and sometimes Mia's brother. *What is Callie going to think of this?*

"You box?" Callie asks, her eyes wide. She's dressed for working out like she's someone who never works out. Incomparably impractical. That's her. Tight leggings, a cropped sports bra that makes my head swim, bright pink sneakers. I want to grab her ass and grind her against me. *And I think she wants it too.* It struck me in the car. Her expression was as pained as mine is every time she walks in front of me. Or maybe I was seeing things.

"I used to box competitively."

And I was fucking good. I don't tell her that. I don't mention that I could have gone pro. I could have been an instructor instead of a businessman. It's not relevant now.

"When did you stop?"

I should have known that she would have questions. Her reporter's mind can't stop ferreting out secrets.

"Years ago. When I went to business school." I remade myself. Shed the harsh accent, the motorcycle, the hobbies that didn't fit with who I wanted to be.

I move to the corner, where the wraps and gloves are kept, and pull out the box of multicolored fabric.

"Come here. I'll do your hands."

She stands in front of me while I take her wrist in my hand and start wrapping her hand with the strip of green fabric. I've done this a million times for myself, but rarely for others. My hands are thick and awkward as I pull the first wrap tight.

"Why did you stop?" *Is it my imagination, or does her voice sound higher than usual?*

I snort. "Businessmen don't box. Boys from New Jersey might, but men like me bet on boxing matches or own the casinos that host them, the TV stations that air them."

"Do you miss it?"

My gaze flicks up to hers. She's studying me, the way she always does when we're close.

"I do," I admit. "There's nothing like competition. I miss winning."

"But you still practice?"

"Every day. And now I'm going to teach you." I feather my thumb over the skin of her inner wrist, where her pulse is racing. She's impossibly silky smooth. Her eyes are wide and trusting as I wrap her other hand.

"Why do I need to learn?" She steps away as I grab the gloves. "Though I admit it would be helpful for when celebrity bodyguards get handsy."

My fist clenches around the gloves. *Because I would have killed that man this morning for touching you.* "Because this morning came way too fucking close. And I know you won't listen if I tell you to stop, so this is the next best thing. You'll train with me every morning. Until you can beat me."

"Beat you?" She sounds incredulous, and I smile.

I duck into the ring and lean against the ropes. I give her a cocky grin that I know will spur her to compete. "I'll tie one hand behind my back, but it won't be easy. And I expect you to train with me even when you're done working here."

Her tongue pokes out of her mouth as she slips the gloves on and enters the ring. "I'm game. I've always wanted to punch a billionaire in the face." She smacks her gloves together and winces.

I bark a laugh. "You won't get your chance today, I promise you that. We're just learning. No sparring yet. You don't even need gloves, but you can wear them if you want."

"Boring." She mimics leaving and warmth bubbles up in my chest.

"Watch and learn. This is your ready stance. I'm left-handed, so my left leg goes back. You're right-handed, so you'll do the opposite. Keep your knees bent and your weight evenly distributed." She nods, watching me intently. "I'm going to run through the punches now. No defense. Just watch."

My right hand snaps out, followed immediately by my left, as my hip carries me through the punch. Jab. Cross. The motion is as natural as breathing for me. Right elbow crooked and my body turns into the front hook. The left hook is more powerful. A heavy bag would be shuddering with the impact, but I have no bag in the ring. I step in for an uppercut, following with my right hip and then my left.

When I turn back, I'm preening a little. Callie's eyes are wide. "You're going to teach me to do *that*?"

I grin. The gym always puts me at ease. "Well, maybe not that. I'm known for the speed of my punches. It takes time to develop the fast twitch muscle. Come on, Thompson. Ready stance."

She awkwardly mimics my stance. "You're going to be a yeller, aren't you?" she grumbles.

"A yeller?"

"You know. Like a football coach. Come on, Thompson. Faster. One-two. You look like a girl out there." She growls the final words and a surprised laugh bursts from my chest.

"I'll let you be the judge," I say mildly. "Hands by your face. When you're done punching, your hand should come back to guard your face." She lifts a hand and I growl, "Closer. Touch your ear. We don't want that pretty face getting ruined."

"You think I'm pretty?" Her eyes track me as I circle her.

I wince where she can't see. *That wasn't supposed to come out.* "I didn't say that."

"Yes. You did. You think I'm pretty." She's practically wiggling with excitement.

"It's not nice to gloat."

"You likeeee me," she croons. "You want to kiss me."

God help me, I do. And I can't remember the last time I kissed anyone.

"Thompson," I bark. "Focus."

"Guess you are a yeller," she grumbles.

I step in toward her and her eyes widen. "You're an insubordinate trainee. I'm going to make you run laps around the building if you keep this up. Do you want to be punished?" Her tongue darts out to lick her lips and my groin tightens in response. "Don't answer that."

Her eyes are laughing at me as I lean against the ropes, a safe distance away. I bark orders at her as she runs through the punches. She's a fast learner and she takes direction well. I can tell she's actually trying to improve.

"Good job," I tell her quietly, when her form on a cross looks particularly good. She does a little dance of excitement.

"Am I a natural, coach?"

"You're paying attention. And trying. That's half the battle."

"I believe in taking the opportunities you're given," she says, practicing the jab-cross combination again. I startle. *Me too.* Callie Thompson, the woman who might be my polar opposite, holds the same values I do. Shock keeps me stock-still against the ropes as I watch her.

She flows through the punches as best she can, and pride fills my veins. She's a fighter, Callie Thompson. Even if she is a fucking reporter.

"Just going to ogle me?" she asks sweetly and I choke on my saliva. That's exactly what I'm doing.

"Keep going," I say darkly. "Fifteen more minutes of shadow-boxing for you. And no more sass, or I really will punish you."

As I duck under the rope and head for the heavy bag, I swear I hear her say, "Do you promise?"

25

Callie

Two days later, Jonah still won't let me punch him.

"Come on," I wheedle. He's in black pants again, leaning against the wall while I shadowbox to warm up. No shirt, which is unfortunate for my focus. Yesterday, he was just in low slung shorts, and I kept getting distracted. He's a symphony of muscle when he boxes. Graceful and brutal all at once. The lethal edge to him only makes it sexier.

His gaze flicks over me as I move. After three days of this, I'm starting to get into a rhythm, my muscles and nerves following the beginning of a what I know for Jonah is a well-worn path.

"No," he grunts.

"I just think it would be satisfying to land a facer." I picture my fist landing on his face. "You deserve it."

"I do." His lips twist. I stop and stare. "If you tell anyone I admitted that, I'll deny it. But I do deserve it."

I shiver at his words, at the way he's baring himself to me. Raw honesty and acres of naked skin. *Is there anything hotter than a man willing to admit when he was wrong?* Probably not.

"One facer," he says. "But I have to show you how to punch properly first. Okay?"

I nod. "Sounds good."

"Now keep going. Faster. Work some defense in there too."

I roll my eyes but speed up, trying to snap out my hands the way he does.

"Stop."

I stop, my breath coming short. Shadowboxing is harder than it looks. He's frowning as he grabs my arm. *Oh no.* His hands wrap around bare skin. He never touches me. He's kept a careful distance since day two, when he made the mistake of asking me to kneel between his legs during an ab workout. Our nearness needs to be carefully prescribed. My knees on his sneakers for sit-ups, my hand brushing his when I pass him something to sign. Never this. Warm, rough skin on mine, his long fingers totally engulfing my forearm. *Focus, Cal.*

"You're twisting your arm too much when you jab," he says. "You're doing this." He manipulates my arm and I can't concentrate on the motion, because he's close, so close. He smells good, like a rainy day, fresh earth, citrus, and *oh, hell.* I'm so dumb and so *wanting.* "You should be doing this." He moves my arm again, fingers stroking over my skin, making nerves jump inside me.

"I see." My voice sounds high and breathy. I think. I can't tell.

"Do you see?" He angles his head. He doesn't let go of my arm. He's running his fingers over the inside of it now. Wrist to elbow. It feels like he's stroking more intimate parts of me, and I shiver with want.

"You seem distracted."

I nearly choke on a laugh. "I just need to warm up more." He lets go of me and steps away, still watching. "Don't you need to work out?" I drop onto the mat, refusing to meet his eyes, and start the routine of bodyweight exercises he has me do each morning.

"Yep." He rustles around and drops onto the mat next to me. *Don't look. Don't look.* I keep my eyes on my feet. "I'm very behind in my workouts, actually." I can practically hear him frowning with annoyance. "You're learning fast, though. You won't need my supervision soon. You can practice on your own."

"Great. Great," I mutter. He's doing push-ups next to me, and I so badly want to look. I take a peek from under my lashes. The hard planes of his body look like they were created to tempt women to sin. He's the most beautiful man I've ever seen, and I can barely breathe. Hair made to tug on, arms strong enough to carry you to bed, a back with muscles for you to dig your nails into.

The proverbial you. Not me. Of course.

I can't have him. He's my boss. He hates me. He wants to destroy me. *But does he?* He wants me to learn self-defense. He apologizes when he's wrong. He meets an old woman for coffee every morning.

The woman. I forgot about the woman.

"So are you going to tell me about your breakfast date this week?"

He does one more push-up before rolling onto his back. "I thought you'd forgotten." He's sprawled out and panting like he just finished a round of particularly athletic sex.

"I've been waiting for my moment," I say primly. "Who was she?"

"My mother's best friend growing up. Judy."

"And she lives in the city? Not New Jersey?"

He levers himself to sitting, and I try to avoid watching the way his muscles roll under his skin. A shadow passes over his face. "Judy has Alzheimer's. She lived in the city with her husband before he died five years ago. Her whole family is in New Jersey, but change is hard for her. Judy has patterns here, like going to the diner every morning. I went as a favor to my mother, and I just kept going." He shrugs, like it isn't heart-wrenchingly wonderful that he meets her every morning.

"Stop looking at me like that," he growls.

"Like what?"

"Like I'm a do-gooder." He practically spits the word, and I have to smile.

"Is that the worst insult you can think of?"

"Yes."

"Doing good isn't so bad."

"But being a do-gooder is. At least I'm honest about who I am. I don't pretend to be a good person and do bad things secretly."

"So, what about training me? That's a good thing."

"Neutral at best," he says flippantly, pulling a smile to my lips. Jonah's humor is there, even though it's drier than most. "I'm behind on my workouts, remember?"

"I'm not neutral at best," I tease. My heart is thudding, and I hope he can't see how he affects me. My face is hot, but I can't stop smiling.

His gaze sharpens on mine. "No, you're not," he finally says. And damn if that isn't the best compliment I've ever received.

26

Jonah

"It's time."

"For what?" Callie eyes me suspiciously. We're in the gym again, on a Friday morning. She's wearing a pink cropped T-shirt that nips in at her trim waist. I can see the top of the dimples at the base of her spine every time she turns around. They draw my eye like I'm a horny teenager.

"Sparring. But you're going to do the punching. Not me." We've been at this five mornings now, and she's learning quickly. She's ready for the pads.

Her eyes light up. "Hell yes." She moves to grab her wraps and gloves, and I watch her go, helpless not to. It's getting ridiculous. Every time she walks into my office, my body comes alive. When she leans over to give me something, I imagine running my tongue along the tops of her breasts. I'm a walking HR violation. I've been jerking off in the shower every morning, which might be making it worse. Last night, I actually fantasized about sweeping everything off my desk and feasting on her. *And there I go again.* These thin shorts won't do much to hide an erection.

I strip off my shirt and slot my hands into the straps on the back of the pads. If I'm going to suffer, so will she. I've seen the way she looks at me when she thinks I'm not paying attention. There's hunger in her eyes. The bare skin does it. I think she still hates me, but she definitely doesn't hate my body. I'm rewarded by her mouth parting as she turns, though she brings her gaze up to my face immediately.

My back is to the wall, and I bring up my hands. "Start easy, Thompson. Jab cross. Like we practiced. I'll raise the pad I want you to hit. No defense and no other punches. Got it?"

She scrunches her nose up like she does every time I give her an order. "Yes, coach."

"No sass. Let's go."

She smacks her gloves together and we begin. She's tentative at first, like I was the first time I hit an actual person instead of a bag. It's easier than it looks, though, and she starts to relax. She follows through with her hip on a cross, and her fist makes a satisfying thump against the foam pad.

"Good girl," I say, and she flushes pink. *Fuck.* She likes it. That was a mistake. I'm too comfortable with her. "Harder. Focus." My voice comes out gravelly.

"I am." She throws the next cross harder. Her hair is escaping in tendrils around her face. Her plump pink lips are parted with her shallow breaths. I want to bite them.

"Harder," I growl. "Force me back."

"You're like a damn—" Punch. "Wall." Her form is perfect on the last jab.

"Good girl," I say again, without thinking.

"You are the worst." She punctuates every word with a thump of her glove on the pad. She's annoyed now. Annoyed and slightly flushed.

"Harder."

"I'm trying. I hate you." She goes for another cross, but she stumbles and the momentum carries her into me. My back hits the wall. Her soft hip meets my groin, her hand punches the concrete behind me. I groan. She freezes. I let my arms fall to my sides, and the pads drop from my hands.

"Are you hurt?" I run my hands down her arms and her hands. Silky soft skin, no sign of injury. My pulse slows. "Punching a wall is no joke. You can break a hand like that."

"I'm fine. Sorry." Her forehead is pressed into my chest, and she sighs. "I just need a minute." She rests her head on my chest, and my body responds. *Shit.*

She shifts, her hip rubbing indecently against my hardening erection, and I grab her waist.

"Don't move." My voice comes out pained. Every brush of her body against mine is like taking a shot of whiskey. My cock in rising in my shorts, and *oh, fuck.* She shifts against me, and I tighten my grip. "Thompson." I say the words through gritted teeth.

"What's wrong? Are you okay?" She leans back, presses herself fully against me. Soft breasts to my hard chest. "Jonah? I asked— oh." *She's looked down then.*

"Yes. Oh. I need you to step away very carefully, okay?"

"Why?" she whispers. Her face is tipped up to mine, trusting, the heart shape of her high cheekbones and her rounded cheeks making her impossibly lovely.

"I can't be this close to you."

"Oh." She sucks in a breath. "You hate me that much?"

I laugh softly. "No, Thompson. I don't hate you." I can't look at her. If I look at her, I'm going to kiss her. I don't kiss, but I've never wanted to break a rule more.

"What do you mean?" she whispers. "Look at me."

I groan and look down. I can't resist her. She's so pretty. Everything I want. "I've been trying so hard," I mutter, almost to myself. "I can't stop thinking about you. Do you know how difficult it is every day?"

Her lips curve. "Probably about as hard as it is for me."

"You did not just say that." She can't say that, because that means she wants me too, and that means... I can't go there. My breaths seize in my chest, my heart thudding like a bass drum in my ears. I'm turned on and confused, and *fuck*. I want her.

"What's wrong with that?"

"I'm your boss." I lower my head. Her hands land on my chest. She digs her short nails into my chest muscles, and my stomach tightens. "I can't." I murmur the words into her ear, loving how she shivers in response. "We can't." She smells so good, and her skin looks so soft and delicious. "Just one taste," I murmur. My lips hover over the pulse point of her neck. "One taste, okay? And then we stop."

"Please," she whispers.

The word is my undoing.

27

Callie

Jonah's lips make contact with my neck, and desire floods me in a rush. He groans like kissing my skin is his holy grail. His lips are soft, seeking. His breath is damp and warm. I press closer on a shudder and tilt my head to give him more access. *Just one taste.* If all we get is this, I don't want it to end. He tugs my ponytail out and spears his hand into my hair, tangling the strands, wrapping them around his hand.

He's sucking lightly on my skin, and it's lighting me up. Sparks dance behind my eyes, and I melt into his chest.

"Good girl," he mutters. The words are gas on an open flame. When he said them earlier, I didn't understand why they turned me on so much. I'm not going to question it. I'm just going to go with it.

He tilts my head to the other side, but doesn't kiss me. I dig my nails into his chest, forcing a soft laugh from him.

"Impatient, Thompson?"

"More," I murmur. I'm not above begging. I'm strung tight and I need his mouth on me.

"Okay." He brushes his lips gently over my pulse. So gently that I can barely feel it. I make a frustrated sound and he laughs again, just a huff of breath, before his tongue flicks over skin. I cry out and sag against him. It's just a tongue on my neck, but I've never felt this way before, like I'm high. Jonah is a drug and I need more. I run my hands over his sides, from the cut of muscle at his groin, up his firm sides. I dig my fingers into his back, and he shudders.

I've spurred him into action, clearly, because he skims one hand up my side, kneading the dip of my waist, higher, higher, until his fingers trace over the top of my breast in the tank top I'm wearing. "Jonah," I breathe. "Please." Slowly, he leans down and flicks his tongue over the skin at my neckline. I jerk like I've been electrified. He makes a low sound of pleasure, grips my waist, and does it again. He's feasting on me and I'm along for the ride. *I guess this is what he meant by I can't stop thinking about you.*

"So good." He groans. "You taste—" A soft bite at the top of my breast before he shoves my neckline down. "So good." His voice is reverent when he bares my breasts. His tongue slowly sweeps his bottom lip. I shiver, holding myself still, waiting for him to act. I'm bared, and I should be cold, but instead I'm on fire for him.

"We shouldn't," he murmurs. His gaze lifts to mine, slightly glazed, a little desperate. He looks like he's pleading with me to stop this. Hell, no. I'm not stopping.

"No one will know." Bold words, but the desire swirling through my blood is making it hard to think.

"If we do this, you do what I say. Understand?" His voice is ragged.

"What do you mean? Like you're into BDSM or something?"

"You could say that." His mouth hitches in a half smile. "Just know that if you listen to me, you'll have the best orgasm of your life. Is that enough?"

"And you won't, um, hurt me?" My face heats. I'm so out of my depth.

He looks horrified. "I would never hurt you." He shakes his head. "I'm not into that. Your pleasure is my pleasure."

"That sounds pretty good." I smile.

"Believe me, it is." He kisses my neck again and grazes my

nipple with his finger, rasping his nail gently over it until I cry out. Like he does everything, Jonah focuses on me completely. My stomach is tight with need, my hips are pressing toward him, like it will soothe the ache. And then he sinks heavily to his knees before me, and my breath stutters in my chest. His hands are careful and his body is almost shaking with need. I'm right there with him. I've never felt this way before—consumed by desire, like I haven't had a drop of water in years and only Jonah can quench my thirst.

I thread my fingers through his silky hair as he runs his tongue along the top of my leggings, where my tank top has ridden up. Shivers run through me at the wetness of his tongue on my skin. He makes a low hum of pleasure before he presses his thumbs into my hips and hooks them under the waistband of my leggings.

"What is this?" This is not what I expected. I thought maybe he would be forceful, aggressive. I expected him to kiss me hard enough to draw blood, fuck me into the wall, but no.

"Let me give you pleasure." He raises his head. His dark eyes are hazy already, half-lidded. He inches my leggings down while I hold his gaze. "Let me show you how good I can make you feel."

My heart is in my throat, fluttering like a bird. I nod, desire making my insides hot and my blood sluggish. Jonah's erection is thick under his shorts, but he ignores it in favor of pushing my leggings all the way off.

"Hands against the wall," he growls, before pulling my lace underwear down to the ground.

He looks triumphant when I'm bared before him. And then he settles himself onto the floor, pushes my knees wider, and buries his face between my legs.

I sob out an embarrassing sound at the first touch of his mouth on my thigh. "I'm all sweaty. Are you sure?"

"Don't question me, Thompson," he growls, but there's no edge to it. He licks a hot line up my thigh, lets out a groan, and twines his tongue over my clit. My hips punch off wall right as he says, "You taste so fucking good."

My face is red with embarrassment, like it was when Eric went down on me. It never got me there.

Jonah raises his head. "Stop squirming." His lips are wet and his eyes are feral. He stills my hips with one large hand on my stomach and licks back into me. Sparks dance in my belly at the contact.

"Relax," he mutters, the words vibrating against me. "Relax, beautiful."

Beautiful. Oh my god.

Before I can think about the implication of his words, he flicks his tongue over my clit and my mind goes blank.

After a few breathless moments, I realize Jonah loves this as much as I do, maybe more.

He groans every now and then, like the pleasure is too much for him. He uses his free hand to force my legs open. His hot tongue makes long swipes through my center, then quick flicks over my clit, until I'm sobbing with pleasure. My lids flutter shut, but I force them open. I want to see all of this. He might be the biggest asshole I've ever known, but here? Now? He's on his knees for me, and I can't catch a full breath.

He murmurs words of encouragement when I cry out, but I can't tell what he says. His tone is low and gentle, like he's coaxing me to orgasm. Pleasure is running through me nonstop, dripping down my spine, pooling between my legs, tightening my stomach. It feels like Jonah is in control of my body, not me.

When he pushes one thick finger inside of me, we both moan. *I'm close.* "Please," I whisper. "Jonah." I think I hear him mutter a curse.

"Not yet," he says. "Not yet, beautiful. You can last a little longer." He crooks his finger just right, and my legs shake. *Too good. Too fucking good.* It's never been like this before. Eric was acceptable in bed, nothing more. Sometimes I had an orgasm, and sometimes I didn't. Part of that was my own damn fault, for being too self-conscious to let go. But with Jonah, there's no space for thoughts. And if even a shred of embarrassment could leak through my desire-fogged brain, his sounds of enjoyment would eliminate it.

"Give me more," he demands, his breaths ragged. "I'm close. I'm so close just from the way you feel."

He's ruthless now, his finger pumping into me, his tongue swirling over my clit. His body is shuddering, and I want him to touch himself. I don't want to be alone in this. I want him to press a hand to the erection under his shorts and—*yes*. He palms himself and his hips buck into his hand.

"Fuck," he mutters, gasping a breath against me. One more pass of his hand, one more clench of that veined forearm, before he groans low in his throat, and squeezes his eyes shut. His shoulders shake. There's a damp spot on the front of his shorts. *Holy shit.* He came from just a few passes of his hand and the way I taste.

Why is that so hot?

And then he sucks on my clit, hard enough that my hips jerk and an orgasm tears through me. It's enough to make my spine bow, and my eyes fall shut as the pleasure spreads through me like lightning, then like honey. I open my eyes to see Jonah watching me, beautiful and brutal. His lips are parted and swollen. His cheekbones are red.

"Oh, Callie," he breathes. "Look at you."

My eyes fly wide at his use of my first name.

He freezes. The moment stretches between us. *Beautiful. Oh, Callie.*

I don't say anything. I don't know what to say. Jonah shoves back from me and rises to his feet. He douses the fire in his eyes. His cold mask snaps back into place.

"Jonah." I don't want it to end. Not like this. But I'm not brave enough to admit it. I want more of his raw honesty. I want to give him pleasure too. *I didn't even get to touch him.*

He looks horrified. And somehow, I think the sex was not the reason, but the use of my name. Like it broke down some final barrier and he hates himself.

"We shouldn't have done that," he says shortly. His lips are still damp from going down on me, and I expect him to wipe his arm on his sleeve, like Eric always did, but instead he licks them, and an expression of pure pleasure crosses his face. "We definitely shouldn't have done that," he repeats.

"Why? Why does it matter so much?" My pulse is thudding in my chest as I adjust my leggings. I need to know his answer. *Is he going to walk away? Am I a fool for getting involved with him?* I'm terrified that the answer is yes.

"Why?" He sounds incredulous. "I don't know, let me count the reasons. I'm your boss. You hate me. I don't trust you."

The words are a knock-out punch. "I thought—I don't know. I thought we might be working on that." My voice comes out faint. *I thought you were forgiving me. I thought we might be friends.*

He shuts his eyes briefly, one of the only signs of weakness I've ever seen him permit himself. "It doesn't matter. We are not friends." He shakes his head, as if to clear his thoughts. "We have chemistry. We got it out of our systems." He's so clinical about it, and I want to shake him. I want to get in his face and yell. *Desire. This feels like more than desire. This was more than desire when you begged me.* Asshole.

Why do I feel hurt by this? He's right. I know he's right, and yet, I feel adrift. And that feeling, more than anything, is what spurs me to say, "Why are you so eager to compartmentalize this? Unless—" I cock my head. "*You* want more."

"I do not."

"Okay, Jonah." I shrug, but my heart is thudding and my skin is hot.

"Don't okay, Jonah me," he growls. "This is how it needs to be. I'm your boss." He rounds on me, eyes flashing. "We hate each other, remember? I'm not a nice person." He says the last like he's trying to convince himself. *Why is that even relevant?*

"You can be a nice person."

"Stop." He sighs. "I'm not like you. Stop trying to lump me in with you."

Anger flashes through me. I step toward him. "*You* were the one who wanted this." I poke him in the chest.

"Are you *mad* at me? Thompson, this is ridiculous." He pushes my hand away and grabs his sweatshirt from the floor. His movements are sharp and jerky.

"Of course I'm mad. You gave me the best orgasm of my life and five seconds later, you're eager to put this all behind you." *Oops.* I didn't want him to know that.

He skates right by that one, shaking his head and stabbing his arms into his sweatshirt. "I just want to be clear where we stand."

I cross my arms over my chest. "Oh, believe me. It's clear. You're still on top. Don't worry, boss. Do you want me to call you Mr. Crown again?" The distance between us is wider than ever before. It's a pit yawning between us, filled with spikes.

"Don't be like this," he hisses. "This is the only way it can be." His jaw is tight and his lips a thin line as he steps back. Little does he know, telling a woman *don't be like this* is a surefire way to get his eyes clawed out.

"What do you mean by *this*? What way will it be?" My eyes are narrowed and my arms are crossed like it will shield me from him.

"We go back up there and we act like this didn't happen, understood?" He gestures upward.

Through the haze of my anger, I can see how important this is to him. *I'm right.* Jonah wants more and he's putting up a wall. *It would be funny if it weren't so sad.* If I weren't so foolishly hurt. This is just like every other person I've been close to.

"You were the one who begged me to let you show me pleasure," I remind him.

His eyes flash. "Well, I sure as hell regret it now."

Hurt lances through me, but I still my face. If he can be cold, so can I. Even though I crave the cuddling after sex, the closeness. I am not an against the wall quickie kind of girl. "Good. I regret it too." I lift my chin.

His eyes glitter. He smells like sex and he looks every inch the cruel, arrogant billionaire. "Thompson. I'll never touch you again. Not even if you beg."

"I would rather eat dirt than beg you." It's true.

"That can be arranged," he says shortly, and stalks out.

∼

Jonah ignores me for the rest of the day. He keeps his door shut and barks orders at me over the phone or in short emails with no punctuation. I leave his stupid sandwich outside his door, and I don't spit in it, which takes an admirable amount of self-restraint.

I'm raging mad. Foolishly mad. So mad I want to quit. Anger and shame are a heady mix in my gut. I do everything he asks of me with ruthless efficiency before he can even think to follow up.

I pull out my phone and email Paul at the diner, who agrees to an interview. I'm excited to feature the diner in the paper, maybe drum up a little business for them. And for us. Readership was down last week, even with the photo of Jonah driving traffic from across the web. I check the page stats like I do at least five times a day, then the comments.

"Good lord," I mutter as I scroll through the comments I have to approve. The website's filter picks up potentially inappropriate phrases.

Yes, Daddy - Marc L

That one makes me laugh, so I hit approve.

I'd let him work me out any day - Rachel M

I roll my eyes and reject the comment. People seem to go wild when there's a level of anonymity. If we showed full names, I'm sure the comments would be tamer.

One woman commented "that jaw," and I have to agree. I flick back up to the photo. Those angry lips went down on me like I was precious. Breakable. *No one has done that for me before.* Jonah's focus was all on me for those twenty minutes, and I felt like I could fly. *But then his reaction.* Shame makes my stomach knot. The way he shut down after. The look on his face, like he immediately regretted his actions.

If he hadn't jumped up, I would've kept going. That has to be the very worst part.

I just have to survive until the weekend. Just a few more hours, and then I get a whole glorious weekend to myself. And that means avoiding Jonah.

28

Jonah

The sight of my locked door pisses me off to no end. It's not that I *want* to talk to anyone. I don't want to hear the occasional conversation between employees. But I'm the boss. I should be able to open my damn door and intimidate people if I want to. Instead, I'm choking down bites of a sandwich that tastes like sawdust and reviewing the notes Callie sent me for my three p.m. meeting.

Really good notes. I make an angry slash, underlining the education and work history of the investor we're meeting with. Somehow she dug this up. Ms. Cahill went to the same high school as Miles. A fact we can use when getting her to invest with us.

Callie probably used nefarious methods to get the information. All reporters for those gossipy papers are the same. They'll do anything to get ahead. She's too fucking competent. *And why are you so mad about that?* And too pretty. *You didn't feel that way when she was panting your name.*

That swishy hair. *Perfect for wrapping around your hand.*

An annoyingly hot body. *That ass you fantasized about in the shower.*

Stupidly plump lips. *The ones you wanted to taste.*

And that's the thought that makes my brows draw down and my fist clench. I'm not tasting anyone's lips. I don't kiss. A hot night of release does not need to involve kissing. Or feelings. Or seeing the woman in question more than a few times.

Callie doesn't understand that. *You gave me the best orgasm of my life, and five seconds later, you're eager to put this all behind you.* The best orgasm of her life. Fuck. I shut my eyes and replay her wounded expression.

Why are you so eager to compartmentalize this? This is how it has to be. Why can't she see that there's no other option?

But those lips. I can picture the way her lashes fluttered closed with pleasure. *Jonah*, she moaned, like I was the center of her universe. That's my fault. Instead of keeping myself locked down, I got what I craved — Callie, coming apart at the seams. I wanted to ruin that perfect demeanor. I wanted her to beg me. And she did. *Please, Jonah.*

My cock is rising in my suit pants, and I dig my fingernails into my palms. She's a reporter. An employee. She'll betray me. *You don't do this.*

I do an admirable job ignoring Callie for the rest of the day, even though her notes help us lock down the investment with Ms. Cahill and her family, and an email telling her "good job" wouldn't be unwarranted. *She doesn't need a good job email*, I remind myself. She's not here to actually help me.

When six p.m. rolls around and she knocks on my door, I bark "enter" with enough force to scare her away. I know it's her by the no-nonsense way she taps. Softer than George but not hesitant. Not nearly scared enough.

"Jonah? I'm heading out."

Please, Jonah. I scowl at her, and she makes a faintly disapproving face, but doesn't say anything else.

"Did you finish the report I asked you to prepare for the Monday meeting?"

"It's in your email."

"What about rescheduling all those calls?"

"Rescheduled. For Tuesday. Ten a.m. to two p.m. with a break for lunch."

"And the shredding?"

"Done. Would you like me to take the garbage out too?" She smiles sweetly, but there's an edge to her voice.

"Go," I grunt.

"Have a great night." She sails out of my office, and I wait until she's definitely gone before muttering curses under my breath.

What does she have to be upset with me about? Because she definitely was. Not my fucking problem. I don't need to examine her feelings. As far as I'm concerned, she doesn't even have feelings.

I press my palms to my eyes. One month. Of six. *How the hell am I going to survive this?*

I need to talk to Miles. I grimace because he's going to be smug and annoying about me asking for his advice, but he's the only one who can help. I stalk down the hall to his office and pace while he finishes on the phone.

"Jonah looks like he's going to kill me any minute now." Miles grins at me as I roll my eyes. "Yeah, keep talking."

I hear a woman's laugh sound faintly from the other end. It must be Lane.

"You want to do what later?" His voice lowers. "I can kick him out of my office right now."

I make an irritated noise, and Miles laughs before telling Lane he loves her and hanging up the phone.

"I'm glad I stopped by before things got X-rated."

"My office has frosted glass." He gives me a self-satisfied smile and tilts his chair back on the back legs.

"Really? How do you get any work done?" I raise a brow, but he's unaffected.

"I'm very efficient. The motivation to get home on time is stronger than ever." Another smile. "So what's up?"

"I think I did something stupid." I sit heavily on the couch in his office. "I uh, hooked up, with Callie."

"Ha." Miles lets his chair thump to the ground. "I've gotta get Jason for this." He calls Jason and tells him to meet us at the office. Jason grumbles, but thirty minutes later, we're sitting downstairs in Kings Cove. Miles slides me a snifter of whiskey and pours some sparkling water for himself. At my raised brow, he tells me he needs to be sober for whatever Lane has planned later. I shudder in mock disgust, but a spike of jealousy digs into my stomach. He's so damn *happy*. Am I missing out? Am I the fool?

"Spill," Jason says. His blue eyes are chips of ice today. He was on a difficult negotiation, and he has to go back to the office after this. It's been a week since he last saw Cynthia, his girlfriend, and the separation is making him miserable. *Yeah, I'm not missing out.*

"I did something stupid," I repeat. "I hooked up with Callie in the gym."

"Woah. Nice." Jason's eyes narrow. "Not nice? Why do you look so pissed? Is it the employee thing?"

"It was a bad idea," I say shortly and knock the whiskey back. "We fought after." I sputter the words around the burn in my throat. The warmth from the liquor settles in my chest.

"Fought? You fought? About what?" Miles's brows are drawn low.

I sigh. "I told her it could never happen again, that we hate each other, that I don't trust her. We shouldn't have hooked up. I shouldn't have gone near her."

"Who cares?" Miles exclaims. "Live a little. She's not an employee. Hate sex can be fun. And you don't need trust to have hot sex with her at the office. You overthink everything."

I tense, but Jason chimes in with, "I agree. Let go, man."

"I wanted to kiss her," I say quietly.

"Ah." Jason gives Miles a knowing look.

"What?" Miles asks.

"It's his rule," Jason explains. "No feelings. No kissing. A different version of the rule I had for years. He'll see the same woman a few times, but he'll never get emotionally involved."

"It's better this way."

"Okay, well that's fucking stupid," says Miles. "But let's go back to the fight." He narrows his eyes. "How pissed was she?"

"How do you know she was pissed?"

Jason and Miles laugh. "Oh, she was definitely pissed. I saw her stomping around all day. But even without seeing that, I would have guessed it. You hooked up and then immediately told her it could never happen again." This from Miles. *Know it all.*

"How do you even know she wants to do it again?" A woman's voice comes from behind me, and I turn to see Lane. She's speaking to me but smiling at Miles.

"You invited her?" My eyes are shooting daggers at my friend, but he has eyes only for his girlfriend.

"Backup. I figured I'd need it." He shrugs and makes space for Lane on the seat.

"You think she doesn't want to sleep with me again?" I never considered the possibility, and now I feel like a fool. Lane shrugs and nibbles on some of the chips the bartender left us. Her nose ring glints in the light as she considers me. I trust Lane. I've known her for years. She's perceptive and thoughtful.

"I think," she says slowly, "that if I were in her position, I'd be hurt. Both by the assumption that I'm going to catch feelings, and by the accusation that you don't trust her."

"But I don't trust her." I frown. "She knows that. We've been pretty open about it. Although—" *Shit. She thought we were making progress toward being friends. Or something.* "She may have thought we were becoming friends. That she was atoning for the article." I grimace. "I've been using her for her connection to Dylan."

"I don't really know who Dylan is, but it sounds like she thinks you're on your way to being friends, and you just want to use her. That's shitty." Lane wrinkles her nose at me. "You're better than that, Jonah."

Her words lance through me. "Why do you say that?"

"I've known you for a long time, Jonah Crown. You're a good man. To some people."

"To your family. To us," Jason interjects, nodding.

"It doesn't matter." I shake my head. "I'm not getting involved with a reporter. Not Callie." *It's my fault my family got hurt by Annalise. I'm not bringing another woman back to meet them.* "It's better this way. If Callie doesn't want me, then good. We're on the same page. I don't want anything with her."

They're brave words that make an ache start near my heart. Her hurt expression from earlier is stamped behind my lids. Every time I blink, I see those blue eyes filled with anger.

Lane shrugs and grabs another chip. "She probably feels the same. Maybe it was just a onetime fling for her, too."

And that, more than anything, is what unsettles me for the rest of the night.

29

Jonah

Callie isn't at work on Monday. I'm used to her being here at 5:45 a.m. sharp, but I shift from foot to foot in the lobby for fifteen minutes, waiting for her. *She's not going to show up.* I have a coffee for her in one hand and an apology ready on the tip of my tongue. An apology that would explain that last week was unprofessional, and I'm sorry for lashing out at her. A plea that we go back to whatever we had before.

My impatience turns to anger as I make my way through my workout. Every time the lights flicker, I think it's Callie pushing open the door. *Why do I care?* I punch the bag harder, until I'm trembling with exhaustion. She's probably avoiding me. This is probably the first day of many when I'll be working out alone.

The dull ache near my heart is back. I hate it. I miss telling her what to do and her little eye rolls of impatience at my orders. I miss her sass and her excitement when she finally gets something right. *Fuck.* I slam my fist into the bag and finish the rest of my routine with ruthless efficiency.

I drop her coffee in the trash on the way out the door. She's not coming back to the gym with me. Why bother? She's not downstairs when I get there either. *She didn't even bother to tell me she wasn't coming.* I should fire her. The idea percolates as I seethe at my desk. She's mad at me. She was the one who started our argument on Friday. She's the one who wasn't remotely affected by what we did, and she's not even here to avoid looking me in the eye.

I *should* fire her. I check my watch. It's nine a.m. Before I can think, I'm up and out the door, texting Lou to bring the car around and shouting at George to cancel my meetings. My rage has cooled to a simmer by the time we pull up to Callie's apartment, but it's still there. The righteous burn feels better than whatever I felt last night. That ache was there all night, like I'd done something wrong, when all I did was stop us before we went too far.

I text her as soon as I'm outside.

JONAH

I'm at your apartment.

A second later, her face appears in the window. She presses her nose to the glass, and then she disappears. I draw myself up, ready for her to kick me out. She yanks the door open.

"Where the hell—" I snap my mouth closed. "You look like shit."

"Thank you, Jonah. So kind of you to say." She leans against the door frame. Her hair is up, her face is flushed, and her eyes are red. She's wearing a huge Columbia T-shirt and sweatpants. *Shit.* She looks like she's been crying. That ache is back, even through my rapidly cooling irritation.

"What's wrong with you?"

"I'm sick." She sounds sick, and she looks worse. "Didn't I send you an email?" She frowns and pulls out her phone. "I could have sworn I sent it. Ah, shit. I left it in draft." She winces. "I'm sorry. I meant to tell you. I've just been so tired. I didn't sleep last night from the body aches, and I really did mean to tell you. Please don't fire me."

Her eyes are pleading, and my jaw nearly drops. "You think I'd fire you for that?"

"Yes?" She doesn't sound sure, and in that moment, she looks so incredibly fragile. My jaw ticks. I came to have it out with her, and now I can't. I sigh.

"I'll be back."

Thirty minutes later, she's opening the door again, suspiciously eyeing the bags under my arm. "What is that?"

"Supplies," I say shortly. "Now let me up."

"Why?" She crosses her arms over her chest. It pushes her nipples against her shirt, and I drag my eyes back to her face.

"Thompson," I say slowly, leaning in to watch her lips part and her breathing hitch. "I *can* fire you. Now let me up so I can help you. I want to talk."

"Fine." She slumps. "But my dad is here. Just don't be—just be nice, okay?"

I'm silent as I follow her up the stairs. The stairway is nothing special, lit with ancient chandeliers with fake candles and covered in worn carpet. She pushes open the door to their apartment on the second floor and I follow, not sure what to expect. The first thing I see is a couch, and a hairy orange beast who jumps down to twine around my ankles. I freeze.

"Not a cat person?" Callie asks. She's moving slowly with her arms still tucked around her.

"I like cats just fine. I respect them and they respect me." I eye the orange beast. "I don't like cat hair."

"I'm sorry for your pants, then." She sits on the faded couch. "I'm not inviting you into my room, so we can talk out here. My dad's in his office."

I scan the apartment. I've seen it from the outside, but from the inside, it's like a time capsule from the 1980s. There's an honest-to-god record player, stacks of newspapers, an ancient TV, and a small kitchen with Formica countertops. *It's tiny.* I don't know how I pictured Callie Thompson's life, but this isn't it. Maybe I didn't picture it at all. *Do you just look for articles about you and scroll to the comments section?* My chest burns. Callie doesn't wake up fully formed and think about torturing me. She's a woman. A real woman who lives with her father, and judging by the way she's tucked herself into a ball, she's embarrassed about it. Her apartment is smaller than my master bedroom, and I think back to our conversation about her budget with a rush of shame. *I'm not paying her.* Can she afford rent? She must be living here because she has nowhere else to go, right? *No, she must like being here.* That must be it. Because if not, it looks a hell of a lot like I'm taking advantage of her.

"What do you want? Sit and stop looming," she says.

She looks irritated at my mere presence, and I want to smile. Instead of responding, I take the soup out and put it on the counter. The meds are next, then the fresh bread, then the green juice.

"What is that?"

"Supplies," I say absently. "Do you think I need to refrigerate this bread?"

"Supplies?" She pushes off the couch.

"Stay there."

"You don't need to refrigerate bread."

"Hmm. Okay." I look at the labels on the medicine. "You can't take these together, you know. They both have painkillers in them. I wasn't sure what you wanted. One is non-drowsy."

"What are you doing here?" she asks tiredly.

I set the medicine on the counter and walk the five steps it takes to the tiny couch. "I'm apologizing. For Friday."

She squeezes her eyes shut. "Please don't," she whispers. "Please don't say you regret it. Let's just move on, okay?" When she opens her eyes, they're pleading.

"Honestly? I came to yell at you." I laugh softly. "I thought you were mad at me, and then I convinced myself you were ashamed and totally unaffected by it." I try for a smile and she stares at me like I've gone insane. "I really worked myself up. And then I found you here. All—pitiful." I wave my hand in her direction. "And the wind went out of my sails. It's very annoying, actually."

"I'm sorry to disappoint." Her mouth curves up at the side. "I thought about it, and you're right."

Hope is a balloon in my chest. *Idiot. You're the one who stopped it.* The balloon deflates. "You agree with me?"

"Yeah." She nods, looking a little embarrassed. "I overreacted. I've never been a casual hook-up kind of girl. I cried after sex once. From all the emotions." She pulls a face. "I don't know why I just told you that. Anyways, you're right. You're my boss, and we have enough difficulty being in the same room together without all that." She waves a hand. "So I agree. You did the right thing by saying it can't happen again."

"I did?" I clear my throat. "I did. Okay." *Ally or enemy?* I need to decide. If I extend this olive branch to her, there's no going back. I'm not dangling her in front of Dylan, I'm not using her for revenge. She's just Callie for five more months, and I'm just me. "Truce?" I say, before I can question it.

"Okay." She smiles, looking so unbearably pretty that I nearly lurch forward. "I'd like that. Truce." She stands shakily, and I steady her with a hand under her elbow. "I need to take a nap now. Make yourself at home."

With that, she disappears down the hall, and I'm left stunned in the living room.

"Hello. I thought I heard voices."

I turn to see her father shuffle into the living room. "Ah, Jonah Crown. Good to see you." He's wearing a faded ball cap and a flannel shirt.

My brows go up. *He's not going to question my presence in his apartment at nine a.m.?* Weird. "And you. I was just checking on Callie since she didn't show up this morning. I didn't realize she was sick."

"She's not feeling well?" He frowns. "She didn't say that. I assumed she was off today or something." He shakes his head. "Typical Callie." His voice drops lower. "She thinks I'm too old to worry."

I'm silent. I don't know what to say. I barely know Callie. We don't even really like each other. So I nod and shove my hands into my pockets.

"Coffee?" Her dad raises the pot in the air. "I'm supposed to be drinking decaf after the heart attack, but I've been putting a little regular in the pot. Don't tell my daughter." He winks.

"Sure." My phone buzzes in my pocket. I'm supposed to be at a nine-thirty meeting with Miles. He's probably annoyed that I won't be there. "You had a heart attack?" I ask.

"Over the summer." He busies himself preparing two cups.

"Milk?"

I nod.

"Good thing Callie was here. She's the one who forced me to go to the hospital."

The ache is back, a lump behind my ribs that I can't shake. I take the coffee and say, "I'm sorry to hear that."

He waves a hand and takes a hearty gulp of coffee. "It's part of getting older. I'm not worried about it." *But Callie is.* She's worried and she's just trying to take care of her father. "So, Jonah, how's it going with Callie?"

Does he know about my plans? How much did she tell him? Shame makes my stomach turn. "It's going well. She's very smart." What every parent wants to hear, right? Maybe he doesn't know anything.

"She is. Headstrong, but very smart." He sighs. "She's the one who started the paparazzi thing a few years back, even though she hates it. It pays our rent now, if you can believe it." He shakes his head. "I never thought people would pay so much for photos."

"Depends on the subject, I'm sure," I say coolly. "I have a meeting I have to get to. Thanks for the coffee." My words are stiff. I don't want to hear about how brilliant Callie is or how good she is at stalking people and invading their privacy. This is why I should have kept her at arm's length.

It's not until I'm in the car back to the office that I think about her father's words. She hates being a paparazzo. She started the photos because they couldn't pay rent. *On that shitty apartment?* I wince. And five years ago, she would have been fresh out of journalism school. Bright-eyed and ready to take on the world. Instead, she's living with her dad, making him drink decaf, and trying to save the family business.

Who am I in this scenario? The hero, saving her business? *No.* I nearly laugh. I'm the big bad wolf at the door, coming to blow their fragile house down. A role I'm comfortable with. It gets things done. It's why I'm feared in business. I'll take fear and respect over affection any day.

But just in case, I email George and tell them to have HR start paying Callie Thompson.

30

Callie

I've never regretted a truce more than I do this week. *Why was I so adamant that we not be involved? Why did I agree with him?* It's impossible to be near Jonah without remembering the gym incident. Every hour is torture. On Monday, we stay late to work on a presentation he's giving that week to a huge investor.

It's seven p.m. and we're in his office. His tie is loose around his neck, and his hair is standing in every direction.

"Are you nervous?" I eye him suspiciously.

"I don't get nervous." He's scanning his notes again and pacing the office.

"You look nervous, though."

"Thompson," he growls. "When I asked for you to work on this project, this is not what I meant." He shoves a hand through his hair. It's delicious when it goes in every direction, and my hands remember exactly how silky it was when his head was between my legs.

"Well, go ahead and do the presentation then. I'm waiting." I cross my arms and raise a brow. He gives me a mutinous look and slumps into his chair.

"We have to win this. I've been trying to get the Danforth Group to invest with us for years. And every time I get close, Dylan does something to make them question our reputation or our abilities. This is the first time I've ever been in a position to present to their board."

I tilt my head as I watch him. He's really worked up. "Why don't I do some research into them? And send me all the materials you've sent them over the years. Maybe we can figure out where you went wrong."

He lifts grateful eyes to meet mine. "We recorded the prior meetings at their request. I'll send you the recordings."

I nod and go back to my desk. I like Jonah when he's like this. All business and treating me like a partner.

I spend two hours watching recordings of Jonah doing what he does best, and it's so fucked up, but the way he commands a room has me turned on and shifting in my seat to ease the ache.

"Thompson," he shouts at nine p.m. "We need to eat. What do you want?"

"You can pick," I shout back, half-expecting him to come stomping over and tell me to go pick up our food.

A few breaths later, he's at my desk. "I asked you a question."

I turn to see his arms crossed as he leans against the door. The triangle of skin at his collar is bared. I remember what it felt like—warm and silky smooth. Delicate over the corded muscle of his neck. "What do you want for dinner?" he repeats. "I don't want to pick. That's what I have you for." He drops a credit card on my desk and strides away.

I finger the metal edges. I'm starting to see through him. The command is a ploy to get me to pick what I want, I think. I'm not sure. I shake my head and order from my favorite steakhouse. I'll have to figure him out another day.

On Tuesday, we eat in the office again. We're head-to-head over the coffee table as Jonah scans the notes I took.

"Environmental concerns? Really?" He tilts his head to look over at my notes, and I tense. He's close. Close enough that I can see those gold flecks in the black-brown of his eyes. Close enough to see that one eyebrow is a little more arched than the other. Maybe that's why he looks so arrogant all the time. His mouth is soft, not sneering, but not smiling either.

"What?" he asks. "Do I have something in my teeth?"

"Uh. Nope." *Eloquent, Cal.* "And yes, they asked you several times about the environmental impact of your California portfolio in the last meeting. I don't think you had the data. When your back was turned, a few of them made notes on their papers about it. If you check the video, the guy closest to you is frowning as he writes. I looked him up. He's their CFO and he's on the board of a couple of environmental charities."

Jonah's mouth drops open before he clamps it shut. "We can use this. I want you at the presentation tomorrow."

"You do?" My head jerks back in surprise.

"I do." His gaze sharpens on my me, his eyes dropping to my mouth. Heat pulses through me. *Kiss me. Please, Jonah.*

He stands and drains his water. He's Jonah Crown, titan of industry again, and *he wants me at a meeting.*

~

On Wednesday, all signs of stress are gone from Jonah's face. I'm overheated and nervous under my best sheath dress, but he's cool, seemingly unaffected. He's wearing a charcoal suit and a blue tie.

"Bespoke?" I ask, when he sees me admiring how it drapes over his shoulders.

"Wouldn't you like to know?" He gives me a cool smile, and I roll my eyes. "Image is power, Thompson." His gaze skates over my dress, lingers on my legs in the sheer tights I chose, dips all the way down to my black pumps. I tense for a comment about my outfit, but when his eyes meet mine, all I see is banked heat. For one heartbeat, it looks like he might push me up against the wall.

Please, my gaze says.

Not a chance in hell, his responds. His jaw tics and he goes back to his notes.

When we meet outside the conference room that afternoon, he holds the door open for me. Our investors are already here. *His* investors. I'm just a passenger, though if my sweaty palms are anything to go by, my body is far too invested in this.

Jonah introduces himself and sits at the head of the table. I'm all the way at the other end, on the side, so I can watch him work.

He is magnificent. I can admit it. I prepared the materials on the table in front of us. I've heard him go into the description of their business at least five times, but here? With a hundred million dollars on the line? I can't take my eyes off him. His investors can't either. He has an easy smile when things get tense, one I rarely see him deploy. He's thoughtful when he needs to be, answering their questions without pretense or arrogance. They're nodding along, as enthralled as I am. He paces the room as he goes through the slides he prepared, but his eye contact is steady, and he knows the material by heart.

Until we get to the environmental data. The man in the black suit, Greg, wants to know about the impact reports that were performed before Kings Lane bought the facility outside Los Angeles. Jonah freezes, his gaze darting immediately to me. I read those reports. Last night, or rather, this morning, at three a.m. They were in the materials prepared for the last meeting. *Help*. His gaze pleads. I lick my dry lips. I can't butt in, as much as it looks like he might want me to. *Remember*, I will him with my eyes.

"My assistant, Ms. Thompson, has those materials," he says slowly.

"The reports were completed two years before the facility construction began. No adverse findings were reported. Mr. Crown asked the owners to perform additional groundwater testing before he purchased the facility two years ago." Somehow, miraculously, my voice remains calm.

Jonah's shoulders lower as Greg nods and takes notes. I feel like I'm floating. The meeting finishes, and Jonah sees our investors out. His head is down when he walks back down the hall. His hands are shoved into his pockets. He looks disappointed. *Shit.* I'm quiet at my desk, my stomach knotting as he paces into his office.

"Thompson. In here."

I twist my fingers around my gold necklace as I enter. He looks so pissed. *Did I say something wrong?*

And then his mouth broadens into a heart-stopping grin. "We did it. They're going to invest."

"Oh my god." My hands fly to my mouth, and I take two steps forward before I can think better of it. I stop so fast, I nearly fall onto his desk. *What were you planning to do? Kiss him?*

He's two steps closer too. I grin at him, and he smiles back, his eyes on my mouth. He runs a thumb over his bottom lip, absently, like he wishes my mouth were on his.

My head is pounding as I leave his office and sit back at my desk. The adrenaline from the meeting and then whatever *that* was with Jonah are making me feel hot and confused.

He doesn't like you. But he's looking at me like he does. Like he wishes we could go back to the gym and repeat the other day.

I need to do something to get rid of this excess energy. Maybe Adriana and Luz can distract me.

CALLIE
Girls' night? I need to let loose.

LUZ
Yes! I'm off for four days starting tomorrow.

ADRIANA
Karaoke?

I grin. I fucking love karaoke, and Adriana knows it.

CALLIE
You know I'm down.

I just need to forget about Jonah. He doesn't want to kiss me. He doesn't even like me.

An hour later, I get an email from him.

> To: Thompson, Callie
> From: Crown, Jonah
> Subject: Good job

31

Callie

"Lemon drop shots. Let's go." Luz makes a waving motion at Adriana and me, and we both groan. We're in a private karaoke room with a bucket of crappy beers and now Luz's favorite sickly sweet shots. The disco ball is sparkling in the multicolored lights, and my friends and I are dressed to kill, even if it's just girls' night.

"You can have mine," Adriana says.

"Mine too." I haven't done a shot since the last time Luz forced me to do one.

Luz waves the tray of shots under my nose like smelling them will make me more interested, instead of repulsed. "Come on, Cal. You said you wanted to let loose. This is the first step."

"You did," Adriana adds.

"Not helpful," I protest, but Luz raises a brow. I dutifully raise my glass to my friends and knock back the shot.

"What's eating you, anyway?" Luz asks, totally unfazed, as I shudder.

"My boss."

"Ugh, I feel you. Dr. Davenport is awful. Today he actually told me—"

"Wait. Literally eating you?" Adriana cuts Luz off and gapes at my pink face.

Both girls stare as the blush deepens, and I grab a beer from the bucket.

"Literally. A week ago. On the gym floor. After telling me I could punch him in the face. But only after I've learned how to properly throw a punch. And then we got into a fight, but now I think we're *friends*? Things are weird." I sigh.

"Rewind." Adriana holds up a hand. "You hate him. You told me you hated him. Yes, he's hot. But also, he's trying to ruin your life." She points the straw from her cocktail at me. Adriana is not a beer girl and never will be.

"Yeah, but he's like really, really hot." Luz is clearly already feeling the effects of her vodka. She's a total lightweight.

"Not that hot," Adriana bursts out.

"I don't hate him." It's true. Not anymore.

"Was it good?" Luz wags her brows.

"Does it matter? He's so going to fire her for this," Adriana grumbles.

"This is why I didn't tell you." I throw up my hands. "I don't know what to think. Or how to feel. He and I agreed it would never happen again. It doesn't matter."

"Was it good?" Luz repeats. Her eyes are huge.

"You're like a dog with a bone." I huff. "It was really good." I squeeze my eyes shut. "Maybe the best orgasm of my life?" I crack them to see my friends still staring at me in shock.

"What happened? Start at the beginning." Adriana takes a long drink of her fruity cocktail.

"I told you about the drunk guy who accosted me last week." Adriana and Luz nod. I'd texted our group chat, but I'd left out the details about Jonah. I was embarrassed and wanting. *And obsessed with Jonah.* I'd been firmly in his orbit for the last week. *Just like I was with Eric.* I mentally kick myself. "That happened outside the diner where Jonah gets breakfast every day. Well, just coffee."

"Psycho," Adriana mutters. Luz smacks her on the leg.

"I was taking photos, and this guy wouldn't get out of my face. So Jonah threatened to kill him, and then he told me he would teach me how to box."

Luz nearly spits her drink on the floor. "He what? You didn't tell me this."

"Because I didn't know what to think. He threatened to kill the guy," I repeat. My pulse thuds uncomfortably at the memory of the icy rage that suffused Jonah's face, the way he didn't hesitate to act.

"I change my mind. I like him," Luz volunteers.

"You're a pushover." Adriana rolls her eyes. "So then you went to the gym?"

I swig my beer for courage. "He boxes every morning. He said he was going to teach me to defend myself."

"And then he went down on you? I'm confused." Luz scrunches her face up.

"Me too," I mutter. "It's just as insane as it sounds. One moment, he was agreeing to let me punch him in the face, and the next, he was yanking my pants down." *Except it wasn't yanking.* It was more of a slow, sensuous slide, asking for consent and caring only about my pleasure. But I can't bring myself to tell my friends how Jonah Crown melted for me. That's a secret for me alone.

Adriana gapes. Luz just grins and does a happy little dance on the black vinyl couch.

"He doesn't hate you." Adriana's eyes narrow.

"Oh, he totally still hates me. He told me so himself."

"No. He doesn't. He protected you. He's going to teach you how to box. And then he gave you an orgasm, expecting nothing in return. Wait, he didn't expect anything in return, right?"

I shake my head.

"He likes you." Adriana sits back triumphantly. "You should use this against him."

"What? No way." The thought of taking Jonah's secrets and baring them to the world makes me feel ill. "And he doesn't like me. He clearly regrets touching me. He even said it could never happen again. And you should have seen the look on his face. So cold. Like a mask." I shiver. "No. This is firmly in the regret column for him."

"And for you?" Adriana cocks her head.

"I don't know." I shake my body out, like I can get rid of the memories. "The fight was awful, but he's right. He's my boss. It's not happening again. Time to move on. Hey, Luz, do you have any more doctor friends you can set me up with? Preferably someone who won't bother to remember my name. James was way too nice. Sam too."

Luz nods enthusiastically. "Yes. Totally. Davenport will give it to you good. He's a total cad."

I laugh and cough on my beer. "A total cad. Sounds perfect. One night with him and I'll forget all about Jonah."

Adriana is still watching me with knowing eyes. "You want him."

"I do." I shut my eyes briefly and inhale for strength. "I so do. Fuck, I'm pathetic. I can't even pretend I don't want to bang him." I look at my friends with pleading eyes. "Do you know how hard this week has been? I can't stop thinking about him naked. When I was sick on Monday, he brought soup to my apartment. Soup and an apology for our fight."

"Wow," Luz whispers.

"I know. And then after the apology, he and I agreed to a truce and swore that we would never touch each other again. I'm an idiot." I sigh, but start flipping through the karaoke book.

Luz chugs the rest of her beer and slams the bottle down on the table. "The music will fix everything. Callie, start us off. And don't pretend to look through the book, because I know you're going to pick Britney."

I start with the same song every time—Britney Spears's "Oops, I Did It Again." A classic.

Adriana groans when the opening bars fill the tiny room.

"Don't start. You know this is how we always begin." I point my finger at her. "Britney sets the mood." I shimmy my way through the song, forgetting about the outside world for the three minutes it lasts. Singing transports me.

I flop onto the couch when Adriana takes the stage. "Man, I forgot how much fun this is."

Luz grins. "There's nothing like karaoke to make you forget your problems." She bumps me with her shoulder. "I forgot how good you are."

"All those years of singing in the shower." I wink, but my heart is heavy. Eric hated when I sang in the apartment. Said it disrupted his work. *Work.* Right. If taking selfies and posting about detox tea and protein powder could be considered work.

I focus on picking my next song, because I don't want to think about my shitty ex. Not when I'm supposed to be enjoying myself.

Adriana sings Queen and then Luz picks Christina Aguilera. We go from early 2000s classics to show tunes, and then back to classic rock. Luz has the vocal abilities of a dying cat, but she puts her whole heart in it. Adriana's face is pink from three fruity, pink cocktails, and we've moved on to our second bucket of beers.

"You should text Jonah," Luz yells over the intro music to an Aerosmith classic.

"Why would I do that?" I knock back the rest of my beer.

"Because we need some men in here. Maybe he has a hot friend he can bring."

"You're drunk. No way."

Luz is a wild child on her nights off, though it's not intentional. She's just up for anything and can't hold her liquor. She'd probably accidentally fall into the lap of whomever Jonah would bring. *And who would he even bring?* Miles is taken. Theo, their mysterious friend, is gone. He has another friend that I've seen a few times. Jason, I think his name is, but I think he's taken too. Somehow, I doubt Jonah is tearing up the town. *That's sad.*

"He's probably at the office. His life is depressing."

Luz shakes her head. "Like I said, you should text him. Everyone deserves a karaoke night." She shrugs and opens more beers for the two of us.

Jonah is probably in his glass tower, buried in work. At nine p.m. on a Friday night. I picture 555 57th Street, the building dark, except for the light from Jonah's office. *I wonder if he ate there. Or maybe he didn't eat dinner at all.*

"Okay, I'm going to text him." The beer is making me bold, and the thought of him alone is too sad to bear.

I pull my phone out, squinting slightly at the screen. I tap out a text that reads, "*What are you doing tonight? We're at karaoke. You should come.*"

"What's she doing?" Adriana asks, when her song finishes.

"Texting her hot boss," Luz says nonchalantly.

Adriana snorts. "You're so gone for him."

"Am not." My head jerks up. "I just think he needs to loosen up. Maybe it will make him nicer."

"Sure. Keep telling yourself that. You like him. You want to have sex with him, and he wants to have sex with you." She shrugs. "You should go for it. You don't have to ride off into the sunset together."

"Oh no. Here we go. The Adriana dating method rears its ugly head." Luz groans and I grin. "Feelings? I've never met them." Luz presses a hand dramatically to her heart.

"Sex does not require feelings," Adriana protests.

"Yes, well, not all of us like to schedule our sexual encounters like we schedule our nail appointments."

"Some of us are extremely busy."

"Busy hitting it and quitting it." Luz cackles.

"Guys." I look up at my friends. "He's calling me."

"Pick it up!" Luz screeches.

I hit "accept" and raise the phone to my ear.

"Hi."

"Thompson?" His voice rolls over me, and I shiver down to my toes. "Where are you? I hear music."

"Karaoke." My tongue is thick and awkward. *This was a bad idea.*

We can work together in the office just fine, but socializing? After hours? What was I thinking? "Do you want to come?"

He's silent for a second. My heart tries to leap up my throat. He's going to say no. Of course he's going to say no. He told me we were just a boss and employee. I read into our success this week way more than I should have.

"What's the address?" he finally says.

Luz picked this place and I've never been here before. "I'm not sure of the address. I'll just send you my location."

"Are you drunk?" He sounds incredulous. And pissed.

"Don't get your panties in a twist, Jonah Crown. I'm allowed to drink after hours."

"So you are drunk. Send me your location." His voice is flat.

"You know what? Forget it." Anger bubbles in my veins. "I don't know why I even emailed you. This was stupid. I thought maybe we were friends after this week. Or something. I thought you might want to go out and have fun. Let off some steam. Lord knows you could—"

"I wouldn't finish that sentence, Thompson," he says silkily. "Send me your location. Or I'll search every karaoke den in the city to find you. And you won't like what happens after that."

"Promise?" I ask snarkily. *He's such an ass.*

His breath is loud in my ear. "That's not my kink," he says shortly and hangs up the phone.

I press a hand to my mouth. Adriana and Luz are staring at me with huge eyes.

"You could cut the tension between you with a knife." Luz grins.

I roll my eyes, but I have to agree. Jonah makes me feel all fluttery and hot. *That's not my kink.* So he does have a kink? Maybe it's giving endless orgasms to women on the floor of his gym. Something jumps in my stomach and I press a hand to my abdomen. I have to be the stupidest woman alive. "This is dumb," I grumble, as I pull open my texts.

He's already sent me two—

JONAH

Location.

Now.

I hit "share location" and look back at my friends. "Something tells me I'm going to regret this."

32

Jonah

Chasing my employee into a karaoke den has to be one of the strangest things I've ever done. When I push open the door to the dark room, my eyes immediately snag on Callie. Her hair is up, her neck is bared, and her skirt is short. She's swaying to the music, sipping a beer. My gaze flicks to the empties on the table. She has to be drunk.

That's half the reason I'm here, and I hate it. My quiet evening at the office disrupted by thoughts of her trying to walk home in the dark, getting accosted by another drunk guy, getting hurt.

Her friend with the curly hair realizes I'm there before Callie does.

"Your boss is here, Cal," she says flatly.

A petite bleached blonde jumps up, unsteadily. "Oh, you must be Jonah. Wow." Her mouth pops open. "He's just as hot as you said he was."

Callie winces. "Luz, please."

Satisfaction curls in my stomach. "You said I was hot."

"Shut up," Callie grumbles. "It's a fact of life. You know it. I know it. The general public knows it."

I smirk, and she rolls her eyes. "Gloating is an unattractive quality in a man."

"Sit." The taller one points at the bench. "And start drinking. You're behind."

I shed my coat and my jacket and settle next to Callie on the vinyl bench. It's a little sticky and I shudder. "Nice place."

"Stop grousing. We're here to have fun." She passes me a beer. "I hope beer is okay for Your Majesty."

I hold her gaze while I slot the bottle between my lips and drain the beer. Her eyes trace over my face while she watches. *He's just as hot as you said he was.* And now that her walls are down, I can see the naked desire on her face.

"See something you like, Thompson?" *Stupid, Jonah.* Why am I baiting her? *Because she thinks you're hot. And because you can rile her up.* And fuck, I love riling her up.

"Just making sure you don't choke," she says sweetly. "This is Adriana." She points at the dark-haired one, who gives me a nod. "And Luz." The blonde waves from where she's picking a song.

"When was the last time you sang karaoke?" Callie sits on the bench, keeping a careful few feet between us.

"Never."

"No way." Luz gasps.

"Do I look like a karaoke kind of guy?" I cock a brow.

"Guess not. Okay, well, you have to go next then." Callie passes me the huge book of songs. "I recommend Bohemian Rhapsody. Can't go wrong with that."

I browse the songs while Adriana starts a rather off-key rendition of a song that I vaguely recognize from a popular musical.

"And this is something you enjoy?"

"Stop it. It's freeing. You just have to not be self-conscious." She wags her brows. "Think you can handle that?"

"I'm not self-conscious."

"Yeah, but you're not exactly relaxed." She sips her beer. Her legs are tucked up under her, her sweater is falling off one shoulder, and she looks like the definition of *relaxed*. She's practically buzzing with contentment, and suddenly, I want to know what it's like to be Callie Thompson. Would she like me better if I were more like her? Would that guy I saw her with last week sing karaoke with her?

"Show me." My voice is rough. "Show me what it's like to be you. To be relaxed."

She sits up straighter. "You mean that?"

"Much as I think I'll regret it, yes."

She smiles and my heart turns itself over. "I get the rest of the night then. And you'll do whatever I want?"

"Whatever you want. Within reason. I'm not skydiving or something like that."

"Scared of heights?" She's still smiling and she's looks so fucking pretty it nearly hurts.

"I like life. And I see no reason to jump out of a plane."

She snorts. "Fair enough. We'll start small. A duet."

I grimace. "Really?"

She stands in a rush. "Jonah Crown. You put your faith in me tonight. I will not let you down. You must do a duet with me."

"What if I don't know the song?"

"Who cares?" She flings her arms out. "Besides, I'll carry us both."

"You will?" My brows go up.

"I so will." She grins at me and my heart thuds in my chest. "I won't let you down." Her eyes are soft and inviting, her smile is hazy. When she extends her hand to pull me off the couch, I take it.

~

THE OPENING BARS of "Can You Feel the Love Tonight?" make me choke out a laugh.

"This is your choice? Really?"

Adriana and Luz are watching us expectantly, and I feel itchy and awkward. Not something I'm used to.

"Do you not know the words?" Callie's eyes are sparkling.

"Oh, I know them. This was my sister's favorite song as a kid."

"Bring it, then." She makes a beckoning motion with her hand and passes me the mic. "Oh, and you have to do Timon and Pumba's dumb parts in the beginning."

I stumble through the first bars, fumbling the silly dialogue, until Adriana and Luz join in, like the world's drunkest peanut gallery.

Callie pumps a fist in the air, and I can't help but smile. My part comes and I manage to sing the lines. It's easier when I'm not looking at Callie or her friends. She gives me an encouraging smile, and then she belts her lines, and my jaw drops so fast that I nearly drop my mic. She's electric. I can't look away. I muddle through the words while she closes her eyes and pours her heart into every word.

I look at Adriana with wide eyes, and she shrugs, a small smile on her face, like this is a common occurrence. Callie owns the room, and I try to keep up, stumbling over the words and jumping in a little too late. But true to her word, she carries us both. *Holy shit.* She can really sing. She can really fucking sing. The final lines come, and she holds my gaze while she sings them.

"Another?" she immediately asks, and the girls cheer.

"Sure. Another."

"You did good. Little stiff in the hips but—" She shrugs. "You're a newb."

"A newb? I'll show you newb. Give me the book."

"Someone's cocky," she crows, but she's smiling.

I know exactly which song I want, so I find the number quickly and punch it in. I loosen my tie and roll my sleeves while the opening bars play.

When the backing track to an Elvis hit starts playing, I bring the mic up with a flourish, start crooning the lyrics, and do my best impression while Callie laughs. I add an extra swivel to my hips while she watches. I look like a fool, but she loves it. She flops onto the bench next to Luz while I perform, and when I finish, I bow with a flourish and the girls cheer.

"Tens across the board," Luz shouts.

"And the singing wasn't bad either," Adriana adds and the group dissolves into giggles.

They're clearly drunk and I grab their last beer, partly to keep Callie from having any more.

"So where to next?"

"I'm heading home." Luz rises to her feet unsteadily, and Adriana follows.

"Me too. I have an early morning workout class," Adriana says.

"Sadist," Callie says with a grin.

"Let me have my driver take you back. You're in the city?" I'm already texting Lou to bring the car around.

"Oh no. It's okay," Adriana refuses. "We'll take the train."

"Shut up," Luz says. "I want to be driven."

"Good choice." These two are in no shape to be on public transit.

We burst into the fresh October air, and Lou is already there. I slip him an extra bill, along with their addresses. He gives me a surprised smile. "Walking, Mr. Crown?"

"I'm not entirely sure, actually. My fate is in her hands tonight." I jerk a thumb at Callie, who is pink-cheeked and bright-eyed in her wool coat.

"I'll pick you up later," he says, and then he's gone.

I'm alone with Callie on the street in Midtown Manhattan. She looks up at me with those lovely blue eyes, and my chest twinges. This feels like a date. Something I haven't done in years. *Don't think about it.* I'm supposed to be living in the moment tonight, letting her lead and all that. Another thing I don't usually do.

"Want to walk a bit?" she asks, oblivious to my inner turmoil.

"Sure." We fall into step, heading downtown. "What made you text me tonight?"

"What made you say yes?" She gives me a sly smile.

"You first."

"I don't know if you're going to like this answer." Her tongue swipes her lips nervously.

"Try me."

"Well. You just seem, lonely, maybe. I was thinking about you in your office working, and I thought it was terrible. Luz was the one who pushed me to text you. She said *everyone deserves a night of karaoke*." She shrugs sheepishly. "Sorry if that was presumptuous. Were you at the office?"

"I was."

"Rough." She gives me a sympathetic look.

"It was by choice." I shrug, but I don't feel casual. I feel pathetic. Something I rarely feel, and I hate it. The brightness of Callie's life makes my own feel lacking.

"You're very driven," she murmurs. "Do you ever rest?"

"Rest?" I scoff. "No. Why would I rest?"

She laughs softly. "That is such a *you* thing to say."

"Yeah?" I flick a glance at her. Her chin is tucked into her coat and she's smiling faintly. Warmth fills my chest at her knowledge of me. I always thought I would hate having someone presume to know me, but instead, it feels good.

"I don't need to rest. I just survive on coffee and revenge," she mocks, mimicking my voice.

"I can still fire you," I say mildly.

She rolls her eyes. "You won't. Admit it." We wait for the light and she smiles up at me. "Say it."

"Say what?" I raise my brows.

"Say you won't fire me."

"Here's the thing, Thompson." I step in and her eyes widen a fraction. "I *like* having one over on you." I wink and start walking again, and she scurries to keep up.

"You're very annoying. You know that, right?"

"Mmhmm. My sister says the same thing."

"Is that why you never see her? Shit. Sorry." Regret is written on her face. "I didn't mean to say that. Ignore me. I can never hold my tongue."

A laugh tears from my throat at her face scrunched up in distress. "It's fine." I shake my head. "I see her now and then, but my family doesn't exactly understand my lifestyle."

"What do you mean?" She turns the corner with purpose. I have no idea where she's leading me, and the desire to ask is on the tip of my tongue.

"My family are regular people. They've never wanted more than what they have."

"Sounds admirable."

"Oh. It is. It's also not for me."

"Because you're more of a black coffee and revenge kind of guy?" She slants me a look.

"I take it with milk, as you know, but yes. Remember when you said you wanted a regular guy?"

"Yes," she says warily.

"Well, that's the kind of guy my family wants me to be. A guy who watches sports and sees them every Sunday for dinner."

"Oh." She avoids looking at me for a second and then sighs. "I was lying." I raise my brows in response. "About the guy thing. That's not the type of guy I would choose." She bites her lip and a flash of heat runs through me. And then something that feels like relief. *She doesn't want a regular guy.* "Anyways. Your family? It seems like they love you, from what I have—ah—seen."

"I'm going to choose to ignore that comment," I respond tartly. "Don't get me wrong. They love me. They're grateful for what I've done for them, but my mom is still waiting for me to stop working and settle down with a nice girl from the next town over in New Jersey. My dad's world revolves around whether the Giants and the Rangers are winning, and whatever auto project he's working on with his friend Larry." The familiar resentment twists in my stomach at my family's complacency. They've never cared about *more*, and more is a drumbeat in my blood, the god I pray to.

"That's kinda nice, don't you think?" Callie flicks me a glance, her blue eyes dark and mysterious in the glow of the streetlamps. "They get to live that life because you live this one."

I open my mouth to disagree, then shut it. Callie waits for the light to change on 5th Avenue, watching me instead of the street. "You think that's nice? Wouldn't you be annoyed if your family was waiting for you to give up the paper and do something else?"

Her face shutters, and she looks back at the street. "They are," she finally says. "He is. My dad is my only family. There's no *they*," she explains.

"And he wants you to stop writing?"

"Don't act like you care." She sighs. "You'd probably love if I stopped writing." She crosses the street into Madison Square Park, and I hurry to keep up.

"That's not true."

She tucks her chin into her jacket and keeps walking through the park.

"Thompson." I stop.

She stalks back toward me and stops in front of me. "What?"

"I wouldn't love if you stopped writing." *Why are you saying this?* Because it's true. I don't want her to stop. She loves it, and I wouldn't want to take that away from her.

"Well, my dad wants me to stop." Her lips are pressed together and her eyes are sad. "He still thinks of me as a little kid, playing paper. I have ideas. Good ideas. Ideas that could save us."

"What's wrong, Thompson? You didn't decide to give up, did you?" The thought of her being beaten down feels wrong, like a stone in your shoe that you can't shake loose. I can't imagine a world in which Callie Thompson gives up. It's not a world I want to live in.

"I hate that you call me that," she says shortly.

"Call you what?"

"Thompson. Like I'm your servant." The street lamp flickers above her head, bathing her in soft yellow light. The tip of her nose is red, her cheeks are flushed, and her hair is piled on top of her head in a mess of curls and wisps.

I step toward her and her eyes widen. "What would you prefer I called you? Maybe Ms. Thompson?"

"That would be better," she says primly.

"What about Callie?" My voice drops on her name and something like longing flashes across her face.

Another step, until she's right in front of me. "What are you doing?"

I brush my thumb over her cheekbone, then under her lip. Her skin is impossibly soft. Just like it was when I kissed her neck in the gym. Her lashes flutter closed with pleasure. "Callie," I murmur. "Callie." Her name is a litany. I sound like I'm begging her, and maybe I am. I lower my head, just a fraction, waiting for her to close the gap.

Her hands land on my chest, and triumph flashes through me. "Callie," I say against her mouth. And then I kiss her.

33

Jonah

This *is why I don't kiss.* That's the first thought that flashes through my head. And then, *she tastes so good.* My mind goes blank at the feel of her plush bottom lip moving over my own. Callie doesn't just accept the kiss, no, she kisses me back. And it's *everything*.

I am unmade and remade when her lips part. My breath stutters in my chest at the first touch of her tongue against mine. My hand comes up to cradle her jaw, and hers presses over my heart. I pull her bottom lip between my teeth and she makes a needy little sound.

"Callie," I groan softly.

"Jonah," she whispers back.

I try to breathe in my name on her lips like it's air. I suck on her tongue and that needy sounds turns to a harsh gasp. I want her to do it again, so I angle her head and I kiss her like she's my last meal and I'm a dying man. I gather her close with a hand on her hip, and she melts against me. I'm a thousand feet tall. The mayor of New York. The king of the world.

I need more. More of her and the delicious way she tastes. More of her little sounds. *This is everything.* Need heats my blood. *We should go back to my apartment.* She'd say yes, and fuck, it would be so good. I need to get these clothes—

"Get a room," someone shouts and we both jerk back. Callie starts laughing and presses a hand to her mouth.

"Oops." She squeezes her eyes shut and scrunches up her nose. "We got a little carried away, didn't we?" She smiles sheepishly up at me, her lips a little swollen.

I brush my thumb over the bottom one, and her eyes go heavy-lidded. "I didn't want to stop," I murmur. I don't want to bring up the fight or our promises that we'd stay away from each other. I had enough of that torture for the last week.

"Me neither." Her lips are curved, and her eyes are sparkling. *I did that.* "But this is the middle of Madison Square Park, and you did promise me the whole night, so don't think a hot kiss is going to get you out of this."

"So you thought it was hot?"

She laughs and starts walking down the path. "Totally hot."

I shove my hands into my pockets to keep from grabbing her. My blood is pumping thick and warm through me, heading straight for my groin, where one part of my body definitely agrees with her. "What specifically about it was hot?"

"Oh no, stop." She won't look at me, but she's smiling.

"Glad to know we're not making this awkward," I say blandly.

"Because what about making out with your hot boss in the park could be awkward?" She smacks a hand over her mouth, but I still hear, "I'm going to stop talking now."

"Tell me more, Thompson."

"I thought you weren't going to call me that," she grumbles.

"After seeing what happens when I call you *Callie*, I think I should use it judiciously."

"Please stop talking."

"I like making you blush." And I do. I've forgotten what it was like to flirt, or maybe I never figured out how. But all I know is I want more of Callie's smiles, her laughs, her red cheeks. I want it all.

34

Callie

Jonah and I seem to have an unspoken agreement that we're not going to make this weird. Maybe on Monday, but tonight, a very public kiss with my very hot boss is par for the course. The burger stand in the park is hopping with people at this hour, and we wait for twenty minutes before we finally sit.

Jonah has at least twice as much food as I do. A huge burger, double fries, and a milkshake. I eye it with suspicion, because I'm not sure where he's going to put all those calories.

"Keep your eyes on your own food," he says, with an arched brow.

"I'm just surprised." I swallow a bite of burger. "I guess I always pegged you for a fancy salad guy, or maybe one of those people who drinks only protein shakes."

He grimaces. "I like food."

"The diner, the deli, now this. You're just a regular guy."

He grunts but doesn't look at me.

"You *are*." Realization hits. "You prefer this. Is this a way to connect with your roots or something? I bet you totally order pizza and eat Italian food all the time."

"Stop psychoanalyzing me."

"But it's so fun," I tease. It *is* fun peeling back his layers, seeing what makes him tick. And I'm starting to think I might like it more than I thought. Particularly when he whispered my name like it was a prayer and kissed me like he had hours to explore my mouth.

We eat in silence for a minute, two people among fifty doing the same thing. I try not to watch him, but it's hard. Jonah draws the eye in a way most men don't. He's sprawled in his chair like he's the king of this little park. A woman across from us sits up straighter when she sees him. A couple of guys are sliding him glances and whispering. Does he notice? Nope. He has eyes for his food, and for me.

"Why did you agree to come tonight?" I ask, when he puts his milkshake down.

He wipes his mouth with a paper napkin, like it's the finest linen. "I'm not sure," he says slowly. "Or I am sure, but I don't like the reason."

I still, waiting with shallow breath to hear his reason.

He sighs. "I was scared." He lifts his dark gaze to mine. "I thought about you out, drunk, with men accosting you. I was just going to drive you home." Something warms in my chest at his admission. His brows draw down as he takes in my expression. "Stop looking at me like that."

"Like what?" I ask innocently, but I feel triumphant. Jonah Crown likes me, and I'm pretty sure he doesn't like anyone.

"Like you know something I don't. You're my employee. I protect what's mine."

Longing flashes through me. I want that. I want to be protected. No one has ever protected me. Not my dad as soon as I hit eighteen and he got more and more distracted by the paper, not Eric, and definitely not my mom.

I reach over and steal one of his fries, and he smacks my hand. "So you would sing karaoke with any employee, is that it?" I keep my voice teasing, but my heart is thudding against the wall of my chest.

"Definitely not." He sighs.

"You like me," I say in a singsong voice. "You want to kiss me."

"Do not quote Miss Congeniality to me again," he says in a stern voice.

My mouth parts in shock. "You've seen it?"

"I practically know it by heart. Christine must have watched it a hundred times."

"She sounds great. I can't wait to meet her."

"You are never meeting her, Thompson. You two would gang up on me, and I would never see a moment of peace." He stands, sweeping up our garbage.

"Well, now you've just given me a new mission in life." I grin and he rolls his eyes, but I see a ghost of a smile on his face.

"Where to?" he asks.

"One more drink?"

Jonah eyes me like I shouldn't be allowed to touch alcohol, before he sighs. "One more. But something weak for you. I'm not carrying you home."

∼

"Shots. Come on." I loop my arm through Jonah's and knock back the cinnamon whiskey shot, before we both start coughing.

"I don't know how you drink this crap. You know it's illegal in Europe, right?"

I laugh. His perpetual grumpiness and his sharp humor do something to my insides. Somehow my knees are tucked between his at a dirty bar on 10th avenue, his shoulders are relaxed, and his face is boyish, even as he pretends to hate drinking. He's done two shots with me, though.

"Only the finest whiskey for Your Majesty, is that it?"

"There's a middle ground between swill and twenty-year old Macallan."

I swig the rest of my cheap beer and shrug. "Too bad. You said the night is mine. You can have the next one."

His gaze turns calculating. "You'd do that?"

I set my empty bottle down slowly. "Yes. I would." *Are you asking me out?* I don't ask because I don't want to scare him. "What would you do on the perfect date?"

"Anything you want," he says in a low voice. Suddenly, he seems dangerously close. Close enough to drown in. His heat, his strength, his delicious smell. I want to wrap it around me.

"Anything?" I tease.

"Literally anything. You forget, Thompson. I can do whatever I want. Not something I take advantage of frequently." His dark eyes drill into me.

But you would, for me. You offered to kill someone, for me.

I stand on unsteady legs, shaken from his words and the drinks. "Walk me home?"

His hands land on my waist. The warmth of his palms seeps into me as he watches me from under heavy lids. His cheekbones are slightly flushed from the drinks, and his pulse thuds in the hollow of his throat. I imagine licking up the base of his throat, all the way under his jaw. He'd probably taste amazing. I shiver at the thought, and his hands tighten on my waist.

"Steady there. And yes, I'll walk you home. Unless you want me to call Lou?"

"I want to walk. I like walking at night."

"And in the morning," he grumbles, but follows me into the night. "Any time it's not safe, you'll find Callie Thompson out stalking strange men."

"Better to be the stalker than the stalkee," I say cheerfully, and he barks a surprised laugh.

"I suppose that's one way to look at it."

"I love New York." I tip my head back to admire the tops of the buildings and the street lamps. "It's the greatest city in the world. And nighttime is special."

"What's your favorite place to walk?"

"My neighborhood. And the High Line. It's closed at night, or I'd say we should walk home on it. I bet the lights are really pretty at night. You walk between the buildings at one point. That's my favorite part."

"Show me," he says in hoarse voice. "This is your night. Show me." His words remind me of earlier. *Show me how to be like you.* And suddenly the roughness of his tone seems more like vulnerability than his usual grumpiness.

"Okay. We can walk up to the stairs, but we can't climb them. It's on the way, anyways."

Jonah taps at his phone briefly, before shoving it into his pocket. When we near the High Line, he ducks into a bodega and buys us two beers. The incongruousness of him fumbling for a fifty in his bespoke overcoat while the bodega cat watches him with wary eyes is enough to make me laugh. He tucks the black bag under his arm and holds the door open for me.

"Something funny, Thompson?" He raises one black brow, and I want to kiss him. His prickliness is like catnip to me. Partly because it means that when he shows me the soft parts of him, they're all for me.

"Just enjoying watching the billionaire go to the bodega."

"I grew up here too, you know."

I gasp. "You did not. New Jersey is not New York, and you know it."

"Don't start," he threatens, but his mouth is tipped up in a smile. "You New York City types are all the same."

"Oh, convenient to claim it when you want to, isn't it? But not when you want to rag on us."

He bumps me with his shoulder. "Screw you."

"I see the New Jersey is coming out." Warmth is bubbling in my chest at his antics, the way he's loosening up. I don't want this night to end.

"You're right. *Fuck you,*" he amends, and I snort a laugh.

We approach the entrance to the High Line, where a man waits by the entrance. "Mr. Crown?" His uniform identifies him as a park ranger and employee of the city of New York.

Jonah shakes his hand, looking unsurprised to see him there. "That's me."

The man grins. "It's your lucky night. Park is open for you. Someone will greet you on the other side."

"We appreciate it." Jonah slips the man a crisp hundred, as if people open closed New York City parks every day for him.

We mount the steps. "How?" I demand. "How?"

He winks at me, the lights of the surrounding buildings making his triumphant smile flash white. "I told you. Literally anything you want. And George called the mayor."

I choke and nearly stumble onto the raised platform that makes up the park.

"Easy there, tiger." Jonah's palm lands on my back.

"You had George call the mayor? Remind me to thank them."

"George likes throwing their weight around. I'm sure they took pleasure in it."

I snort a laugh because George would enjoy that. I can picture their crisp tone now, always half-distracted on the phone, like the person on the other end doesn't matter.

"You're crazy," I whisper.

Jonah shrugs and shoves his hands into his pockets. "I don't do things like this." We walk past the tall grasses that make up the plantings along the path. We're several stories up, walking between the buildings, as if we live in the sky.

"I'm glad I forced you out tonight."

"Me too, Thompson." He gives me a faint smile. "Though I think my workout tomorrow might suffer after all the drinks."

"You're drunk?"

"Not on your life." His smile is hazy though.

"You're totally drunk," I crow.

"So are you," he counters.

"Maybe so." I shiver and rub my arms.

"That coat is too thin."

"Don't growl at me. It's perfectly fine. It's just windy up here."

"Take mine." He's already shrugging out of it.

"No, no. I don't need—"

"Take it." He reaches around to settle the overcoat over my shoulders. The warm weight of it makes me sigh with pleasure.

"Better?" His dark eyes watch me intently. His hands are on my shoulders, like he can't force himself away.

"Better," I whisper. It smells like him, woodsy cologne, faint hints of citrus, male skin. I want to bury my nose in it, breathe him into my lungs. "Are you cold?" He's only in his suit jacket and a scarf, both gray wool, but not warm enough for the cool evening.

"I'm fine," he murmurs distractedly. His thumb comes up to brush my cheekbone. I freeze, my pulse fluttering in my throat. His eyes are half-lidded and locked on my mouth.

The pad of his finger ghosts over my lips. I can't help but part them. I want to bite his finger, but I restrain myself.

"I want to kiss you again." His voice is a mere whisper in the dark.

I step closer. "I want that too." I want that free-falling feeling I had when he kissed me in the park.

Kissing my boss is a bad idea.

As if he can hear my thoughts, Jonah says, "We shouldn't. Once was a fluke. Twice is the road to perdition." The pad of his thumb moves over my skin, making my breath hitch.

"We shouldn't," I agree.

"I'm your boss," he mutters. He skims a finger under my jaw, like I'm precious to him.

"You want to destroy me," I whisper. He's so close. His eyes are slumberous with desire. I can make out every lash, the tiny flecks of lighter brown in his eyes, each hair on his stubbled jaw.

"And you want to destroy me." He doesn't look like he cares, though.

I tip my head up to his. "Right now, I just want you."

He draws in a sharp breath. He dips his head down. His breath whispers over my lips, smelling faintly of whiskey. I sway toward him.

"I don't kiss," he mutters. "But I've never wanted anyone the way I want you. I can't stop myself."

"So don't."

He groans low in his throat, like I'll be his undoing, and seals his mouth to mine.

Jonah kisses me like he's imagined doing it a hundred times. Unyielding, drinking me in, like this kiss is as necessary as his next breath. He pulls back to murmur, "Callie," in that broken whisper, before kissing me again. The sound of my name in that low voice makes me shiver.

His lips are plush but firm as he tastes me. Hesitantly at first, until I kiss him back, and then he makes a needy sound in his throat and spears his hand into my hair. His lips move over mine, teasing, licking, until I can't help but fall against his chest.

He wraps his arm around me and bands me to him. I'm on my tiptoes and he's holding me up, but god, this is the best kiss I've ever had. Free-falling was right. My stomach is tight with desire, the way he grips my hair only stoking it higher.

The stroke of his tongue along the seam of my lips has mine parting. His tongue slicks against mine, heady and delicious. I want to fall into him and never come up for air. I think he'd let me. He kisses me like he wants to meld our bodies together, and I love it. I tentatively pull his bottom lip into my mouth, and he makes a feral sound. His other hand drops to my hip, kneading, pulling me against his hard body.

He wrenches his mouth away and sucks on my neck. Goosebumps follow, my nipples coming to points. I press closer, like I could climb him, and he growls his approval. Need is rushing through my veins, like I've chugged a bottle of whiskey. My head spins as he pulls my stomach against his erection. He's running his lips over my throat, and damn him, I want more.

"Jonah." I pant. "More."

"You're drunk." He stills, his lips pressed to my throat, his heart thudding against his jacket and my hand.

"Not that drunk." *I'm pretty drunk, but I'm definitely not telling him that. He'll stop and I want more of what I know he can do with that tongue.*

"I don't want a drunk fuck." He pulls back. His lips are swollen, and his breath comes in harsh gusts. "If we have drunk sex, you're going to regret it on Monday."

"That's not true." But I don't sound certain. I sway a little in his arms, and his face softens.

"I don't want you to hate me in the morning. And you *will* hate me." He brushes his thumb over my lips, and I chase his hands with my mouth. "Behave, Thompson. I'm taking you home. Lou will pick us up at the exit. You need sleep and I need to deal with this." He gestures down to where his erection presses against his wool slacks. Heat flashes through me at the thought of him dealing with it. That veined bicep and his hand around his shaft. The way his lids would flutter closed with pleasure as he worked himself up.

"Will you think of me?"

"Fuck." His eyes close briefly. "I will. I definitely will."

35

Jonah

Callie is practically weaving on her feet by the time we exit the High Line.

"Tired?"

"No way." She yawns. "That wasn't a real yawn. Ignore it. I want to keep walking."

"Come on, tiger. I'm taking you home." Lou is already idling at the exit. I texted him when Callie insisted on opening the beers I got.

She protests a little but lets me pull her into the car. The dark interior closes around us, and I sigh with pleasure.

"I'm just going to take a nap," she mumbles.

"Do not drool on my upholstery."

"Prickly," she responds, but shuts her eyes.

And yes, I am prickly. I have to be, because seeing her in my coat, in my car, her head dangerously close to falling onto my shoulder, makes possessive need claw at my stomach. *You don't do this.* I shut my eyes and replay the scorching kiss behind my lids. I don't do this. I don't kiss women. I certainly don't mess around with anyone who plans to betray me, woman or otherwise. *But does she plan to betray you?* I watch her lids flutter slightly. Her plush lips are parted. She might look innocent in her sleep, but I know she's trying to dig up as much detail as she can on the company. She can't help herself. *Fuck.*

I tap my fingers on the seat as we approach her apartment. I need her out of this car. She's too tempting. She smells good and her soft breaths make me want to pull her onto my lap. *And what, have her sleep on your chest? Not fucking happening.*

We pull up to the brownstone, and I murmur her name.

"We're at your place."

"No," she says sleepily. "My dad. I don't want him to see me drunk. Too embarrassing. Take me to Adriana's please."

"Is she awake?"

"She will be. I'll buzz her until she gets up."

"Doorman building?" I need to know if she'll be drunk on the steps of another brownstone in the wee hours.

"No. It's fine. I've done it before."

She shifts and her head falls onto my shoulder. I freeze. *Shake her. Kick her out of the car. Remind her of her place in your life. You're the villain, remember?* My hand clenches on my thigh. It's either that or settle her against me. *You don't do this.*

But the thought of her, drunk, tired, waiting for her friend to let her in. I can't.

"Lou. Take us home."

Within minutes, I'm stepping out of the vehicle and scooping her carefully into my arms. She settles against my chest like she was meant to be there. Her warm breaths puff against my neck as I mount the steps to my apartment.

She wakes when I start climbing the staircase, and I gently set her down. I own a fully renovated brownstone, two actually, that have been combined into one soaring, modern, apartment building. A glass-topped addition on the roof provides a generous amount of sun that filters down into the building during the day. The bedrooms are on the second floor.

"Where are we?" Callie blinks sleepily.

"My house."

She cranes her neck to see into the living room, and I grab her hand. "Not now. You can be nosy in the morning. I want to sleep."

I lead her up the stairs into the primary guest bedroom and curse under my breath when I see the disarray.

"What's wrong?" She blinks sleepily at the messy room.

"The guest bedrooms are being renovated. New mattresses."

"I can sleep on the couch."

I sigh. "There's one in the master suite. Come on."

Leading Callie Thompson into my bedroom is weird. She's darting glances left and right, at the massive California king, the reserved decor, the old books, the door into the sitting room where the couch is.

"Bathroom is on the right." I point at the first door.

She looks at me uncertainly. "Are you sure about this?"

I'm already pulling an extra comforter out of the closet. There are no extra pillowcases. *Fuck it.* She can use mine.

"Am I sure about what?"

"Me. Sleeping here. In your, um, bedroom." She's biting her lip and I want to suck it into my mouth.

"Frankly? No." My voice is gravelly with need. I'm exhausted, and I've been fighting my attraction to her for weeks.

"I should go."

"Thompson. If you set one foot out that door, I will fire you. You're here. I'm tired. You're tired. Now go to sleep." I toss the comforter unceremoniously onto the couch in the sitting area and stalk from the room.

I press my hands over my eyes in the bathroom. *Don't do anything stupid.* She's my employee, for fuck's sake. She shouldn't be going to bars with me, or singing with me, or kissing me. *Fuck.* I methodically strip off my clothes, and my cock jerks. I grit my teeth. Clearly my body has the wrong idea.

I brush my teeth with more force than is strictly necessary, and when I shove open the bathroom door, Callie is there.

"What?" I say flatly.

"Can I borrow something to sleep in? I don't want to sleep in my work clothes. Or just my underwear." Her face is pink.

"Probably a good idea," I mutter. I toss her an oversized workout shirt from the dresser, and she disappears into the sitting room.

Twenty minutes later, I'm lying on my back in my massive bed, wide awake despite the half gallon of alcohol I consumed. *It's her.* The pea under my mattress. The reason I don't get anything done. I can hear her breathing from the other room. The door is just five feet away. *Is she awake?* Is that shirt riding up over her ass? Fuck, I feel like a pervert. She shifts restlessly on the couch and before I can think better of it, I'm up and at her door.

"Do you need anything?" I ask.

"Sorry. Am I bothering you? I can't sleep." She sits up. The silky material of the shirt clings to her breasts, highlighting her peaked nipples. My mouth waters. Literally fucking waters. *Pathetic.*

"Why can't you sleep?" My voice comes out harsher than I intend.

"Well, it's a couch. I'm trying." She sounds irritated. Finally. A comfortable place to be with her.

"Sleep on the bed."

"But you're on the bed."

"And I'm not getting any sleep with you tossing and turning all night."

She stands and the shirt barely hits her mid-thigh. *Ah, fuck. What was I thinking?*

"Where will you sleep?"

"On the other side. It's a California king. Just get in the bed, Thompson. I'm not going to ravish you. Fucking hell." I mutter curses and settle back onto my side before she slips under the covers. I freeze. The temperature is instantly ten degrees warmer. Her steady breaths fill the space. *This is worse.* Why would I suggest this?

"Jonah?" she whispers.

"What?" I bark.

"Thank you. For everything." She finally, blessedly, falls asleep.

I WAKE to a warm arm thrown over my stomach, a woman's cheek cradled against my chest. *What the hell?* And then, through my sleep-addled brain, *Callie.* I freeze. She's asleep, if the evenness of her breathing is anything to go by. Asleep and half-draped over me. *Fuck.* And my arm is curled under her and around her shoulders like she's mine. The rest of my body seems to agree. She shifts slightly and my cock hardens further. *Shit. Leave, you fool.* But I don't want to leave. I want to stay, and show her pleasure, explore that connection I felt when we kissed. I hover on the edge of indecision, until she murmurs, "Jonah," in her sleep, and I'm done for.

36

Callie

I'm having the best dream. I never have dreams like this, and I never want it to end. I can't really see Jonah's face, but I know the warm weight pushing me into the mattress is him. His hands are everywhere, his hot breath is on my neck, and I love it.

"Callie," I hear. Lips on my neck, a hand on my jaw. I arch to meet dream Jonah. His lips are just as soft as they were when he kissed me, and *oh, right there.*

"Jonah." His name is a gasp of air.

I'm tumbling into the pit of desire between us. His muscled chest is a solid wall at my back, and even in my dream, he smells delicious. I push back into him and he makes a surprised sound. *Wait, is he awake? Oh shit.* I freeze. My eyes open. *Not a dream. Very much reality.* A reality in which Jonah's heart thuds against my back, and his arm is wrapped around my stomach. But just like the dream, I'm wet and aching between my legs, and he's hard against me.

His mouth is at my ear. His teeth close over the lobe and the pinch has my breath stuttering in my chest. "Well, don't stop now," he growls. "It was just getting good." His lips move over my throat, and I release a shaky sigh.

"We shouldn't."

"Why not?" His voice is a rumble at my back.

I'm having a hard time remembering why this is a bad idea, especially with the way he's tugging me back into his body. His hardness cradles my softness, his thick erection providing delicious friction.

"Because last time, you said it was a mistake."

He stills, and then surges over me, one leg between my own, his eyes intent on mine. "I take it back." He brushes his lips over mine. "I take it all back. Please, Callie. Trust me again."

I squeeze my eyes shut.

"I said I would make you beg, but I take it back. I'll beg you. I'll get on my knees. I need you," he says. Another kiss, my lips parting to let his tongue delve into my mouth. "Please. Say yes." He bites at my bottom lip.

If I do this, I'm going to fall for him. This is bad. But I can't stop. "Yes," I whisper.

"Thank fuck." And then his mouth is on mine again, this time, hard, demanding. He coaxes my lips apart and when I touch my tongue to his, a ragged groan dredges up from his chest. We're a tangle of tongues and teeth and grasping hands.

I'm pushing his T-shirt up with my hands. I need to touch him. I didn't get to touch him before, and it's been all I could think about for weeks. The skin of his stomach hot and smooth under my fingers. Muscles roll under his skin as his hips press into me. I gasp into his mouth and he chuckles. He's hard where I'm soft, confident when I'm not, and I need more.

"Slow down," he whispers. He pulls back to look me in the eye, smiling like he's not trembling with need. Like we have all the time in the world to explore each other. I arch up toward him in frustration. I'm crazed for him. The weeks of waiting broke something inside me, because I can't stop touching and seeking.

"I can't slow down," I groan out.

"I'll make you." His eyes are laughing at me.

"How can you say that? This is all I've thought about for weeks." I circle my hips again, craving the feel of him.

"Oh, me too." His mouth hitches up at the side. He skims seeking fingers down my arms, then over my hips. He leans down to bite gently at my nipple through the thin material of the borrowed shirt and *holy shit*. My body jerks like I've been electrified. He laughs softly.

"The last few weeks have been torture. All the more reason to take it slow." He captures my lips with his, and I try to urge him on with my teeth and my tongue, but he's undeterred. His kisses are deep and drugging, pulling me under, until I'm sighing and squirming under him.

He nuzzles down the side of my neck, almost *tender*, and my heart lurches. I didn't expect this. I thought we'd tear at each other's clothes, that he'd take me from behind. Instead, he's savoring me. His teeth grasp my other nipple and I cry out. The damp cotton on the tight peak creates delicious friction. It's almost too much.

"Jonah," I plead, tugging at his shirt.

He rises up to pull it off, and I suck in air. I got a small glimpse before, but now, the chest I've wanted to touch is *right there*. I trace over his abs with one finger, making him shudder and sigh. That vee of muscle at his groin feels just as good under my palm as I imagined. He sucks in wind like he's dying, but lets me explore him.

"This is your one chance," he says. "Then you're mine."

I shiver. "What does that mean?" I trace the ridge of his cock through his briefs. He bows his head, neck tense, tendons straining. His body is pure grace—thick muscle, lean limbs.

"Pleasure dom," he grits out. "It's called a pleasure dom."

"I've never heard of that." I'm stroking him through his shorts. He's on a short leash. I can practically see him trembling with anticipation, restraining himself.

"It means I want to give you pleasure. More than want. Crave it. I won't finish if you don't. As many times as possible."

Holy shit.

"Okay?" He asks, his voice gravel.

"Okay."

He smiles and helps me slip my shirt off, then my shorts, and then I'm under him, nearly naked, while he kneels between my legs. The crispness of his hairs create delicious contrast to the sensitive skin on my inner thighs. I want to rub myself against him. I want to feel him everywhere.

The expression on his face is slightly awed as he runs a finger over my stomach, then up under my breasts, making me shiver and gasp. "You're so pretty, Callie." His eyes meet mine, and the black depths are already a little glazed. "I want to devour you."

"Please," I whisper.

The plea unlocks him. He shoves off me and strips off his pants and briefs, his movements confident and economical. When he turns back, his erection juts proudly from between his strong legs. It's long, thick, and so hard it taps against his stomach as he climbs onto the bed. He ignores it, in favor of flipping me over and pressing my face into the pillow. One hand in my hair, the other palming my ass.

"Stay like this, Cal."

"Okay." I turn my cheek so I can watch him. He sweeps my hair over my shoulder, and presses his lips to my back. Cool air caresses my overheated skin. I shiver with anticipation. I'm vulnerable like this, in a way I never let myself be with Eric. Jonah hooks his fingers under my underwear and eases them down. I can't see his expression, but I hear a soft groan of pleasure before he brushes between my legs. It feels like I've touched a live wire. Sparks fly, heat spreads through me.

And strangely, despite how I'm bared to him, I feel utterly protected. *I trust him.* For all his faults, I know there's no reason for embarrassment with him. He's brutally honest and no one could make him do anything he doesn't want to do. Which means he really wants this, wants me.

One big hand pushes my knees wider, and then his tongue slicks through my core, over my clit, and back again. My hips buck and he presses me back down.

"Oh god," I breathe.

"Try again," he mutters, before licking me again. Warm wetness mixes with desire as I arch against the bed. He tongues my clit, and I murmur, "Oh, Jonah."

"Good girl," he growls against me. "You taste—" He makes a ragged sound of approval, and then spears his tongue into me in a way that makes me scream his name. He laughs softly.

"You like that?"

"No one has ever done that." I'm panting slightly. My body is shaking with need, already.

"Fools," he hisses, before he does it again.

He brings me to the edge with his clever tongue, and then he presses one thick finger to my entrance, and pushes slowly in. I'm gasping into the pillow at this point, trembling with the need to finish. My limbs are warm and heavy and sparks dance behind my eyes.

"Come on, Cal." He sucks on my clit and crooks his finger, and I break apart, moaning his name. The orgasm is sharp and jarring, unexpected in its intensity.

"Another," he murmurs, stroking lightly.

"Another? I don't think I've ever had two."

"Two?" I can hear the smile in his voice. "Oh no, you'll have more than two. But we'll start small."

He strokes me gently, just the tip of his tongue moving over me, the pad of his finger, until I'm pushing back against him.

He presses his finger back into me, and I clench around him. "Jonah." He crooks it and thrusts while he sucks on my clit, hard. "Jonah," I cry again. "That feels so good." My words make him shudder and I decide right then and there to tell him exactly how he makes me feel. If he's going to give me this, I can give him that. Another orgasm is building, the desire a heady rush. I'm free-falling into him and the feeling he can give me, with no expectation of anything in return. *Wonderful man.*

He brings me right to the edge, again, with just soft flicks of his tongue and light thrusts, almost absurdly gentle, like I'm made of glass. "Please," I moan. "I need you, Jonah."

"What do you need?" he growls the words into my skin.

"I need you—ah. Right there." I pant. A second finger joins the first, and *oh no*, I'm going to come again. Pressure is building between my legs, there, so close, and then I break, flying into pieces as I scream his name.

He strokes my back as I come down, light and soothing. I flip over and he lets me. His eyes are heavy lidded, but a cocky grin is on his lips.

"You're very proud of yourself," I mutter.

"You're hot when you come," he shoots back. His eyes darken as they roam over me. "Are you up for more?"

I love that he keeps asking. This is all about me, not about him.

"Please."

His eyes flare and he reaches over me to pull a condom from the drawer by his bed. A rip of gold foil, the hiss he makes as he rolls it onto his length, and then he's *right there*. My hands dig into his shoulders, and his neck strains, and he pushes into me, just an inch.

"Oh, wow," I whisper. He's bigger than I thought.

"I know." His voice is tight.

I shift, trying to work myself onto him.

"Cal." The word is spoken between clenched teeth. He presses his forehead to mine, shaking with strain. The muscles of his arms stand out in stark relief. I run my hands over them, and he relaxes a fraction. "I don't want to hurt you."

I wiggle again, lifting my hips, until he sinks in another inch and hisses a breath. "You're not hurting me." Another inch and I gasp at the pleasure. "Please, Jonah," I beg. "You feel so good."

"Fuck, don't wind me up like that." He keeps his forehead pressed to mine as he sinks deeper, pushing me into the mattress, like the world's best weighted blanket. As he slides home, we both groan.

"So good," I whisper.

"I know. Watching you come got me close." He rolls his hips and pleasure arcs through me like lightning. Another roll, his face pressed into my neck, his hand pinning mine to the bed. Then messy thrusts, my nails digging into his back, his breath damp in my ear. Raw, and primal, and gasping. *So good.* And *right there.*

"You take me so well." His voice is rough.

"I love the way you feel."

He groans his approval at my words and increases his pace, until we're both straining and hanging by a thread.

"More, Jonah, yes."

"You're perfect."

And then he's rasping hoarse sounds in my ear, sounding like he might come at any moment, and pleasure is making my legs shake, the sensation spreading from where he's filling me up, to where his stomach brushes my clit, where his lips meet my neck. A final thrust breaks me apart. I gasp his name, and he throws his head back in pleasure. The orgasm is a wave cresting through my blood, the desire sharp and sweet, then warm and drugging. His hips are still pumping helplessly into mine, before he collapses over me.

"Callie." He presses his lips to my neck. "Callie." He sounds like he's half out of his mind. "How?" He raises his head. Our eyes meet and in his I see awe, desire, and a new realization. It's the same conclusion I've come to––the same warmth filling my chest, terrifying and amazing, all at once.

Everything has changed.

37

Jonah

Callie presses her face into my chest while I smooth a hand down her back. *Too good.* I'm spent, but my body is already thinking about round two. Callie is limp in my arms, her breaths puffing against my skin. I am triumphant. There is nothing better than watching her fall apart.

"When did you become a pleasure dom?" Her voice is soft, like she doesn't want to break the cocoon we're in. Early morning sun streams in through the windows that face the garden.

"Become?"

"Or, decide that's what you liked, I guess."

I run a hand over her hip as I think. "I'm not sure. I've always preferred my partners' pleasure to my own. But I didn't really learn the term until later in life. It can be annoying for some women, though." A fact I've accepted. This is what I need, and it works for some, not for others. "I definitely choose carefully when I sleep with people. It's an experience. Part of why I said I didn't want to have drunk sex with you. I like to be fully present and in control."

She stills in my arms.

"What?"

"I just really liked it, that's all."

I pull back to see her cheeks tinged with pink. Fuck, she's pretty. Soft curves and wild, dark hair. Her lips are swollen and her eyes are hazy. *I did that.* Masculine pride fills my chest. "What did you like about it?"

She bites her lip. "I liked how much you liked it, honestly. And the three orgasms helped too."

I laugh softly. "Wait and see how you feel when I'm asking you for five or six, or more. Or bringing you to the edge and then leaving you hanging."

"You'd do that?" She sounds shocked but excited.

"And more." *Until this is over.* Because it will end. And fuck, I don't want to think about that right now, because she's in my arms and I'm weak where she's concerned. "What else?" I ask.

She buries her face against my chest. "Well, this is awkward. Um. I liked how you were all in. One hundred percent focused. My ex didn't focus on me that much during sex."

"Asshole," I mutter. Possessive anger replaces the pride I felt. The thought of that prick, Eric, touching her, and doing it badly. "He didn't deserve you."

"Sorry for bringing him up."

"Don't apologize." I sigh. I'm being an asshole. Callie doesn't owe me anything. I rub circles on her back while I calm the anger boiling through me.

"Want breakfast? I'm sure the, ah, chef, left us something," I say.

"Chef?" She laughs, and pulls back so she can see my face. "You have a chef?"

"Don't start. I knew you were going to laugh. I'm uh, actually learning to cook." I rub a hand over the back of my neck, uncomfortable with how deficient I am at normal human things. I bet even shitty Eric knew how to make eggs.

"A chef, a driver, a secretary, private security. Anything else I should know about? Do you have someone to hold your towel in the gym? Oh, wait."

I grimace. "You'll notice I didn't make you do that on Friday."

"Oh yes." She grins and rises from the bed, hips swaying. "You're turning over a new leaf."

She's joking, but the truth of her words lances through me. *Maybe I am.* Would that be so bad? Would she like me better if I did? *She might.*

She follows me to the walk-in closet, where she watches me choose exercise pants and a sweatshirt. Her sigh when I grab the sweatshirt stops me. "Something wrong?"

"Just, um, I think it would be a shame if you wore a shirt. Pants are enough, don't you think?" She looks hopeful and I start laughing.

"Here." I toss her the garment. "You wear it. Then you don't have to wear your clothes from yesterday. And you can ogle me."

"Yes, please." She slips the sweatshirt on, wiggling as it slips over her thighs, just covering her butt. "This is nice."

"You are shameless." But I say it without heat.

"I have to be." She shrugs. "Reporter, remember?"

The reminder darkens my thoughts as she follows me into the kitchen on the first floor. It's huge, with floor to ceiling windows that open into the atrium, and then the garden.

"Did I say something wrong?" she asks. I turn, shoulders tense, to see her worrying her lip. "It's because I brought up reporting, isn't it?"

"Don't worry about it." I don't want to get into Annalise right now and all my fucked-up baggage from that relationship.

"I think I should go." She moves to go and I stride forward, catching her hand, pulling her against me.

"I hate that your instinct is to run away when I'm being a jerk." My words are a little rough, the honesty surprising even me.

She considers me. "So you admit that you can be a jerk?"

"I am…not an easy man, Callie. I think you know that. I'm not nice and I don't want to be."

Her eyes move over my face. They're so blue and thickly lashed.

The prettiest eyes I've ever seen. "I told myself I'd only go for nice guys. No more bad boys."

I freeze. "I can try," I say carefully. *What are you doing? What the fuck do you think you're doing?* "I could try to be nice, for you."

"You're missing the point." Her lips curve up. "I was going to say that while you might the baddest guy of all, I don't want you to change."

My pulse thuds in my chest. "You're joking. I made your life miserable. Thompson. We really need to talk about your sense of self-preservation."

Her smile grows. "And now I can tell you call me Thompson every time you want to put some distance between us."

I scowl. "Not true."

She presses her fingers to my lips. "This is not a buddy cop movie, right? Isn't that what you said?"

I shut my eyes briefly. "I was being an ass. I'm not going to torment you anymore."

Her face falls slightly.

"What's wrong? Don't tell me you miss being abused by me?"

She scrunches her face up and pushes at my chest. I tighten my arms in response.

"Um, yes?"

"What?" The word comes out strangled. I finally let her go and move to the espresso machine. One touch on the silver panel starts the brewing process.

She leans against the counter across from me, and my eyes arrow to her bare legs. I want them wrapped around my waist. I steel myself to be nice and normal.

"I like going toe-to-toe with you. You treat me like an equal. Even when you're demanding that I do things for you."

My eyes widen in surprise. "I respect you, Cal. You're smart as hell. I wouldn't have an incompetent person working with me."

"But you're not going to torment me anymore? Because I really could help with your work."

"I know you can. I do need your help. But not today." I take a deep breath. "Today, I want you to show me what you love about New York. Since I'm just a clueless boy from New Jersey."

"Stop." Callie laughs. "I didn't mean it like that, and you know it."

"I like giving you shit." Too much, I think.

"So you want to be a tourist, eh?"

I pass her a coffee and grimace. "Don't make me do anything embarrassing, please. I'm already regretting this." But I'm not, not really. I want to spend time with Callie. I don't know what normal people do on weekend mornings in New York City, and suddenly I'm desperate to find out.

"I was thinking maybe a ride in one of those rickshaws with the music blaring. Perhaps *New York, New York*? And then we can go to the top of the Rock. Oh, there's usually a really long line there. You'll love that."

"I don't do lines," I say coolly. "If you want to do that, then I'll have a private tour arranged." More like George can arrange one, but whatever.

"No." Callie shakes her head, her eyes flashing. "Sometimes you just have to get down and dirty with the masses." She steps into my space, looking stubborn and sexy in my sweatshirt. I keep myself from reaching for her, but barely. "You forget, I think, what it's like in the real world. You've shut yourself in that glass tower and this townhouse. You need to *live*." Her voice is fierce.

"And living means waiting in line?" I arch both brows.

"Living means walking because the subway isn't working, even if it's raining. It means dealing with inconveniences and successes being all the sweeter for them."

Her eyes are earnest. She really means this. *Her way.* A normal man would wait in line. A regular guy. "I trust you." I sigh. Trusting her might be the death of me, but I'll give it a shot. "I guess I can start by trying to make you breakfast. I'm a bad cook, though, I warn you. And you're giving up, let's see—" I open the massive fridge. "Ah, steelcut oats with berries and maple syrup. Oh, and turkey bacon."

Suddenly, I feel embarrassed, awkward even. I hate it. "I can make eggs. And toast."

She gives me a brilliant smile, like I just offered her champagne and caviar. "Eggs and toast it is."

∼

"So how are you learning to cook?" Callie perches on a barstool while I carefully crack eggs into a bowl. I'm all thumbs when I do this. I'm terrified to drop the damn eggs. I've only successfully scrambled them once.

"Mark, my chef, is teaching me. An hour a week. So far, I can make breakfast and pasta. That's it." The words are absent while I hunt for a whisk.

"Not bad." She watches me over the lip of her coffee mug. Her presence in the kitchen I barely use is unsettling me more than normal. I want to impress her, and somehow I think the chauffeured car and the fancy townhouse aren't doing it. But maybe breakfast will. "Do you not know where anything is?"

"Ah. No. What do I look like to you, Thompson? A chef?" My words don't have any bite to them, and she huffs a laugh.

"I can help. If you want."

I look up at her and point the infernal whisk in her direction. "Sit. I'm cooking. Though I don't know why anyone needs four whisks."

She chokes a laugh and my chest swells. "Something funny?" I drawl the words, and when I raise my head, her eyes are glinting with happiness.

I like you, her face says.

You can't like me, mine replies. I'm not made for *liking*. I turn to the bowl, whisking furiously, tilting it awkwardly.

"You look like a natural." Callie's compliment goes straight to my chest.

"I'm not."

"Your parents never taught you?"

I shake my head. "Nah. My mom is traditional. She taught Christine but not me."

"Does Christine like it?"

"She does. Gives her a chance to hold something over my head, too." I look up, smiling faintly. "And now she's having a baby, so she's a real domestic goddess. She'd kill me if she heard me say that, though."

Callie smiles and my pulse speeds. She gives those smiles away to everyone she meets, but the ones I receive feel hard fought.

"What does she do?"

"Runs a PR firm. With her wife." I dump the eggs into the saucepan. *Low and slow.* That means five on the dial? Six? Fuck it. Cooked is cooked. I set it to five. "I don't know how anyone could work with a spouse or a partner. I certainly couldn't." *And definitely not after Annalise.* I stir the eggs more angrily than I mean to at the thought of how she and Dylan stole my company from under me.

"I could, I think." Callie sounds dreamy, like she's imagining a neat little world in which no one ever argues and no one has any secrets. "I mean, it might be nice, building something with someone you love. I work with my dad on the paper, and it's tough, but more rewarding because it's family."

"You don't want to murder each other?"

She bites her lip, looking uncertain. "It's tough. My dad is set in his ways."

I set our plates on the counter and settle in next to her. "And?" I take a bite of eggs and grimace. "Damn, this is bad."

Callie tries it, daintily. "No. It's good. Stop being such a critic." She takes a bigger bite.

"Stop avoiding the question. Tell me about your dad."

She sighs, those navy eyes shadowed. "He's been doing this for a long time. He loves being a reporter, but he's in his late sixties now, and he's stuck in the same habits. Newspapers have changed a lot since he started writing." Her shoulders slump. "The paper has been dying for years. If you hadn't come along, I think we would have stopped printing."

My chest aches at her words, the way she's so fragile. "You have the money now, though."

"It doesn't matter if he won't change. Why keep publishing for fewer and fewer readers? I have ideas that could help us, but he won't let me implement them."

Protectiveness sinks hot spikes into my stomach. *Fix it. Fix it for her.* I shake the thought away. What am I going to do? Give her a print division at Kings Lane and have her grow? She'd love that. She'd blossom. And I almost want to tell her I'll solve all her problems for her.

"Like what?" My emotions make my voice rough, and Callie looks up at me in surprise, her mouth full of coffee.

She swallows, looking skeptical. "You want to know? You're not going to, I don't know, retaliate?"

"No." The truth of it rushes through me. "I'm not going to retaliate. I want to understand."

"Well, first of all, we need to focus more heavily on digital media and getting quality advertisers. To do that, we need to invest more. I don't think we should focus on print at all. But my dad disagrees."

"There's something nostalgic about printed papers. I imagine that's why he likes them."

She gives a funny, surprised look. "Yeah. That's exactly it."

"But you don't?"

"I would sacrifice nostalgia for success. I'm practical. He's not." She shrugs.

"I understand." I shovel another bite of poorly cooked eggs into my mouth. "I've done the same. Many times."

She gives me a small smile, like the fact that we're similar is comforting, instead of terrifying.

"What would you do? If you were in charge? In terms of content."

She fiddles with her coffee mug. "The gossip stuff is fun. I'd still do it."

My chest tightens, but I nod. I don't want to push her away, even though it's not what I wanted to hear.

"But I'd do more. The paparazzi gig started as a way to make money. I realized I could make a lot selling pictures to the Post. And we really needed the money. My dad was having health problems at the time, and our health insurance lapsed. It was up to me to make things work." She sips her coffee. "So I did."

"I underestimated you," I say quietly.

"A lot of people do," she says calmly. And suddenly, I *hate* that I'm in that group.

"So, what would you do?"

"I'd focus more on the immediate neighborhood. We can't be all things to all people, but we can be a really important source of information for our neighbors. My dad does a few long-form articles about the city as a whole, but we're never going to compete with bigger outfits. I'd focus on the Upper West Side, including our celebrity residents." She gives me a sly smile, and I roll my eyes.

"You've raised it to him, I assume? Since you're not exactly shy."

"Nailed it. And yeah, I have." Her face falls and she looks back at her plate. "He doesn't want to change. Or he doesn't trust me. He could retire, but he won't. Because he won't let me run the paper alone."

"Have you thought that maybe he doesn't have anything else?"

"What?" She looks up at me.

"I mean, your mom is gone, right? He's been a newspaper guy for years. He doesn't have much else. Plus, it's your thing. Together. Maybe he's not ready to give that up."

Callie is opening and closing her mouth like a fish.

"Something wrong?"

"You're very perceptive. More so than I thought." She narrows her eyes at me. "And you might be right. I never thought about it like that." She sighs and sips her coffee.

"What else would you change, if you could?" Callie is intelligent and calculating when it comes to her business, and I want to hear her ideas.

She perks up at my question, her eyes bright. "So many things. Right now, the website is an afterthought. My dad is focused on these long think pieces that don't appeal to digital readers. People get halfway through and don't keep reading. We need more traffic on the site. Gossip, neighborhood news, photos."

"Ah. Like the photos of me."

Her cheeks redden. "Yeah. Those do really well. The best, actually."

I raise a brow. "The best?"

"Don't gloat," she says primly.

"Tell me how I'm the best."

"Well, the photos of Miles do pretty well too. Especially when he goes to events. Those tuxes." She shakes her head, like she finds Miles attractive. I shove back from the counter. My hand wraps around her wrist, tugging her up, so she's looking into my eyes. Her pulse thuds in her wrist, and I feather my thumb over it. "Do you think he's attractive?"

"Why do you care?"

"Answer the question." Possessiveness is making my insides hot and uncomfortable. I take a long gulp of water to cool the burn.

"Sure. He's attractive. If you have a pulse." Her eyes are sparkling.

"Baiting me, Thompson?" I back her up until she's against the wall. Her chin is lifted, baring her neck. So bold. So smart. Everything I want.

"Your photos do better." Her lips curve in a knowing smile. "Twenty-five percent more traffic."

"And?" My voice is gravel.

Her eyes flick over my face, drop to my lips. Hunger is written there, and I fucking love it. "You're way hotter than Miles."

"Be a good girl and tell me why you think I'm hot." My lips hover over hers, promising rewards.

"Why?" she whispers.

"Because it turns me on to hear the things you like."

"Oh." Her breath whispers against my lips. "I like your body." I run my lips up her neck, reveling in the softness of her skin, the scent of her hair. She smells a little bit like sex and my laundry detergent. *Mine.* She smells like she's mine.

"What about it?"

"Greedy," she teases.

"I am greedy." I tangle my fingers in her hair. "I don't share. I want all of your pleasure."

She shivers and closes her eyes, like she's imagining what *all of your pleasure* means. "I like your arms. The way they flex when you work." Her voice sounds dreamy. "And your shoulders. Even your collarbones. Everything is bigger on you. Stronger." I shudder at her words, my erection already tenting my thin pants. "I like when you have me like this." I lift the hem of her shirt and brush my hand over the soft skin of her stomach while I bite at her neck.

"Like what? Touch me while you tell me."

She's panting now, as turned on as I am. Her hands come up to my shoulders and she digs her little nails into my skin. The pleasure-pain goes straight to my cock, making me groan.

"I like feeling caged by you. It's hot. I know you'll never hurt me. And the way you focus on me. It's so good." I claim her mouth as she says the last words, trying to breathe in the compliments, drown myself in her approval, the way she craves me.

"Good girl," I murmur. She kisses me like she really does believe I'm the hottest guy she knows, and pride beats through my blood. She twines her hands through my hair, presses herself to my body, makes needy noises in her throat. I pull her bottom lip between my teeth and she moans. I cup her breast in my palm and she cries out.

"So sensitive. Are you wet for me?" And I need her to be, because for the very first time in my life, I don't think I can wait. Normally, I'm all about control, but right now, she's shredding it.

"Touch me and find out." She kisses me again, bold and delicious, her soft lips trying to give back exactly what I'm giving her.

"Fuck." I groan and press her against the wall, before I delve my fingers between her legs to find her soaked. The desire that rushes through me is indescribable. "I feel how much you want me, and I love it." I circle her clit, slick and swollen. The blood pounding through me is making it hard to think, hard to go slow.

"Jonah," she breathes.

"I've got you." Her hips are already chasing my hand, thank fuck, because I'm trembling with need.

I shove my pants down in one swift movement and free my aching cock. I'm already lifting her off the floor, notching myself to her entrance. We both groan as I press into her. *So good.* My breath is stuttering in my chest, but I will myself not to finish before I've barely gotten inside her. *Ah, fuck.* She's slick and hot and squeezing me.

"Condom." Shit. I'm an asshole.

"Don't stop." She presses her head back against the wall. "I have an IUD. And I'm clean."

"Me too. You're sure?" Her half-lidded eyes meet mine and in them I see trust and unquenchable need for me.

"Please, Jonah," she whispers against my mouth.

I slide deep, and we both cry out. She's already clenching around me, as on fire for me as I am for her.

I buck up into her in short, hard thrusts that make her move across the wall. I'm close, so close, after mere minutes of being with her. *It's never been like this before. Never.* My skin feels like it's on fire, the tug in my groin tells me that this orgasm will feel like a free-fall from a steep cliff.

"Cal." I pant. "Are you close?" I roll my hips and fumble to circle her clit with my thumb. She cries out, a little panting sob, and clenches around me. "Thank fuck," I mutter. I set a driving pace, rolling my hips in a rhythm that ratchets us both higher. My fingers play over her clit and drink in her reactions until she moans, "Jonah," and clenches around me, hard. *Fuck.* The pleasure of her orgasm has a sharp bright edge, dragging me right to the brink, whether I want it to or not. One more thrust, to make sure she's finished coming, and then I follow her over, my cock swelling and jerking inside her, the desire spiraling up from between my legs to fill my body to bursting. I'm limp and spent when we finally stop panting. I slip out of her and let her down gently. "Stay," I whisper against her neck. "Stay there."

I get a cloth from the kitchen, and then sink to the ground to clean her. The gentle strokes make her tremble.

"Do you need more?" I raise my head to see her watching me with hazy eyes. I press a kiss to her thigh. She smells like sex, like *me*, and my chest swells.

She shakes her head, and a little part of me is disappointed, because I think I would very much like to keep Callie Thompson in my bed all day.

I'm so fucked.

38

Callie

Lou drops us at my apartment, but I don't want to leave. Being with Jonah is magical, like a cocoon of wonderful things in a sea of insanity. An anchor in a world that moves too fast. He stares up at the window where Samson watches us with eager eyes. I guess Jonah feels the same way I do, though neither of us broaches the topic. He lingers outside my apartment, even though he could be whisked away in seconds.

"Are you going to invite me up?"

"No way." I shake my head. Nerves jump in my stomach at the thought of Jonah being in my space, my dad's space. One time was enough.

"Why not?" His lips press flat. He's not used to being denied things.

"My dad. And I—" I swallow around the lump in my throat. "I'm not ready." And a whole host of other reasons, including the fact that while Jonah might want me, he sure as hell doesn't trust me.

His expression darkens, and for a second I think he's going to argue with me. But then he says, "Fucking Eric."

"Yeah." I give him a sad smile. "Fucking Eric."

"All right, Thompson. I'll let you go, for now. But first—" He captures my hand and tugs me against his body, wrapping his massive overcoat around us so I'm cocooned against his cashmere sweater and his delicious warmth.

I'm helpless to resist him when he's like this. Open and protective. His layers peeled back. So when he dips his head down, I raise mine and I let my eyes flutter shut in anticipation. He presses a light kiss to the corner of my mouth. "I see the appeal," he murmurs.

"Hmm?" Pleasure is drugging me, along with the heat of his body, his scent.

Another kiss on the corner of my lips. "I've never wanted to kiss anyone before. Until you." He captures my mouth. "And now, I can't seem to stop."

My chest cracks at his admission, and I press up on my tiptoes to kiss him back. His arms band around my back, and his mouth moves over my own. For someone who never kisses, he is divine. His tongue is hot and clever. He makes noises in the back of his throat like I'm destroying him. He finally pulls away, his eyes wild, his cheeks a little red.

"Fuck, Cal." He presses his forehead to mine, inhaling a shaky breath. "See you on Monday."

I step away and he lets me go. I watch him drive away, then sigh and let myself back into the dreary building. I trudge up the stairs to the second floor, where the worn mat and the shoe rack welcome me back. *You love this apartment. Stop. Get a grip.* But when I unlock the heavy door, for the first time in a long time, I don't feel glad to be home.

"Callie?"

"Hi, Dad."

"There you are." He appears in his office door, his face creased slightly with worry. "Where were you last night?"

"Ah, with a friend. I texted you." I sigh, and go to strip off my jacket, then remember Jonah's sweatshirt is under my coat. "I'm not a little kid anymore."

"I know you're not." His voice is gentle and it makes me want to rage. I'm sick of the non-confrontation and the never discussing things.

"Well, you still treat me like one." I cross my arms over my chest, looking like the child I claim not to be.

"What's that supposed to mean?"

"You never listen to my suggestions. I have so many things I want to do with the paper, and you won't take any of my advice. I could help us. I could expand. And every time I bring it up, you shut me down. Do you even want me involved?" My eyes are hot and scratchy when I finish, and I will myself not to cry.

He regards me uncertainly. This is the first time I've ever been so honest. "Of course I do." He scrubs a hand over his face. "I'm set in my ways, Cal. I'm sorry. You know that. Give me some more time, and I'll come around."

All the fight goes out of me. "I know, Dad. I'm sorry." My shoulders sag. "I can be patient."

As I strip off my coat in the bedroom, I think to myself, *for how much longer?*

39

Jonah

Fight night is the best. The air of anticipation. The feeling that we're doing something clandestine.

The lights flicker on in the gym as I push open the studio door, Jason hot on my heels, his friend Andrew behind him.

Fight night is an insane tradition that Theo invented. We used to do it once a quarter, until the split lips and black eyes became a liability. Callie photographed me with a spectacular purple bruise once, and the speculation ran rampant for weeks. Now, we have rules. Punches are kept below the neck. Ten rounds, a thousand dollars to fight, winner takes all. The thousand dollars are just to make sure you really want to fight. Because once you're in, there's no tapping out. Only passing out. Theo's crazy like that. And even though he's not here to enforce the rules, we still play by them.

"I fucking need this." Jason drops his bag on the floor and walks to the wraps, already keyed up and ready to go.

"You good, man?" This from Andrew, who has an easy confidence about him. His gloves hang from his gym bag.

Jason can be a ball of anxiety and anger on bad days. I know because I've gone drink for drink with him on enough of them, or punch for punch. He's usually more relaxed now that he's with Cynthia.

"Yeah." Jason shakes his body out, still in his warm-up clothes. "The fucking firm. My last bonus season. The hours are ramping up. I can't wait to be done."

I wince. Jason works like a dog, especially now that he's between Texas and New York. "Just a few more months. And the office space you picked out is great."

He gives me a real smile. "Thanks."

I turn to Andrew. "You box? Jason told Miles he was bringing someone who could actually fight. I'm tired of kicking their asses every time we spar."

Andrew shrugs, grinning, and starts to wrap his hands. "For fun. I learned in college. I don't know that I'm good enough to beat anyone. But Jason said you were itching for a real fight."

Jason is a mind reader. We've always been more aligned in our moods than Miles and me, even though Miles is my best friend and business partner.

Speaking of the devil, he swings in the door, dressed in all black and looking murderous.

"Let's do this." He tosses his bag in the corner and starts stripping off his outer layers.

"What's eating you?" Jason asks.

"Lane. She won't stop trying to give me back the Montauk house." Miles gifted his girlfriend his family home in some sort of insane bid to win her over. "I told her I don't want the damn house. She's making me talk to an estate planning lawyer tomorrow. I should just marry her and then everyone can have the fucking house." He tosses his coat on the ground, and Jason starts laughing.

Andrew looks at us with wide eyes, like he's walked into a den of lunatics. "I thought this was *your* fight night."

I smile, baring my teeth. "Everyone's grievances are welcome at fight night. Let's do this."

We glove up, and then Andrew and I step into the ring. He's taller than me by an inch or two, with long arms and the muscle of someone who works out a lot. He guards his face like he's done this before.

"Careful there. He's being modest but he spars at a boxing gym all the time." This from Jason.

"Ready?" I bring up my guard.

Andrew grins, nods his head, and comes at me with a swift jab-cross that outdoes anything Jason or Miles could throw. I roll back, but barely, and come back with an uppercut, pulling it at the last minute so he doesn't get hurt.

"What the hell?" Andrew looks annoyed that I didn't hit him.

"No hits above the chin," I explain.

I'm light on my feet as we fight, a flurry of fists and bobbing heads. A left hook slams into Andrew's ribs, followed by a powerful cross that hits me in the collarbone.

"Fuck." I disengage and shake myself out.

"You good?" Andrew is panting slightly.

"Yeah." I give him a sharp grin. "You're not bad."

"You holding back?" He raises his eyebrows.

"Little bit." I crack my neck. I'm itching for a real fight today.

"Let me have a try." Miles hoists himself up and ducks under the ropes. He's a bit broader than Andrew, but his arms are shorter. I know his reach. I can beat the crap out of Miles on a good day.

"You sure?"

"Yep." He gives me a dark look, and Andrew steps out of the ring. "What's eating you?" He circles me, guard up. "That text you sent. Sounds like you really needed a distraction." He means the one where I practically begged for my friends to beat me up.

He feints the jab and I dance back. "I do. It's Callie."

"I knew it," Jason crows. "I fucking knew it."

Miles's eyes hold mine while he tries to read me. "What's going on with her?" He comes at me with a quick jab-cross, followed by a left hook. I duck and his final punch glances off my ribs. I hammer a hook of my own into his side, and we break apart, breathing hard.

"She stayed over last night." *And we had the best sex of my life. And I kissed her. I liked it and I think I want more.*

"She did?" Miles's brows go up. "Wait, you slept with her? Hold on." He stops, lowering his hands.

I nod, not sure how he's going to react.

"I can't believe it." He shakes his head. "After all your going on about how she's a reporter, an employee, and now you're sleeping with her?"

I scowl. "If you're going to make fun of me—"

"No." He bends over, a soft laugh gusting out of him. "No. I think it's great. I'm just surprised."

"Was it hot?" This from Jason.

"Of course it was hot." Miles grins. "Look at him. He's obsessed with her." He starts laughing.

"I am not. How can you even tell?"

"You're practically begging me to punch you in the face so you stop thinking about her." Miles keeps laughing.

"Well, you're doing a shit job of it," I growl. Jason starts laughing too.

"Oh no. I'm not getting goaded by you," Miles says, as he shakes his head. "What are you going to do about it?"

"I came here to fight, not talk about my feelings."

"Classic avoidance tactic," Jason says. "Ask me how I know."

"So?" Miles raises a brow. "Where did you leave things?"

"Nowhere. We left them nowhere. I asked to be invited up to her apartment, and she declined. Now hit me."

Miles shrugs and comes at me with a right hook. He's right-handed so it's the most powerful punch he can throw, and I don't dodge in time. The impact has me doubling over with pain, gasping for air.

"That's more like it." My voice comes out strangled. I blow out a breath. "I think I like her." I raise my head to see Miles giving me a knowing smile.

"You're not sure?"

"I don't do this," I say shortly. I bring my hands up, and he does too, and then I come for him with a jab-cross-left hook combination that he manages to block, before tapping me gently with an uppercut to the chin.

"You don't do what? Feelings? Relationships?"

He's going to make me say it, that prick. "Love. I don't do love."

His head jerks. "Who said anything about love?" He leans back against the ropes. Jason is watching us with calculating eyes, seeing too much.

"I could fall for her. And I don't want to."

"It's worth it," Jason volunteers. Andrew is nodding next to him. "You know I didn't want love, and it's the best thing that's ever happened to me."

My insides are a tangled knot as I glance between my friends. "Your priorities change, though. I can't deal with that." I go to run a hand through my hair, then remember the glove.

"They change for the better." Andrew's voice is confident, knowing. "Change isn't always bad."

I look back at Miles, the one of our little group who has always been the steadiest. "I agree." He considers me for a moment, those clear gray eyes seeing straight into me. "I say go for it."

"I do too." Jason is looking at me with sympathy. He and I are so similar. *Do I trust him? Do I trust Callie not to betray me?*

"Be sure." This from Andrew, who might be more level-headed than both of my insane friends. "Go for it. But be sure. Otherwise you'll hurt her."

My chest seizes at the thought of hurting Callie more than I already have. *Be sure.* But I'm not sure. The only constants in my life are my work and my revenge. What would it look like to add a third constant to that? *It could be so good.*

"Come on." Miles claps me on the shoulder. "Let's show Andrew the bar downstairs."

"You promised me a fight," Andrew says lightly. "I barely got bruised."

"Yeah, well now Margo won't yell at you," Jason says.

"Oh no, she doesn't yell. She'd just kiss my bruises and bandage me up." His tone makes it clear that more than just kissing is happening. Jason and he laugh as we pack our bags.

I want that. I want Callie's soft hands on me, skimming over my skin. She'd be serious about the bandaging, I know she would. I'd have to coax her to stop worrying about me. Fuck, that could be fun. We ride the elevator down and I'm halfway to pulling out my phone and texting her to meet me. *Be sure.* I put it away before I dive head-first into something stupid.

"Are you sure we can go in there like this?" Andrew asks, when we reach the interior door that leads into the bar.

"Most definitely." Miles grins. "You'll see."

"It's good to be them," Jason adds.

We nod at the bartender, Matt, as we pass through the bar. Heads turn in our direction. My skin prickles with discomfort at the attention, and I tuck my chin into my hoodie.

"What's with all the staring?" Andrew asks. We push open the door in the back of the bar and into the plush space of the back room. Andrew lets out a surprised breath when the wall sconces light up, illuminating the massive wood and velvet table and chairs.

"They're famous," Jason says shortly. "It gets old really fast."

Miles snorts. "Tell me about it. The paparazzi have been hounding Lane ever since our relationship went public."

My jaw clenches. "Fucking photographers."

Jason slides me a look as we sink into the seats. A bottle of whiskey and four glasses are already on the table, along with sparkling water and bar snacks. "Isn't Callie one of them?"

"Yep." I pour a finger of whiskey and knock it back.

"Bit of a conflict of interest, don't you think?" This from Andrew, who is pouring himself some water. Jason mentioned that Andrew doesn't drink much. Must be nice. I intend to get drunk enough to stop my thoughts from running toward Callie every two minutes.

"I hate it," I say in a low voice. Even though I know why she did it, and I understand her reasons. They're the same as my own motivations––protecting my family. Guilt and anger and sympathy are an unsettling combination. Maybe liquor can help with that too.

"Jonah has some ah, hang-ups, when it comes to reporters and paparazzi," Jason adds. That's putting it mildly. But I'm grateful that no one asks me to elaborate.

"You think she'd ever give it up?" Miles asks.

I think back to the passion in her voice when she talked about the changes she wanted to make to the paper, the way she fiercely defended it all the times I derided her.

"No." I turn my glass in my hands, watching the amber liquid sparkle in the dim lighting. "She loves it too much. She would never give it up. Even though it's failing, she'll do anything to save it." *Even sell herself to me.* The guilt is back. I knock back more liquor.

"Oof." Andrew winces. "That's tough."

Understatement of the year. Uncertainty spirals through me, along with Andrew's words from earlier. *Be sure.* I'm not fucking sure. I've never been less sure. I'd rather get roaring drunk and not think about Callie anymore.

"Enough about me. Miles, tell me what's going on with Lane and the house," I say.

He pinches the bridge of his nose. "She's too damn noble." He looks pained. "She claims I'm always sacrificing for everyone, and she doesn't want to take the house away from me. I want her to have the house. In case I'm not there one day."

"You're so whipped."

"Shit, I guess so. This is ridiculous." He sounds so irritated that I have to laugh.

I'm happy for him, but do I want the same thing?

∼

Two hours later, I'm holed up in my office. Miles tried to convince me to go home, but the term sheet for a meeting on Monday needs my review. And I didn't want to go home to my empty house, anyway.

My eyes flick to my phone, like they have been every few minutes since I got upstairs. I could text her. The whiskey is making me bold and careless. *Be sure.* I'm not sure, but I need her. I can be sure next week. I've known her for a fucking month. Why do I need to decide if I want to spend my life with her? My friends are idiots. I shake my head. Fuck it. I'm not even sure what I'm going to do when she gets here. I just want to be near her.

The decision sends anticipation fizzing through my blood. I pick up my phone and tap out a message. One simple sentence that should have her running, but not for the reasons she thinks.

JONAH
I need you at the office.

40

Callie

Jonah's message has me scrambling for my jacket.

> **JONAH**
> I need you at the office.

What game is he playing? Does he need me to do work? Ten p.m. on a Sunday doesn't seem unusual for him. Am I still at his beck and call? If I'm not, does that mean *this* is becoming something else?

I shout a goodbye to my dad, who I've mostly been avoiding since our fight, and run down the steps of our apartment.

> **CALLIE**
> I'm on my way. But I have to take the subway, so it'll take a bit.

The trains on the weekends are notoriously slow, even though it should be a straight shot and a brief walk to the office.

He sends back a message not a moment later.

> **JONAH**
> In the future, Lou will pick you up.

He sends Lou's number to me.

High-handed, imperious, demanding. I fucking love it. His clipped tone would have annoyed me a month ago, but now it sends warmth tingling through me, curling up through my chest. Jonah has lodged himself firmly behind my ribs. His protectiveness and his sharp humor are a warm ache. I text back when I'm on the train.

> **CALLIE**
> Bossy.

> **JONAH**
> Hurry up, Thompson.

I can practically hear him growling the words and I smile to myself in the crowded car. The subway is busy with stragglers who were out enjoying one of the last warm weekends before fall turns from crisp to cold. Even on a Sunday night, people are weird and wonderful here. *I fucking love New York.* And here I am, going to meet my boss at the office. I feel like I have a delicious secret.

The hallways are dark when I arrive, but Jonah's door is open, golden light spilling out. The office is creepy at night, and I rush toward his door. I come to a stop in the doorway, taking him in. Black sweatshirt, hood up, silky black shorts riding high on his thighs. He's lounging in the chair like a king in his kingdom, legs sprawled, eyes hooded. A tumbler of whiskey is in his hand, a bottle sitting on the desk.

"Hi." My pulse speeds at the way his dark gaze rakes over me. "You needed something?"

"You," he says roughly. "Come here."

Anticipation is a rush of blood to my head. I shed my coat, loving the way he watches me from his seat.

"You called me here for sex? That seems unlike you." I walk

toward him, feeling confident and sexy under his gaze in a way I never did with my ex.

"Not sex." His eyes flare as I stand in front of him. "I just wanted to see you."

Something funny worms its way into my chest. "Yeah?" My lips curve up. "What have you been doing? Why are you here?"

He sets his whiskey on the desk and tugs me onto his lap. The chair is big enough for both of us, with my knees around his hips, my skirt hiked up around my waist, his nose almost touching mine. And damn, I know he didn't call me here for sex, but his thin shorts hide nothing and his cock is already half-hard under me. I want to wiggle down onto him and hear his breath hitch, but his hand on my hip stops me.

"I was trying to review something. We had fight night earlier. And I drank a fair amount of whiskey."

"Only you would work drunk." I shake my head. "And fight night? What's that?"

"It's a tradition Theo invented. When one of us has something on our minds, we box. Fight night." He says it like it's perfectly normal.

"You're deranged," I whisper. I run my fingers through his hair, and his lids drop closed. His hair is silky-soft, thick and waving. "Did you win?"

"Not sure." He lets out a soft groan as my nails scratch his scalp.

"That seems unlike you as well. You always know who comes out ahead."

"Hmm." His mouth curves up at the side. "You know me so well, Thompson. How?"

"I've watched you for a long time," I say softly. "I know you hate it." Before he can respond and I can be hurt by his comment, I run a finger along his jaw. "What's this?" Dried blood on his skin, a small cut.

"Hmm?" He sounds half-asleep, his eyes shut, his breaths even.

"You have a cut."

"Oh, that. Andrew clipped me in the jaw. He's new. Kept forgetting we're not allowed to punch above the neck. You're responsible for that rule, by the way."

"I am?"

"Yeah." He smiles faintly. I've never seen him smile so much and it does something funny to my stomach. "Do you remember taking a photo of me with a black eye?"

I groan. "That was from fight night?" Embarrassment courses through me. I took a bunch of photos of Jonah that morning, with his ball cap pulled low, his bruise a spectacular color that matched the faded purple-blue fabric of his hat. I implied all manner of things about him in that article, speculating he got into a bar fight, or worse.

"Yeah." His eyes open, still hazy and half-lidded. "We decided it was best to keep things secret after that. Wouldn't want the paparazzi in our business." He squeezes my hip, a warning maybe, or affection. Hard to tell.

"Let me bandage you up."

"It's small, Thompson. I'm fine."

"I want to help you." My fingers trail over his jaw. His skin is soft and stubbled, scented like citrus body products and sweat. If I licked him, he would taste delicious. I shiver slightly, before I clamber off his lap. "Consider it my apology for the photos and the article."

"First aid kit is in the bathroom."

"You have a bathroom in your office?" He nods, gesturing at a handle that I assumed was for a cabinet, but no, the wood panel opens into a hidden bathroom, complete with a massive shower, a changing area, a toilet, and a sink.

"Damn. It's good to be you."

"It is." He grins at me lazily, watching me still. "Get back here."

"Relax, Your Majesty." I resettle myself on his lap, and he sighs slightly. Content, I think. Like a lion after a big meal.

I rip open the antiseptic packet and press it to his jaw with no warning.

He hisses a curse. "Little warning next time?"

"I seem to remember you enjoying doing this to me," I tease. I swipe the pad over his skin, cleaning his cut.

He laughs softly. "Don't torment me, Thompson. It turns me on." As if agreeing, his erection jerks against my leg. "See?"

I smile and set the used pad on his desk. "I thought you said no sex while you were drunk."

He groans softly and runs a hand up my thigh, fingers playing along the edge of my lace underwear. His hand is warm and rough. "I did say that, didn't I?"

"What about other things?"

His sharp intake of air tells me that he likes the idea of other things very much.

"What other things?" His eyes are sharp and hungry, no longer lazy and satisfied. His desire makes me bold, like a woman I don't recognize. I like who I am in his eyes. His equal, respected, a woman to be feared and desired.

"Do you remember that first day in your office?" I slip my fingers under his hoodie to find him bare-chested. Hot skin, all muscle. "You asked me where I went?"

"Yes. Your eyes had this look in them." His breath hitches as I trace the hair on his stomach that leads into his shorts. "Like you were picturing something delicious."

"I was," I murmur, tugging at his waistband. "I was wondering what it would be like to get on me knees under your desk and take you in my mouth."

He makes a choked sound, his lids dropping. "Fuck. If I'd known —" His words cut off as I run a hand up his erection and climb off his lap. He lifts his hips to let me pull off his shorts, and then he pulls off his sweatshirt with one hand, his abs and arms flexing in one sinuous motion.

My breath comes a little faster as I take him in. Lean lines, not an ounce of fat, powerful shoulders, those arms that held me against the wall while he fucked me. A perfect cock, thick, long, hard against his thigh.

"I love the way you look at me."

I smile and pull off my sweater, my skirt, my boots, while he watches, until I'm just in my black lace underwear.

"All of it," he says, eyes hungry. "I want it all off while you suck me."

That voice. Like sin. I strip off my underwear and kneel in front of him. My pulse is already throbbing between my legs, demanding more. I ignore it as Jonah pushes his hips to the edge of the chair so I can take him in my mouth. The instant the flared head of his cock meets my lips, he makes a low noise. The sound arrows straight to my core. His insistent desire pulls my own to the surface.

I twine my tongue over the head, reveling in the taste of him, salt and musk, and the feel of him, silky skin, hot and smooth. I take him as deep as I can and he groans again. *I love this.* Driving him crazy is a new high. He likes hitting the back of my throat, I think, so I keep doing it, again and again, my hands slick with spit, the salty taste of pre-come in my mouth. His hoarse breaths mingle with the sounds of his cock sliding through my hands. His fingers are digging into the chair, his chest is rising and falling in soft pants. When I raise my head, his eyes are slumberous with desire. I keep eye contact with him as I suck him into my mouth again and his eyes flare wide.

"Fuck, Callie." His voice is a ragged whisper. His hand spears into my hair. I lave my tongue over the head of his cock and his hips lift. He's swelling, jerking in my mouth. "I'm close, but I need you to tell me what you enjoy." He shuts his eyes briefly, face twisting with pleasure. "I need to know that you like this. Are you wet?"

I press a single finger between my legs and moan at the contact. His own need has ratcheted mine up higher than I thought possible.

"Let me taste."

I lift my hand, and his lips close over it, warm and firm. A rumble of enjoyment comes from his chest, and I press my thighs together. His face is slack with desire at the taste of me.

His tongue twines over my fingers, and I mirror the movement on his cock. His hips are jerking now. He's close, so close, but I need to push him over the edge. *I crave your pleasure.* More than his own. I let him pop out of my mouth, smack against his stomach. I delve both hands between my legs, feeling bolder than I ever have before. But something in me wants to please him. I flick my fingers over my clit, already close. I'm slippery and swollen, and watching Jonah watch me is a whole new level of hot.

His face looks pained, his hands clenched. I moan, riding my hand, my stomach tightening.

"Fuck it," Jonah growls. In one smooth motion, he surges out of the chair, pins me to the floor, and drags his cock through my folds. My body jolts, my hips buck. He fists his cock and enters me in a long stroke that has sparks arcing through me.

He plants his hands on either side of my head and kisses me, long and deep, before rolling his hips into me in hard thrusts. I'm moving across the floor, the rug abrading my back, and I don't care. I claw at the parts of him I can touch—his hands on my hips, his veined forearms.

The orgasm is waiting for me, the highest peak of a precipice and a delicious fall.

"Jonah, I—" I gasp as he strokes into me.

"I know." His words are rough. "I'm close too. Give me your pleasure. All of it." He circles my clit with one finger, and I rocket up the mountain and off the precipice faster than I thought was possible. My eyes are shut, my body is straining. Through the haze, I hear Jonah muttering soft curses, trying not to come.

"I can't last." He chokes out the words, his thrusts turning messy and helpless. "I want you to come again."

"I will," I pant. "Touch me." I never would have demanded that before Jonah, but with him, everything is different. He obeys with those clever fingers, his face screwed tight, his muscles straining.

"Callie," he groans, shaking. I'm right there with him. I'm warm and glowing, and so very close.

"Jonah," I whisper. The orgasm spreads through me, slower, growing in intensity, until it shakes me like a thunderstorm.

"Thank fuck," he mutters, before his cock jerks inside me and he gives a hoarse shout.

I have the presence of mind to open my eyes.

Watching Jonah Crown come has to be the hottest thing I've ever seen.

Muscles stand out in stark relief, his head is thrown back, his lips parted. Like some sort of feral god. At least until he slumps over me and kisses my stomach, nuzzles through the hair between my legs, and licks into me like I'm precious. "One more," he murmurs. "One more."

I'm spent, but the touch of his tongue on my clit makes me buzz.

"I can taste myself on you. I love it." His voice is low, tugging at my insides, his dirty words raw and honest. And so he does the impossible, drawing a final gasp of pleasure from me with the flat of his tongue, his fingers, even his teeth, until I sob his name and clench around his fingers for a final time.

"Good girl, Cal," he murmurs. I want to bask in the warm feeling his words evoke. I'm floating in a sea of afterglow, hazy, disconnected. I barely notice that he's lifting me from the floor, carrying me to the shower, until warm water is cascading over us. He settles me between his legs and washes me with gentle strokes while my head rests on his chest.

"So you didn't call me here for sex?" I tease. His chest is a slick wall of muscle at my back, warm and steadfast. I never want this to stop.

"No. I can't resist you." He sounds annoyed at himself, and I smile.

"Why did you call me then?" I yawn and curl in closer to him. I could totally fall asleep like this.

"I told you. I wanted to see you. I drank something like seven glasses of whiskey and texted you. Don't read too much into it."

I laugh softly. "Yes, Your Majesty." I'm not reading into it but that warm ache is there behind my ribs. I'm the person Jonah Crown texts when he's drunk.

He doesn't speak for several minutes. His hand smooths over my arms, my sides, until I'm floating between awake and asleep.

"What did you have to look forward to today?" he finally asks.

"Adriana got a puppy. I took it for a walk this morning in the park. But other than that, I avoided my dad."

He makes a hmm sound in his throat for me to continue.

"We got into a fight after I came home from your apartment. He's so stubborn. He asked me where I was, and it turned into me accusing him of treating me like a child. We already clash over the paper. Living there is not helping." I blow out a breath.

"Can you move out?" His hands keep rubbing my arms, soothing me. His voice is a rumble at my back, his skin is slick and warm, and I never want to leave.

"I don't have the money. I've been saving, but I used my savings to pay off a third of the loan. A day before we found out you wanted to invest." His hands still. "I'll keep saving, though. I'm not a big spender." I shut my eyes and press my cheek to his chest. "Keep going, please."

"You'll have your first paycheck next week," he says roughly.

I still. "You're paying me?" This feels like a turning point. "When did you decide to pay me?"

"When I saw the apartment."

I cringe. "I wish you hadn't."

"Why?" He soaps over my shoulders, kneading the muscles until my head falls back. "What's wrong with your apartment? It told me more about you. And I got to chat with your dad." He makes a considering sound. "It was a little weird that he didn't ask why I was there."

"He's just...not that kind of dad," I finish lamely.

"Explain." Jonah's voice is hard.

"He's not a worrier." I sigh. "He never has been. Most dads would have oiled the shotgun the very first time Eric was photographed with his arm around another woman."

"Fucking Eric," Jonah bites out.

"Yeah." I sigh. "That's just my dad. I love him, but living with him isn't easy."

"You'll be a millionaire soon. You can move." Jonah presses his fingers to the sides of my neck and strokes. I sigh at the delicious strength of his hands, at the way he's caring for me.

"That's not apartment money. My dad doesn't have any retirement savings, and who knows what will happen to the paper?"

"You should be more selfish." His voice has an edge to it, like he's annoyed.

"You sound like my friends."

"They sound intelligent," he grumbles. "No sense of self-preservation. That's you."

"You can bother me tomorrow about it." I yawn.

He lathers my hair with strong fingers. The shampoo smells like him. Citrus and eucalyptus. Manly, expensive. He scratches his nails over my scalp and I moan.

"I'm going to smell like you tomorrow."

His lips brush over my pulse, his breaths steady in my ear. "I know. Is it fucked up that I like it?"

"Possessive," I murmur.

"I told you, Thompson. I don't share."

"What does that mean?"

His arm tightens on my stomach. "All your pleasure is mine. No touching yourself, and definitely no touching others. No more dates." He spits the word. "Understood?"

You're mine. His words from the other day echo in my head. And instead of being alarmed, like I definitely should be, I smile and nod my head.

41

Callie

On Tuesday, Jonah tells me I'll finally get a chance to spar with him.

"I've been waiting for this." I grin at him and he raises a haughty brow.

"You think I'm going to go easy on you?" His voice is arrogant, as usual. Jonah might soften sometimes for me, but he is still so unabashedly himself. *I love it.* I loved the anger in his voice last night when he told me I needed to be more selfish. He's selfish. And I think he would be selfish for me too, if I let him. His cold exterior is better than any nice guy.

I smile at him and his eyes widen before they narrow on me. The planes of his face are brutal in the overhead lights of the ring, but he's handsome. So unbearably handsome. I want to trace his face with my fingers, not punch it.

I take a step forward to do just that, but he barks, "In the ring."

I clamber in, under the ropes, and Jonah follows me. He drops his gloves on the ground and pulls off his sweatshirt.

"Not fair," I breathe. My eyes roam his body. I may never get tired of looking at it. Golden skin, that vee of muscles leading in to his shorts.

"What's wrong, Thompson? Distracting you?"

"Do you have to be naked to box?"

"No. But if you want me to be—" He tugs at the waistband of his shorts, and I make a horrified sound. He smirks.

"No." I shake my head. "I want a fighting chance. Which means—" I pull off my own gloves and shirt, until I'm standing before him in the hot pink bra that matches my leggings. "Ready." I give him a winning smile, but he doesn't even see it. No, he's too busy cataloging every part of my body with his eyes. *Ha.*

"What do I get if I win?" I'm securing my gloves, ready to fight.

His head jerks up, his eyes dark with desire. "You're not going to win."

"Give a girl something to fight for."

He considers me. "Okay. If you can get one punch in, I'll tell you a secret." *A secret.* My very favorite thing. Jonah knows exactly how to tempt me.

"Oh, I like that. And if you win, I'll tell you one." I wink at him, before we bump fists and move to the center of the ring.

"Guard up. I'm not going to punch you, but you should be ready for anything. Like a real fight."

I raise my hands obediently, keeping my knees bent, trying to move like Jonah showed me. I go for a jab, but he dances away.

"Again," he says. "Use the jab to keep me at arm's length. Otherwise—" He steps in close and before I can react, kisses my neck. "You're dead." His eyes are sparkling when he darts back.

I stick out my tongue, but extend my left arm, using it to keep him away. "Good. Now come in for the cross. Right in the face. Come on." He's eager for this, and suddenly I see why he does fight night. He's alive in the ring, electric in a way he isn't in meetings. I go for a cross, trying to carry through on my hip, the way he showed me. He pulls back easily, just a quick pop of his hips.

"Come on, Thompson." He beckons. "You hit like a girl."

"Ooh. You didn't." I narrow my eyes and go for another jab-cross combination. He ducks, and irritation flares.

Twenty minutes later, I still haven't landed a punch and Jonah is barely breathing hard. I, however, am a sweat-slicked mess. My face is hot, my hair is frizzing out of its bun. Jonah's skin glistens with a light sheen of sweat, from ducking and dancing away from every punch.

"You're very annoying," I say, panting slightly. "Was this your signature move in the ring? Just annoying people to death?"

"You want to see my signature moves?"

"Anything to end the humiliation."

"Let's go." He swings out of the ring and heads to the heavy bag. "Watch. Speed, then power. When I hold my hand out like this—" He demonstrates. "It's called a post. I have long arms. Not as long as Jason's friend Andrew, but pretty long. I can keep an opponent at a distance, then use my speed to go in when they least expect it." His words are matter of fact, not bragging. But then he lifts his hands and lunges at the bag so hard it shudders on its chains.

"Damn," I breathe.

"Yeah." Now the look on his face is a little cocky. "Again."

I'm fired up now from watching him box, but I'm distracted. Sweat is sliding down his body, and it's practically pornographic. After a particularly inelegant lunge toward him, I bend over to catch my breath. Jonah lounges against the ropes.

"You should box again," I say between panting breaths.

He doesn't respond, and when I look up, his face is shuttered. "You should," I press. "You love it. I've never seen you like this."

"Like what?" he bites out.

He's not going to like this, but I need to say it anyway. "Alive. You're so alive. You told me you missed it."

"Billionaires don't box," he says shortly, looking away.

"Oh, come on." I roll my eyes. "Miles has his surfing. Theo has something, I'm sure. Lots of your competitors have hobbies."

"Rich person hobbies," he bites out. "When I boxed, it wasn't pretty. I boxed for money. I boxed in underground fighting rings. Yes, there were sanctioned competitions, but most of the time, there was no glory. Just blood, sweat, and shouting."

I shiver at the thought of Jonah there amid the dirt and sweat and bodies. The image is primal and terrifying. "I bet you came out on top, though."

"Yes," he says shortly. "I did. I was the best for a long time."

"Of course you were," I murmur. His eyes cut to mine, his gaze questioning. "Come on." I wave my hand in the air. "You have to know that you're terrifyingly competent."

His mouth hitches up. "Scared of me, Thompson?" He prowls forward, each muscle graceful and lean.

"Never." I tip my chin up and put a glove out to stop him. "Don't distract me. I want you to try it again, okay? For me."

He pushes my glove aside and gets in my space. He's a seething god on the outside, and the best man I know on the inside. Where others see anger, I see loyalty. What might be perceived as coldness, I recognize is protectiveness. Of himself, of others.

"For you?" He dips his head so his lips hover over mine. "I'll think about it, for you."

I shiver and arch into him at the contact. He's damp skin, hard muscle, and harsh beauty. I want to bury my face in his neck and breathe him in forever. He presses his lips to mine, and I sigh into his mouth, until I pull my hand back and punch him in the side.

He grunts, and his head jerks back, before he laughs and kisses me again.

"Good one." He winks. "Come on. Let's stretch."

We flop onto the mat and I sigh. "This is the best part."

He laughs. "The stretching? Yeah?"

"Totally. I feel very relaxed. Must be all the endorphins. I know it's not all the yelling."

"Heaven forbid your boss tell you what to do," he murmurs, but his lips are curled up at the sides. Despite himself, I'm pretty sure Jonah Crown likes hanging out with me.

42

Jonah

Fuck, she's pretty. All bright smiles and humor, even when she's pretending to hate sparring with me.

"A secret for a secret," I say. I want to know more about Callie, even though this wasn't the deal.

"Secret. Hmm." She bends over her leg, giving me an eyeful of her round breasts. My skin prickles. I'm getting addicted to her. Last night I wanted to text her again, and barely restrained myself.

"Did you know I was in a music video once?"

My brows go up. "What kind of video?"

"Oh no." She laughs. "Not like that. Some guy I went to college with recorded an album, and he needed backup singers. It was fun. My fifteen minutes of fame."

"I would have thought you hated being in front of the camera."

She startles, her head jerking up to meet my gaze. "Yeah. Now I would. I wasn't always shy. I guess Eric did that to me."

Anger heats my insides. She's only given me crumbs of information about her ex, but it sounds like he did a number on her.

"Was it just that night at the party, or is there more to that story?"

I ask the question carefully, even though I want to spring up and find Eric right this second.

Her shoulders sag a little. "It's pretty obvious, right? He was the worst."

"It's a little obvious. If you're paying attention."

"You always are. I like that about you." She gives me a half smile. "He talked down to me a lot. I think he felt inferior, since he didn't have much direction in life. And it wasn't reserved for just me. He said mean things about a lot of people. But he never wanted me to steal the spotlight from him, so he used to say I was better behind the camera and not in the spotlight. At a certain point, you start to believe it." She shrugs, like it doesn't get to her, but anger fills me to bursting.

My emotions must show on my face, because she says, "What?" Her eyes are wide.

"The offer stands. Say the word and I'll take him down." My voice is rough. I'm trying not to scare her.

"Thank you. But I just want to forget about him. He doesn't deserve my attention."

"He doesn't," I say viciously.

"What about you?" she asks. "Any horrible exes in your past?"

I freeze. "Other than Annalise?"

"Was she horrible?" Callie looks up at me from under her lashes as she leans over her other leg.

"Certifiably awful," I confirm. I should tell Callie about the photos that were leaked, the texts, but I can't. *I can't.* I've never felt weaker than I did after Annalise. "She's the reason I don't date."

"Ever?"

I shrug, but my shoulders are tight. "Ever. I do one night stands here and there, but mostly, I work." The words sound pathetic as I say them, and I wait for her to judge me, to tell me to get out more, like Lane and Miles always do.

"Me too." She gives me a half smile. "I'm mostly working. Especially after Eric. I told myself I'd focus more on the things that mattered to me. Like the paper."

Fuck. I hate that it's the paper. I hate that this woman who sees me so clearly is the last person I can have. Because I want her. The need for her makes me dizzy. *Just one more week.* One more time in bed with her, then I'll... What? *Cut her out of my life?* Fuck.

"You understand me," I say, my voice gravel.

"Yeah, well, you do work a lot." Her mouth tips up. "More than I thought possible."

"I need to be on top. It's the only way."

"But you are now." Her brow wrinkles in confusion.

I slant her a look. "I'm what? At the top? No, I'm not."

"Looks that way to me," she says lightly.

I frown. "I guess I could see why you think that. Miles is certainly satisfied with what we have, and Theo, well, I'm not sure he's ever been that focused on business, but no. There are so many competitors. Dylan is personal, but we have whole swathes of the market that are waiting for us. There's always more to do." I shake my head. There's a pit in my stomach every time I think about how much more we have to achieve. A pit that threatens to swallow me on lonely nights, but also a fire that keeps me going.

"Why?" she asks. "I mean other than the obvious. Money, power, etcetera. You're swimming in those. So why?"

I shove off the floor to grab a foam roller from the corner. I can't be still for this.

"It's the only way to protect my family. You understand that, I think." When I finally look at her, her face is soft and open. "I brought Dylan to their doorstep. It was my fault." My voice comes out choked, and fuck, it's like this every time I think of the past.

My hand clenches on the foam roller so hard that the nubs dig painfully into my skin.

"It wasn't your fault," she says quietly, but forcefully. "You couldn't have known what he would do."

"I brought him close to them. I was the one who told him my sister's secret. I betrayed her trust. I ignored all the signs that he wasn't the person I became friends with. I ignored the jealousy. It's my fault that he had the ammunition he had to hurt my family. He'll never have that ammunition again. No one will. Look at me now. No one would dare touch what's mine. The only way I can protect them is by being the best. The biggest business, the most ruthless competitor, the richest man." My chest is tight at the memories.

She shakes her head. "You're punishing yourself."

"Maybe I am." I sigh. "I can be hard, Cal. Intense. I think you know that." My throat works while I stare down at her, those lake blue eyes of hers seeing everything.

"Oh, I know." Her lips curve. "You're a right asshole when you want to be."

A smile tugs at my mouth. "You've seen me at my worst."

"And I still like you." She bites her lip. Warmth blooms in my chest at her admission, and the soft way she's looking at me, even as my rational brain tells her to stop. *I'm not made for liking.* I'm going to break her heart if this continues.

"Do you want a secret of mine?" I want her to smile again.

"Oh yes." Those blue eyes sparkle with anticipation.

"This one can't go in the paper, Thompson. Understood?"

"Yes, boss." She nods solemnly.

"I used to ride a motorcycle."

"What?" she chokes out and then flops onto her back. "You've done it. You killed me. I've officially expired."

I nudge her with my toe.

"Leave me alone." She shuts her eyes. "I'm picturing you shirtless on a motorcycle. I can die happy."

"I most definitely did not ride it shirtless. That's a great way to get injured. Road burn is not pretty."

"Shut it." Her full lips are curved up, like this is the best fantasy she's ever entertained. "So when did you stop?"

"Years ago. It didn't really fit with the personality I tried to cultivate." *Why am I being so honest with her?* Even Miles doesn't know about the motorcycle. "I was very different at nineteen."

"What were you like? I can't picture it. In fact, I assumed you were born wearing a bespoke suit."

I grin. "I wore a chain in high school."

"No way." She sits up. "A chain?"

"Oh yes. I wore a chain, I had a thick New Jersey accent, and I thought J. Crew button-downs were fancy."

"Heaven forbid." She's smiling though. "Did you take your girls on dates to Olive Garden?"

"You know, I think I did. But only if I really wanted to impress her."

She starts laughing and my chest warms. I don't talk about my past. Christine says I'm ashamed of my roots, but it's not that simple. I'd rather just pretend it never happened. The man I am today is respected, feared. The boy I was then had no idea what the world held. Naïve and overly confident. The worst combination.

"When did you get rid of it?"

"I didn't." I wink. Callie's mouth forms an O and I want to kiss her. And then, even though I haven't been on it in years, and I must truly be losing my mind, I say, "If you're a good girl, I'll let you ride it."

∽

ON WEDNESDAY, Callie tells me that the first batch of documents from our FOIA request has been received.

"We need to start going through them." She's tapping her pen against her lips while I lounge on the couch next to her.

"Hmm?" She's stunning today. Her dark hair is up and her dress is a deep navy that brings out the color of her eyes. It's definitely not work appropriate, like all of her outfits, which makes it my favorite.

"Are you listening?"

"I'm fantasizing about peeling that dress off you and seeing how many orgasms I can get out of you before my next meeting."

Her jaw drops, and her cheeks go pink.

"Focus." She pokes me in the thigh.

"Poke me again, Thompson," I growl. "See what happens."

"I need to start combing through the documents. I just need to figure out where to start." She flips pages. "When I'm doing this for the paper, I usually start with the most personal stuff, but this is business." She makes a thoughtful sound.

My stomach sours a little at the mention of her work. I try not to think about it, but it's always there. *Be sure.* Andrew's words echo in my head. I'm still not sure, and she's not asking, so limbo is where we'll be. A limbo in which I think about her constantly and fantasize about her in my free time, and even during meetings.

She heads for her desk and I head to my meeting, and for the first time in years, I'm bored. I'm never bored. Boredom is for people who are too stupid to take interest in the world around them. I can't fathom boredom. And yet, as I negotiate against this investor, with only half my brain, the other half wonders what Callie is having for lunch, whether she might want to go to a concert that Christine keeps badgering me about. *The baby shower.* The thought pops into my head. I will it away. But it keeps coming back. I could take Callie. She would love Christine. She'd have fun. She'd make it halfway bearable for me to pretend to like tiny cupcakes and small talk.

But if I take her, I'll never hear the end of it. My mom will assume we're dating, and Mia will make inappropriate comments at my expense. My grandma will ask me every Sunday for two years when that *nice girl* is coming back for dinner.

Be sure. Fuck.

43

Callie

"I'm here," Luz trills. "And I want all the details." She bursts into the wine bar that Thursday, the wind gusting in behind her as the door opens. The space is cozy with small groups of friends, the windows fogged up from conversations around us.

"Finally." Adriana shimmies in her seat. "An emergency meeting. Spill." She gives me a direct look.

In answer I slide my phone to my friends. On the screen are Jonah's messages.

> **JONAH**
> I need you at an event next weekend.
>
> Not like last time.

The message is from hours ago, but I still haven't responded. Adriana looks at me with knowing eyes. I slept at her apartment that night after Eric and I broke up. "What does he mean by not like last time?"

I take a healthy gulp of white wine to fortify myself, the slide of cool liquid down my throat unsticking my tongue. "He means last time when he took me to an event. I showed up looking like I'd been dragged across the island of Manhattan by my hair. And I had a panic attack." I fiddle with my napkin, not wanting to meet my friends' eyes. "He did it intentionally. He wanted to embarrass me."

"That prick," Adriana says in a low voice.

"But he apologized. He begged for my forgiveness actually. On his knees."

"Woah." Luz's eyes are wide. "So you obviously forgave him."

"I did. And our relationship has changed since then."

Luz and Adriana give each other a look. "You're sleeping with him."

My cheeks are hot as I nod. "I like him." I press my glass to my face. "I like him a lot. And I think he likes me too."

Luz lets out a squeal. Adriana sips her wine thoughtfully. "I knew it," Luz says. "I knew it. Adri, didn't I tell you she was going to fall for him?"

"Fall for him? No. That's not this." I shake my head, but Luz is undeterred.

"He's so handsome. I bet he has a huge dick."

I choke on my saliva.

Adriana grins. "He so does, doesn't he?"

"He so does," I whisper, my eyes dropping shut in mortification. "This is bad, you guys."

"Bad how? Go to the ball, Cinderella. What's the worst that could happen?" Adriana is so matter of fact about everything, and usually, I am too. But something shifted after Eric. A fundamental part of me can't leap before looking, not when it comes to love.

"The worst is that I fall for him, and he breaks my heart." I blow out a breath. I said it. My secret fear. Because his messages might seem like those of a boss to an employee, but I know they're a promise. To protect me, to make sure I'm okay. The man who sent those messages is someone I could easily fall for. "If I fall for him, he will consume me."

Adriana and Luz look skeptical.

"Guys. He's like Eric times a hundred. He's a force of nature. You haven't been in the room with him, but he takes up all the air. He's the only one people focus on. And being with him would mean being in the spotlight. All the time. My needs would always come second. Just like they did with Eric. His life would swallow mine up. Hell, it already is. I can't stop thinking about him."

"Okay, but look at it this way." Luz leans forward. "It could also be amazing.

"But at what price?" My voice is fierce. "You know I've been struggling. I'm not proud of how hard I took that breakup, but I've fought for my independence since then. I don't want to give that up for Jonah. Especially knowing that if things ended between us, the fallout would be one hundred times worse than Eric."

"Would you have to? Give up your independence?" Adriana's eyes are calculating. She's not one to be taken in by promises and the thought of true love.

"I think he'd make me give up the paper." My heart beats faster at the thought. "And why wouldn't he? If I were a billionaire's girlfriend, I'd have no reason to work. Most people would call me insane for even thinking about it."

"Has he said that?" Luz's face is scrunched up. "Maybe he wouldn't mind. I mean, lots of rich guys have partners who work. It's not unheard of."

"It's not that." I shake my head. "He hates reporters. And I don't think he can get over that, even for me. You should see the way he shuts down every time I mention the paper. I don't think he'd be okay with it, and I can't handle that."

"Well, shit," Adriana murmurs.

"Shit is right." I take another gulp of wine. It's making me warm and fuzzy, but not enough to feel settled.

"I think you should go," Luz volunteers. "Nothing is irrevocable. If you change your mind, you can always leave." She shrugs.

I'm not so sure. Jonah is like a force field. He draws me in whether I want him to or not, and that's the scariest thing I can imagine.

~

I WALK HOME from the wine bar and end up wandering. It's an unusually warm night, the last gasp of warm fall days before the November chill. My neighborhood is bustling with families buying groceries, couples walking home hand in hand.

Jonah sends me another message while I walk.

> JONAH
> Thompson.

That's it. Nothing else. It feels like a secret code between us. The name no one else calls me. It's a sign of his caring, masquerading as gruffness. My chest aches at the possibility of losing what I have with him before it's even started. My feet must know something my mind doesn't, because they carry me to his townhouse. The windows are dark except for those on the upper floor. I picture him there, alone, except for his chef.

Before I think better of it, I pull out my phone and text back.

> CALLIE
> I'm outside.

I wait for minutes, shifting from foot to foot in the crisp air. He doesn't respond. My heart settles somewhere in my stomach, and I turn to go. I'm ten feet down the block when I hear, "Thompson."

It's him. My foolish heart soars back up into my throat, and I turn. He's in lounge pants, slippers, and a huge wool coat. The high collar frames his jaw. He's holding a bottle of water in his outstretched hand.

"Hi." I smile despite myself, feeling a little silly for showing up at his house.

"Take the water," he responds gruffly.

"Why?"

"I know you went drinking with your friends tonight. Thought you might need it."

My smile grows and I take the water. "You know, Jonah, you're not so bad." *I like you. All your harsh pieces and your soft heart.*

"Don't read into it," he says crisply and tucks his chin into his overcoat. "I need you hydrated for tomorrow morning. Maybe you'll finally beat me."

I roll my lips to keep from laughing. I've been trying to land just one punch, but I'm no closer than I was on Tuesday morning.

He turns toward Central Park. "You coming?" he tosses over his shoulder.

I hurry to keep up. "You want to walk?"

"It's better than sitting in my apartment reviewing documents, so yes." He slides me a look that says he has other reasons too, but I better not mention them.

We enter the park at the closest entrance, not chatting, just breathing, keeping pace. Jonah is shortening his strides for me, I can tell. When we reach the first set of benches, he asks quietly, "Why didn't you respond to my messages?"

"I'm not sure I can go to an event." His jaw tightens at my words. "Even if it's not like last time," I say quickly. "I know you're not trying to humiliate me. I know. I just—I'm not meant to be in the spotlight," I finish lamely.

Jonah turns on me, his eyes fierce. "I could kill him for making you think that." His throat works, his gaze searches mine. I try to look away from his knowing eyes, but his hand comes up to my cheek. "Callie," he murmurs. "Look at you."

My breath hitches at his words. The same ones he said to me that day when he looked at me with reverence.

"You're so beautiful. But more importantly, you're brilliant. Always watching, always analyzing. I wish I had half your ability to read people. How could anyone make you believe that you deserve anything less than their full attention?"

My eyes are hot as Jonah continues. His gaze softens, his thumb brushes over my cheek, warm, slightly rough. "Let me take you. I need your help. But more importantly, let me show you who you could be if you didn't care what the world thought."

"Why?" I whisper, tears threatening to spill over.

"Because it would make me happy." He looks so earnest, in a way I've never seen him. His hand is a warm anchor. When he focuses on me like this, it feels like nothing in the world can go wrong.

"Okay." I blow out a breath. I'm shaky and warm from Jonah's words. *Careful, Cal.* I shove the doubts down. "I'll go with you."

Relief flashes over his face. He pulls me to him, opening his coat to wrap me in it. We stand there under the streetlight for minutes, Jonah's lips on my hair, my face pressed to his chest.

"I have a business trip tomorrow. I'll be back Sunday morning. George will help you with stuff for the event."

Two days without him. Damn, I'm pathetic. And I'm not sure what help I'm going to need, but I'll go with it. "Is George getting overtime?"

"Oodles of it," he says, sounding disgruntled. "Miles is a pushover."

"Miles is great."

"Don't test me, Thompson," he growls, tightening his arms.

I laugh. *I like you.* I want to tell him, but I don't know how he'll take it. *I'm falling for you.* The words are bubbling up behind my lips, but it feels insane. *Too risky. Maybe tomorrow.*

44

Callie

Turns out, "not like the last time" means a massive amount of work. On Friday, I'm told I'm needed at Jonah's townhouse. Lou picks me up in one of the cars and takes me from the office to the Upper West Side. Lou has driven me a few mornings now, and I usually opt to keep the privacy divider down so I can ask about him what it's like being a driver for the rich and famous.

Today, he's got a story about his employer before Jonah, who would make him circle the block for hours while he met his mistress in the car.

"That's wild," I exclaim, smiling, as we head up town. "Poor you. Being subjected to that."

"It was eye-opening to say the least." He grins and shakes his head. "None of that with Mr. Crown, though. Just early morning wake-ups and the occasional trip to New Jersey."

"He's never, ah, had women over?"

"Not since I've known him. Not really his thing." Lou shrugs as we turn onto 87th street. "Seems lonely though, if you ask me."

I have to agree, but I don't say it. Jonah does seem lonely, and the picture Lou has painted is not a life I would want. I thank him and step out of the car into the afternoon sunshine. A woman is waiting for me on the steps of his townhouse, with a clipboard and a headset. *Wow.* I blink. Not what I expected.

"Callie Thompson?" She extends her hand as I mount the steps to the building. She's in a black sheath dress and heels, with sleek hair that reminds me of the inside of a seashell. All pinks and faded lavender. "Katie Jones. I'll be your stylist today. We have an exciting afternoon ahead of us."

I shake and squint at her. "Stylist? I thought I was just getting some files from the home office?"

"Oh no. Follow me. We have a lot to get through." She breezes through the doorway without waiting for me to follow. I trail her through the lobby, which looks like an atrium. Sun-filled, all glass from the third floor up, and full of plants. I didn't get to snoop much when I was here that night, and I turn slowly to take it all in. After just two visits, I've decided that this is the most beautiful home I've ever been in. It's serene and understated. It even smells like Jonah—citrus and warm wood.

I duck into a massive living room that extends all the way to a garden in the back. It's indoor/outdoor, with wood that blends seamlessly from the floor onto the deck, and garage style windows. In the living room are racks upon racks of clothes, displayed with shoes under them. Even a little table of jewelry.

George is sitting on the couch, looking bored to tears.

"There's Cinderella," they say.

"What is this?" My mouth hangs open. "Did you set this up?"

George purses purple-painted lips. "Despite what the movies would have you believe, it is not my dream to help little straight girls find their inner goddess. This was all Jonah."

They raise their brows like they know exactly what is going on between us. I thought we'd been keeping it under wraps, but I guess not.

I give them wide eyes and a neck slicing gesture when Katie turns to the first rack.

"Like I care," George mutters. "At least if he's sleeping with you, he's not bothering me."

I choke out a laugh and admire the racks. Silky dresses in every shade of the rainbow, little jeweled heels, massive diamond necklaces. I run my fingers over one dress in deep blue. The artful folds pin at the shoulder and fan out to the waist. Beautiful.

"Want to start with that one?" Katie asks.

"Sure." I finger the dress and swallow hard when I see the number of zeros peeking out on the price tag. "Um, I can't afford this. Is it a rental?"

She cocks her head, like I'm daft. "This is paid for."

My mouth drops open again and George snorts. "All of it? But what if I don't like it? What if it doesn't fit?"

She shrugs. "Mr. Crown will pay for anything you keep. Everything else will be returned."

I'm frozen in shock, until Katie tells me to follow her to a changing area she's set up in a small sitting room off the main living area. She hangs five dresses and leaves a pair of shoes. "Try these on and show me your favorite of the five."

I pull my phone out of my bag with shaking hands. I snap a photo of the clothes and text Jonah.

CALLIE

What is this?

His response comes immediately, like he was waiting to hear from me. I picture him lounging in his chair during a business meeting, with that lazy confidence he adopts when it suits him. No one would dare yell at him for texting during a meeting.

JONAH

I told you. Not like the last time.

My pulse hammers in my chest.

> **CALLIE**
> This is too much. You can't do this for me.

> **JONAH**
> I can do whatever I want.

God, that confidence. Arrogance even. He owns the world and he softens for no one. *Except for me.* The thought makes me jolt.

I try on a green dress, then a red one, each a cascade of luxurious fabric that makes me feel like a goddess.

> **CALLIE**
> The dresses are beautiful. Thank you.

> **JONAH**
> Send me a photo.

My lips curve. I pull the camera away and take a selfie. Before I can think better of it, I send it to Jonah.

I wait long minutes for his reply. I'm slipping on the blue dress when I finally get it.

> **JONAH**
> It's rude to be hard in a business meeting. Or so I've heard.

I laugh and slap a hand over my mouth. The blue dress is partly on, and my breasts are pushed up above the top, almost baring my nipples. *Am I about to do this?* I guess I am. It's fun and joyful and a little bit bad. I fire off another photo and the response comes immediately.

> **JONAH**
> Fuck.
>
> A little lower next time.

A knock sounds and a horrified *eep* comes out of my mouth. I rush to zip the blue dress and let Katie in.

She assesses me like only a professional can, while I fidget under her scrutiny. "That's lovely. Classic, elegant, flattering. I want to put you in some bold earrings to go with it. The bigger, the better. And of course you'll need to try on a few backup dresses and then whatever else strikes your fancy."

"Backup dresses. Of course," I mutter, but follow her out.

George gives me an approving nod but doesn't say anything else. Presumably they're here to make sure Katie gets paid.

When I'm back in the room, I text Jonah again.

> CALLIE
> Where am I supposed to keep this stuff? I have a tiny closet.

I guess I can have Katie return the dresses, but a little part of me wants to pile them all into a heap and jump into it. No one has ever done anything like this for me.

> JONAH
> You can keep it all here.

Does he mean—no. My thoughts scurry while I think of a response. *He can't mean at his place, like I'm his girlfriend.*

> JONAH
> I can hear you thinking. Send me another photo. This meeting is boring.

His insistence brings a smile to my lips. I decide to be very bad, instead of a little bit bad. So I put on the dangling earrings and lay on the divan in the corner. I take as artful a shot as I can manage. Nothing explicit, just cleavage, an earring, the curve of my ass.

I fire it off to Jonah with a message:

> CALLIE
> Your turn.

I lay there for several minutes, but of course he doesn't respond. He's in a meeting. *What did you think he was going to do?* Lock himself in the bathroom and strip? *He's a billionaire, Cal.* Whatever he's doing is probably worth more than all these dresses combined.

And in that moment, I feel like the cliché of a billionaire's wife. At home, with a world that revolves around my husband. I pull off the earrings and dress in my street clothes. On the way out, I thank Katie and tell her I'll keep just a few items—the dress, some underwear, a pair of shoes. She looks shocked, but doesn't argue.

George raises a brow. "You didn't want all of it?"

"I don't have space for it." I shrug nonchalantly, the ache in my chest growing with every minute that Jonah doesn't answer me.

"He's not going to like this." George purses their lips.

I steel my spine. "Honestly? I don't care."

45

Jonah

My phone stares at me accusingly from where it rests next to the bed. It's unlocked with the photo of Callie in the blue dress filling the screen. It's my favorite photo of the ones she sent, because it shows her face—her mischievous smile and sparkling eyes. But I still haven't responded.

Coward.

Be sure.

If I send one to her, what will she do with it? Will it end up leaked to the press? Annalise had some photos that were dangerously close to the one Callie is asking for. I wasn't as famous at the time, or they would have been front page news, along with the dirty texts I sent. I shut my eyes and sip the whiskey that's balanced on my stomach. The hotel room is luxurious, the best LA has to offer, and I don't care. I haven't used the spa, I haven't checked out the bar, hell, I haven't even eaten. *I miss her.*

Which is fucking stupid. But a fact. And I think she might miss me, too.

Your turn.

I want to send her something. I want to keep playing this game. Callie makes me feel so alive. And now, alone in my hotel, I can finally admit that my life is better with her in it. She wouldn't leak the photos. She's not Annalise. I'm sure of that. She's kind and decent. She cares about her neighborhood, her family, her friends.

Before I can think too much of it, I pop an arm behind my head, pull up my phone camera, and take a photo.

46

Callie

I'm ashamed at how I scramble for my phone when Jonah's name appears on the screen. I take a deep breath, expecting a message about how he doesn't do that, or maybe ignoring me completely.

I nearly drop the phone when I see what he sent. His shirt is open, his broad chest is bare. The dim lighting lovingly caresses each ridge of muscle. *Holy shit.*

CALLIE
Didn't think you were a selfie kind of guy.

JONAH
So you don't like it?

CALLIE
Oh no, I love it.

I roll my lips. I love it and I want more.

> **CALLIE**
> Another one?

I wait, my heart threatening to beat out of my chest, and my body buzzing with anticipation. When I finally get his photo, the breath leaves my chest.

A mirror selfie. His hands gripping the bathroom counter, his pants slung low enough to show the veins above his groin. But best of all is his expression. Feral intensity, half-parted lips, arrogant dark eyes.

Fuck.

I lay back against the bed. I need more. I'm flushed and aroused and *damn,* I miss him. I want to send him something back, but I'm too nervous. Old Callie would never have done this, but new Callie? I shut my eyes and imagine Jonah's face in the park the other night. *Beautiful.*

I can do this. For him.

I slip on the new underwear from today and the matching bra. Both are navy lace, with sheer panels. I take two artful shots, just the curve of my hip and the side of my bra.

> **CALLIE**
> Thank you for these.

> **JONAH**
> Fuck.
>
> Stop teasing me, Thompson.

I can practically hear him growling the words and I smile. I want more, but I can't. I'm not a nudes kind of girl.

> **JONAH**
> You're going to pay for this.

> **CALLIE**
> Revenge?

He doesn't respond and I get ready for bed. I have an early morning tomorrow, interviewing Paul at the diner and then heading to another one on the East side.

When he finally texts back, it's a video. I click and frantically turn the volume down when I see the content.

Holy shit.

He's naked. The phone is propped up. That intense look is back on his face and his hand is wrapped around his cock. I drink him in greedily. The long lines of his body, his strong hands, the fine muscles of his forearms.

"Thompson." His voice is like smoke. "Look what you did to me." He strokes, his eyes fluttering shut, his lips parting.

"You got me so close with those photos. But you know what I'm thinking about right now?"

Another stroke, his hips pushing forward. His face is slack with pleasure, like he's imagining something amazing. Need shimmers in my stomach.

"The way you taste." His tongue swipes over his lips and the breath stutters in my chest. He's unraveling already, his thrusts long and deep into his hand, his shoulders shuddering. *I'm getting him close. He's thinking about me. That's so hot.*

"Fuck," he groans. He tips his head back. "I'm going to—"

The video ends and I nearly shout. I go limp against the bed, breathing hard. I'm slick between my legs and frustrated. I need to come. I let my hand skim over my stomach, drawing shivers to the surface, little sparks of desire. Before I can go lower, I get another message.

> JONAH
> Do NOT touch yourself. All your pleasure is mine.

> CALLIE
> You're evil.

I'm so turned on and I would murder to see the end of that video.

JONAH
You love it.

Heaven help me. I do.

~

THE NEXT MORNING, my dad volunteers to come to the diner with me. We're buttoned up against the cold and walking the fifteen minutes it will take to get there. My dad is slower physically, but still sharp.

"So where'd you get this idea, Callie?"

"From Jonah."

"Your boss?" His brows go up. "Interesting."

"He goes here every morning. I thought it would be nice to do something on the disappearing diners in our neighborhood. Paul actually knows a few other owners in the area and offered to connect us."

"Good idea." My dad nods his approval and I practically buzz with pleasure. "We can branch out to the other boroughs too."

"No, Dad." My voice comes out more forcefully than I intend, and my father's head snaps up. "I mean, no, because I really think we should focus on local neighborhood items."

"Callie," he says. I steel myself for another conversation about how he wants more for me, how he won't accept my ideas.

"Don't." I speak around the lump in my throat. "I know you're going to tell me that you don't want this for me, but I want this. I love reporting. I have so many ideas. Really good ones. Did you know that the neighborhood that reads our paper the most is this one? Even on the website, Upper West Side residents are our most voracious readers. And the articles that get the most traction are the local interest pieces, not the ones about city politics. And the celebrity gossip? People love it. Why do you think I spend so much time getting photos of Jonah? Yes, I sell them, but to the people around here, he's a local. They care." My dad stiffens as I speak.

I've gone too far. My blood rushes in my ears as I think back to

Jonah telling me this is all my dad has. I'm undermining him. *What would Jonah do?* He'd stick up for himself. I know he would. And he'd stick up for me too. *You're smart, Cal.* I lift my chin while I wait for my dad's response. I might be a mere reporter from the Upper West Side, but there's a billionaire out there who closed a deal last week because of me.

My dad's eyes are calculating. "You know, Callie, I think you're right."

"I knew you would—wait. You do?"

"I do." He sighs. "To tell you the truth, I've felt like we didn't have direction now for years. I've tried, Cal, I have. But I'm tired. I don't have it in me to stake places out for a photo, or interview people all day. Hell, I'm winded after a brief walk."

"That's not true," I protest, my heart clenching at the thought of his health.

"It is. The fact is, this paper has been like my child for a long time." He settles his ever-present cap on his head. "After your mom left, you and the paper were the only things I had." His voice is rueful. "I tried to force you to fly because I didn't want this life for you. It's lonely being a reporter, Callie. The hours are weird and demanding, and you might be forced to choose between your integrity and something else."

I squirm internally but keep my face calm. That's exactly what I've been struggling with. I was planning to investigate Jonah, but it never felt right.

"I love it, Dad. I want this."

"I believe you, Cal." He gives me a smile. "You've always stuck by me. You've earned this. But don't think I haven't noticed how hard it is for you to live with me. That's not the life I want for you. I can hand some of the reins over for the paper, but I want you in your own place."

"But you need me."

He shakes his head. "Not at the cost of yourself."

In my head, I hear Jonah telling me be more selfish, so instead of arguing, I say, "Okay."

My dad smiles. "Starting this week, do you want to publish your articles as editor-in-chief?"

I can't help the smile that spreads over my face. "Hell yes."

~

I'M PRACTICALLY FLOATING by the time I get home later. My dad peels off to meet a friend of his for a beer, and I settle in with my notes from Paul's interview. He was a great interview subject—honest, funny, thoughtful. The article is going to be a crowd-pleaser. My fingers fly over the keys as I type. I have so many ideas for articles about this. We could do a whole series about the different diners, and we could ask local residents about their favorite meals from each. *Maybe even Jonah.*

The thought makes me smile, and I pull out my phone to tell him.

CALLIE

Mind if we interview you about the diner?

I pause before I send it. This is a mistake. I delete the message. Jonah hates the paper and every time I bring it up, he goes cold. *He's not going to do an interview.* I toss my phone aside and ignore the ache in my chest while I finish the article.

I'm in bed later, watching a movie, when Jonah calls. I jump at the sound of my phone ringing, and then carefully press accept. Maybe he didn't mean to call me.

"Callie." His low voice rolls over me.

"Hi, Jonah."

"What are you doing?"

"Lying in bed. I'm watching a movie." Just saying the word "bed" to him makes my cheeks flame.

"What did you do today?" I hear rustling on the other side of the line.

"Are you in bed too?"

"I am. It's eight p.m. here, and my last meeting finished an hour ago. My flight's in a few hours." He makes a contented sound as he settles into the bed. "I wanted to talk to you."

A smile plays on my lips. "You called to chat with me?"

"Tell me about your day. Did you get photos of any pizza rats?"

I laugh at Jonah's reference to a famous video that circulated a few years ago. "We interviewed Paul at the diner. We're doing a piece on the disappearing diners of the Upper West Side. And I talked to my dad. I'll be publishing this one and all my future articles as editor-in-chief."

Just saying the words makes my heart beat faster.

Jonah is silent for a minute. *He hates this.* My stomach knots with regret.

"I'm proud of you," he finally says.

"What?" I nearly drop the phone in surprise.

"Fishing for compliments, Thompson?" he teases. "I said I'm proud of you. You stood up to your dad. That's not easy." His voice is warm and soothing, and I want to wrap it around me like a blanket.

"It wasn't as bad as I thought actually."

He hums. "Tell me."

"He told me that the paper had lacked direction for a while. And you were right. It's the only thing he's had in his life for years, other than me. Am I doing the wrong thing by taking it away from him?" It's the question I've been too afraid to ask, and it drops like a stone in the silence between us.

Jonah pauses. "I don't know, Callie." He sighs. "He loves it, and you can still do it together. But you have to ask yourself whether it makes you happy, or whether you'd be happier striking out on your own, I guess. Or maybe doing something completely different."

"Jonah Crown talking about happiness. Didn't you tell me you were a black coffee and revenge kind of guy?"

"Don't start," he says tartly, and I laugh.

"Thank you, Jonah. You're a pretty good advice giver."

"Of course I am."

"And so modest too." I'm grinning ear to ear at the way he plays with me. *I miss him.*

"What are you doing tomorrow?"

Does he miss me too?

"Nothing big. Just some work and maybe seeing Adriana's puppy. Why?"

"Cancel your plans. Come with me."

"To where?" I can't stop smiling. Jonah's insistence is so *him*.

"Baby shower. New Jersey."

"Wait. Really?" New Jersey means family. *He wants me to go to a baby shower with his family? What is this?*

"Yes, really. Yes or no, Thompson?"

"Will I get to ride on the motorcycle?"

"Yes. Whatever you want. Just come with me." He sounds as desperate to see me as I am to see him.

"You sweet-talker, you. I'll do it." I laugh and he huffs a breath into the phone.

"Good."

Satisfaction fills me. "I don't want to hang up," I whisper.

"So don't," he says in that blunt Jonah way.

"I have to go to sleep. I have to get up early tomorrow and get ready for a baby shower my weird boss invited me to."

He laughs. "So go to sleep. I'll be here."

My heart clenches, but I settle under the covers and put my laptop away. I stare at the empty space where I wish Jonah were. "What did you do today?"

"Meetings. Endless meetings. They were boring, and if I tell you about them, you'll definitely fall asleep."

"Tell me."

I can hear that he's smiling while he tells me, and I wish I were there to see it.

And that's how I fall asleep with the phone next to me and Jonah's voice in my ear.

47

Jonah

Callie is a vision when I pick her up. Her hair is twisted up in a messy bun, her eyes are soft, her lips are glossed.

I grab her around the waist and pull her up against me. "I fucking missed you."

She stills, her lips parting, but I'm not sure how she'll respond, so I kiss her, groaning slightly when her lips make contact with mine. I delve my tongue into her mouth and tighten my arms around her back. She responds like it's the best kiss she's ever received, like I was gone for a year instead of two days. Her hands are in my hair, and her breasts are pressed to my chest, and fuck, I want to drag her into the back of my car and raise the privacy screen.

"In the car, beautiful."

She settles herself on the seat and greets Lou like an old friend.

"Making friends?" I ask.

She smiles serenely. "He's been telling me some great stories. Sounds like you're actually the easiest client he's ever had. Shocking, I know."

"You know. I've never thought to ask. I should." Hot shame fills my chest. Callie is undoubtedly a better person than I am.

"Since when do you own a small limousine?" Callie asks, interrupting my thoughts.

"Since today," I say. "I had it special ordered. Originally, because riding in that tiny car with you was torture, but now—" I press the button to raise the privacy screen.

I tug her onto my lap and cup the back of her neck with my hand. "Look at all the fun things we can do."

"Oh no." She laughs. "What if Lou hears us?"

"I have it on good authority that the soundproofing is excellent." I give her a lazy smile. "But if you don't want to—" My other hand drops from where it was toying with the hem of her dress. Need for her is fire in my blood. My body is humming with anticipation, but I can be patient.

"I do want to." She bites her lip, her eyes already eager with desire. "I'm scared, Jonah." She traces my jaw and I hold myself still. "I'm scared that this is going to blow up in my face. It's too wonderful. I like you too much."

I freeze. I like her too. More than I want to admit. This is too new for me. I don't date, I don't tell women I like them, I don't buy cars just so I can make out with them in the back.

Be sure.

And suddenly, I am. I wrap her fingers with mine, squeezing lightly. "I like you too. Trust me, Callie. Please. Don't overthink this, okay?"

"Easier said than done," she mutters.

"It's an order." I brush my thumb over her lips, savoring the plush feel of them. "I'm your boss. And I'm ordering you to stop thinking, Thompson. I can give you at least five orgasms in the back of this car, then a whole bunch more tomorrow morning. We never have to leave the bed. I'll even make you breakfast."

"On a Monday?" Her mouth parts in surprise.

"I'll play hooky if you will." I grin, my heart thudding. I'm desperate for her after a mere forty-eight hours away. She quiets the part of my brain that is always buzzing, always seeking. I've never played hooky from work before, but the thought of a whole day with her to myself sounds like heaven.

She's blushing but smiling. "Okay," she whispers.

"Good girl," I whisper back, just to watch her lids drop and her body sway to me. "Shut your eyes, Cal. Let me do this for you."

She lets her eyes close. "Good girl," I croon again, in her ear this time, and she shudders. "You're so strong. You're always doing so much. When was the last time you let go?" I skim my hands up her impossibly silky skin, seeking the clasp of her bra. I shift her over my lap, where I'm already hard, drawing a little gasp from her throat. I bite gently at her neck, knowing she's overwhelmed with sensation. Pleasure only I can give her. And fuck, I want this to be so good for her. I want to show her everything my body can do for her.

She inhales sharply as I brush the backs of my fingers over her breasts, and then lets her head drop into the crook of my neck. I shift her weight so she's comfortable against me, and I ignore the way my erection is pressing against my zipper. This is all for her.

I take my time with her, caressing her soft skin and undressing her with persistence that has her gasping into my shoulder. When I finally kiss her, we both groan. *Take it easy.* I force myself to go slow, when I want to drown in my desire for her. I gentle my mouth and she makes frustrated noises. Her hands tug at my hair, and in response I bite her lip.

"Jonah," she protests. "Please."

"No." I kiss her again, twining my tongue with hers in the way that I've noticed makes her forget all reason. "I'm doing this the way I want. The more you rush me, the more I'll draw it out. Enjoy this, Callie."

"Okay." She lets out a shuddery sigh and traces her fingers over my jaw and down under my collar. Her eyes are half lidded as she explores me. *She likes my body.* I spend a lot of time on it, and her appreciation turns me on. I hold myself still, letting her explore me.

"Like what you see?" I give her a cocky smile as her eyes lift to mine.

"I do." The breath sighs out of her as she presses a hand to my chest. "You're wearing way too many clothes."

I shake my head and press my lips to the soft skin where her neck meets her shoulder. "I told you. This is about you. I can make you soar." I suck gently and she cries out. "Let me take you there."

After her shaky nod, I push her dress up to her waist and settle her more firmly over my lap. My cock jumps in my pants at her nearness. I will myself to settle and focus on kneading her soft skin, biting at her neck, overwhelming her with sensation. She rocks her hips over me, and pleasure rushes from the contact. "I'll soothe the ache, sweetheart, I promise." I slide down the seat until I'm under her, my head tipped back on the leather. *There are benefits to the limo.*

"What are you doing?"

I knead the globes of her ass. "Sit on my face, beautiful."

"I don't know." She squirms. "I thought most guys hated that." I can barely focus on her words. She's soft and wet and *right there.* I already know she tastes amazing.

"I *need* this, Cal." I kiss up her thigh, making her gasp. My stomach is shimmering with desire. This is the best part. The slow climb, before I see how many times I can make her fall.

"If you're sure."

Instead of responding, I growl and give her ass a light smack. She falls forward, right into my mouth. *Hell yes.*

I lick into her, starting slow, building a rhythm before I break her apart. She'll be sensitive at first, until I can bring her to the peak. Sure enough, as I taste her, she relaxes. But not enough. She's still holding back.

I grip her hips. "Do you trust me?" I growl.

"Yes." she pants.

"Then let go, Callie."

"I can't," she sobs.

"Do you want me to make you?" My voice has an edge to it. I *need* her to comply. "You can tap my shoulder if you want out."

"Yes, Jonah." The sound of my name makes me shudder. "Make me stop thinking, please."

I yank her down over me and bury my face in her, loving that her wetness is spreading over my face and chin. I nibble at her clit, lap at her thighs, swirl my tongue at her entrance. She's tense and magnificent during the first orgasm.

"Another," I grit out. I'm making my body wait, which is part of the game, but fuck, it's so hard.

I suck on her clit and press my index finger into her until she clenches and rides my hand.

"Good girl, Callie." She gasps. I fucking love how much she likes this. The soft moans, the way she shudders when I use my tongue just right. "You like that?"

"Yes. Jonah, please."

"Fuck." The soft curse falls from my lips when I look up to see her face slack with pleasure, her perfect body moving over me. I thrust my fingers in gently, and then harder, until she shakes through another orgasm. I'm so hard it's nearly painful.

"One more, sweetheart. Give me one more."

"Okay." Her voice is a sigh. "You're really good at this. I feel amazing."

The praise lights me up. "Tell me what you like. While I do it." I delve my tongue inside her, and she shrieks, but bites her arm.

"*That,*" she says in between pants. "That feels so good. I've never felt that before, but *holy shit*, the angle—oh, Jonah, right there."

I'm fucking her with my tongue now, one finger pressing her clit in the way I know will make her go off like a bomb. I'm still learning her body, but it feels made for me. My hand on her hip controls her body, grinding her into my face. She's shaking and trembling, and when I replace my tongue with two fingers, she groans.

"Like that. I like the way you're controlling me," she says. "I like the way you feel. But nothing is better than you."

"What do you mean, me?" I want her to say it while I push her off the cliff.

"Your cock." She gasps. "I like the way you fill me up."

My body jerks. *This woman is perfect.*

"Just for that, I'll let you have it."

I gentle my mouth as I undo my slacks with shaking hands. I lift my hips just enough to shove my briefs down. My erection throbs against my stomach.

"I need you, Callie." I settle her on my lap, expecting her to be limp and spent, but while her eyes are hazy, she arches her back and rubs over me. Her cheeks are pink, her hair is mussed, and her skin is marked from my mouth. *Beautiful.*

"It's going to be deep from this position." We're sitting on the floor, her legs around mine, and I'm *so close.*

She grinds down onto my cock. "Please, Jonah. I want to feel you."

I guide her up with my hands and then notch myself to her entrance and push in. We both shudder at the feeling.

With her on top, it's not just me taking her, it's her taking me too. Her eyes fly wide at the first inch. I grit my teeth. She's hot and wet, and I was almost ready to come in my pants when we started this.

"You feel good, Cal. Give me a little more." She sinks down and our groans of pleasure mingle together in the quiet interior. When I'm fully seated, I pause, giving her time to adjust, running gentle hands down her back. She presses her forehead to mine, and I take her mouth in a deep, drugging kiss. It's not enough. *It may never be enough.* I'm inside her and I crave her. I want to be deeper. I want us to share one body. I want to feel her pleasure like it's my own.

I guide her hips with my hands, helping her rise and sink down in a steady rhythm. She's hot and wet and clenching around me, and *fuck,* it's so much.

"Jonah." She gasps.

I can't respond. I'm strung too tight, too overwhelmed. I kiss her again.

I dig my fingers into her hips as she moves over me. Desire is moving slowly through me, like a tsunami, ready to drown me. *Too soon.* I don't want to come this soon. I want this to last forever. Forever is impossible with how she feels, though. The curves of her body fill my hands, her wet heat ripples around me, her soft cries drag me closer to the edge.

She makes a little frustrated sound and increases her pace.

"That's it, sweetheart. Use me for your pleasure. Take what you need." I spear a hand into her hair and kiss her, even as my stomach coils tight and my legs shake. When our tongues touch, she moans and clenches around me and finally, *finally*, I let myself go. I press my mouth to her neck so Lou won't hear me shout. The orgasm is lightning up my spine, sending sparks through me. My body jerks and my cock pulses and *fuck,* it's so good. It's never been this good. *It's her.*

We come down together. I comb my fingers through her hair as she draws deep, shaky breaths. She traces her fingers over my neck, and my lids drop shut.

"So good," she whispers.

"The best," I agree.

We stay like that for long minutes. Callie's head rests on my neck, and I rub her back. Her soft breaths puff out against my skin. When we finally untangle ourselves, I pass her tissues and a bottle of water from the door.

"You came prepared." She smiles.

"If you say I was planning to ravish you in my limo, I'll deny it," I say solemnly. *It's totally what I was planning.*

"You know, I've never had a man buy me a car just for sex." She laughs and I give her an arrogant smile, because I know she likes it.

"Get used to it," I say. "Remember what I told you? Anything you want."

Her cheeks are delightfully pink as she adjusts her dress and buckles her seatbelt.

"So, whose baby shower is this?" she asks. "I assume someone you know?" Her eyes are teasing. In my desperation to see her, I didn't give her any details, and I definitely didn't give Christine a head's up.

"My sister's. She and her wife are due soon."

Callie's brows go up. "The sister you rarely see."

"She wanted me to bring a date." I shrug, like bringing Callie to meet my family is just another day, when in reality, it's a big fucking deal. What if she hates them? What if she says something bad about them? The last person I let close to them did.

"To a baby shower?" She grins. "Totally normal. So what

happened to the *you're never meeting my sister, Thompson?*" She does a passable imitation of my voice, and I roll my eyes.

"I changed my mind. But don't even think about ganging up on me."

"I would never," she says seriously, but her eyes are laughing.

The trip to New Jersey is mercifully short. Soon, the car is winding along tree-lined roads, with neat houses and small lots giving way to cookie-cutter mansions and hedges. My skin prickles uncomfortably as we drive through the town. It's just a few main roads.

Callie's hand lands on my knee. "Jonah."

"What?"

"Your knee."

I grimace. "I didn't even realize I was shaking it."

"What's wrong?"

"Is it that easy to tell?" I blow out a breath. I'm unsettled and I fucking hate it. This is why I avoid family dinners. I hate being reminded of the past. Driving down these streets makes feel like a teenager again.

"It's pretty obvious." Callie's mouth lifts in a half smile. She looks so pretty with her bright blue eyes and her freckled cheeks that I want to pull her onto my lap. Her thumb rubs a circle on my knee, anchoring my thoughts.

"I grew up here. You'd think my parents would have accepted one of the many offers I made for them to move. St. Barth's, Vail, San Francisco, Tribeca. Anywhere but here."

"Maybe they're comfortable here. I mean, it's really pretty. It reminds me of a suburb from a movie, actually."

"And just as closed-minded," I mutter, before sighing heavily. "I don't like the person I was when I lived here. I don't like being reminded of that." I meet her gaze, serious and considering, and wait for her to disagree, to tell me I'm wonderful, or some other platitude.

Instead, she nods and says, "That, I understand. I don't like who I was just a year ago, but that person made me who I am today. Would you be Jonah Crown, the Prince of Darkness without being Jonah

Crown, boy from wherever this is in New Jersey?" Her lips tilt up as she teases me and warmth fills my chest.

"Come here." I unbuckle her seatbelt and tug her onto my lap, hoping Lou doesn't choose this exact moment to get in our very first crash.

Callie's blue eyes draw me in, her soft skin so smooth under my fingers. I run my hands lightly up her arms. She brushes her thumb over my jaw, looking at me like I'm the only thing in her world.

"You're a force of nature," she murmurs. "You know that, right?" She looks annoyed. "No matter who you were in the past, the man you are today is someone I admire."

My chest tightens painfully. "Yeah?" My voice is gravel in my throat. "Even after everything I did to you?"

"I see why you did it." She threads her fingers through the hair at my temple. "I admire you for it. Secretly protecting those you love, pretending to be awful so people are scared of you." She leans down and presses her lips to my jaw. The scent of her hair fills my nose, and my hands twitch with the need to crush her to me.

"You make me sound foolish," I grumble.

"Not foolish," she murmurs. "Big-hearted. Bigger than you want to admit. Big enough to keep everyone around you safe."

"That list is small," I reply. *But you're on it.*

"I know." She smiles at me. "I like that it's small. Someone who is kind to everyone isn't special. Someone who is kind to a select few, well—" She raises her shoulders. "If they care about you, you've won something amazing."

My eyes widen. My blood rushes in my ears. Callie is looking at me like she might be falling for me. *I'm falling for you too.* Her eyes are warm, and her lips are gently smiling.

Possession rises. I've just had her and I want more. I want it all. I want her with me every day and in my bed every night. Satisfaction coils in my stomach. Callie Thompson doesn't realize it yet, but when I set my mind to something, I always get it.

I don't even realize the car has stopped until Lou says, "We're here."

48

Callie

I'm totally falling for him. I watch Jonah as he speaks in low tones to Lou, then claps him on the shoulder and shoves his hands into the pockets of his suit. A suit with a T-shirt and sunglasses pushed up onto his forehead, like a model. Everything about him speaks to me. His looks, sure, but his quiet strength, his fierceness, his sharp humor, even the ruthlessness.

He gives me an amused glance, and I smile sheepishly. I'm totally staring and daydreaming, when I should be focused on meeting his family. The house is neat and traditional, with cedar shingles and white windows. A lawn, a garage to the side, a few trees.

"Idyllic," I say, craning my neck to see if there's a backyard. "I was always jealous of you suburban kids with your swing sets and your trees."

"Playing with pigeons, were you, Thompson?" Jonah's eyes are laughing at me, and I swat at his arm.

"Let me have this. I love leaving the city."

"You know I have a house upstate, right?"

"What? No. I had no idea."

He raises a brow. "That missing from your file on me?"

"I can't drive," I say primly. "I'd never be able to stalk you efficiently."

He smiles. "I'll take you. And you don't need to drive. Not with me."

Before I can respond, a woman's shriek sounds and my head snaps up. His sister rushes out of the front door, screeching, "J, you're here." She comes to a halt before us, her eyes wide, her dark hair a wild cloud around her head. "You brought a guest."

Jonah's hand is on my back. "You didn't tell your sister?" I ask, assuming that's who this is. *This is weird.* He didn't tell them I was coming.

"He doesn't tell me anything." Christine frowns. "Wait. I know you. I saw you outside the restaurant that night."

"Christine, this is Callie Thompson," Jonah responds evenly.

"Callie T— oh." Her mouth parts in shock. "The reporter. But I thought—"

"Stop speaking," Jonah interrupts, glaring at her. I roll my lips to keep from laughing. Presumably he told Christine about his plans for me, but she didn't realize things had changed between us.

Christine rolls her eyes but gestures for us to go ahead of her. "He's so cranky. I can't imagine working for him. Did you want to punch him on the daily?"

I let out a surprised laugh. I'm not sure what I expected from Jonah's family, but this is definitely not it. "I deserve an award for not spitting in his coffee."

Christine laughs, then pulls me into the kitchen, where there are trays full of meatballs, chicken parm, pasta, bread. Cupcakes are piled high on the counter to the right.

"Wow."

"I know," Christine says. "Our mom went overboard." She's pretending to be annoyed, but I can hear the love in her voice.

Jonah trails us, looking a little out of place, even in his parents' home. He nods at the guests, glances at the food, and shoves his hands back into his pockets.

I turn to him. "Would you introduce me to people, please?"

"Sure." His shoulders lower a little bit, and I decide to stick by him today. For whatever reason, he needs support while he's here, and he deserves it. "But be prepared for inappropriate comments."

I see what he means when he finally introduces me to his mother. She's surrounded by her friends, larger than life, with slightly graying dark hair and a round face. "He finally comes home," she exclaims. "I never see him." She shakes her head and glances at her friends, who are looking on disapprovingly. "Not so much as a phone call. And he's brought a woman." She presses a hand to her chest. "I'm going to faint from shock."

"Mom," Jonah says, in a warning tone. "This is Callie. Please don't scare her."

"Callie." She takes my hands in hers. "Tell me that my son is treating you right."

"Fucking hell," Jonah mutters.

"Don't curse around your mother," she says sharply, not letting go of my hands. She looks back at me expectantly.

I'm tempted to make a joke about how Jonah only wants to torment me, but instead I just say, "He's wonderful."

Jonah lets out a choked sound, but covers it with a cough.

His mother smiles. "He is, isn't he? I'm so glad he's bringing a nice girl home. He never does. Well, not since—"

"Mom," Jonah says more forcefully. She snaps her mouth shut and gives him a disapproving look. *What was she about to say? Did he have an ex-girlfriend maybe? Annalise?*

Jonah practically drags me away, through the kitchen, out onto the porch. It overlooks a neat backyard with a few trees and a carefully manicured lawn. "She was nice," I say, partly to needle him.

He snorts. "You know I will never hear the end of this. It's going to be *where's that nice girl Callie* from now until the end of time."

My smile falls slightly at the implication that I won't be there. *Of course not, Cal. Be serious. This isn't a thing.*

"Coffee?" Jonah is pouring us some from a carafe that's been set out. "Or there's hard stuff. But I thought you might want a ride on the motorcycle later."

"I so do." I can't picture Jonah on a motorcycle, but I want to see it for myself.

"What do you think so far?" His question is nonchalant, but his eyes are shadowed. My chest pinches for him. My answer matters.

"I like them," I say honestly. "I mean, I never had a big family. I always wondered what it would be like growing up in the suburbs, with bikes and neighbors. Did you form a gang with the other boys?"

"Totally. Our old house is just a few streets away." He's smiling, holding my gaze, and I feel like we're the only people in the world.

"Lucky." I sigh. "Growing up in the city is weird. All that stuff you see in the movies doesn't happen. No making out in cars, or climbing trees, or having huge sleepovers with all your friends. I mean, my apartment can accommodate exactly two additional bodies."

Jonah looks thoughtful. "I guess I never thought about it that way. I was so focused on leaving."

"You're fortunate," I say quietly. "I would have loved a sister. Or an annoying brother. Or a mom always in my business."

His arm lands on my shoulders, heavy and warm, as he tucks me against his side. "When did she leave?"

"You know when she left."

"I'm sorry for that. That was shitty of me. I was looking for leverage, and I wanted it any way I could get it."

I nod and swallow the lump in my throat. "Do you really want to know?"

"Please," he says in a low voice. He pulls away to look at me, and his eyes are pleading.

"She left when I was six. I don't remember her that well, but she wasn't a great mom. She was pretty absent, actually. I don't remember her being around much when I was little. She worked on Broadway. Not as a star, just as a chorus member. She loved to dance and sing. I guess that's where I get it from." My chest is tight, the way it always is when I think about her too much.

"And you've never heard from her?"

I shake my head. "Never." My voice comes out hoarse. "I wish I could stop being upset about it. Even after all these years."

Jonah's face twists in sympathy. "You never wanted to reach out to her?"

"I've looked at her social media. She has a new family. Two kids. One even kind of looks like me. If she wanted to come into our lives, she could. She knows where we live. She knows my name. But she just left." My voice breaks on the last words, and Jonah puts his coffee down before pulling me against his chest. He smells like citrus and cedar. His T-shirt is soft against my cheek, and I curl my fingers into it. He's so warm. Strong, like he could never break under the weight of the world. I inhale deep lungfuls of air as he holds me.

"I'm sorry." He presses his lips to my hair. "I don't know how anyone could ever leave you. I certainly couldn't."

I tense. *What does that mean?* I'm scared to ask, scared he'll take it back, but a tendril of warmth curls through my chest.

49

Jonah

Mia interrupts us, looking annoyed, which is normal for her. She's petite and blonde and extremely pregnant, which has not improved her mood whatsoever. She smiles at Callie, scowls at me, and gestures for us to come inside.

"We need you for the cake cutting."

"Why?" Callie whispers to me as we follow Mia down the hall.

"Family tradition," I mutter. "Guest of honor has to cut the cake. I'm the, ah, sperm donor for them."

Callie's face softens. "How lovely."

A smile tugs at my mouth. "Pretty cool, right? That reminds me —" I hurry to catch up to Mia. She turns, still looking irritated. "I had the documents for me to give up paternity drafted. If you want to sign, we can fill in the name when he's born." Giving up paternity is a necessary step, and Mia's greatest fear was that I would change my mind about it.

"Thank you," she says quietly. I shrug awkwardly and follow her into the kitchen, where everyone is gathered.

Callie looks questioningly at me. "She was nervous I wouldn't want to give up paternity," I explain. "She wanted to go with an anonymous donor, but Christine didn't. I'm trying to show her that she doesn't need to worry."

"You're wonderful. You know that, right?" Callie's eyes are shining with emotion. I shake my head, but I'm smiling as I step away.

Christine is waiting expectantly. I wrap my arm around her and press a kiss to her hair. "Proud of you, sis." My voice comes out rough but Christine gives me a happy smile.

"Let's get on with it," Mia says. We wrap our hands around the cake knife. Christine, then Mia, then me, and cut into the massive chocolate cake with one definitive slice.

"A good cut," my dad exclaims. "He's gonna be strong-willed. Like Jonah." Everyone laughs and I duck my head. My eyes search for Callie in the crowd. She's pink-cheeked and her eyes are bright. *Does she want kids?* Maybe. She'd be a good mom. She'd teach them how to sing and how to navigate the city and how to never give up.

Mia's sharp elbow digs into my side. "Move. I need to cut pieces for everyone."

I ignore her and focus on Callie. I jerk my head to the left and give her a smile. She gives a tiny nod. We meet in the hallway behind the kitchen.

"Let's get out of here."

"And go where?" She's grinning. "Won't your sister be mad?"

"I'll text her. Come with me for a ride." I grab her hand and tug her down the hall, out the back, and to the garage. It's musty and smells like oil and dirt. It's full of my dad's tools, yard supplies, an extra fridge. The motorcycle is in the corner, under a tarp.

"Wow." Callie's eyes are wide and excited as I uncover it. "What, um, kind is it?" She screws her face up. "I have no vocabulary for this."

"It's a cruiser." I run my hand over the black leather seat. It's worn and faded but soft from use. "It's designed for daily riding, even commuting. But it was the fastest model available the year it was made. It goes 145 miles per hour. I couldn't afford a new one, but I got it used."

"Do you miss it?"

"Yeah." I say it without thinking, but it's true. *Huh.* "Yeah. I miss it a lot actually."

"You could still do it, you know. Just because you're rich doesn't mean you can't still do things like this. Who cares if it's a used bike? Or even if you just go around the block?" Her voice is fierce.

"Maybe," I say uncertainly. I pull helmets out of the bin behind us and settle Callie's on her head. I tighten the straps, my fingers brushing over her soft skin. I can't help but press a kiss to her lips, which makes her sigh and melt into me. "Make sure the helmet is on securely, please."

"You're such a worrier," she says, without heat. I can tell she likes it.

I wheel the bike out into the sunshine and swing a leg over. My heart is thudding in my chest, and my palms are starting to sweat. "It's been years since I've done this. I don't know—"

"Stop worrying." Callie settles in behind me and wraps an arm around my waist. Her weight grounds me and I loose a shaky breath.

"Both arms, Cal. I don't want you to fall."

She huffs and complies, pressing her cheek to my jacket. "Good?"

"Good." I rev the engine. It sputters slightly but turns over. The roar of the bike is louder than I remember. It's impossible to speak, so I just squeeze her leg, and then we're off. I can't control the bike like I used to, at least at first. It requires more balance than I remember, and definitely more core strength. I feel the vibrations from my toes to my teeth. Callie's arm is a tight band around my stomach, but I can't ask if she's okay. We edge down the road at thirty miles an hour. We're in a subdivision, but soon it opens onto a main road.

"Faster," Callie shouts.

I don't know if that's a good idea. I speed up to forty. We pass houses, a school, the country store, then farm after farm, stands of trees, open fields. The bike roars under us. I'm constantly fighting it, trying to stay upright, trying to make it comfortable for her. *I can't believe I used to drive this to work.*

"Faster," she yells again. "Come on. Faster."

Fuck it. We're on an empty road. It's a straight shot. I let the bike loose. There's a brief moment of fear when I think the bike won't respond. Then the jump forward makes my stomach press against my ribs and my heart leap into my throat.

Callie lets out a whoop of happiness, and I grin.

"More."

The speedometer climbs until we're going eighty. The breeze stings my cheeks, the wind whips her hair, and fuck, I feel good.

Better than good. Amazing. Because I'm doing this with her.

I ease off the throttle until we're back down to a reasonable thirty, then twenty, then meandering along until we come to a stop at the park I used to go to as a kid.

I help Callie off. My legs shake, and her breath is gusting. But her eyes are bright.

"Well?"

"That was fucking awesome," she says. "Again. Please, Jonah."

I can't help but laugh. "I didn't think you would like it. Adrenaline junkie." I shake my head and unbuckle our helmets with unsteady hands. The adrenaline is still coursing through my body.

"It was so much fun. I want to drive. Can we take it back to the city with us?" She's so happy and unfettered. It makes my heart gallop and my body buzz.

I pull her in for a kiss, claiming her mouth with the intensity of someone who just did something death-defying and stupid and lived to tell the tale. "Fuck, I love you," I murmur against her mouth. She stills. An ache, but a pleasant one, starts in my chest. This feels right.

50

Callie

I love you.

"What?" I pull back just enough to see Jonah's face. When I see his expression, I don't need him to repeat himself. It's obvious how he feels. His mouth is tipped up in one of those smiles that is becoming more and more common, his eyes are soft with emotion.

"I love you," he repeats.

I open and close my mouth like a fish. I don't know what to say. *Love?* I think back to when Eric said it first, and how shocked I was, how I let myself fall for his lies. I was so enthralled by the idea of love, that I didn't stop to consider the reality. *Would it be the same with Jonah? Would his needs come first?* I don't think so, and yet doubt worms its way into my mind. *Would he make me give up my dreams? Would he make me close the paper?*

I want to say it back. I want to fall for Jonah without thinking, but I can't look before I leap, not in this.

"Jonah, I just—"

He presses a kiss to my lips. I sway into him, trying to show him with my body that I could love him, but I need time. "I don't care if you don't say it back. You don't have to declare your feelings now. But give me a week, okay?" He doesn't look angry, and thank god for that, because a lesser man would have gotten on his bike and ridden away.

"A week of what?"

He rubs a hand over my lower back, comforting me. "Showing you what it's like to be mine." His voice is strong, assured, and suddenly I know what it's like to be Jonah's sole goal. I don't know if I can resist him.

~

WHEN WE GET BACK to the house later, Christine pretends to be annoyed, but I can see she's secretly pleased that Jonah took the bike out.

His mother rolls her eyes and mutters something about it being a death trap. When we gather around the dinner table later, it's to eat leftovers from the baby shower and enjoy the remaining wine from the open bar.

Jonah asks me what I want before making his own plate, and I see his mom watching with approval, and with no small amount of speculation. His grandma is there too, watching me with hawk-like intelligence and sharing the occasional look with her daughter.

"So Callie, do you want kids?" his mom asks.

I cringe internally. Two hours ago, Jonah said he loved me, and now his mom wants to know if I want kids. "I do," I say slowly. "I have a lot to achieve before then, but I want a big family."

"That okay with you, J?" Christine teases.

I expect a cutting remark, but instead Jonah looks at me, steady and sure, and says, "Yes." His eyes glint. In them I can see confidence, and no small amount of arrogance. *I'll win you*, those eyes say. *Whatever it takes.*

Happiness tangles with nerves inside of me. He's so certain, but I'm not.

"I want you at the birth," Christine suddenly says.

Jonah looks around, like she's speaking to someone else. "Sure, okay." But his voice is hollow.

"You could try to sound a little excited." Christine frowns at him, and my heart pinches.

"I am." He lets his fork drop onto his plate. "I'm excited for you." He pushes back from the table. "I'll be right back." He strides from the room and Christine jerks her head toward him. I raise my brows. I don't think following him is the right idea, but staying here will be more than uncomfortable.

I find him on the back deck, staring out at the yard. The air has edged from crisp to cold, and I shiver as I come to stand next to him. He silently removes his jacket and drapes it over my shoulders, letting his hands linger at my neck.

"Come to convince me that babies aren't terrifying?" He slants me a look that says he knows why I'm out here.

"Nah. I'm just outside because I didn't want to be collateral damage. It's safer out here."

His eyes fly wide and he laughs, tipping his head back with joy. Warmth blooms in my chest. *Is this love?* That feeling of being the half of a whole? Of being the only person who can make someone laugh when things are hard?

"What's wrong with babies anyways? Seems like you're okay with kids." My pulse speeds even as I ask the question. Maybe what Jonah said about kids is all for show. He doesn't seem like a kid kind of guy.

"Aren't they a little small?" He looks at me with shadowed eyes, and my chest aches. "I just—" he swallows and looks down at his hands. "I've never held a baby. And I want to, for Christine and Mia. They've wanted this baby for so long. He means everything to them. But I'm scared."

Oh, Jonah. "Why are you scared?" I ask carefully. I wrap my arms around myself because I want to fling them around him, but I'm not sure he wants that.

"What if I hurt him? Or what if he doesn't like me?" Jonah blows out a breath. "A five-year-old I can handle. I can get him gifts, show him boy stuff. It's simple. But a baby?" He shakes his head. "They need affection. Skin-to-skin contact. I read about it." He shoves a hand through his hair, tugging on the silky strands. My throat tightens at the thought of Jonah googling babies and freaking out that he wouldn't be a good uncle. I want to cry for him.

"Christine wants me to be there for him. I have everything ready for his college fund. I even know what type of bike I'd buy him. But she wants more. I don't know if I can do *more*." He looks at me with helpless eyes, and I can't help but step into him and press my face to his chest. I loop my arms around his waist and squeeze.

"You're going to be fine. Parents aren't born knowing how to parent, you know. Uncles aren't born knowing how to uncle. You'll figure it out as you go. And I'll be there."

I lean back so I can look at his face. "I'll be there," I repeat. "You won't be alone."

His face softens. "Yeah?" His lips curve in a lopsided smile.

This is love. That feeling of stars bursting in my chest when he smiles. The quiet comfort of knowing I have someone by my side. *Am I brave enough to tell him? Am I brave enough to go down this road and not lose myself along the way?*

"Yeah." I confirm.

∽

"Stay with me," Jonah insists when we get back to the city.

"Stay with you? Really? You don't want your privacy?"

"I just want you." His eyes are serious, his expression determined.

So I agree, and staying with Jonah turns out to be magical. He eats his meals in the dining room inside the atrium, which functions like a greenhouse in the winter. Vines cascade from the ceiling down three stories and dangle above our heads. That night, his chef makes us steak salad and serves a light red that I'm sure costs more than I want to know.

Jonah has clothes delivered for me from Katie and her team. Pajamas, sexy underwear, comfortable clothes, slinky dresses. Every night, I try on a new set of lingerie and distract him from reading in his bed. To my delight, he pops an arm behind his head and lets the sheets pool around his bare stomach while he reads. On Tuesday, I wear a lacy red set, and he groans like a man undone before he pounces on me and goes down on me with luxurious slowness. The brush of my hand on his cock has him spilling into it with his teeth clenched. Watching him come apart is without a doubt the sexiest thing I've ever seen.

On Wednesday, he tells me we can play hooky from the office. His mouth is on my neck, his erection digging into my back. This is how I wake up most mornings. Jonah might start on his side of the bed, but he migrates to mine in the night, like he doesn't want to stop touching me.

"Hooky again? Are you okay? Let me check if you have a fever," I tease.

"Let me show you how fun I can be." He nips at my ear and rolls me onto my stomach before stretching me deliciously around his thick cock. We watch movies on his massive couch, and I find out that while he might be a ruthless asshole when he wants to be, he loves comedies. The dumber the better.

"Wayne's World? That's one of my favorites." My legs are slung over his on the low couch. It reminds me of a giant marshmallow. A bit silly, but damn comfortable.

In response, he quotes the famous line about being frank, and I laugh.

We work out every morning and every night we use the sauna in his home gym. He shows me what he learned from his masseuse, and I force him to let me massage him back.

The very best part of being with Jonah is his undivided attention. When he speaks to me, it's like I'm the only person in his world. He makes eye contact when he speaks, he mulls over what I say before responding, and he always cares about my answers to his questions. The nice clothes and the big house are fine, but what I could get addicted to is *him*. His intensity, his single-minded focus on everything, from my past to my pleasure, his raw honesty, and his ambition.

I watch him work at all hours and realize that he does it all for the people around him. His company, his employees, his family. The weight of everything is on his shoulders and he carries his burden proudly.

I could love him just for that. I'm watching him type out an email at his kitchen counter. When he finally finishes, he shuts his laptop with a sigh.

"What?" he asks, seeing me watching him.

"You care. A lot."

His brows go up.

"You pretend not to care." I point a finger at him. "But you do."

"I like money," he says nonchalantly.

I shake my head. "It's more than that. You're a good man, Jonah Crown."

He stands and stalks toward me, still in his green suit from today. So handsome, especially with his hair gelled back and his jaw stubbled with five o'clock shadow. His gaze goes predatory. "Trying to change me, Thompson?"

"Just calling it like I see it." I tip my chin up.

He nudges me back against the wall until I'm pinned there with my wrists in his hand. His thigh is between my legs. Just the barest motion has need cascading through me.

"I'm not good. Take it back," he growls.

I nearly laugh. "You are for me."

"True," he murmurs, dipping his lips to my neck. "Only for you."

51

Callie

Walking into an event on Jonah's arm is surreal. Nerves make my palms sweaty, but Jonah is a steady presence beside me. His tux is midnight black, his hair combed back in the way that makes him look more intense than usual. His eyes are black ice as he watches the crowd in the ballroom. A little bit predatory, a little bit irritated. Just the way I like it.

People sneak glances at us, but he doesn't seem to notice.

"Jonah," I mutter. "People are staring."

He arches a brow. "Of course. You look hot. They want to know who you are and if you're taken, or if you're here on business."

"And am I?" I tease.

His face darkens briefly. "You are very much taken. Don't test me, Thompson. I'll drag you into a closet and show you just how taken you are." My pulse jumps at his words. *Taken.* I love it. "But if you want to network, you can be here in your own right. It is a media event, after all."

"You'd do that?" *Even though I think you still hate what I do?*

He dips his chin. "Of course. You don't belong to me." He tilts his head. "I won't let you fade into the background." His eyes are serious and steady on mine. He knows exactly what he's saying. *Pick me.* He's different from Eric. He'll put me first.

I give him a brilliant smile. "Thank you."

"Careful how you wield that thing, Thompson. You could blind a man."

My smile grows at his grumpiness. "So what are we here for?"

"Dylan," he says shortly. His jaw flexes as he scans the room. "I don't see him yet or his board members."

We're still waiting for the remainder of our FOIA documents, and Jonah has been trying to contact the employee who sued Dylan, but we haven't had much luck.

"Board members? I thought you wanted to go after him directly?"

"It's a backup plan. If I can't ruin him, I'll buy the company." His shoulders slump. "The first step is approaching the board members and offering to buy their shares. They shouldn't be so damn difficult to talk to. But he's got them locked down tight."

"Maybe he has something on each of them."

Jonah gives me a sharp look. "I didn't think of that." He tilts his head, considering. "Find their secrets, then use the leverage." He looks grimly satisfied at the prospect.

"I didn't say that," I murmur.

"Too late. You're in it now. Remember the female board members you read about? Melissa and Erin? I need you to get close to them. Maybe follow them to the bathroom. See if they say anything bad."

I nod. This is a skill in my wheelhouse, whether Jonah likes it or not.

∽

"THERE HE IS." Jonah's voice is dark and low in my left ear. His hand on my waist tightens. I look at the entrance and spy Dylan's gelled blond hair and large frame. He's tall but paunchy, with skinny arms and all the markers of wealth. As he approaches, I take in his expensive suit, his ostentatious watch, his garish silk tie.

"Not much of a dresser, is he?" I mutter, and Jonah laughs into my hair.

"He thinks he is." He squeezes my waist. "Go time."

He steps into the aisle with cool confidence. "Dylan."

Dylan's head jerks and his face twists with hatred before he smooths it away. "What do you want?"

"Just want to chat," Jonah says mildly, but I can tell how angry he is from his tone. I could practically spoon up the tension between these two. "How's business?"

"Better than ever," Dylan says smoothly. *Liar.* His profits are down this quarter, and his company's valuation is dropping. I read the reports Jonah gave me. "How about you?"

"Good, good, though I can always do better." That's the real Jonah. The difference between the two of them has never been more apparent. It might look like dark versus light, but I know it's a matter of earning what you have versus being given it. Of taking everything on your own shoulders versus using others to get what you want.

"Listen, we're thinking of hiring a new CFO for Kings Lane and a résumé was passed on to us. Steve Park. I think he worked for you?" Jonah furrows his brow like he's not entirely sure. I freeze. It's the employee who Dylan assaulted. I'm not sure what Jonah intends to learn.

Dylan's face shutters. "That prick?" He laughs coldly.

"He did seem a little aggressive. I heard a rumor he caused trouble at Green Media. I don't want any part of that."

"Aggressive," Dylan scoffs. "More than that. He was insane. Claimed I beat him up. Check the fucking records. I never touched the guy. He was obsessed with taking me down. He falsified documents. Crazy bastard." He shakes his head, like he was totally innocent.

"Falsified documents? That's pretty bad." Jonah frowns and looks at me.

"That can be damaging," I agree. "Maybe if it was just small stuff..." I trail off, hoping Dylan will fill the silence.

"Small? Ha." He grabs a glass of champagne from a passing waiter and downs it. *Lovely.* "You call tax filings small? Asshole."

I control my reaction, but I see Jonah's eyes widen. *Tax filings.* To go with the tax fraud. There's something here.

Dylan's mouth presses flat. "Don't think I'm not onto you, Jonah." He steps toward me and Jonah tenses. "You're going to hire Steve and try to get information out of him. He knows nothing."

"Not interested," Jonah says coolly. "I just want to protect my business."

"Sure." Dylan's face is ugly with hate. All his suave composure is gone. "I saw her outside my apartment." He turns to me and leers. "I thought you were just a hot reporter, but now I realize you're his pet."

"Step away from her," Jonah says with icy calm. His eyes are flat with rage.

"Or what?" Dylan grabs my wrist and I yank away, but his grip is clammy and viselike.

Jonah's hand lands on Dylan's arm and twists. Dylan yelps as his wrist is bent back at an unnatural angle. "Or I'll break your fucking wrist."

"You're a thug," he pants, pain lacing his voice. Jonah twists harder.

"Maybe so." Jonah's smile is a baring of teeth. "But right now I'm glad to be one if it means I could knock you out. Don't ever fucking touch her again." He drops Dylan's arm with a shove and turns back to me.

He's shaking with anger as Dylan walks away. "Are you okay?" I ask.

"No." He blows out a breath. "I should be asking you that." His hand shakes as he runs it down my arm, feathering warm fingers over my skin. He's careful. So careful. Like I'm precious to him.

"I'm fine. Do you want to leave?"

"Not yet," he says shortly. "Let's find the information we need."

I'M LEAVING the bathroom an hour later when I run headfirst into a man's large frame.

"What the hell?" he exclaims, at the same time I say, "Sorry." I take a step around him and freeze.

"Eric." It's him. In the flesh. He's pretty and cruel with those pouty lips and that artfully tousled blonde hair. His eyes are small and flat, lit with anticipation now that he's seen me.

"Callie Thompson." He peruses my body, boldly, then gives me an insulting smirk. "Learning how to dress, I see."

My breaths seize in my chest. All the confidence I've earned back over the last twelve months drains out of me in a sickening rush. *Say something.* But all I can remember is the last time I saw him when he told me, "you'll come crawling back."

"I was wondering when I was going to run into you at one of these events. Surprised you wrangled an invite."

"She's with me." Jonah's cool voice comes from behind me. He strolls up, looking elegant and unruffled in his tux.

Eric's mouth parts in surprise and vicious satisfaction courses through my veins. Of course he knows who Jonah is. The whole world knows.

"Whoring yourself out now, Callie? Since I know he didn't bring you as a date."

Jonah's jaw flexes. His eyes are black pools of rage. My pulse speeds, and I turn pleading eyes on Jonah.

"Callie is the head of media for Kings Lane. She's here to make connections. And you are?" He frowns faintly, looking at Eric with bored eyes. I could kiss Jonah at that moment. Instead of losing his mind like a boyfriend would, he's making this about me and how competent I am. He knows exactly how to make Eric eat his words.

Eric puffs up, clearly thinking he's about to network with someone who obviously hates him. *Why didn't I see how dumb he was at the time?*

"I'm a brand promoter for—"

"Hold that thought." Jonah holds up a hand. "I see a canapé I really need to try." He puts a hand on my shoulder, and I follow him numbly in the opposite direction of the canapés. He knows exactly where he's going, because soon he's pushing open a door into a small event space. The room is scattered with couches and extra chairs.

He turns on me with concerned eyes. "Are you okay?" His palms land on my shoulders, as if he's checking to make sure I'm not hurt. I'm shaking slightly.

"Breathe, sweetheart," he says.

Sweetheart. Oh god. I shut my eyes briefly.

"Would you do that? Make me the head of something? Hire me for real?"

Jonah's expression turns thoughtful. "I would. You're smart and dedicated. Kings Lane would be lucky to have you. If you wanted it, of course."

"Could I still publish if I worked for you? Or would I have to give up the paper?" The words rush out of me. I have to know. I'm falling for him and he says he loves me, and *oh god*, the paper. Panic rises as I wait for Jonah's response.

"Why would you need to keep publishing?" His face is carefully blank.

My heart plummets somewhere into the vicinity of my ankles. *He doesn't understand.* He may never understand. *Does he trust me?* I'm falling for him, and if he doesn't trust me, it's going to break my heart.

"I love it. Could you live with that? I'd still want to publish celebrity gossip and silly things that make people smile. Serious articles too. But I like being a source of entertainment for people. I know it seems hard to understand, but there have been times in my life when I just needed something silly and fun to focus on. It's important to me to keep doing that for others."

He frowns. His thumbs rub absently over my shoulders, but I'm too numb to appreciate it.

"Jonah?"

"I don't think I can." His eyes are shadowed when he finally meets my gaze. I suck in a breath.

"You'll never be okay with me being a reporter."

He looks away briefly. "I don't understand why you need to keep doing it. You could have everything you want if you're with me. You'd never have to work again."

Such a Jonah thing to say. "And yet, I wouldn't have the thing I care about the most," I murmur.

He reels back, like I've hit him. "You sound like my sister."

"Well, she's a smart one. Money doesn't solve everything. This is my passion. I love this. It matters to people. It matters to the world. Why would you take it away from me?" My pulse is hammering in my chest. I want him to understand, but I don't think he will. I have to try, though. I can't end things without trying, even if I feel like this conversation is a runaway train coming dangerously close to speeding off the rails.

"I can't, Cal." His throat works. "There's something you should know." He sits down heavily on one of the sofas, his head drooping. When he finally looks at me, his gaze is bleak.

"I told you about Dylan and Annalise. But I didn't tell you everything." He says her name like it's poison. "Annalise was my girlfriend at the time. I was in love with her. I was going to propose. I'd saved up for a year to get her a ring. I was so fucking stupid." His words are bitter, and I ache to comfort him. "She was sneaking around with Dylan. He convinced her to sell photos of me to the press. Photos and videos." He says the final word with extra emphasis. My stomach turns over.

"I've seen the photos. That was her? That's awful."

"It was. Text messages between us, mocking commentary about me and my body and things I did in bed." His voice is hoarse and sympathy twists through me. "You want to know why I work out so much? Because of her."

"I'm so sorry, Jonah," I whisper. My eyes are hot and scratchy. "No one deserves that." I put my hand on his shoulder, and his shoulders bow. It's one of the only times I've seen him look broken. "I could kill her for doing that to you."

"So you see why I can never trust reporters? Especially Page Six reporters?" His eyes are pleading with me to understand, but all I hear is him drawing parallels between me and this woman he hates.

I tense. "You think I would do that? You think I would sell nude photos of you to the Post? I would *never*." I step back. "I've never once published anything with the intent of hurting you."

"Except for the article in October," he shoots back. His mouth twists with unhappiness.

"One time. That was a mistake. It won't happen again." I'm shaking now. *How can he profess to love me and think so poorly of me?*

His jaw clenches and he doesn't respond.

"You don't believe me," I say, with dawning realization. "You think I'm like her. When you sent those nude photos to me, what was your first thought? That I would sell them to Dylan?"

"Yes," he says bleakly. "My first thought was that they would end up on the front page."

"I was all in," I choke out. "I was thinking about how much I missed you and I wanted you." My voice is rising with my anger. "And you were thinking about whether or not I would betray you? I would never sell photos of you again, Jonah. I'd sooner publish them myself."

He jolts like I've punched him. My words are stupid, said in anger, and meaningless. I should take them back, but anger and hurt twine through me in a potent mix that makes it tough to swallow my pride. Jonah shoves his hands through his hair, mussing the strands I know feel like silk against my thighs.

"At the time, I told myself I knew you wouldn't publish them. I know you're not her, Callie, I do." He looks at me with pleading eyes. "But I don't think I'll ever forget how I felt when those videos were published. So yes, a tiny part of me regrets sending them," he finishes quietly.

I choke out a breath. "How could you paint with such a broad brush? How?" My cheeks are wet with tears. I didn't even realize I was crying. "You say you know I'm not like her, but you're still acting like I am. It all makes sense now." My voice is shaky. "Why you hated me so much. The way you tormented me. What was your plan, Jonah?"

"You knew I hired you for revenge. I told you."

I did know, and yet, I thought he was beyond that. I thought he was all in. But love without trust is meaningless. I learned that lesson with Eric. My chest feels like it's going to crack.

"I didn't realize it was like this," I burst out. I was all in when he was scheming. An innocent lamb led to the slaughter, except I'm not innocent and he fucking told me exactly what he planned to do. And like an idiot, I thought hatred could turn into real love. *Men don't change.*

"Were you planning to use me? Was I supposed to go after Annalise too?"

"No, sweetheart." He rises from the couch, and I step back warily. I don't want him near me. Not when he doesn't trust me.

He raises his hands placatingly. "I hired you initially with a stupid plan of using you to get back at Dylan. I thought maybe he'd hire you, and I could get you to give me information."

My jaw drops. *He's so much more ruthless than I ever imagined.*

"Callie. I'm over that. It was a stupid plan. I should never have used you. I love you. If you just stop the articles, I promise I'll forget it ever happened."

"So I'll give up everything I've worked for and just be consumed by your life? I've been there before. I don't want that again." My heart is racing. I can't go back to living in a man's shadow. I won't. Not even for Jonah.

He steps toward me, but I back up unsteadily. His eyes are wild. "Please, Callie." He stops, clenching and unclenching his fists, like he wants to grab me, but he knows I'll hate it.

"I can't do this," I choke out. "You want this on your terms. I'm not that girl anymore. I have to go."

I give him one last look before I leave. He looks broken, stunned. But he doesn't follow me as I walk down the hallway into the night, even though a little part of me wishes he would.

52

Jonah

I wake to my phone ringing. I feel like shit. Gritty eyes, cotton mouth, sweaty palms. Maybe I'm getting sick. *Not fucking likely.* I glance at Callie's side of the bed as if she'll be there.

"Mr. Crown? We've identified a cyber security threat. Are you near a computer?" My head of security's voice is clipped. This is the tone Sean uses when something bad is happening. *Fuck.*

"What time is it?"

"Five a.m. Are you near a computer, sir? We need to know how to proceed."

"Sure, yeah," I mutter, pressing a palm to my eye. I stumble to my laptop, which sits on the couch. I reviewed documents and drank until I fell asleep. All to forget about Callie and the horrified look on her face. Thinking her name makes me feel like an elephant is sitting on my chest.

"We're sending you a link, sir. Please pull it up."

The light of my laptop hurts my eyes, but I dutifully click the link that Sean sends me. "What is this?"

"We found it on the New York Star website. You told us to monitor it twenty-four hours a day, so we were able to act quickly. It was published five minutes ago. We can use a distributed denial of service attack to take it down."

I scroll with shaking hands. *Callie's website.* My stomach sours as the photos load. The photos I sent her. My nude torso is displayed in grainy quality on the screen. And the other photo. The one where I'm hard under my sweats. *Fuck.* There's an article accompanying the photos, but the words blur before my eyes. I can't read this.

The photo quality is better, but I could substitute this moment for that morning six years ago. The sinking feeling in my stomach. The ache of betrayal. The shame of being exposed. The only difference is now no one will see the evidence. *I hope.*

"What the fuck?" I whisper. My blood rushes in my ears. She betrayed me. After all her promises, she fucking betrayed me. *Just like Annalise. Just like I knew she would if I let her get close to me.*

I'm going to be sick. I swallow to clear the saliva in my mouth.

"Print the article. Save it. I want this preserved." *So I never forget what she did.*

"Very good, sir. And what do you want us to do about the website?"

My pulse thuds. *I would never sell photos of you again. I'd sooner publish them myself.* She told me exactly who she was. She loves the paper. She picked it over me. I pushed her and she picked it over me. *Damn her.*

"Shut it down. We own the LLC. Do whatever you have to do, but I want it gone." My voice is hoarse. Pain and anger dig twin claws into me. I want to rage, I want to find Callie and shake her. I never want to see her again. *Fuck.*

"Understood, sir."

I hang up and call Miles again and again until he answers. I'm on the verge of shutting down. My hands shake.

"Everything okay?"

"I'm sorry to call you. I don't know what to do. Callie betrayed me."

"Fuck. What happened?" Miles is whispering. He's probably in bed with Lane. I shouldn't be bothering him but I don't know what to do. He's been through this before with me. This is the exact conversation we had years ago. And just like then, I'm gutted, my heart cut open for the world to see. *I thought it would hurt less the second time around.*

"The photos. She published photos I sent her."

"What kind of—oh shit."

"Yeah."

"Shit." I hear him rustling around, and then a door shutting. "What can I do?"

"Nothing. I'm going to call Aiden. Her paper is done."

"Are you sure?" He's silent for a minute. "She'll never forgive you."

I let out a hoarse, unhappy laugh. "I don't care. We're through. I never want to see her again." I let my head hang down. "I thought she was one of the good ones. I told her I loved her." My breath is ragged in my chest. *She said she would never betray me.*

"I'm sorry, man. Are you sure I can't help?"

I shut my eyes, drawing in deep breaths. "I need a minute. I can deal with the fallout later. I just need some time." *To get myself together. To see if there's anything in the first aid kit in my bathroom to tape me back together.*

"I'll be here when you need me." Miles hangs up. I let my head drop into my hands.

She fucking betrayed me. After all her promises otherwise.

I'm not like that.

I would never.

Her outrage that I was comparing her and Annalise when they are exactly the fucking same. How could I be such a fool? Callie met my family. She saw ultrasounds of the baby. My blood slows in my veins. *My family. The baby.* What if she went after them? What if she goes after them?

She still has a badge. She can still get into my office. She could be there right now, plotting to take me down. My breaths come short in my chest. She has a fucking video. She could make millions from the video. And now she needs the money, because the paper is gone, and her loan was never settled. I never fucking paid it, because I'm an asshole, and she definitely deserved it, but this is a fucking mess.

Adrenaline courses through me. I fire off messages to my mom and Christine and Mia.

"Do not speak to Callie Thompson if she contacts you. Tell Dad."

I pull up the documents Aiden sent me when Callie started for me. I sign them with quick strokes of the stylus on my tablet. One paper to dissolve the LLC that owns the New York Star, one signature to cancel the trademark. Pain slices through my stomach. Another stroke of my pen to pull her press pass. Another to shut down her website.

I slump over the table when the papers are sent. *It's done.* It's all done. Now I just have to survive.

53

Callie

I throw myself into the paper with unmatched dedication. If my dad is surprised at the fact that I'm doing nothing but working, and on a weekend, he doesn't say anything. I still haven't decided what to do on Monday.

We still need the money, and I hate being a quitter. But I don't know if I can see Jonah and not break down. Part of me is tempted to give up everything for him, and I hate it. I hate how tempting his offer was. *Love me, and everything will be okay.* I find myself taking deep breaths every time I think about how lost he looked as I walked away.

Fuck, I love you.

I love you too. I've imagined being brave enough to say it back a hundred times. I'd fall into his arms and he'd kiss me like he was never going to let me go.

Did I just ruin the best thing I've ever had?

Maybe, maybe, says each beat of my heart. But my brain still says I was right to stand up for myself, right to reject Jonah. *My terms or not at all.* It's what he would do, isn't it?

I feel like I'm slowly going insane. Sunday rolls around and I'm still in Saturday's clothes. My hair is messy and my skin feels dirty, but all I want to do is lay in bed and watch movies until I fall back asleep.

Tomorrow. I'm going to see him tomorrow.

I press my palms to my eyes and swing my legs over the edge of the bed. When I walk quietly into the kitchen, I see my dad's keys aren't on the hook, and I let out a sigh of relief. He's gone, but he's going to start asking questions, especially if I don't go to work tomorrow.

Focus, Cal. If I get fired, we need a backup plan. I need photos for the Post, and they need to be better than ever. I need to get my head in the game. Today, I'm going to get outside and take photos, whether I feel like it or not. But first, I have to check the website and make sure the printer got the money I sent.

I yawn over my computer, gulping my coffee in hopes it will kick-start my brain. When I log into the bank account for the paper, it shows a sizable refund from today. *A refund?* It's from the printer. *That's odd.* My hand hovers over my phone. I should call and ask, but a selfish part of me wants to keep the money and not question it too much. My payment bought us time on the loan, but it still hasn't been paid off. It's an axe hanging over my head, waiting to slice.

With a sigh, I dial the printer. Matt, the owner, is usually there on Sundays.

"Callie, what's up?"

Matt is a straight shooter, and I like him for it. He's easy to deal with.

"Matt, I hate to say this, but I see a refund in the account from you guys. I think your accountant made a mistake."

"No mistake. Let me see." Rustling noises come over the line. "Yeah. You guys terminated the contract. Last edition runs this week. I thought you knew?" He sounds apologetic, but certain.

"I didn't cancel it. Did my dad?"

"Nah. The cancellation was signed by someone named Jonah Crown. Says here he owns the LLC that owns the paper. We thought it was weird, so we checked the public records for you guys and realized he was telling the truth. I didn't know you were owned by a larger company."

Time slows to a drip. My heartbeat is loud in my ears as my mind races. Jonah canceled the contract. Jonah.

"When?" My voice is hoarse and I clear my throat. "When did the cancellation come through?"

"Ah. This morning, it looks like. Yep, the document is signed and dated for this morning. Weird that the bank actually processed a refund on a weekend, but yeah. We're sorry to see you go."

"Us too," I say woodenly, even though this printing contract has caused nothing but trouble. *Jonah. Jonah.* Betrayal makes my insides crumple. I can't believe this. *Can you not? With the way you rejected him? The way he always gets what he wants?*

If he was determined before, he's going to be even more determined now. *Maybe it's a mistake.* I don't want to jump to conclusions. But when I refresh our email, I see a notification from our domain provider saying the domain sale has been accepted and the transfer has begun.

Sale? What the fuck? The loss of the printing contract is one thing, but losing our website? I frantically click into our site and get a red notification that the domain transfer is in progress. I can't publish any new content.

I sit back against my chair, stunned. *He did it. He killed the paper.* He was holding back this whole time, and when I gave him enough incentive, he ruined us. It probably took him five minutes.

I picture him in the limo back from the party, sending emails in that clipped manner of his. Ruining me was a moment's work for Jonah. An annoyance at the end of the day.

I press the heels of my hands to my eyes to keep from crying. *I am not going to cry over him. He doesn't deserve it. Men don't change.* I'm a fool. Jonah told me in no uncertain terms who he was, and I didn't believe him.

I want you to suffer.
This is not a buddy cop movie.
I am not a good person.

Idiot. I'm such an idiot.

The longer I press my lips together to keep my chin from wobbling, the worse I feel, and the more anger starts to tangle inside me. I welcome it. I'd rather anger than betrayal.

I squeeze my eyes shut. *I love him. I lost him. He hates me.*

The ache inside me doesn't dull when I click out of the website. On my screen is the last article I started about Jonah. A brief piece about Kings Lane with a photo of Jonah in a suit right above it. His eyes are devilish, his face is set. He's staring at the viewer like he hates them.

Like he knows it's me behind the camera.

54

Callie

I think I'm going to be sick. The rush of the elevator rising isn't helping. I've dressed well for my execution, in my favorite blue dress. My cheeks are heated and I press cold fingers against them, trying to calm myself. I thought maybe he'd leave it at ruining the paper. *Fool.* Jonah Crown does nothing by half measures. I received a clipped email last night with instructions to arrive at ten a.m. and wait by the elevators. It didn't come from Jonah. It came from HR. He can't even be bothered to fire me himself.

When the elevator opens onto the 52nd floor, I'm greeted by George. Instead of a smile, I get a stony glare. I feel like the enemy. *I guess I am the enemy, though I'm not entirely sure why.*

"I know the way to the conference room."

"You're not allowed to wander the halls here without an escort," they say crisply. There's sadness in their voice, though. My heart clenches. George and I could have been friends. *Not anymore.*

I duck my head as we pass people at their desks. Silence falls as we pass the little groups, then whispers start up behind me. *I think I'm going to be sick.* My stomach is sloshing.

I waited for Jonah to call yesterday, even though I wasn't sure I wanted to pick up the phone. I held out foolish hope for hours, alternating between turning my phone off and trying to sleep away the day, and staring at it while I waited for him to call.

I love you. Let me show you what it's like to be mine.

When I saw the email from HR, I thought perhaps I was being summoned to hand in my badge and get my belongings. But now? It's clear Jonah wants me to suffer. He picked the conference room farthest from his office, which he never uses, but which requires me to pass every cubicle on this floor in a sick parade of shame.

George silently opens the conference room door, and I steel my spine before walking in.

Seeing Jonah is like being punched in the gut. Damnable hope rises and is rapidly squashed as I catalog his appearance. Cruel stare, smirking mouth. He's spread lazily in a chair. He doesn't bother to stand when I enter, instead gesturing to a chair at the opposite end of the long conference table. *So that's how it is.* My breakfast turns to a hard lump in my stomach.

Miles is there, too, along with a woman I think is Caitlin, the head of HR, one of the internal lawyers, and an unknown man who looks like he might be a security person. *Looks like Jonah brought a crowd.* Their faces blur and I look away.

I seat myself and press my hand between my thighs to keep them from shaking. This feels like an interrogation. Caitlin's face is serene, but Miles's normally pleasant expression is sour.

"We have an NDA for you to sign." When Jonah finally speaks, his words are crisp.

"I'm being fired?" I assumed it was coming, but I have to be sure. *Right back where I started, but now, he's taken everything.*

He barks an unamused laugh. "Yes, Ms. Thompson. You're being fired." Anger flashes through me. What right does he have to mock me, when he ruined me? His eyes are glittering with malice, and his cruel amusement at my expense makes me bold. Foolishly bold, perhaps.

"On what grounds?" I raise my chin.

"You really want to know?" He looks pleased at the prospect.

I nod. "I've done everything you asked. I didn't report on anything confidential. I didn't act out at work."

Jonah smiles, more of a baring of teeth than a real smile. *I miss his smiles. Oh god.* I press my lips together.

"Nothing confidential? Are you sure?" His eyes are flat and black, his face is shuttered.

"I'm sure."

His face hardens. "As it turns out, Ms. Thompson. I'm firing you for fraternization."

"Fraterni—oh my god." I whisper the last words, my face heating. Miles and Caitlin are staring at me with distaste, and my breaths are shallow in my chest, until I feel like I'm going to faint. I need to get out of here. Fraternization. Sleeping with Jonah. He's firing me for sleeping with him. It's cruelly elegant in its simplicity. *I'm an idiot. I fell for him even though he told me not to, and now I'm paying the price.*

I scan his face for any hint of softness. Maybe this isn't real. Maybe I'm dreaming and the man who professed to love me isn't ripping out my heart. His expression is dark, cruel, and satisfied. *I'm going to be sick.* This isn't a joke. This is very real, and Jonah and I are through.

Someone else might fight. Maybe I'm weak, because I don't want to. I've learned you can't fight people when they really want to do something. It just brings more pain. My mom wanted to leave, and she did. I've never tried to get her back. Same with Eric. And now Jonah. Better to hold your head high and move on.

"Give me the paper," I say dully. "I'll sign it." Anything to get out of this room. *Who do you think you are?* I can feel their eyes on me, witnessing my shame. Just like the last time. My hands shake and I clench them together. The lawyer is looking at me like I'm a crazy person, but he slides me the paper.

I scan it with unseeing eyes. All I see is $18,000 and pages of legal jargon.

"We'll pay the remainder of the loan," Jonah explains. "In

exchange, you will never disclose anything you learned at Kings Lane. Do you agree?"

"Yes." My voice comes out flat and emotionless, by some miracle.

Jonah tilts his head. "You'll never report on me. Do you agree?"

"Yes." I clench my hands together so he can't see them shake.

He's frowning now, but he continues. "You'll release any claims you have against the company. And you will never, ever, come near my family or speak about them in the press. Understood?"

"Okay."

Jonah is looking at me with a wrinkled brow, like he expected more resistance. "Nothing to say?"

Does he want me to fight him? I don't have it in me.

I shake my head. I don't care. I'm not planning to report on Jonah anymore. I just want to forget him. "I would never report on your family." I don't meet his eyes as I sign the paper. I write my name on the dotted line and date my signature. I raise my head to meet his eyes, my own hot with unshed tears. I will myself not to cry as I gather my belongings. Jonah stares at me like I'm dirt on the bottom of his shoe.

"Why?" I whisper. "All from that fight? Because I rejected you?" My face heats as Miles and Caitlin watch this private shame unfold. I guess they already know about us sleeping together. *How much worse can it get?*

"Rejected you?" Jonah barks a cruel laugh. "Ms. Thompson, you tried to ruin me."

"What do you mean?" I scan his face, looking for some clue. I feel like everyone in the room has the full, awful picture, and I'm left in the dark.

"This." He smacks a piece of paper down on the table hard enough to make me jump. "Do you not remember this? Since you published it a mere forty-eight hours ago?"

He slides the paper toward me, and I see the photos printed in black and white. *Oh my god.* I press a hand to my mouth.

"You think I did this?" I choke out the words. "You think I printed nude photos of you?"

"You deny it?" He raises a brow, affecting calm, but his chest must be cracking like mine is. *Oh, Jonah.*

"How long were they up?" I ignore his question. I need to know if anyone saw. Poor Jonah. I hate him, but my heart hurts for him. *It happened again.* "Did anyone see?"

His eyes flare with surprise. "They were quickly removed," he says tightly. "Don't play dumb, Ms. Thompson." Every time he says my last name, it's like a bullet through my chest. *Callie. Oh, Callie.* "I don't know what your game is," he continues, shaking his head. "But you can stop. These were on your site."

"I would never." I gather my bag and my coat. Jonah doesn't believe me. After everything, he still thinks I'd betray him. I guess I was right to end things. Much good it did me. My heart is in pieces after all.

"Check the byline, Jonah. It reads Callie Thompson. I've never signed an article with my real name. And since I became editor-in-chief, I changed my byline. If you don't believe me, at least believe that. I'm proud of my work." My lips twist unhappily. "After everything you told me about Annalise, I understand. I guess it never would have worked." I give him a sad smile, even as his eyes flare.

"Callie. Wait." He rises in a rush. "If you didn't print it, who did?"

Pain is a dull knife behind my ribs as I turn to him. "I don't know. But I deserve more than someone who doesn't love me enough to trust me. Goodbye, Jonah."

I turn on my heel and walk out. When I get into the elevator, I finally let the tears come.

55

Jonah

"Is there any chance this wasn't her?" I round on Sean, my head of security. "Any at all?"

"No." He shakes his head. "There's no other—"

"Check your email," Miles interjects. "Here." He passes me his phone.

My stomach plummets.

There, in black and white is an email from Dylan. I see only the first few words, indicating the leaked photos were just a taste of what he'll do to me and Callie.

I drop the phone and run for the door, pushing it open so hard it slams against the wall. I have to talk to her. "Callie," I yell. I reach the elevators. She's gone. I mash the button and pace nervously for the whole awful ride to the bottom. Then I'm sprinting through the lobby, scanning for her, my heart pounding. I see a flash of dark hair, but it's someone else. *Fuck.* People are staring, but I don't care. *I need to explain. I need to explain. I love her. I ruined her. Oh fuck.* I slam through the double doors onto 57th Street. *Where is she? I don't see her.* Fuck. My shoulders slump. I try calling her, but it goes straight to voicemail. She probably has me blocked. I text her anyway.

JONAH

Come back

Please

I can explain

Please, Callie

Nothing. Fuck.

I ride up to my office, ill and shaky, like I just boxed ten rounds with a stronger opponent. *She thinks I hate her. She thinks I don't trust her. I took away everything she loves, and she did nothing to hurt me.*

You asshole.

Shame makes my stomach turn.

Miles comes storming into my office.

"What the hell happened in there? Fraternization? Really?" He's angry and I have to agree with him. "What the fuck? This was Dylan? You told her about Annalise?"

"I fucked up." I slump onto the couch and then stand so I can pace. Adrenaline is still coursing through me from my desperate bid to find Callie.

"I ruined her, Miles. I destroyed her paper. She loved it. After I called you Saturday, I took it all away. The printing contract, the website, her LLC, the press pass. Everything." My shoulders slump. "When she came here today, she thought this was about the fight we had." My stomach roils. "Friday night. She asked me if I could live with her working as a reporter, and I said no. I told her about Annalise and I implied—fuck. I implied they were the same." I basically flat out said it. "And then the photos. I was wrong."

Miles's face is hard. "You fucked up," he says flatly.

"I know." I shut my eyes and let the guilt wash over me. "I love her."

"Well, she certainly hates you. That's a guarantee. You just publicly fired her and accused her of sleeping with someone. Wait, you didn't mean you, did you?"

I nod and open my eyes to see my best friend staring at me in shock, and no small amount of disappointment. "That's fucked, Jonah." He shakes his head. "You loved her and you destroyed her."

"I know, okay? I know. I can worry about that later. I just have to get her back."

"Oh no," Miles says. "There's no getting her back after this."

My heart clenches. "I have to. I need her."

"I asked you to be sure. You were sure. Fuck." Miles sounds as pissed as I am.

"All I saw was Annalise and those awful articles. You remember those? The ones about how I was bad in bed and how she thought my body was disgusting."

His face softens with sympathy. "Yeah. I remember." Miles sits next to me, and I let my head drop into my hands. "I get it. I saw how devastated you were. But Callie didn't. Did you see the look on her face just now? You betrayed her." He releases a heavy breath. "I don't know if you can get her back."

"I can't accept that." The thought of losing Callie forever makes my chest pinch.

"Then you need a plan. A really good fucking plan. I'll call Lane. I suggest you talk to your sister."

Miles claps me on the shoulder, affection evident in the way his hand lingers.

All I know is that I definitely don't deserve it.

56

Callie

The first days after the meeting, I'm numb. I don't leave my room, I don't eat, I just sleep. I sleep and I worry about our future. I can start another paper, I can sell photos to the Post, but we need to pay rent, and Jonah was easily my best subject. My brain veers away from the topic of Jonah every time I think his name.

My dad and I need a plan.

I finally tell my dad the news on Wednesday morning. We're having coffee in the kitchen, regular for me, decaf for him.

"Dad." I blow out a breath. I need to rip this off like a Band-Aid. "The paper is gone. Jonah closed it. And it's all my fault."

"What did you say?" His brow wrinkles in confusion.

"I got, um, involved with Jonah. But it didn't work out. I shouldn't have done it."

"Oh, Callie."

"No, Dad, let me finish." I take a deep breath. "I finally figured out what happened. Jonah sent me some photos. I uploaded them to the cloud automatically, so they were available for the site. You know I do that with the photos I take on my phone."

My dad nods and a pit yawns in my stomach at the words I'm about to say. "Jonah's business rival hacked the site. I called the domain provider." I can't even look at my dad. "He published the photos and Jonah thought I did it." My chest aches with the weight of my regret. I shouldn't have fallen in love with Jonah. I shouldn't have uploaded the photos. As much as I want to hate Jonah for this, I understand. He was cruel, but the evidence was damning. The thought of being so exposed makes my skin crawl.

"He retaliated by shutting down the paper." Now that I've had a few days, I've realized the extent of Jonah's destruction. "Our website is gone, the printing contract is canceled, and the press passes were pulled." That hurt most of all. I'd fought hard to be recognized as a legitimate paper for years. The press pass was a culmination of those efforts. Gone with a stroke of Jonah's pen.

"Oh, Cal." My dad puts a hand on my shoulder, and I squeeze my eyes shut. "It's not your fault. I knew letting Jonah invest in the paper was a risk. He could have sold it or closed it whenever he wanted. I don't blame you."

"I blame myself," I whisper. "You loved that paper. I'm sorry."

He sighs. "I'm more worried about you. I've barely seen you. How serious were you and Jonah?" His sharp blue eyes assess me and I look away.

"I loved him," I admit, my voice cracking. "I fell in love with him, and he fell in love with me, and it ended horribly. And the worst part is, I still love him."

My dad winces but loops an arm over my shoulders. "Love doesn't just go away, Cal."

That's exactly what I feared.

∼

THE NEXT MORNING, after I've stuffed my hair under a beanie and slogged out the door to take photos, I see a sleek black car idling at the curb. My stomach sinks. *I know that car.* Just like I know its occupant. *Why is he here?* I tuck my chin into my jacket. *Maybe he won't recognize me.*

"Callie."

I turn, against my better judgment, and take Jonah in. My heart clenches at this sight of him. He's in a suit, but there are blue circles under his eyes. His hair is standing in every direction, like he spent all night running his fingers through it. His eyes are shadowed with regret. *Too fucking bad.*

"Come to torment me again, Jonah? Haven't I suffered enough?"

"I came to apologize."

"I don't want to hear your apologies." The words taste bitter, but I turn on my heel and walk away.

∼

Jonah's there again the next day, though it's an hour later than the day before. This time, with a coffee for me.

"How did you know when I was leaving?" It hurts to look at him. Another suit today. This one rumpled.

His face colors slightly. "I slept here. I got the coffees when I saw your light go on."

My mouth drops open. "You slept in your car?"

"It's a comfortable car. And I needed to talk to you."

"Are you going to give up?"

His throat works. His eyes are intense. "No."

I sigh. If I want any peace, I'll have to hear him out.

"So talk," I say, my voice hard. We walk down the street, side-by-side. I sneak glances at him, my stomach knotting every time I see how handsome he is. *How am I going to get over him?*

"Callie." He stops in the middle of the sidewalk, forcing me to stop too. Pedestrians are giving us annoyed looks, so I back up until I'm against a building and he's facing me. His face is lined with guilt. Exhausted in a way I've never seen before. He reaches out, like he's going to touch me, before he lets his hand drop. The distance between us feels way too close, and yet, a chasm that can't be crossed without bloodshed.

"I'm sorry. I don't expect you to forgive me." He grimaces as if he's in physical pain. "What I did was...unforgivable. I realize that." His voice is heavy with recrimination. "You know about my past. I think you understand why I reacted the way I did. But that all pales in comparison to how I treated you." He pauses. "I love you," he says in a low voice. My body jolts at his words. I shut my eyes. "I know you don't want to hear it. I won't burden you with it anymore, but just know that I was in a dark place when those photos leaked the first time. And this time—" His throat works. "I was destroyed. But it's still no excuse for assuming you did it. I'll do everything in my power to get your paper back for you, okay? I promise. I'm sorry."

I stare at him for long seconds, my pulse thrumming. *I miss him.* But I can't forgive him. Not when he deliberately caused me pain.

"Those photos were in the cloud because of me," I respond. He steps forward and I hold up a hand. "I just want you to know." My lips twist in self-recrimination. Jonah didn't deserve that. "I'm sorry. I'm partly to blame. You were right." The words drop between us.

"No, Callie. No, you're not." He looks so earnest and serious, as if hopeful that maybe we have a path forward. I want to press my face to his chest and ease this pain, but I need to crush this hope before it can grow.

"I'm not going to forgive you," I say. I cross my arms over my stomach, as if I can protect myself.

"I don't expect you to." He shakes his head. "I'll spend the rest of my life making it up to you, though." He gives me a sad smile and walks back to his car.

∽

I GET dinner that night with Luz and Adriana. I called both of them after the incident at the office, but I haven't seen them in a few days.

"How are you holding up?" Luz gives my arm a squeeze. Her big brown eyes are worried.

Adriana's face is hard. "Want me to kill him and make it look like an accident? Scratch that, it doesn't need to be an accident. No jury in the land would convict me." She made the same offer when I told her about Jonah's betrayal.

"I saw him today." I hug my wineglass to my chest.

"And?" This from Luz, who is drinking her white wine in nervous sips.

"He apologized. He said he loves me." Pain lances through me at the words. "I wasn't interested in hearing it." Except I had wanted to hear it, and his reactions made perfect sense, and I hated myself a little for wanting to fall into his arms afterward. If only things were that easy.

"What did he say?" Luz asks. She's much more inclined to be forgiving. Adriana has more of "kill first, act questions later" kind of vibe.

"He apologized. He said he would spend the rest of his life making it up to me. His ex—" I pause, not sure if I should tell Adriana and Luz about what happened. "You know the photos of him that came out a few years back?"

Luz wrinkles her nose, while Adriana nods. "Yeah, the nudes. Texts, photos, the works. It was pretty bad. We learned about it during a crisis management seminar actually." She winces. "The public backlash was pretty bad. That was right around the time there were the embezzling rumors, right?"

I nod, my shoulders tight. "It was his ex. She left him for his business rival, and they worked to take him down. She leaked the photos."

"Holy shit." Adriana's mouth drops open.

"I know." I gulp my wine. "So when he saw the photos on my site, he lost his mind. I can't blame him."

"I sure as hell can. He should have known you'd never do that."

I knot my fingers together in my lap. "The thing is, I told him I'd do it."

"What?" Luz asks.

"We got into a fight on Friday. He compared me to Annalise and I told him I'd sooner publish photos than sell them to Dylan."

"Oh my god," Luz whispers.

"Still. He should have given you a chance to explain." Adriana shakes her head, but Luz make an expression that tells me she understands.

"I feel bad for him," Luz says. "I think he really fell for you, Cal. He must have lost his mind when the photos were posted. Even though what he did was awful. And he did apologize."

"It doesn't matter, Luz. Those are words. He's showed me who he is with actions."

Adriana is poking at her phone. "So if he proved to you with his actions that he was a good man, you'd take him back?"

I bite my lip. "If he could show me with actions that he changed, I'd think about it," I say slowly. *If I could be certain that he would trust me and stick by me, maybe.*

"Well, you might regret saying that." Adriana slides her phone toward me. "Look at the alert I just got."

Shock makes my face go slack. "Billionaire Jonah Crown arrested for assault." Jonah's mugshot is terrible. One eye is purple and swollen, but his other stares defiantly at the camera. His collar is rumpled, his hair mussed. I press a hand against my mouth as I read.

"Eric. He assaulted Eric. He found him in a bar and beat the shit out of him." My stomach does somersaults that make the wine go sour. *For me.* And a sick part of me is glad that Jonah did what I could never do.

"Barbaric," Luz mutters, but her eyes are shining.

"Knock it off, Luz. You're practically panting."

"Sorry." She winces. "I just think it's hot. And much needed." She scowls. "Eric deserved to have his bones broken."

It is hot. The thought of Jonah avenging me makes my insides fluttery. *God, I'm so weak.*

"This just proves that he has some anger issues to work out." I shake my head and drain my wine. "This isn't change."

Adriana and Luz are looking at me with sympathy. "I want to move on." I press my palms to my eyes, and Luz puts a hand on my shoulder. "I need to figure out my next move. I just have no energy. I'm so tired, you guys." I grimace. "I laid in bed all day yesterday. But we need rent money."

"Danny needs someone for a few shifts a week at the coffee shop," Adriana volunteers. Her friend owns a coffee shop a few blocks from my apartment. "You could do it to take your mind off things. Just until you find something else."

"There's no shame in needing a break," Luz interjects. "We're here for you."

My eyes fill with tears at my wonderful friends. I'll be okay, and I'll get over Jonah eventually.

57

Jonah

Miles bails me out of jail. He's pissed, his jaw working as he signs me out and stalks back to the waiting car. Luckily, the press haven't gotten wind of my arrest—there are no reporters waiting outside the jail. No Callie. Miles's driver gives me a brief nod, clearly shocked at my antics.

"What the fuck were you thinking?" Miles asks when we're settled in the car's interior.

"I wasn't." I shut my eyes and lean against the cold window. The glass feels good against my swollen face. Eric landed one good punch before I broke his arm. I clench my teeth. I should have broken all his fingers too. I started with the hand he touched Callie with at the event, but he could stand to break a few more bones.

"This is not like you," Miles says quietly. "You're scaring me. I think you should take a break from work."

My eyes fly open. My best friend looks genuinely worried. I heave a sigh. "You're probably right. I'm so fucked. I can't stop thinking about her."

"Callie?"

Miles's eyes are sympathetic.

"Didn't Lane and you break up? How did you handle that?" I remember when Miles was a mopey mess around the office.

"Lots of alcohol and self-recrimination."

"So you get it," I say bitterly. "This is it for me. She doesn't want me. She's not going to take me back. I said I was sorry and she accepted my apology and told me she would never forgive me." My chest aches at the memory.

"I'm sorry," Miles says. "But is this all you've got? One apology and a bar fight? You're the man who once told me that failure to achieve your goals was simply a lack of effort." He raises a challenging brow.

"I don't know. I need to respect her wishes. I'm not going to stalk her."

"Has she told you to leave her alone?"

"No. And I can't help but feel like she wanted me to chase her after the event. I should have chased her. I should never have let her go." My voice is fierce, certain.

"So don't."

58

Callie

The next morning, Jonah is there again, looking sinfully handsome in a dark wool coat and cashmere scarf. His eye is swollen shut, but even that can't dim his beauty. *Don't notice him.*

He silently passes me a coffee, and I sigh as I accept it.

"We ran out of beans this morning, otherwise I would throw this in your face," I say.

"I know. I wouldn't mind." He smiles faintly. "Can I drive you?"

"Aren't you going to work?"

He looks sheepishly away. "I'm on leave. I, uh, can't be trusted in this mental state. You know, with the eye and all." He gestures at his face.

I turn toward Amsterdam Avenue, and he keeps pace, walking a few steps behind me.

I stop and cross my arms. "Are you going to trail me every morning?"

"It's not safe for you to be out this early. Think of me like your bodyguard."

I narrow my eyes at him.

"You should have seen the other guy," he says flippantly. *Eric.*

"What happened?"

"Don't worry about it," he says tightly. "He won't harass you anymore. He offered to move out of that apartment. If you want it back." His voice makes it clear the offer was coerced. My pulse speeds. Jonah got into a very public altercation to avenge me, when he hates notoriety. Something flutters inside me at the thought. No one has ever done that for me before.

"Why?" I whisper. My heart feels like it's somewhere in the vicinity of my throat. "I told you I wouldn't forgive you."

He steps forward. "Because you're mine. Even if you don't want me. I'll spend forever clearing the path for you. It's what you deserve."

He turns and walks away, leaving me stunned on the sidewalk.

∽

THE NEXT DAY, he's a minute late, and I find myself lingering on the steps. *Go. Don't wait for him, you fool.* But I breathe a sigh of relief when he shows up.

He leaps out of the car, his face relaxing when he sees me. "Sorry. I had to stop at Judy's apartment."

"Is she okay?"

"Oh yes. Just had a fall last night and my mom wanted me to check on her. She's alone. It's hard getting older alone." He shakes his head, looking serious and sad. My stomach dips. *Alone.* Like me and Jonah.

"Are you ever going to stop pursuing me? Like you said, being alone is hard. Don't you want to find someone to make you happy?"

My heart rolls itself up into a ball at the thought of him with someone else.

"You're the only person who has ever made me happy." His jaw works. "Do you want me to find someone else?"

No. No, I don't. I want him for myself. It's so fucked.

Instead of responding, I say, "I'm starting at the coffee shop on the corner tomorrow. So I won't be here in the mornings anymore."

I don't wait for his response before I go back inside and shut the door. I'm not telling him to meet me there. I'm not. But a tiny part of me knows I'll be disappointed if he isn't there.

59

Jonah

I can hear the baristas whispering about me. It's Callie's second day at the coffee shop, and I'm at the same table I chose yesterday. I chased some sucker with a laptop away. It's perfectly positioned so I can watch Callie while she works. She's clearly done this before because she works the coffee machine with ease and smiles at customers while she rings orders. Every man who smiles at her makes my fists clench.

Do you want me to find someone else? She hadn't answered, but the way her eyes darkened makes me think she would be equally upset if I found someone else. *There will never be anyone else.* Life is dull and gray without Callie. It's her or no one.

I go back to my laptop, idly checking my email. I've had George forwarding me key emails without telling Miles. It's going to end at some point, because George is more loyal to Miles than they are to me. Miles is going to freak out when he finds out. At least that day will be interesting.

But damn, my life is fucked. No work, no Callie, nothing. All I do is work out and fantasize about getting her back.

A coffee thumps down on my table. "Is that you leaving hundreds in the tip jar?"

I look up slowly, knowing who I'll find. Callie's annoyed, and fuck, I love to see that fire in her eyes. Her hands are on her hips, and her hair is all wisps and curls in her messy bun. For just a minute, I want to pretend we're back to our old selves. Me making fun of her, her pretending to hate it.

"No, must be some other billionaire," I drawl.

She scowls. "You're scaring the patrons."

I look around and raise a brow. "Am I?"

Her scowl deepens. "Yes. It's your huge black eye."

"Concerned for me, Thompson?"

Her face flushes, her mouth parts. "Don't call me that."

"Why not? Afraid you'll like it too much?"

She opens her mouth to speak and then clamps it shut.

I pull out my wallet and lazily count hundreds into a small pile. "Is this enough to compensate for the table?"

Her eyes flick to the stack. "I don't need your money, Jonah."

"I want you to have it," I say quietly. "Anything you want is yours. Name it."

Her eyes light. She thinks she's got me, I can tell. I nearly smile. An annoyed Callie is better than a sad Callie. "I want you to show me that you value journalism. And *not* with money."

"Okay. I can do that." I've never met a challenge I couldn't overcome. "Game on, Thompson. Now take the money." I hold the stack out to her. Her tongue darts out to lick her lips, and she sighs before pocketing the cash.

"I'm putting it in the tip jar," she warns. "And because we need the money."

"Wait. What did you say?"

She frowns. "You fired me, Jonah. The paper is gone. A thousand dollars, or whatever this is, is a drop in the bucket. This isn't even rent for this month." Her shoulders sink. "Normally, I'd have way too much pride to take this from you, but this week?" She shakes her head. "Pride is for the rich."

"I told them to pay you, Cal. As soon as I realized what happened, I had the money wired. I'll do it again. I'll send you an electronic payment from my personal account right now." I sound desperate. I guess I am desperate. The thought of her worrying about money makes my heart clench. "Is that why you're here? For the money?"

"Did you think I was doing this for fun?" Her voice is bitter. "You took everything from me, Jonah."

Her face is cold when she walks away, and a tendril of doubt worms into my heart. I've been so confident that I could convince her to take me back, but what if I can't?

60

Callie

"Your billionaire is back."

Danny jerks his head at where Jonah sits in the corner. This is the second week of him lurking at a table in the coffee shop. He looks good enough to eat, wearing another one of his carefully chosen outfits. Today it's a hunter green suit with some sort of graphic knit T-shirt. There are a couple of women sneaking glances at him from across the room. I can't blame them. He's reading on his tablet and sipping an espresso, like a Vogue Italy shoot come to life. Watching them watch him makes my stomach knot. I had him once. He was mine. For two glorious months.

You could have him again, my traitorous brain whispers. *Forgive him.* I'm not even mad at him anymore. I've never been one to hold grudges. Jonah's actions were awful, but understandable. It's the lack of trust I can't get over. That and the fact that I know if I give in, I'll be giving up a piece of who I am and be wrapped up in his life all over again.

"I'm sorry," I tell Danny, as he works the espresso machine. "I can tell him to leave."

Danny shrugs, his tatted arms moving deftly through the motions of pulling a shot. "He's not bad for business. But he better order more if he wants to sit there all day."

That's enough for me to throw my rag down and stride over to Jonah's table. I cross my arms and tap my foot until Jonah's head slowly raises. He gives me a heart-stopping smile, his eyes crinkling at the edges. He's so handsome, maybe even more handsome now that I can't have him. His hair isn't gelled back today. It's mussed like he's been running his hands through it.

"Sit with me." He gestures to the chair next to him.

"You're going to get me in trouble with my boss," I respond.

"I'll buy coffee for everyone here. For the rest of the day," he responds evenly. He will too. Jonah pursues things with single-minded focus. And now his focus is on me. I suppress a shiver. It shouldn't thrill me to be in his sights, but damn him, it does.

I roll my eyes in response, but I know Danny will love the extra revenue, so I can't say no.

"I know you want to yell at me, Thompson. I'll let you. Just sit. Please." His soft words and the way my name rolls off his tongue unlock me. *I miss him.*

I can tell he misses me too, by the way he catalogs my face. He's scanning for wounds, but he must know they're all on the inside.

"You make good coffee," he finally says. "When did you learn?"

"I waitressed when I was at Columbia. Both times." I pulled his shot this morning, and the service person in me had to make it well.

"Do you like it?" He sips his coffee and watches me with those dark eyes.

"You know," I say slowly. "I don't mind it. I like interacting with people. I like seeing the regulars. I'm still thinking about my next move, but this is an okay temporary replacement."

His mouth twists unhappily before he reaches into his pocket and pulls out a bulky, folded piece of paper. "Here. Before I forget. For your next move."

I unfold it and foolish hope bursts in my chest. "A press pass." I run my fingers over the official badge, with my photo and name printed on it. "How did you get it so quickly?"

He looks embarrassed for a minute. "I used a lot of political capital. Let's hope Miles doesn't need to be bailed out of jail anytime soon."

"Thank you, Jonah." I raise my eyes to meet his. Something passes between us.

I'll never give up, his eyes say. He's all arrogance and confidence when he looks at me like that.

You'll need to do better than this, my eyes shoot back.

His mouth hitches up. *Game on.*

"What would it take to get you back?" he asks, leaning in, filling my vision with his broad shoulders and his perfect face. All I smell is him—his cologne and his expensive body products. I want to press my face into his neck. *Shit.*

"Change," I say. "Real change." I'm not giving him more than that. He can figure out how to change on his own.

"All right, Thompson." He gives me a cocky grin. "Tell your boss everything is on me for the rest of the day."

"You're very annoying," I grumble.

"Mmm. I know you hate me. Tell me more." He leans in again, his eyes sparkling with happiness. "Tell me how much you hate me, Callie."

It's on the tip of my tongue to tell him, but it would be a lie. So instead, I awkwardly clear my throat and say, "You're not going back to work?"

"I'm working from home. Something I'm trying." He shrugs elegantly. "I've been talking to Christine and once the baby is here, I'm going to be in New Jersey more. I'm learning to be more, ah, flexible." He fiddles with a sugar packet. "Anyways, here's my credit card." He hands it to me and picks up his tablet. "I have another twenty minutes before I have to log in. These back issues of your paper are interesting."

"What?" *Surely, I didn't hear that correctly.*

He raises his tablet in the air with a half smile. "I have the back issues of your paper. I started with the first issue published after you got involved." He glances down. "This is the August 3rd issue from three years ago. I'm not even in here, Thompson. I'm offended."

My mouth opens and closes, but no sound comes out.

"Looks like it was a slow news week that week." He frowns down at the tablet. "Though I remember this building being demolished on 87th street. I didn't realize you were the one who broke the news about the building permits being falsified. Nice work."

"There must be hundreds of issues," I say inanely.

He glances up, with a small crease between his brows. "Two hundred plus, I should think. I'm a fast reader. Don't worry about me. I have more free time now that I'm not going to the office."

"You're reading all of them?"

"That's the plan," he says lightly, but his gaze is steady.

"Why?" I whisper, my pulse thudding.

"Because you matter." He speaks with quiet intensity. "I want to understand what you do. I dismissed it before. I won't make that mistake again."

He picks up his tablet and raises a brow. "See you at lunch, Thompson?"

And despite my better judgment, I say, "Yes."

<hr />

"A SCHOLARSHIP TO COLUMBIA JOURNALISM? Really? I told you it couldn't be solved with money."

Jonah's black eye is fading, slowly. He looks almost casual today, in a cashmere sweater and wool slacks. Suede loafers complete his professorial look. He's back at his table, like he has nothing better in the world to do than to wait for crumbs of my attention. *It's flattering.* I shake myself. *It's fucked, is what it is.*

"Read the rest of the press release." His voice is silky, his eyes glinting.

"Fine." I huff and drop into the chair, scrolling on my phone. Columbia's journalism department blasted this message out to us this morning. The largest donation ever made to the school. The scholarship will be named...*for my father?*

"Really?" I raise my eyes to meet Jonah's. "You named it for my dad?"

He nods. "He instilled a love of journalism in you. I figured it was only fitting. You were a scholarship recipient, right?"

I nod mutely.

He gestures at the phone. "They told me this scholarship would provide tuition for five students per year. Preference will be given to students who are from the five boroughs. And preference will be given to aspiring female journalists."

He carefully explains the scholarship conditions to me, how my dad and I can be involved in choosing the recipients if we want. He's so serious about all the details, and a lump lodges in my throat.

I swallow past the tightness and focus on his words. Jonah is going to provide two internships in a newly formed media division at Kings Lane Capital. And a personal mentorship on how to run a successful business. My eyes heat with tears. *Wonderful man.*

His eyes flare as he takes me in. "Don't cry, Callie. Please. I wanted to show you how much I value you." He brushes a thumb over my cheek, wiping away the tears spilling. "I was wrong. The work you do is important. If you ever want to come lead the media division for us, the job will be open for you. And you can run a gossip column to rival Page Six out of our office as well."

"I can't believe this." My voice comes out choked.

"I told you, sweetheart. Anything you want. Take me back, or don't. I'll never stop." He says the words like he's at peace with me never taking him back, but his eyes are burning. That intensity, that Jonah fire, it's back in his gaze.

"Thank you," I say shakily. I get up to wait on customers, but my thoughts and my gaze keep straying toward Jonah. I'm not sure how much longer I can resist him.

THERE'S a motorcycle outside my house the next morning and a man leaning against it, clad in black jeans and black leather. There's a helmet on the seat and one tucked under his arm. *Jonah.* I barely recognized him in his bad boy outfit, but it's him.

"What are you doing here?" I shout from the front door, even though Mrs. Delano on the first floor is totally going to tell my dad I was "causing a ruckus."

"I know you're off today," he yells back. "I asked your boss. Come with me."

"You're very annoying," I shout back, but my heart does a little pirouette at how handsome he is, at how ruthless and single-minded.

"Come yell at me down here, Thompson."

I'm already halfway down the stairs as he speaks the words. "Nice outfit. Is the leather jacket bespoke?"

"You know me well," he says with a blinding smile. "Will you be warm enough in that?" He glances at my wool coat.

"Warm enough for what?" I can't help but tease him a little.

"You're coming with. I'm kidnapping you." He says it like it's a foregone conclusion.

"Jonah—"

"Please." He raises pleading eyes to mine. "Please come with me. I brought the bike back to the city yesterday, and I just need to share it with someone. I'll take you right back after."

Did I ever wonder what Jonah looked like with his layers peeled back? This is it. The raw honesty, the soft center of him, the parts only I have seen. They're special.

"I don't think I can ride a motorcycle in a wool coat."

"Take mine."

I make a sound of protest, but he's already shrugging out of it. He tucks my coat in the case at the back of the bike.

"You won't be cold?" I zip the leather up to my chin and inhale lungfuls of his scent.

"I'll be fine. Helmet?" He passes it to me and helps me settle it on my head. "This okay?" he murmurs as his fingers brush my jaw. I nod as warmth spreads from where he's touching me. I miss his hands on me. I miss his arms pulling me close. My heart is in my throat as he checks the visor and makes sure the helmet is settled before putting on his own.

He steadies the bike for me as we get on, and then I'm pressed to him, with my front to his back, and my arms around his waist.

"Hold on."

With a roar, we're off. Riding in the suburbs was one thing, but riding in the city? It's completely different. Jonah weaves through delivery trucks and cabs, making a few irate drivers honk at us. He opens up the engine when we reach the West Side Highway, and my stomach presses itself against my spine. He's solid and warm beneath me, and for a few minutes I pretend that nothing went wrong, that he's mine and I'm his and we don't ever have to go back to the real world.

We ride all the way to Riverdale, where Jonah finally stops the bike at a park, and helps me off. My legs are numb and shaky from the ride, and I stumble into his body. "Careful, Cal," he says as he steadies me. The ache in my chest grows at how protective he is, how caring.

"What made you bring the bike back?" I ask, as we swap coats.

"I miss it." He shrugs, but I can see how uncertain he is, like maybe it's wrong for him to enjoy this. "It was nice, that day with you. Image isn't everything. I forget that sometimes." His mouth twists and my heart lurches at the reminder of how *image* has ruined everything for us. "I looked into some boxing gyms too."

"You did?"

"Don't sound so shocked." He gives me a look as we make our way up the path and into the park. "I can still fight."

"I know. I just—I'm happy for you."

"Yeah," he says, but his eyes are shadowed. I know what he's thinking, because it's what I'm thinking too. Happiness is hollow without him. And the thought of him moving on and doing all these things without me, I fucking hate it. I want to be there to watch him overcome his fears.

"I'd give it all up, you know, if you wanted me to," he says quietly.

"What?" I stop on the path.

He turns, mouth pressed in a line, hands shoved in his pockets. "The job. I'd give it up. If you want someone more...*regular*. I don't have to keep working. I could be a boxing instructor, and you could do whatever you wanted. You could run a paper from our apartment instead of the Kings Lane offices."

Our apartment.

"Jonah, I don't know what to say—"

"It's okay." He shrugs, but his shoulders are tight. "Don't say anything." He keeps walking, head down and hands tucked away, like he's scared he'll grab me if he lets himself relax.

"I don't want you to quit for me." I blow out a breath. "I'm just scared. Scared I'll lose myself to a relationship again. I put myself second when Eric and I were together."

"How?" He sounds murderous.

"Let me count the ways." I grimace. "He hated my favorite restaurant, so we never went. I missed deadlines for the paper because I was out at events with him and he didn't want to leave. I pretended to like everything he liked. I lost myself somewhere along the way. When things ended, I realized just how much."

Jonah rounds on me, and I stop just before walking into his chest. His expression is earnest, those dark eyes intent on mine. "I will never let you lose yourself. Even if we're not together. I promise you, Callie."

Even if we're not together. The thought is a weight on my chest. I believe him. All the times he owned his faults. Every time he apologized. Every time he quietly cared for me, brought me supplies, asked me what I wanted for dinner, helped me to feel like the most beautiful woman in the room.

How could anyone make you believe that you deserve anything less than their full attention?

"Have you decided which direction to take your business?" he asks a few minutes later.

"I'm not sure." I sigh. "The New York Star made a name for itself, but now that it's gone, I wonder if letting it go is the best thing after all."

Jonah tenses. "I hate that I played a part in that. Whatever you need to start again, I'll provide."

I roll my lips between my teeth as I consider. "I talked to my dad," I finally say. "He's okay with me doing it the way I want. I guess the issue is, I don't know what I want. In some ways, the paper was a weight around my neck, and I might hate the way it ended, but maybe ending wasn't bad. So now, I'm just... at loose ends."

"The media division is waiting for you," he responds. "If you want it. You can publish whatever you want. You can name the paper whatever you want. You can buy up local papers that are failing and revitalize them." He gives me a small smile. "I know you have ideas. I know you want to make a difference. I believe in you."

Tendrils of warmth spread through my chest. I want that. I want to make a bigger impact on the world. I want to use my expertise to help struggling local papers.

Suddenly, it feels inevitable that I'll fall for Jonah again, and instead of feeling terrifying, it's starting to feel *right*.

"Thank you, Jonah."

He smiles at me, a little hopeful, a little sad. "I can take you back now."

I'm not ready. "Just a little longer," I say.

∿

I GET an email that night from an unknown sender.

Tell your boyfriend to stop coming after us, or I'll ruin you.

I jerk like I've been slapped when I open the attachment. It's a photo of what looks like a legal document. A motion maybe? We're listed as a party. My blood rushes in my ears when I see who the plaintiff is. Green Media.

Dylan Green is suing us. For thirty million dollars.

61

Jonah

Callie's face is pinched with worry when I see her the next morning. I get up to order, watching her move more slowly than usual. She looks tired and sick at heart.

"What's wrong?"

Her head jerks up. Her eyes look haunted. "I'll show you."

She makes my coffee and meets me at the table. "Look at this." She slides her phone over to me with a trembling hand. I scan the email and the attachment, rage coursing through my veins as the implication hits me. This is my fault. I convinced Sean to try hacking Green Media's servers. Dylan is escalating.

"I'll fucking kill him. He does not get to involve you in this. Again."

"I don't think there's anything you can do. I read the complaint. He's going to sue us."

"I'll fix it." I cup her face briefly with my hand. "I promise you, Callie. You won't suffer because of me."

∽

I CALL Dylan from my home office. It's a mirror setup to my office on 57th Street. I rarely use it. I still have the prick's cell phone number, and he picks up on the third ring.

"Jonah Crown. I thought I might be hearing from you."

His smarmy tone is gas to the fire of my anger. I can picture him with his loafers up on his desk, ill-mannered ass that he is.

"Dylan," I grate.

"How's it hanging, man?"

I grind my teeth and inhale for patience. "What do you want from me? In exchange for not threatening Callie. Or her father."

"I want you to stop coming after me." His voice is deadly quiet. I know he'll keep his promises to ruin Callie. He's a douchebag, but a vicious one. "I know you're behind all my employees quitting, and that little stunt with my COO. It's done. Sign an agreement, or I'll come after her, and I won't stop until she's homeless and penniless. Maybe even in prison."

My blood turns to ice. He'll do it. And I want to fight him, I do, but *Callie*. Her worried face swims in my mind. I can't take a chance that she'll be hurt.

"I'll need to extract my own promises from you in exchange," I grit out.

"I figured. You might have grown up poor, but you're as ruthless as they come. I always admired you for that, Jonah."

"Fuck you," I say, and hang up the phone.

Am I really going to do this? Will I give up my revenge to keep her safe?

∼

CHRISTINE MEETS me for lunch the next day before she meets Mia for a birthing class. I saw Callie again this morning, and the worry in her eyes made me sick at heart. I have to fix this.

"You look like shit," Christine says bluntly, before seating herself across from me. We're at the very back of Silvio's, where he won't let anyone disturb us.

"Thanks," I mutter. "I didn't sleep." I tossed and turned and kept my phone at maximum volume just in case Callie needed me. I would kill to be the man she calls when she needs someone to rely on. And now with fucking Dylan interfering again, it's like the pictures leaking all over again, but worse, because this time, he's coming for the woman I love.

"What's eating you?" Christine pokes around in the breadbasket for the focaccia they serve at lunch.

"If I gave up my revenge against Dylan, how would you feel?"

Christine's head jerks up and her mouth drops open. "Why?"

"He threatened Callie."

"He's threatened me over the years. And you. Miles, Theo, the company." She tilts her head. "What changed?"

"Coming after Callie is the one thing I can't abide." A short, unhappy laugh bursts from my chest. "Ironic, really. I can't have her, but turns out she's where I draw the line. And I guess—" I blow out a breath. "Being with Callie makes me want to live in the present, not the past. Revenge doesn't seem as important now."

"It's not." Christine shakes her head.

"But I promised." My throat is tight. "I never made him pay and I should have."

"Be happy, big bro." She squeezes my arm. "Be happy and forget about him."

"Happy." I snort. This is the same conversation we had last time at Silvio's. "I was happy with Callie. Without her, I don't think I know how." Christine makes a pained sound, like she feels every inch of my sadness.

"I'm sorry. Don't give up."

I give her a nod, but in my heart, I know that Callie won't take me back. *It doesn't matter.* I can still protect her. I can still keep Dylan from hurting her. That's all that matters.

When I get in the car later, I email Dylan and cc Aiden.

> To: Green, Dylan
> From: Crown, Jonah
> I accept your terms. The agreement will be with you today.

I fire off an email to Aiden with instructions on the agreement and slump into my armchair. *It's done.* Years of pain, years of worry. Just gone.

It was worth it. For her, it was worth it. Callie is worth anything. And strangely, I feel lighter. This is good. Even if she doesn't take me back, this feels right.

62

Callie

"You're on my doorstep again?" I can't help the little flip my stomach does when I see Jonah. He's dressed in workout gear, arms crossed over his chest.

"Thought you might want to box with me. It's your day off, right?"

"Yes." I don't ask how he knows. He always knows, because he always pays attention. *Do I want to box with him, though?* I'm dangerously close to falling for him again. *You have fallen for him, idiot.* I'm fully, madly in love with Jonah Crown.

"You promised, Thompson. I let you off easy these last few times, but technically you're supposed to box until you can beat me. Remember?" He raises his brows in challenge.

"Fine." I sigh. "Let me get my workout clothes."

We walk to Jonah's townhouse together. He points out the delis he likes near me, and I show him the places I've written articles about. After the third person who greets us on the street, Jonah rounds on me.

"Do you know everyone?"

"Of course." I smile. "I've lived here my whole life. And I'm always out on the street, talking to people."

He shakes his head, but his mouth is curved up. "Never change, Callie."

When we get to his townhouse, he leads me to the boxing studio. It's smaller than the one at the office, with no view.

He wraps my hands in silence, the way he did that first day we boxed together. The brush of his fingers over my wrists sends my heart galloping. *He's so close.* He smells so good. I want to bury my face in his chest. I want to kiss him. My eyes flick up to his. He's scrutinizing me as he wraps, carefully turning my hands in his, like I'm precious.

"All right." He steps away swiftly when the wraps are done. "You get to punch me in the face today."

"Don't you think you've taken enough of a beating recently?"

He scoffs. "One punch. Come on. You know you want to. I'll even wear a helmet."

"I don't want to." I'm not conscious of saying the words, but they're true. I shake my head as Jonah advances on me.

"Punch me in the face, Callie. Do it." His eyes are burning into me as he stalks forward. I retreat until my back hits the ropes.

"No," I say.

"Punch. Me." He bites the words out.

"I can't," I sob out.

"I deserve it." He steps in to me, presses his forehead to mine. I shut my eyes and revel in the feel of his warm body so close to mine. His breaths puff out on my face. I want to breathe him into my lungs and never breathe out. "I'm so, so sorry, Callie. I love you. I will never stop loving you. That mess with Dylan. That was my fault. He won't bother you again." He steps back, his eyes swirling black. "Now punch me."

"What did you mean, he won't bother me again? What did you do?"

"I agreed to his terms." Jonah's face is tight.

"Which were what?" My heart hovers somewhere in my throat while I wait for Jonah's response.

"I agreed to give up my revenge." Jonah looks away, his jaw working. "I talked to Christine. She didn't mind. It's done. He got away with it." His shoulders slump. I turn his words over in my head.

"But the photos."

He gives a sharp shake of his head. "I don't care about the photos. Losing you was worse than the photos being published."

"He deserves to pay," I say fiercely.

"You deserve to be happy more." Jonah's mouth hitches up. "Don't you think so? Don't you think choosing happiness is better? I want to live in the present, Cal. When I'm with you, I want to see things through your eyes. And keeping you safe is more important than getting back at Dylan."

"You gave up your revenge, for me?" My voice is incredulous. "You worked for years for that. It was the sole focus of your life."

He shrugs elegantly, like it cost him nothing, when I know it cost him everything. His gaze burns into mine. "You're the sole focus of my life, Callie. I know you don't want to be. And I—" His voice breaks, and my chest cracks along with it. "If you want me to stop, I will. I'll walk away. I'll help you but I'll never make my presence known. If you ever need a shoulder to cry on, I'll be there. If you ever want to punch someone, I'll be the fist that does it. I will never fall for anyone else. If you get married, I'll hate him, but I'll still be by your side. I love you." He whispers the last words. "All I want is to love you." He shuts his eyes, like it's too painful to look at me.

"Jonah," I whisper. My eyes are full of tears, and my words come out sounding shaky. "Jonah. Open your eyes." He looks at me, and the pain in his gaze nearly brings me to my knees. "I love you. I never stopped." I step toward him, and he opens his arms to me. I press my face to his chest, the way I want to do every time I see him. But then I step back and look up at his face, because he deserves to hear these words clearly.

"There is no one else for me. I want every piece of you. All the ruthlessness and the ambition. Your sarcasm and your humor. The way you're secretly a good man, even though you pretend otherwise. I will never stop loving you."

He crushes me to him. His heart pounds under my cheek. "I thought you'd never come around," he says. "I was prepared to spend the rest of my life waiting."

"I know you would have," I say. "But now, you don't have to."

He kisses me, with one hand on my jaw and the other at my back. "Callie," he whispers. "I want you. I need to feel you. I need to feel that this is real, that you won't disappear." He kisses the side of my jaw, bites the lobe of my ear. "I dreamed about you." His voice is ragged. "I dreamed you took me back. Tell me I'm not going to wake up."

Oh, Jonah. "It's not a dream," I whisper. "I love you, Jonah Crown."

He kisses me as I finish saying the words, like he wants to drink them in. His mouth is hot and needy, and his hands roam my body like he can't believe I'm real. He strips off my workout clothes with shaking hands and shucks his own. I'm equally desperate to be skin-to-skin. He sinks to the floor with me on his lap and pushes eager fingers between my legs.

"I need you, Callie," he says into my neck. He sucks on the skin. "I don't know how to be anything but myself, but you—" He groans as my hips grind down onto his hard cock. "You make me better."

"I love you, Jonah."

My belly is swooping and swirling with need. Every brush of his fingers ratchets me higher, until I think I'm going to come on his fingers with his mouth on my neck.

"Take what you need, sweetheart," he murmurs. I grab his erection with greedy fingers, loving the hot, smooth skin and the insistent hardness. He huffs a laugh as I line him up and sink down.

"Oh, Callie," he groans. "Easy there. I won't last."

"Good. Don't." He fills me inch by glorious inch, with his forehead pressed against mine and our eyes closed to heighten the pleasure. When I finally sink all the way down, he lets out a ragged breath before easing me up. The drag of his cock through me and the press of his stomach against my clit has me shuddering with need.

I throw my head back and move in earnest over him. My nails are digging into his shoulders, and my body is shaking.

I open my eyes to see Jonah watching me. His face twists in pleasure, his mouth opening on a breath.

"Jonah, I'm going to—"

"Tell me you love me," he says fiercely.

"I love you," I sob as I tighten around him, the orgasm spreading through me like bottled happiness. The words undo him, and he bucks up into me in sloppy thrusts.

"I love you," he says as he jerks inside me. "I love you."

"I'll never let you go," I say.

"Good," he responds, his breaths heaving, a small smile on his lips. "Good."

63

EPILOGUE

Jonah

"I am not scared of babies," I say, before taking a healthy sip of my martini and glaring at Lane.

She's tucked against Miles because they can't stop fucking touching each other, and she's giving me shit from across the table at Kings' Cove.

"You sure?" Lane gives me a dubious look. "You seem a little off."

"He's very nervous about tomorrow," Callie points out. "Isn't that your second martini? You don't even like martinis."

I grunt and take another sip. "They get me drunk faster." And with Mia being induced tomorrow, and Christine freaking out, I'm all nervous sweat and anticipation. I'm not scared of babies, I'm fucking terrified. I watched a bunch of videos with Callie and instead of making things better, they made it worse. He's going to be small and so very breakable. Christine will want me to hold him and befriend him, and what the fuck do you even say to a baby? I'm sure as hell not using that dumb baby voice everyone adopts.

"Pleasant as always, Jonah," Lane says, and makes a face.

"Only for you, Lane," I retort.

Callie slants me a secret smile, and I raise my eyebrows in response.

I know what that look she's giving me means. *Never change. I like you the way you are.* She tells me often enough.

I wag my brows. *Want to go home and I can show you just how much I like you too?*

She quickly looks away, and I smother a laugh.

A heavy tread on the polished wood floor has me turning in my seat. It takes me a second to register our visitor, because I haven't seen him in months.

"Theo?"

Our youngest co-founder smiles at me and comes to stand at the head of the table. He's dressed like typical Theo—all black. With his height and the broadness of his shoulders, he looks like a pro athlete, not a businessman.

"Miss me?"

Miles blinks away his surprise and stands for a hug. Because Miles is, at his heart, a hugger.

"Theo, this is Callie Thompson." Callie shakes Theo's hand and looks at me with inquisitive eyes.

"So this is the guy you were referring to in the comments section that day?"

I groan. "Can we please not talk about that?"

"Causing trouble, Jonah?" Theo grabs my martini before I can react and drains it. A gold band winks from his hand.

"You're married?" I choke out the words. "I can't believe that." Theo is a player, a bon vivant.

His face shutters. "Me neither. Hey, Miles, you going to drink that martini?"

Miles passes it over. "Married to whom?"

"Cat," Theo says shortly. "Not my choice."

Lane straightens. "Wait. Cat Peterson? From the wedding?" She looks at Miles. "He knows Cat? She never said anything to me." She frowns.

"Oh, I know Cat," Theo says, his voice flat. "I've known her all my life. I can't think of anyone I want to be married to less." He drains Miles's drink.

"Cat is nice," Lane says. "I mean, I know she caused trouble for Miles at the wedding, but I like her. We hang out. She's a good person. Fucked up family, though." She points her straw at Theo. "Don't be mean to her."

Theo snorts and presses the call button for a server. "Me, be mean to Cat?" He shakes his head, his too-long hair falling in his face. "I'm going to ignore her and hope this year passes as quickly as possible."

"A winning strategy," Miles says.

"Shut it," Theo says without heat. He's the easy-going one of the three of us.

"How was Australia? Get any good photos?" Lane asks.

"Loads." Theo grins, his good humor already restored. That's why he's the only one we trust to do overseas expansion. He can put anyone at ease and he never gets mad. "I'll show you. I might not be a pro, but you don't need to be when animals will scamper right up to you."

"Should we toast to the happy couple?" I ask.

Theo shrugs, looking world-weary and sad, before he straightens and flashes me his ever-present grin. "As long as you're buying."

There are sharp edges beneath the surface, and Callie must realize it too, because she gives me a concerned look.

I shake my head. *Stay out of it.* Theo's demons are his own.

～

As it turns out, newborn babies are really fucking small. Baby Noah is lying on Christine's chest, and she looks so fucking happy and not scared at all. I'm scared. I'm fucking terrified.

"Are they all this small?" I ask.

Callie laughs, a happy sound that goes straight to my heart.

"He's actually a big baby," Christine says with a tired smile. "Eight pounds, four ounces. Pray for my wife's vagina." She winks, and I groan while Mia barks a laugh from where she's lying on the bed.

"I do not need that imagery."

Christine and Mia smile at each other and then Mia jerks her head at me. "Time to hold the baby."

"I don't know—"

"Come on," Christine cuts in. "It's easier than it looks."

"What if I drop him?"

"You won't drop him," Christine says airily.

"She's very cavalier about this." I frown at Mia. "Are you sure you should be leaving her alone with the baby?"

"Shut up," Christine grumbles.

I look at Callie, whose lips are curved up with happiness. Her eyes light up when they meet mine. "I want to hold him too, so hurry up."

Christine passes him to me and I hold the back of his head, just like I saw on the YouTube videos I watched. And when he's lying against my chest, my heart feels like it might burst from loving him. His tiny heart beats next to mine, and he moves in his sleep. He's so trusting and small, and I've never been so overwhelmed in my life.

"How does it feel?" Callie asks.

I look at her and let the love I feel for her shine through my eyes. "Let's have a hundred," I say, and she bursts out laughing.

∽

"Did you mean what you said earlier about having kids?" Callie asks while she gets ready for bed later.

"Hmm?" I look up from the book I'm reading. It's a spy thriller. I'm making my way through this author's backlist and enjoying every second. I look up to see Callie doing her skincare routine in nothing but one of my T-shirts. I drop the book immediately. I can get her to stop the nighttime routine, if I just can lure her closer. My success rate at distracting her into having sex with me hovers around ninety-five percent. Ninety-seven percent if I'm not wearing a shirt when I go to bed.

"Kids," she repeats. "Do you want a hundred?"

"With you?" I meet her eyes, and I've never felt surer of anything in my life. "Yes."

She clambers on to my lap, smiling at me like I'm her favorite person in the world. "I love you, Jonah Crown."

"I love you," I repeat, as I bring her head down for a kiss. She tastes minty from her toothpaste, but under it she's delicious and so *Callie*. "I want to keep you in my bed for a year," I murmur.

She swats at my hands where they're slipping under the hem of her shirt. "Don't you think you're doing things out of order?"

I bite gently at her neck, then lick over the spot. "What do you mean?"

"You're already talking babies, but there's so much more before that." Her voice comes out breathy. I love getting to her.

"Move in with me, Cal. Marry me. I need you with me forever." I cup her face with my hand as her eyes widen.

"Don't you think this is going too fast?"

"Do you?" I raise a brow.

"No." She bites her lip. "It feels right."

When she kisses me, everything settles in to place.

64

EPILOGUE

Callie

6 months later...

A knock sounds on my office door. My very new office door that opens into a light-filled office full of plants.

Before I can answer, Jonah pushes into the space.

"Barging in with no warning?" I smile at him.

"Seeing as I own this building, yes," he drawls. He's so handsome, in a sharply masculine way that still makes my stomach feel weird when I see him for the first time after hours away. Like right now, when he's looking at me like he wants to bend me over the desk. Which he's done many, many times. Owner of the building and all that.

"Want to walk home?" He shoves his hands in his suit pockets. He's a little rumpled from a long day. His sharp jaw is shadowed with stubble, his hair is escaping from the confines of its gel. His tie is peeking out from his pocket, and his shirt is unbuttoned.

"I still have to work on the final article for Friday." My eyes flick to the computer, where my half-written draft stares at me accusingly.

"Can't be all work and no play," Jonah responds.

"That's rich, coming from you." I shake my head, but turn off my monitor.

"I am rich. Thanks for noticing." He smooths his jacket, and I can't help but laugh.

"Come on, Thompson."

We make our way out of the office, waving goodbye to Matt, who jumped at the chance to leave Green Media and work for us. The office is in Meatpacking, more of a converted apartment building than a real office. I couldn't go to work every day in a glass tower like Jonah.

He holds the lobby door open for me, and we slip into the fresh spring air. Without asking, we both head for the High Line. Ever since that night, it's become our place to walk after work.

"So how has your first month been? Am I a horrible overlord?"

I grin over at him. "Totally horrible. The one-touch espresso machine in the office kitchen is the worst part."

His mouth lifts. Jonah insisted that he was serious about starting a media division and that there was no one else better positioned to run it than me. We have our own publication, but I'm meeting with a small local paper from New Jersey tomorrow to talk about bringing them in. I'm a little out of my depth, but Jonah insists I'll learn.

"Nervous for tomorrow?" He bumps me with his shoulder as we near the steps leading up to the High Line.

"A little," I admit. "This is my first time doing anything like this. Acquisitions and stuff."

"You know reporting though. You know about running a paper. You're the best person to talk to them." Jonah's quiet confidence buoys me. "Besides, I'll be there to make sure you don't fail."

Warmth spreads through my chest as he ushers me up the steps to the platform, his hand on my back, his palm heating me through my thin jacket.

"I love you," I say, the words tumbling out.

"I know," he says, and I choke out a laugh.

"So modest," I tease.

"Have you thought more about my question?"

I clamp my lips together to keep from laughing. He will not appreciate laughing. "Which one?"

"You know which one," he growls.

"Jonah." I stop at one of the benches lining the path. "You asked me to marry you three months in to dating. And again the next month. And then every week. You asked me yesterday at breakfast."

"You want a bigger proposal? Maybe some fireworks? I could shut down the Met or something."

"No. No. I liked yesterday's proposal." He'd burst out of the bathroom in nothing but a towel and demanded I marry him.

"Number forty-nine." He nods.

"You're counting?"

"Of course," he says crisply. "You hated thirty-eight. Far too public. I made a note. It's okay. I'm very persistent when I want something."

"I know you are." I can't help but smile. "But don't you think this is a bit much?" I can tell from his expression that he doesn't think any of this is a bit much.

"No, I don't." He raises a brow for me to continue.

"It's just—" I make a helpless gesture.

"Oh, I see. You want me to ask again." He glances down, his brow creasing. "I really like these pants. I don't think dirt stains will come out of the knees."

"Jonah, no, that's not—"

"I'm going to keep asking, you know."

I shake my head and smile. "I know." I loop my arm through his and lead him down the path.

"Maybe a string quartet next time. What do you think?"

"Didn't you do music already?" I scrunch up my nose at him.

"Ah, yes. Number thirteen. I sang you a song. That was particularly ill-advised." He shudders. "No music."

"No music," I agree.

"But you'll say yes one day, right?" He glances at me, looking raw and vulnerable for a heartbeat, before he's back to Jonah Crown, king of New York.

"I so will."

"But you're going to make me work for it."

"Just a tad." I give him a sunny smile and he growls under his breath. "It's good for you to have goals, Jonah."

He grabs me around the waist and hauls me up against him. My hands land on his chest, where I can feel his heart thud under his jacket.

"You're it for me. I love you."

"I love you, too."

Jonah dips his mouth to mine, and kisses me like he's addicted to me. Maybe he is. All I know is nothing has ever felt this right.

He presses his forehead to mine as he murmurs, "I'll chase you forever, Callie. Even when I have you. I'll never give up."

The End

Want to see what happens when Callie finally says yes to Jonah's proposal? Sign up to my newsletter and get the free bonus epilogue. You can sign up at www.sophiatravers.com.

If you want more hot billionaire romance, check out Miles and Lane's story in One Billion Reasons. He's her brother's forbidden best friend, and he needs a fake girlfriend for his ex's wedding. Too bad Lane hates him, and there's no way in hell she'd share a hotel room with him for a week.

Printed in Great Britain
by Amazon